A WHIFF OF MURDER

Books by Angela M. Sanders

Witch Way Librarian Mysteries

BAIT AND WITCH

SEVEN-YEAR WITCH

WITCH AND FAMOUS

WITCH UPON A STAR

GONE WITH THE WITCH

THE WITCH IS BACK

WITCH AND TELL

Lise Bloom Mysteries

A WHIFF OF MURDER

Published by Kensington Publishing Corp.

A WHIFF OF MURDER

ANGELA M. SANDERS

KENSINGTON PUBLISHING CORP.
kensingtonbooks.com

KENSINGTON BOOKS are published by

Kensington Publishing Corp.
900 Third Ave.
New York, NY 10022

All Kensington titles, imprints, and distributed lines are available at special quantity discounts for bulk purchases for sales promotion, premiums, fund-raising, educational, or institutional use. Special book excerpts or customized printings can also be created to fit specific needs. For details, write or phone the office of the Kensington Special Sales Manager: Attn. Special Sales Department. Kensington Publishing Corp., 900 Third Ave., New York, NY 10022. Phone: 1-800-221-2647.

KENSINGTON and the KENSINGTON COZIES teapot logo Reg. US Pat. & TM Off.

Library of Congress Control Number: On file

ISBN: 978-1-4967-5646-6
First Kensington Hardcover Edition: March 2026

ISBN: 978-1-4967-5648-0 (ebook)

10 9 8 7 6 5 4 3 2 1

Printed in the United States of America

The authorized representative in the EU for product safety and compliance
is eucomply OU, Parnu mnt 139b-14, Apt 123
Tallinn, Berlin 11317, hello@eucompliancepartner.com

In memory of Janeen Provo, a model of grace and kindness.

A WHIFF OF MURDER

Chapter 1

The customer hesitated near a display of oracle cards. With her parchment-white skin and equally pale, wispy hair, she might have been a phantom.

But what really drew Lise's attention was the scent of violets that wafted from her in airborne ribbons. The odor was sickly sweet, as if the flowers had been left to rot in a vase. In other words, the stranger was grieving.

"May I help you?" Lise asked.

The customer picked up a box of cards with angels on its cover, then returned it to the pile. "I want to attract abundance. I wonder if the Lucky Lotus has some kind of potion for that?"

No, Lise thought. *Not the Magnet Oil.* She ratcheted up her smile a few degrees. "What kind of potion would you mean?"

"I'm not sure." Despite her nonchalant shrug, she watched Lise closely. "Something I couldn't find anywhere else. Something with real power."

"Perhaps you'd be interested in our crystal jewelry? We carry a rose quartz necklace that attracts love. It would look great with your coloring." Anything to keep away from the heinous stench of Magnet Oil.

"That won't work. I'm allergic to metals. No potions?"

If her skin was too sensitive for jewelry, the Magnet Oil would raise hives before she could say "Wow, that burns."

"Our book selection—" Lise began.

Dyann emerged from the beaded curtain separating the Lucky Lotus's back room from the shop. As if to announce her arrival, the shop's playlist changed from pan flutes to an Irish jig. "What you need is Magnet Oil, and you're in luck. I just made a fresh batch. Lise, bring us a bottle."

Lise reluctantly stooped to open the cabinet where they kept the unlabeled brown bottles and handed one to Dyann.

People who came to the Lucky Lotus for Dyann's aura readings expecting an Earth Mother–type in an Indian skirt and Birkenstocks were disappointed. Her style was more Beverly Hills housewife than yoga matron, and her wardrobe was expensive enough to be labeled "boho" instead of "hippie." That said, she was all-in on the woo.

Dyann ran a finger down the bottle. "Magnet Oil is special."

"What's in it?" the customer asked.

"It's from a recipe I received in a vision from my spirit guide, Running Bull, a Native American elder." Dyann let her focus soften, as if she were communing with him at that very moment. "It was a gift, a gift to help people like yourself attract whatever it is you need in your life."

In fact, the oil was a fifty-fifty blend from industrial-sized jugs of Love Evermore and Evil Be Gone, ordered by the crate from a firm in China specializing in Santeria-inspired goods. Last week Dyann had insisted Lise help her decant it into sample spray tubes, and Lise's resulting migraine had taken days to dissipate. She was still finding vials in her pockets.

"I'll take a bottle," the customer said.

"Apply it after you wake up and again before you go to bed," Dyann said. "As you rub it over your chakras, say the words 'With this potion, I magnetize my greatest good.'" Dyann set the bottle on the counter. "Perhaps you'd like a backup? We're running a special. Buy one, get the second half off."

"Then I'll take two," the customer said.

As Lise crouched to retrieve another bottle, Dyann said, "Lise, when you get a moment, would you see me?" The beads clacked as she disappeared into the back room.

The customer's waft of violets had already lightened, as if Astoria's marine air had infused it. Even the thought of relief from her pain had bettered the customer's mood. Working at the Lucky Lotus was teaching Lise how deeply the need for hope plumbed. If a bundle of sage or a labradorite ring helped someone weather their trauma, so be it.

Once the customer had left, Lise went to the back room. "You wanted to see me?"

Dyann looked up from her desk, an unraveling dream catcher next to her. She tapped her pen on a sheet of paper. "I need you to sign this. By the way, that customer?"

"Yes?"

"She came in for Magnet Oil, but you tried to sell her a necklace. What was that about?"

"It was a strategy," Lise said, thinking quickly. "Sure, she wanted Magnet Oil, but wouldn't she be happier with both Magnet Oil and a necklace? Besides, holding off for a minute makes the Magnet Oil feel more exclusive."

Dyann regarded her with doubt. "An upsell?"

Lise nodded. "Sure." Her gaze crept to the clock on the shelf behind Dyann. Two hours until she could go home.

"I guess so," Dyann said reluctantly. "You might wear one of the necklaces, too. I'd give you ten percent off. Employee discount."

"I'll keep that in mind."

Dyann eyed Lise's clothing, a men's button-up shirt and a denim skirt. "I know you're here for the spiritual education, but you might wear something more in keeping with the shop. Maybe one of our T-shirts?"

Lise had picked up the habit of wearing men's button-ups when she worked planting scent gardens. Cotton shirts were loose and comfortable and kept off the sun, and it was hard to find women's clothing to fit someone as tall as she was. Plus, the shirts were a dime a dozen at thrift stores, and she'd much rather wear them than a T-shirt that read "WITCHES DO IT IN CIRCLES." Dyann probably wasn't nuts, either, about her freckles, making her look younger than her thirty years, her lack of makeup, or the simple braid down her back.

"You wanted me to sign something?" Lise asked.

"Right." She handed Lise the pen. "At the bottom of the page." Dyann sneaked a look at her. "I can't wait to see what he does."

"Who is that?" Lise asked, guessing her response.

"Richard." Her ex-husband. "He'll be furious." Strangely, instead of triumph—or even vindictiveness—Dyann's expression radiated joy. "He'll kill me when he finds out."

"No kidding?" Lise responded without enthusiasm.

She'd worked at the Lucky Lotus since earlier that summer, but already she'd witnessed two assaults on Richard—the surreptitious installation of a bird feeder above his beloved Camaro and the delivery to his house of anchovy pizzas from four restaurants. Richard had returned the favor by taking out an ad in the *Astorian* announcing that the Lucky Lotus now offered "sensual massage." Lise dreaded answering the shop's phone.

"This is the big one." Dyann smiled at the paper on her desk. "I'm changing my will. I'm going to announce it tonight at Murphy's birthday party."

Lise seized this opportunity for a new subject. "You're having a party for your son? How nice." She'd met Murphy twice, both times when he'd shown up at the shop to ask for money.

"At the Fort George Brewery. He's turning eighteen." She leaned forward. "Today he would have inherited everything. If I'd died, that is."

Lise watched, a bland smile on her lips. Yes, Dyann had been kind to her, encouraging her to learn more about her ability to smell emotion. However, as right as it had seemed at the time, taking this job was a mistake. The irritation of weathering Dyann's attacks on her ex, of pretending not to care while Dyann found new ways to torment him, overrode the small gains she'd made in understanding her gift.

Lise willed the front door to chime so she could leave the back room. If a customer walked in now, she'd even be willing to peddle Magnet Oil.

"He'll still get an allowance—I'm not a monster—but I'm leaving most of my money to Blavatsky Manor. Richard will have a fit." Dyann's glee soured. "He threatened to bring his girlfriend to the party. She came in the other day, waving around an engagement ring. I got even, though."

"I'm not familiar with Blavatsky Manor," Lise said, ignoring the bit about the girlfriend. There was no way she was going there.

"It's a retirement home for psychic mediums. Appropriate, don't you think? I mean, given my interest in the spiritual?" One hand went to her diamond-studded yin-yang pendant. "Honestly, all Murphy does anyway is play video games and feed his snake. Plus, I worry that . . ." She shook her head. "Anyway, it won't hurt him to know he won't have a free ride when I'm gone. The kid needs to learn how to be a man." This provoked a happy snort. "Not that it's a skill Richard could ever teach him." She pushed the sheet of paper across her desk. "I want you to witness this for me."

Lise lifted the paper to read, but Dyann placed her arm over the text. "You don't need to see it. Just sign."

Lise shot her a curious glance. Dyann had just told her what was in the changed will. Why hide it? "Okay." She signed and returned the pen to Dyann. "Don't you need two signatures?"

"I'll get the other one tonight at the party. It's going to be quite a gathering."

"Oh?" Lise said, hoping she hadn't expressed too much interest.

"Me, Richard, Murphy, that friend of Murphy's from the snake place, and a palm reader from Blavatsky Manor. I want her there when I make my announcement."

Lise inhaled honey, cinnamon, and anise over Dyann's jasmine-heavy perfume. That explained a lot. Dyann had been into the Mayan ceremonial liqueur again.

"Oh," Dyann said, clearly remembering something. Lise braced herself for more anti-Richard venom, but Dyann pulled a thick book from a tote bag at her feet. "A customer brought this in, and I thought you'd like it."

A History of Magical Gifts, the cover read in faded gold letters. The book had to be a hundred years old, and the scent of vanilla and mildew rose from its yellowed pages. Dyann could be so irritating, then she'd come through with a thoughtful gesture like this.

"Thank you." Lise held the book to her chest.

"Maybe there's something in it that will help you figure out your own gift," Dyann said. Her smile cloaked a profound sadness, dark and sharp, like cedar wrapped in aged patchouli leaves.

At last, the front door's chime sounded. "Thank you again," Lise said. "I'd better go."

Chapter 2

After work, Lise locked the shop's front door, leaving Dyann in back to prepare for her son's birthday party. Taking the job at the Lucky Lotus in Astoria, Oregon, had so seemed right, if not inevitable. Now Lise had to wonder if she'd fallen into the same ambush of hope as so many of the shop's customers. She had a longing to know where she'd come from and who she was. Maybe it had led her to confuse coincidence with destiny.

Victorian homes in varying states of repair dotted the hills edging town. Wood fires and fallen leaves were weeks away, and the season's last crickets still chirped, but autumn was in the wind. A knot of clouds gathered, and a gust ruffled Lise's hair. Perhaps it would rain tonight. This evening two cargo ships were anchored in the depths of the broad Columbia River below, waiting for guidance through the shoals to the Pacific Ocean. Beyond them, forested hills rose on the Washington side of the river.

Lise climbed the hill toward home. Home—Corrie House—was a two-story Victorian pile built for what must have been an agoraphobic sea captain. A peaked attic, Gothic-arched windows, and an octagonal tower rising from its east side contributed to its reputation as "that haunted place on the hill." The house stood apart from others, and Lise and her two housemates had to park on the dead-end street below and wind up a path worn into the shrubbery and through a small clearing to reach home.

Yes, Corrie House was a climb from town, but Lise loved it here. With her bedroom window open, wind from the ocean washed away the residual smells of the day and cleared her head.

She mounted the stone steps to the house's foyer and passed through the double front doors to open a second door with a stained glass window with three missing panels.

"There's a letter for you on the table," her housemate Fran said.

Fran, mousy bangs hanging over her eyes, sat on the floor at the entrance to the sitting room with its door handle and lock in pieces around her. The lock, molded in brass with designs of vines and a Tudor rose, was almost certainly original to the house. She wiped a rag on some sort of bolt.

"I didn't know you could fix locks," Lise said.

Fran looked up, revealing luminous eyes behind gold-rimmed glasses. She quickly turned away, her face again hidden by her overgrown bangs. "Yeah. The latches in this place are in bad shape. The tumbler springs are completely missing in this one. Teddy said I could work off part of my rent."

Lise sifted through the mail on the waterfall bureau in the hall and found her letter under a grocery store circular. *Yes.* It was from the DNA firm she'd sent her saliva sample to. Maybe this time she'd get answers about her birth family. Maybe she'd find someone who shared her abilities, who wouldn't look at her strangely when she asked why someone smelled anxious. Her last two DNA tests had been a bust. One said she was one hundred percent Nigerian, Chinese, and Swedish—each. The other said she had the DNA of a squirrel.

She dug her thumbnail under the envelope's flap and unfolded the single page.

"Dear Lise Meitner Bloom," the letter read. *"We are sending this letter because our attempts at email continue to be returned. We regret to inform you we are unable to match your DNA. We have refunded your fee."*

Again? Lise dropped the hand holding the letter. And what was up with the email? She was sure they had the right address. It's what she'd used when she'd asked them to rerun the test. It had worked then.

She shoved the letter into her tote and made her way to the stairs to climb to her room. Voices from the kitchen interrupted her before she'd gone more than a few steps.

"Lise, come join us. Burt brought a bottle of scotch."

Lise only paused a moment before saying, "Gladly."

"See if you can convince Fran to come, too."

"No, thank you," Fran shouted from the entry hall.

The house's owner Teddy—Theodora Bright on her mail—sat at the kitchen table with Burt, her gentleman friend. Despite Teddy's age, it was easy to see the delicate-featured angel she'd been when she'd lounged in Morocco with the Rolling Stones and hung out backstage at Woodstock. Today her waist-length white hair was twisted into a loose chignon. Burt had the weathered look of someone who had spent decades on the ocean. His cane leaned against the wall.

"Darling," Teddy said, "look at you. Why so sad? Dyann, again?"

"It's been a day," Lise said.

The house's two tabby cats, Grace and Charm, were settled one each in Teddy's and Burt's laps. Lise couldn't tell them apart by looks, but Grace, the female, usually smelled faintly of rosemary from her napping spot in the garden.

Lise pulled up a chair. The kitchen chairs, like everything in the house, were mismatched. This one was spindle-backed and painted red, like the kitchen cabinets. Behind the linoleum-topped table sat a down-stuffed armchair. It was an ideal place for reading with a cup of coffee in the morning, but it was more often a cat bed. Rag rugs were scattered over the scarred floorboards.

"Tell us more," Burt said.

"It's the Lucky Lotus," Lise said. She didn't need to bend their ears with her failed efforts to trace her biological family. "Dyann is driving me crazy."

"Here, honey." Burt poured an inch from the bottle into a small jelly jar with stars molded into its sides and pushed it toward her. "A gift from a cargo ship captain I helped out of a jam once. It's good. Now tell us what's wrong."

The scotch smelled of peat, sure, but of something more—of heather, wool, and rain.

"She's at it again. Dyann is. For someone who claims to be so spiritual, she is ridiculously nasty toward her ex-husband." Lise set the glass on the table, and Charm stepped from Teddy's lap into hers. She ran her fingers through his silky fur. "I wonder if I made a mistake taking that job. Summer is over, too. Pretty soon it will be too late to plant, and I have exactly zero landscaping clients. I feel like I'm stuck at the shop."

Rent at Corrie House was low, but her savings were lower. She really couldn't afford to quit.

"Richard is a piece of work," Teddy said. "But so is Dyann. I'm not sure why they ever split up. They're made for each other." She shook her head. "What's happened now?"

"Dyann had me witness a change to her will. She's cutting her son's share, all to spite her ex. She was so gleeful, like she couldn't wait to see how angry Richard would be."

Lise wasn't sure about the full extent of Dyann's estate, but it had to be large. She'd heard many times about how, a decade earlier, when Dyann was still the secretary at her ex-husband's car lot, she'd played the lottery numbers printed on the reverse of the fortune in her cookie from that day's take-out chow mein. The ticket had won the jackpot. When the restaurant went out of business shortly thereafter, Dyann had adopted its name for her shop. The fortune, *"What you sow you shall reap,"* was now framed in her office.

"Vindictive," Teddy said.

"She's not a bad person, but it's not worth the emotional blackmail."

"Life is too short to be miserable," Burt said. "You should leave. You'll find something else."

"I know, but Dyann has been good to me." Dyann had listened with interest to Lise's discussion of her strange ability to smell emotion and even taught her its name, "clairalience." That said, she was moody and demanding, and the stench of the Magnet Oil alone was enough to drive her to quit.

"Burt's right, darling." Teddy leaned back to give Grace room to shift from Burt's lap to hers. "If you're worried about the rent, don't be. You can work on the garden here until you find something else. Lord knows it needs it."

"Maybe I should move back home." Lise didn't know why she'd said that. There was no returning to Seattle now.

"Don't you like it here?" Teddy asked.

"I love it here."

She did. As soon as she'd pulled open Corrie House's tall double doors and walked through the foyer into the entry hall, she'd felt as if the house were drawing her in, as if it had been waiting for her. Teddy's thrifted portraits of strange women—anonymous ladies with sad faces, flowers in their hair, awkwardly painted dresses—lined the walls, seeming to whisper "welcome." Even the faded rug, its rose pattern worn through in spots, had urged her feet forward.

"Then stay," Teddy said.

Lightning flashed, followed by a low rumble. Tonight they'd have a storm.

"You got home just in time."

Burt refilled his and Teddy's glasses and capped the bottle.

"As I said, you should quit. It seems like every time I'm here when you get home"—more evenings than not—"you're miserable. Leave. You'll find another job, something that doesn't leave you feeling so dejected." The scotch had deepened the rumble in his voice.

"Burt has a point, Lise. Dyann will find someone to replace you. God forbid she'd actually work the floor herself."

"Here." From the counter, Burt swiped the notebook they used for grocery lists. "We're going to draft your resignation letter right now. You take the pen. Then you'll email it to her tonight. Okay?"

Lise obeyed. Burt's military air made him hard to ignore.

"I, Lise . . ." Burt paused. "What's your last name?"

"Bloom. Lise Meitner Bloom." She'd been named for a German nuclear physicist. Her brother was Albert Einstein.

"Keep the letter to the point," Teddy advised. "You don't need to convince her, and you don't want to give her any room to argue. If I were you, I'd simply say, 'This is my two weeks' notice. My last day of work will be' "—she glanced at the calendar stuck to the refrigerator with a magnet—" 'October tenth.' "

The scotch loosened Lise's hesitation. She transcribed Teddy's words. Yes, this was perfect. As she wrote, her despair lifted. The Lucky Lotus had been a dead end. She would pin notes about her landscape work on bulletin boards around town. She would fill the town with perfumed gardens, and when walking its hills she'd breathe lilacs, *Edgeworthia*, and bourbon roses washed with ocean air. The flexibility of freelance gardening would give her more time to track down her biological roots.

Burt raised his glass. "I hereby toast Lise Meitner Bloom and her glorious future."

"Here, here," Teddy said.

Lise raised her glass. "I'll drink to that."

* * *

Lise settled into bed and hoisted to her lap the book Dyann had given her that afternoon. Burt had left hours ago, and Teddy had retreated to the house's former sitting room and parlor, now her private quarters. Lise imagined her doing restorative yoga or reading the volume of Mary Oliver's poetry she'd caught sight of when Teddy was having coffee in the kitchen.

In the room next door, Fran was doing whatever it was she did at night. Sometimes Lise heard her moving around in the early hours, but with Fran's reclusive ways, it was hard to know what she was up to. She'd let drop hints that she was writing a novel. Fran's brother was a famous late-night TV host—Lise had learned the hard way not to ask about him—and she worked at the bookstore, but that was about all Lise knew about her. That, and thanks to seeing her surrounded by tools and brass door fittings, that she was handy with locks.

Lise returned her attention to *A History of Magical Gifts*. Its pages were brittle, and a few were loose from its spine. Dyann had been so kind to think of her. She felt a pang of guilt. Was she wrong to leave the Lucky Lotus?

She hadn't taken the job for its relentless Yanni—peppered with Enya and didgeridoo—nor for the recent furtive phone calls requesting massages, and certainly not for the oils that messed with her ability to smell. She had wanted to learn more about her gift, and Dyann had encouraged her. Besides giving her the book, Dyann had suggested podcasts and television programs on magic and had even given her a few days off to visit Josie Way, a librarian in nearby Wilfred who was rumored to be a witch. After a harrowing experience with Josie, another dimension of her abilities had been released. She'd discovered she could smell not just emotion but also, at unexpected times, history.

As for the Lucky Lotus, the resignation email was sent.

Teddy and Burt had both cheered when she'd pressed SEND. It was too late now to change course.

Lise scanned the book's table of contents and flipped ahead. "*Cases of clairalience,*" the page read.

"Clairalience is a rare phenomenon, much overshadowed by the other clairs, particularly clairvoyance and claircognizance. It is characterized by the ability to smell people who have passed as well as to smell angels and demons."

Lise paused. So far, this had not been her experience, although the Magnet Oil might be classified as demonic.

"However, additional cases adjacent to classic clairalience have been reported. In 1747, Isabel Stone, a young woman in Devon, was known to have the ability to smell illness on the inhabitants of her village. Unfortunately, as many of those whom she diagnosed as ill eventually died, Miss Stone was hanged as a witch.

"A member of Queen Victoria's court, Lady Macallen, was rumored to be able to smell love and was well respected as a matchmaker. She asserted that love smelled of roses and champagne. The author is not certain if her skills were entirely due to clairalience or if this was a cover for claircognizance, but she was toasted at many weddings and had eight baby girls named after her.

"Finally, an 1892 journal for the American Society for the Paranormal notes that a New Orleans housemaid had a gift for smelling straying husbands. She was in popular demand with society ladies."

None of these exactly mirrored Lise's knack for smelling emotion, but they edged around it. She'd tried discussing clairalience with her scientist brother and father, and they were puzzled. Their worlds were made of formulae and Bunsen burners. As much as she loved them, she felt like an angelfish swimming with trout. She was always apart—more emotional, more oriented toward the senses.

Her father suggested she might have a form of synesthesia, a condition where one sense triggers a reaction in another sense. However, this theory didn't feel true to Lise. Her birth parents, if they were alive, might be able to tell her more. If she could find them.

She had been adopted when she was an infant. Her mother had died when Lise was five years old, and her father was frustratingly vague when she asked about her origins. "I don't know, Lise. I really don't," he'd say, and, once, "I wish you could ask your mother." Then she'd smell the violets of grief rising around him, and her heart would tighten.

Tonight, rain *tap-tapp*ed on the window. She turned off her bedside light and slid down under the covers until her feet butted against the bed's footboard—a hazard of her height.

Everything had seemed so fated, so right. Astoria, Corrie House, the Lucky Lotus, meeting the witch, the well-timed escape from the fiasco back home—it had all seemed meant to be. But she was no nearer to finding her roots, and the Lucky Lotus was turning out to be a big zero. Maybe she'd been wrong about it all.

CHAPTER 3

As she walked down the hill toward the Lucky Lotus the next morning, Lise reveled in petrichor, the dirty-clean scent of the earth after rain. Heat from the sun lifted steam from the sidewalks still wet from last night's storm.

The kitchen had been empty when Lise had gone downstairs to make coffee. She'd propped open the back door so the cats could go in and out, and the morning had been full of birdsong. Normally, she didn't bother with fragrance before going to the Lucky Lotus, but this morning before she'd left, she'd pondered her collection of perfume, rescued from estate sales and thrift stores, and finally dabbed Fille d'Eve, an old, skin-like chypre in an apple-shaped bottle, behind each ear. She wore it as armor.

She'd practiced her lines. She would thank Dyann for her graciousness and the opportunity to work, but she'd tell her it was time to move on. After all, she would have to quit sometime—it wasn't as if Lise was planning to work at the Lucky Lotus forever, just until she'd built a gardening clientele. She'd tell Dyann that fate had brought her into Lise's life for spiritual guidance and that it was now the moment for a new student to step in. Yes, Dyann would like that.

At the Lucky Lotus, Lise unlocked the shop's front door. In

two weeks, she'd unclip the key from her ring and say goodbye to it forever.

She flipped on the light switches, bracing herself for the odorous residue of Magnet Oil. But she smelled . . . something else, something acrid yet earthy, something that tightened her chest. It was truffled, like compost, but also caustic. Frenzied. What was it?

Lise turned on the shop's sound system. The eerie tones of a pan flute filled the store.

Light shone from the back room. Dyann must already be in. This was unusual. She didn't normally come to the shop until after noon—if she came in at all. Lise grimaced. Hopefully, she wasn't creating a new batch of oils. Maybe that was the odor.

"Dyann?" Lise dropped her purse behind the counter and looked toward the back room. "You're in early." Silence. Lise's breathing slowed, but her pulse climbed. Something was wrong. "Dyann?"

No reply.

She had to do it. Despite the dread rising in her bones, Lise approached the beaded curtain. Its wooden beads clacked as they parted, then dropped behind her. The smell was more intense here.

No Dyann. Lise let out a heavy breath. The back room was still. In Dyann's excitement about her son's party, she must have left without turning out the lights.

Lise did a quick survey to make sure everything was as it should be. To the right was a shelf with the Lucky Lotus's paltry back stock—a few boxes of incense, meditation CDs that would never sell thanks to streaming services, a headless Ganesha statue, and a broken plate with a unicorn on it. Next to that was a table with an altar to a goddess Lise couldn't remember. To the left sat Dyann's desk. Its surface was tidy, except for her open laptop and a small glass with the amber residue of, Lise guessed, Mayan ceremonial liqueur. On the wall behind the desk hung a framed photo of Dyann as a Miss Oregon runner-up, with a satin sash crossing her chest as if she were an item packaged for sale.

What had Lise been expecting, anyway? Dyann splayed dead on the floor? She remembered Dyann's warning of the night before: *Richard will kill me.*

Lise chided herself for her nervousness. She simply dreaded Dyann's response to her resignation email, that was all.

The door to the alley was ajar. Had someone broken in? If so, they weren't here now. Maybe that's what had set her on edge.

She crossed the room to shut the door and noticed Dyann's Mercedes convertible parked outside. It was definitely Dyann's—no one else in rainy Astoria would have been foolish enough to drop that kind of money on a car that would have its top up for all but a few weeks a year.

Dyann's car was here, but where was Dyann? Perhaps she'd gone down the block for a coffee. Lise was about to close and bolt the door when it struck her that the convertible sat awfully low to the ground. She opened the door wider and stepped out. Yes, someone had slashed the car's rear tires. A note was tucked under a windshield wiper, but after last night's rain, it was a sop of paper and running ink. Richard's revenge, no doubt.

"Give me a break," Lise said aloud. She saluted herself for her good judgment for resigning, despite her doubts. The Lucky Lotus was a toxic waste dump of drama.

She returned to the shop, this time bolting the door. When Dyann came back, she could come through the front like everyone else.

Then Lise froze. Jutting from under the desk were sugar-white legs, one with a pink patent leather mule dangling from it. Lise glanced up at the framed photo of the almost Miss Oregon and back down at the legs. They were Dyann's, all right.

The earthy-frantic odor thickened, burning Lise's eyes. She flattened her palms to the door's cold metal side. She wanted to run, to dart into the alley and flee, anywhere, but she couldn't.

"Dyann?" Lise's voice faltered.

Do it, Lise. Look. She rounded the desk. Maybe Dyann had passed out, that was all. It wouldn't be the first time she'd overindulged in the Mayan ceremonial liqueur, although she'd never taken it this far.

However, Dyann wasn't simply sleeping off a bender. How Lise knew, she couldn't say, but a split-second glance at the wide-open, glassy eyes and the parted lips, still stained fuchsia, told her to call the police, not an ambulance.

Dyann was dead.

CHAPTER 4

That afternoon, Lise plunged her shovel into the ground behind Corrie House, counting on exhaustion to settle her mind. She'd already dug up half of one garden bed, churning rocky soil around two overgrown rose bushes and an ancient lilac run through with dead branches. Sure, Dyann had grated on her nerves, but she'd never wanted . . . this.

When the police had arrived that morning, they'd taken Lise's contact information and a quick description of what had happened, then sent her home, saying an officer would be in touch. This was protocol when someone was found dead, they told her, even if from natural causes.

She pulled up another shovelful of rocks and clay. Work was the best way she knew to keep the intrusive thoughts at bay.

Three more feet of digging and she would reach the end of the bed. She glanced over the yard. Burt had mown its center, leaving a patch of bristly weeds and grass under which a stone patio remained to be dug out. Garden beds full of nearly unidentifiable plants ringed the lawn, and a shed—at least, Lise assumed it was a shed; there was no way to tell from the few feet of exposed, weathered siding—struggled to reveal itself from under rampant honeysuckle and blackberry vines.

With this mess, she could earn a few months of rent. At a

minimum. Anchoring her foot on the shovel, she pressed it again into the soil.

Dyann. Dead. She couldn't believe it.

Movement in the kitchen window caught her attention. Fran's face and a wave. Fran appeared on the tiny back stoop off the kitchen door.

"Lise. Someone's here for you," she said.

Fran stepped aside, and a uniformed police officer and a woman in classic Pacific Northwest wear of performance fiber pants and a short-sleeved button-down shirt came down the steps. She'd been expecting them.

Lise slipped the gardening gloves from her hands and rose. And did a double take. *Damn.*

"Lise?" asked the woman in plain clothes, clearly the detective.

Couldn't be. "Signe?" Lise said.

The women stared at each other. The detective was the first to regain her composure. "Lise. It's been a long time. I recognized your name, of course, but I never thought it was you."

No greeting, no "How are you?" When Lise had graduated high school, she'd hoped never to see Signe Rasmussen again. It wouldn't have mattered as much if not for the disaster earlier this spring. Maybe Signe didn't know about that—at least, Lise fervently hoped not.

"I understand you found Ms. King's body this morning," Signe said.

"Yes," Lise replied. Signe? In Astoria? She dropped the shovel to the ground.

"You were working as a clerk at the Lucky Lotus." Signe smelled like carnations and curdled milk. Disdain.

"Yes," Lise repeated, trying not to sound defensive. "I was."

"Can we talk somewhere inside?"

"Yes," Lise said once again, still in shock. "Of course. Come into the kitchen."

Fran had vanished, and the kitchen was empty. Lise motioned toward the red linoleum-topped table where she, Teddy, and Burt had shared tumblers of scotch only the evening before. Charm jumped from his napping spot on a chair and padded toward the hall.

"How did Dyann die? Was it her heart?" Lise asked as Signe took the chair the cat had just vacated. The uniformed police officer pulled out the chair next to her and set an electronic tablet on the table.

"I'll ask the questions, if you don't mind." Signe lifted a hip and pulled something fleecy from the seat of her chair.

Grace's favorite cat toy, a catnip-stuffed carrot. "I'll take that," Lise said.

Lise suspected she looked terrible—bleary-eyed from the unexpected, brief but violent fit of tears earlier that afternoon, with a dirt-smeared face and her hair pulled back in a messy ponytail. Meanwhile, Signe looked like she'd walked out of an ad for the police academy, holding a "star pupil" trophy.

Signe slipped a business card from her jacket's breast pocket and slid it across the table. DETECTIVE, ASTORIA POLICE BUREAU it read. "Tell me what happened this morning."

"When I came into work, I found Dyann dead in the back room."

"Step-by-step, please. When did you arrive?"

Lise folded her arms over her chest, more for self-comfort than as a gesture of defiance. "I got to the shop a little before ten. That's when we open."

Signe nodded.

Lise summarized her morning, from arriving to a quiet shop to finding the back door off its latch, to the shock of discovering Dyann's body. "Then I called 9-1-1." A sudden flash of Dyann's legs, her shoe askew, tightened her throat. "Plus, the odor. I had to get away from it."

"What odor?"

Lise tried to find a way to describe it. "Really strong, and both earthy and buzzy at the same time. You didn't smell it?"

Signe looked at her with curiosity—and a frown.

Lise lifted Signe's business card. "You're a detective. Does that mean she didn't die of natural causes?"

"You were planning to quit," Signe said.

"Yes. I . . ." Lise changed courses. It seemed disrespectful to trash Dyann now. "The job wasn't working out for me. How did you know?"

Again, Signe refused to answer. "And why was that?"

Lise's voice rose. "What does that have to do with anything?"

The police officer stopped typing and looked at Lise, then Signe. Signe turned to him and nodded toward the tablet, giving a definite message of "mind your own business." The officer returned his fingers to the keyboard.

"Ms. King was unhappy with your decision," Signe said. "As to why we know you were planning to quit, she was typing a response to your letter of resignation when she died."

Lise flattened her palms to the tabletop. "Are you saying the shock that I was quitting gave Dyann a heart attack?"

"She was poisoned." Signe's words were sudden.

If Signe was watching her for shock or a tearful admission of guilt, she would be disappointed, because Lise was angry. "You show up here to blame me for my boss's death just because I planned to quit?" Then Signe's statement began to sink in. "You're sure? You're sure she was killed?"

"The medical examiner will say for certain, but indications are that, yes, she was poisoned. She'd been drinking some sort of alcoholic beverage, and her reaction was similar to that of someone who'd ingested a toxin." At Lise's continued stare, she added, "She appeared to have had a seizure and possibly a heart attack."

A seizure would explain the strained look on Dyann's face and her tightened jaw. Lise remembered the sludge-bottomed glass on Dyann's desk. If she'd been poisoned, it had to have been in the Mayan ceremonial liqueur. She imported it, illegally, she'd bragged, through a contact in the Yucatán. Not exactly FDA approved.

"You saw her car, right?" Lise asked. "Her tires had been slashed. There was a note under the windshield wiper."

"You looked at the note." A statement, not a question.

Teddy appeared at the kitchen's entrance. She raised an eyebrow at Lise, then backed away.

"It rained last night, and it was too blurry to read. But, yes, I looked at it. I didn't know Dyann had been murdered. At that point I didn't even know she was dead." Who would have poisoned Dyann? She was irritating—overemotional, reactive, self-absorbed—but underneath the princess attitude was a competent businesswoman with a kind heart. Then Lise remembered something. "Yesterday, before I left the shop, Dyann had told me her ex-husband would kill her."

"You just remembered this?" Signe asked.

"No, I mean, yes." Signe had not changed one bit, Lise thought. "It's just—I thought she had a heart attack or something. I didn't know someone had knocked her off." Knocked her off? Where had that come from?

"Explain, please," Signe said. The police officer stepped up his typing.

"Dyann said she was changing her will. She had me witness it. She planned to leave money to a charity she knew her ex-husband would hate. Besides that, she drastically cut back the money she planned to leave their son."

"You saw this will?"

Lise drew a calming breath. "Yes, but just the change to it."

"The codicil."

"Right. I saw that it existed, but I didn't read it. I'm simply telling you what Dyann told me."

"There was no codicil at the Lucky Lotus or on Ms. King's person," Signe said.

"I don't know what she did with it, but I signed it."

"I see." Signe exchanged a glance with the uniformed police officer before returning her attention to Lise. "What charity was the new beneficiary?"

"A home for retired psychics," Lise said. "I can't remember its name. She was planning to reveal it at her son's birthday party last night."

The police officer stopped typing and looked up. "Blavatsky Manor."

"What?" Signe said.

"That's the name of the outfit. The Blavatsky Manor for Retired Psychic Mediums. My cousin had a job there as a custodian, but she didn't last long. She said the place was a freak show."

"That's the one," Lise said. "I don't know anything else. Only that she said, and I quote, 'He'll kill me when he finds out.' She seemed to think it was funny."

"We're not interested in Richard King."

Lise felt her shoulders drop. "Why not?"

"None of your concern. We talked with him this morning and are satisfied he wasn't involved. Just answer my questions. Do you know where this birthday party was?" Signe asked.

It took her a moment to remember. "Fort George Brewery. She said she, her ex, her son Murphy, a friend of her son's—something to do with snakes—and someone from Blavatsky Manor would be there. Oh, and maybe her ex's girlfriend." A combustible combination for sure.

"Thank you for your help." Signe rose. "We'll be in touch."

"Is the Lucky Lotus closed? I mean, are you busy there? I'd like to return for my things."

"We'll be finished later tonight. Anytime tomorrow morning should be fine."

Someone had poisoned Dyann. She'd died responding to Lise's resignation email. Signe Rasmussen was investigating Dyann's death.

They passed into the Bordeaux-painted hall, and the amateur portraits Teddy had collected of women stared at them in desolation. Lise knew just how they felt.

CHAPTER 5

From the conservatory off the parlor-slash-bedroom, Teddy watched the police detective and her sidekick leave. The front door seemed to slam shut of its own accord, powerfully enough that the uniformed officer looked back in surprise. Honestly, Teddy thought, not for the first time, Corrie House was like a cranky old woman. It had definite opinions about who was welcome and who shouldn't darken its step.

Once the police were out of sight, Teddy returned to the kitchen. Lise sat at the kitchen table and stared at its surface as if the future were written there.

"Honey, are you all right?" Teddy asked.

Lise rose and looked out the back window. "I don't feel good about this."

Fran wandered into the kitchen and, Teddy noted, in an unusual move decided to wipe down the counter. Usually, Fran hid out in her room until late at night and left evidence of her nocturnal ramblings in a sink littered with peanut butter–dabbed plates and tumblers with milk in the bottom.

"It was a shock finding Dyann dead," Teddy said. "It's only natural you'd be out of sorts."

Fran stepped aside to let Lise fill a water glass before pretending to scrub the faucet.

"It's not that. Well, part of it's that," Lise corrected herself. "I don't trust Signe."

"The detective," Teddy said.

Fran had stopped pretending to clean the sink and stood, sponge in hand, watching Teddy and Lise.

"Lise, you look like you could use a good talk, and Fran could use a listen," Teddy said. "Am I right, Fran?"

Fran looked at her feet. "I just want to know what's going on around here."

"Perhaps you two would join me in the sitting room. Fran, will you put on water to boil? I dried rose petals this summer, and they make a nice tea mixed with chamomile and mint. It's in the tin near the stove."

Fran scrambled to fill the kettle. She was an odd one, Teddy noted. She paid her rent on the minute and you'd barely know she was in the house, she was so quiet. But she had imagination for miles, and Lise's situation had evidently captured it.

Ten minutes later, the three women were in Teddy's sitting room. Lise lifted the cup of tea to her nose and inhaled as she looked around the room. Fran baldly took it all in—the crocheted tablecloths as curtains, the chipped gilded mirror over the fireplace, the patchwork velvet throw on the Victorian sofa, the ormolu clock with its circling angels and golden orbs ticking gently on the mantel.

Teddy had always thought the sitting room looked best at night. She especially loved it when Burt was here, looking as out of place as a street dog in a duchess's boudoir.

Fran lifted a framed photo from the table next to the cocoon of an armchair she'd settled in. "Is that guy a rock star? And look at you. You're so pretty."

A lifetime ago. Teddy thought she'd always be young and beautiful, skinny-dipping in the woods of New York and staying up until the sun spilled orange over the morning.

"He was in a band called the Rolling Stones," Teddy said.

"You don't know who Keith Richards is?" Lise said. "Really?"

Fran shrugged, letting her hair fall over her eyes again. She replaced the photo on the side table and leaned forward to pour herself a cup of tea. The teapot had a chipped spout and a crack on its handle that threatened to give way, but it had come with the house, and its motif of butterflies and twining morning glories had been too lovely for Teddy to throw it out.

"Tell me what's on your mind," Teddy told Lise. "You knew the detective, didn't you? I saw it in how you looked at her."

Fran's head tipped up to listen.

"From high school," Lise said. "In Seattle, where I grew up." A few hours north. "We were in the same class, and we didn't get along."

Teddy waited. Clearly, it was more than simply not "getting along" or Lise wouldn't have suddenly looked like a cornered mouse facing a tomcat when the detective had shown up. High school was, what, at least a decade ago for Lise? Whatever had happened between them had burned deeply.

Fran wasn't as patient. "So what? What's the big deal? Not everyone in high school is a bestie. You're not telling us everything."

Lise looked at Fran but didn't reply. She took a deep breath, as if preparing herself for a jump from the high-dive board. Then she retreated. "I'm thinking about moving back home."

"Darling, no." Teddy needed Lise's rent money, even if it was on hold while she worked in the garden, but it was more than that. "I thought you liked it here."

"I do." Lise leaned forward, and her face was full of fervor. "I do like it here. I just think . . . I made a mistake. All of it."

Fran crossed her arms over her chest. "You still haven't told us what the deal is with the detective."

Maybe, Lise thought, all of this business—her gift, fate, finding her roots—was complete BS. As her scientist father liked to point out, human brains had evolved to find causal links between things that were related only by chance. For instance, when a person considered buying a blue Corolla, suddenly that person saw them everywhere. In other words, fate was an illusion.

After the fiasco at home—"fiasco" was as specific as she'd let her mind get—her father had proposed his theory that she was synesthetic and made an appointment for her to meet with a colleague at Stanford to study her brain. Not only would it get to the bottom of her ability to smell emotion, but it was also a great excuse to leave town.

It was on Lise's drive south to meet this colleague, taking the coastal highway to be near the ocean's crisp air, that her car had stalled out in Astoria. When she'd stepped outside at a gas station, she'd inhaled a bouquet of irises, violets, vanilla, and, sparking it to an unmistakable signature, anise. It was L'Heure Bleue, a fragrance more than a hundred years old. She knew this perfume. She owned a tiny bottle she'd taken from her mother's dresser after she'd died, even though she'd never known her mother to wear perfume.

Despite the scent, there was no one around, no emotion to tune into. Besides, she'd never before connected L'Heure Bleue with a feeling. It was simply a beautiful fragrance. At once, she knew this town had something she needed. There was no longer a question of continuing to California. She would stay here.

She'd had the same feeling of inevitability when she'd come to Corrie House. When she'd seen her bedroom, upstairs at the back of the house, she'd felt enveloped by a warmth like easing into a deep bathtub. Except for the lingering scent of dying violets—someone here many years ago had grieved—the room felt happy. It was sparsely furnished with a double bed and a chest of drawers. The room also held a waist-high walnut cabinet fitted with shelves.

"I can move that, if you'd like," Teddy had told her. "It came with the room."

The scent Lise had smelled when she first landed in Astoria returned, just for a moment. *Home,* it whispered. *Here.*

"No, it's perfect," Lise had replied. She could use it to store her growing collection of vintage fragrances. She opened the cabinet's doors. To her surprise, there, in the back corner, was a tiny perfume bottle. It looked old—possibly as old as the 1940s. She eagerly pulled it out and twisted it open. It smelled of roses, cinnamon, and lavender. DANGER, the label said. What an odd name for a perfume.

Teddy had stepped forward to look at the bottle. "Where did that come from? I swear I cleaned out that cabinet."

"Never mind. When can I move in?" Lise had asked. This was nearly three months ago.

"Are either of you listening to me?" Fran asked.

"Of course, darling," Teddy said at the same time Lise said "Sure."

Fran crossed her arms over her chest. "What's the detective doing in Astoria, anyway? You know her from Seattle."

"Signe. Signe Rasmussen is her name," Lise said. "I don't know why she's here. Job, I guess."

"Bad luck," Teddy added.

"It's embarrassing." Lise lifted the edge of the shawl on her chair's arm and let its fringe run through her fingers. *If only they knew the truth.* "Just another blow. We were rivals. I was supposed to be an up-and-coming landscape designer with an unusual specialty. Instead, what am I? A cashier at a New Age shop. And now I'm not even that. Meanwhile, she has her life figured out." Lise pulled the teacup to her nose and inhaled the comforting scent of rose petals and chamomile. "Plus, she wouldn't listen to me when I told her about Richard."

"Oh, darling," Teddy said. "Luck is certainly not on your side. Not today, at least."

The thing was, Lise had been sure she'd followed fate's track, and now this. Dyann was dead—murdered—and the detective in charge of the investigation might have little reason to believe anything Lise told her. So much for a new life.

"You're mopey because you and the detective didn't get along in high school. That's it?" Fran would not leave this alone.

"It's more than that," Lise said. "More, but I don't want to talk about it."

"Darling," Teddy said, "let's let Lise handle this her own way."

"Fine," Fran said. "What are you going to do now?"

"Nothing," Lise said. "What can I do?" Work in the garden, hope Teddy was serious about her offer to let her work off her rent.

Despite Lise's response to Fran's question, Fran's attention had been diverted. She pointed at the clock on the mantel. Its circling angels were still, its golden hands arrested. "Would you look at that?"

The clock had stopped cold.

Teddy rose and twisted a key in the clock's back. "Funny. I wound the clock just this morning."

Never mind, Fran thought. Who cared about the clock at a time like this? Lise was a patsy. This Signe lady was going to pin Dyann's murder on Lise and immediately apply for promotion. She was probably fabricating evidence as they spoke. Fran knew. She'd read this book and plenty like it. Hell, she was planning a similar twist in her novel *Dead Bolt*.

Fran turned to Lise. "You can't let her get away with it."

"With what?" Lise said.

"People don't change." Fran looked first at Lise, then Teddy, when she'd returned to the sofa. "You're deliberately hiding something from us, but I get the hint that Signe-the-detective pulled a fast one on you. What is Signe's goal?" Without waiting for a reply, she said, "To get ahead. She has evidence that you had a motive for killing your boss. That's all she needs to stamp 'done' on this case and wait for the promotion to roll in."

"Fran," Teddy said, "Signe works for the police department. Her life's work is to stop crime."

Fran shook her head. Didn't these people know anything? For an old lady, Teddy wasn't bad, she admitted. The raggedy boho look she'd assembled in the sitting room actually worked, and Fran was even beginning to like being called "darling." Fran had heard her music, too, when she was taking apart the front door's lock and the parlor window was open. It was old rock and roll, but classic stuff. It could be worse, like the piano Fran heard the house sometimes play, too, in wispy fragments when no one else was home. She was not a fan of the waltz.

"People don't change that much," Fran repeated. "I've seen it before." Read it before was more like it, but didn't they say truth was stranger than fiction? "You'd better have your facts solid. It would be good if you knew what was in that will. Better, if you found the codicil and knew if it was ever signed."

"Lise, what did happen when you found Dyann?" Teddy said.

As she asked, Teddy stretched out her legs and crossed them at the ankles. Grace the tabby nudged her way through the pocket doors connecting to the dining room and jumped on her lap. People thought no one could tell Grace and Charm apart, but Fran could. All she had to do was watch to see how Grace swished her tail high while Charm kept his low. Grace was more of a prancer, too.

Although the evening was warm—perhaps one of the last of the season—Lise pulled the fringed shawl from the sofa's back and draped it over her chest. "I did what I always do when I get to the Lucky Lotus to open shop." Lise repeated what she'd told the detective. None of this was new to Fran, since she'd been listening in the hall when Lise had talked with the detective.

Lise frowned. "The strange part was the smell."

"The smell? You mean of the spilled—what did you say? Inca something?" Teddy asked.

"Mayan ceremonial liqueur. Dyann took regular snorts before she did aura readings to, you know, let her 'commune with the spirits.'" No, it was something else. Something I've never smelled before."

"The police have the email to you," Fran said. "Plus, you found the body."

"How did you know about the email?" Lise asked.

"She was listening, honey." Teddy rested a hand on the arm of Fran's chair. "As was I. From the hall. It sounds like Dyann wasn't very happy about your decision to leave the Lucky Lotus."

"What we need to do is gather evidence to protect you," Fran said. "You say Dyann told you her ex would kill her?"

"She was positively giddy about it," Lise said. "Plus, her tires were slashed and a note left on the car. Classic Richard."

"You." Fran nodded at Teddy. "Do you know anything about Dyann? You must have crossed paths with her." With Teddy's patronage of the Labor Temple diner and bar, she would have heard rumors.

"Just a little bit."

"Like what?" Fran asked. Grace, having had enough of Teddy, leapt to Fran's chair in search of, maybe, a softer lap.

"That they had a nasty divorce," Teddy said.

"Duh," Fran replied.

"Plus, Richard has been hanging around with Sylvia Borlotti. The bartender at the Labor Temple saw them there a few weeks ago."

Borlotti. Wasn't that some kind of bean? Fran had seen Sylvia's name on handbills around town as a singer.

"Dyann told me Richard's girlfriend would be at the party last night," Lise said. "She must have meant Sylvia Borlotti."

"If anything, you'd think Dyann would be after Richard, not vice versa," Teddy said.

"Dyann *was* after Richard," Fran pointed out. "Maybe Richard was afraid Dyann would do something to Sylvia and had to stop her. Or maybe Sylvia was jealous of Dyann, so she bumped her off." She shook her head. "No, it has to come back to the changed will. It always does. When there's money, there's a motive. The romantic subplot is a red herring. What do you know about the new will?"

"Red herring?" Lise's brows drew together.

"Subplot?" Teddy said.

"The new will," Fran repeated. "What did she tell you?"

"Murphy gets an allowance, but the rest goes to a home for retired psychic mediums."

"You're joking," Teddy said. "There's a home for retired psychics in town?"

"That's it, then," Fran said. "What the detective needs to do is follow up on the slashed tires first. Check if anyone heard or saw anything. Then nose around about the charity. Was the will finalized?"

Lise shrugged. "I don't know."

"We have the time of death," Fran said. Seeing Lise and

Teddy's blank faces, she added, "What? The detective said she was in the middle of a reply email to you, right? Her computer would have registered the time."

"You're good at this," Lise said.

"Common sense, that's all." That and the accumulated knowledge of having read several hundred crime novels. "Anyway, gather what evidence you can. That's my advice."

Lise gazed toward the end table. She couldn't actually be absorbed in the ancient photo of Teddy with a bunch of hippies with guitars. "I don't know."

"Don't know what?" Fran said.

Lise looked up quickly enough to startle Fran. "Dyann told me straight-out that Richard would kill her, and Signe says she was poisoned."

Fran nodded. "And you need to know more? This is a classic setup, people. You want to sit back and let yourself be dragged to the electric chair, that's your business."

"Stick around, darling," Teddy said to Lise. "I know it's tempting to run away."

Teddy cared about Lise, Fran knew it, but she wouldn't be surprised if she had her eye on her financial bottom line, too. The house needed a lot of work. Expensive work. "Teddy's right. You saw Dyann every day. You saw how Richard and Dyann threatened each other." Fran tapped the coffee table. "You know Dyann in a way the detective never will. If you were smart, you'd collect your own evidence."

Both Teddy and Lise stared at her.

"You guys are looking at me weird. Is something wrong?"

"I don't think I've ever heard you say so many words at a time, darling," Teddy said. "You obviously feel passionately about this."

Fran had gone too far. She tucked in her chin, letting her hair splay over her glasses.

"Fran has a good point," Lise said. "Dyann took a chance on me. I owe her."

Lise sounded more sure than she had all evening. Fran was willing to bet she didn't want to miss the chance to pull one over on the detective, either. "That's the attitude."

Not that Fran would ever stick her neck out like that. No way.

CHAPTER 6

Lise walked down the hill toward downtown and the Lucky Lotus. In a day and a half, she reflected, how a person's world could change. The day before yesterday, she had been traveling the same sidewalk, wondering, as she did many days, if she'd made a mistake in taking the job. Yesterday, she was resolute about giving notice, if a little fearful of Dyann's response.

Today she was on her way to nose around about murder.

At least, maybe. Fran had made a few good points yesterday afternoon. It was possible Lise would see something out of place at the Lucky Lotus, something the police would have missed because they didn't know how the shop ran. She admitted she wouldn't be upset to drop a piece of prime evidence on Signe's desk with a smile and a "Sorry you missed this."

Besides, Lise had a good excuse for visiting the Lucky Lotus. Someone needed to put a note in the door saying that the shop was closed until further notice, and her coffee mug and cardigan were still there.

Astoria's downtown was a ten-block stretch of buildings two main drags deep, lined in old shop fronts, many with tiled entrances bearing the names of long-dead businesses. Seagulls shrieked from the aged posts rising from the river, where piers had once stood to receive cargos of salmon for the canneries.

At the Lucky Lotus, she locked the shop door behind her and made sure the sign was flipped to CLOSED. The shop was warm with the sun through its front windows, but it felt lonely here and unusually empty.

She only hesitated a moment before passing through the beaded curtain to the shop's back room. She turned on the light. The acrid odor from the day before was gone. She forced her gaze to the floor behind Dyann's desk. It had been pulled away a few inches and the small glass and Dyann's laptop removed, but that was the only visible difference from any other morning Lise had opened the shop. However, today Dyann would not be strolling in near noon for aura readings or to order more tchotchkes.

Now what?

The codicil Lise had signed was nowhere in sight. The police had taken the computer, so there'd be no checking to see if the updated will was on it. That was, if Lise could even guess Dyann's password. She slid open the desk's top drawer in case the password was jotted down somewhere. All she found was a Post-it note with "Richard is an asshole" jotted on it.

But wait—here was a calendar. Dyann had been old school about keeping her appointments on paper. Lise knew this from booking aura readings. She flipped to the week before and ran her finger down the page. There it was, a meeting at Blavatsky Manor with someone named Maxine.

She turned the page to the current week. Dyann had a facial scheduled at nine o'clock the morning of the day she died and a note to call someone named Ornette. Other appointments were what Lise might have expected: manicure, personal training session, reminder to issue Lise's paycheck.

The police would have all this information, of course.

She wondered who else had signed Dyann's changed will. Perhaps she'd succeeded in getting the second signature at

Murphy's party, as she'd planned. She would have relished forcing Richard to watch as the server wielded the pen.

Lise cracked open the door to the alley. Dyann's Mercedes was gone, likely towed to the police yard for processing.

"What are you doing here?"

Lise spun to find Signe Rasmussen staring at her from behind the beaded curtain. She had been so engrossed in digging around Dyann's area she hadn't heard the front door open. "Picking up things I left." Thankfully, the cardigan was still draped over her arm, and she lifted it to demonstrate. "What about you? You said the police would be finished here."

The wooden beads clattered as Signe passed through them. "Just making sure everything is in order." She lifted her gaze to the shop's key, still in Lise's hand. "I assume you're taking your key to her son?"

"Yes," Lise said, happy to have this excuse. "I can leave it in her mailbox."

"Do that," Signe replied.

"Do you have any suspects?"

Signe began to say something, but seemed to change her mind midstream. "That's police business. Lock up here when you're done."

Lise hesitated, although Signe seemed to be waiting for her to leave. Finally, she said, "I was surprised to see you in Astoria."

"Is that so? I might say the same."

Signe clearly didn't care for nostalgic conversation, and Lise didn't have the nerve to mention the events from earlier this summer. "Did you return to Seattle after college?"

Signe's strained smile didn't waver. When it became obvious she wouldn't reply, Lise took a last look around the back room. She wanted to stay, to see if there was anything here that pointed to Richard's guilt, but Signe wouldn't leave until she did. And when Lise left, she'd not be able to return.

Signe lifted the beaded curtain aside. "After you."

* * *

In front of the Lucky Lotus, Signe got into a police-issued black SUV, and Lise crossed the street on foot. Dyann's house wasn't far, and, frankly, Lise welcomed the walk. Anything to shake the irritation and undeserved guilt she now felt. As in high school, Signe was a master at communicating disdain without a saying a word.

Lise glanced into the bookstore where Fran worked and caught Fran waving wildly from inside. She gestured for Lise to enter. Fran had a gift for disappearing, and if it wasn't for her arms windmilling, she might have vanished into the shelves of books ringing the store.

Lise had always liked Margie's Books. The store's selection was lovingly honed to a quirky mix of best-sellers and subjects the shop's owner loved. As a result, Margie's had a robust offering of books on dog training, crafts, and World War II as well as a few shelves of spicy romances. Margie had given over a section to Fran to stock with crime novels, and Fran had happily complied, ordering a selection of golden age mysteries with just enough contemporary novels to keep customers happy.

A pug snored from one of the four armchairs gathered in the store's center, while a girl likely not old enough to read flipped the pages of a picture book.

Fran pushed aside a volume she'd been reading. She'd quickly flipped it to hide its cover, but Lise had caught its title on the spine.

"*Talking to Spirits*? I didn't know you were into that sort of thing," Lise said. "We had a bunch of books at the Lucky Lotus you would have been interested in."

"Never mind." Fran pushed Lise toward the cookbook section, where it was quiet. "I've got news."

"About what?" Lise asked.

Fran looked at her in disbelief. "Are you kidding? About the murder, dummy. Did you go back to the Lucky Lotus?"

Fran's floppy hair was a shade of mouse-gray only slightly deeper than that of her skin. But those eyes were large and luminous brown, eyes Renoir would have longed to have painted. Too bad her bangs so often covered them.

Lise nodded. "I picked up a few things, but Signe—the detective—showed up. I'm going to take my key back to Dyann's house."

"That's all?" Fran asked. "You didn't get the chance to look around for more?"

"I wanted to, but I couldn't. Not with Signe there." Lise should have brought Fran with her, although she hated to think about what Signe would have made of that. "But, before she busted in on me, I found Dyann's calendar. She met with someone last week at the Blavatsky Manor retirement home."

"No will?"

"The police took her laptop."

"They would. How about a password? If you could get your hands on that laptop, you might be able to find evidence. Not just the will but also threats from her ex. That's where you need to focus your effort."

Fran was clearly more comfortable issuing commands than taking part. "Too late now." Lise pulled the spine of a book on spice blends. She could nearly smell the saffron threads on its cover. "But I did look in her desk drawer. All I found was a Post-it with 'Richard is an asshole' written on it."

"Her password," Fran said. "Definitely. Anyway, Charlene from the butcher shop came in for her volume on game meat in the Ottoman Empire. We talked about Dyann."

"Excuse me," a man in a Yankees jersey asked. "Do you have anything on baseball?"

"Far right of the store, in the back. Check the shelf there," Fran said without breaking eye contact with Lise. The man wandered off.

"Margie stocks books on baseball? That's new."

"Nope. But looking for them will keep him busy for a minute." She removed Lise's fingers from the cookbook and pushed it back into the shelf.

"Charlene didn't see anything, did she?" Lise asked. The shops would have been closed by then. The antiques mall and shoe store locked their doors at six, the same time the Lucky Lotus did.

"In fact, she did." Then Fran froze.

Lise turned to see a bearded man stroll toward the music section. Fran watched him, lips parted, then yanked her attention back to Lise. A sheer wisp of rose wafted around her.

"Do you know him?" Lise asked.

"He works at the tattoo shop," she whispered as her gaze crept back to the bearded man. "He's so . . ."

Apparently not finding what he was looking for, the man left. Fran's focus on him only broke when the door closed behind him.

"Charlene," Lise reminded her. "She saw something?"

"Right. Yes. She spotted Dyann's ex's car down the block. Late. Not in the alley, but in the street."

The man seeking the baseball book returned to Fran. "Couldn't find anything about sports at all. The sign says those books are romantic suspense."

Fran reluctantly dragged her attention to the customer. "Must have sold out. Better luck next time."

"Charlene," Lise said. "She was sure it was Richard's?"

"Red Camaro. Bumper sticker saying 'So Many Dicks, Not Enough Richards.'"

His car, all right. "Signe said Richard couldn't have killed Dyann, but she didn't say why. I assumed it was because he was somewhere else."

Fran tipped her head up again, revealing those startling eyes. "His car sure wasn't."

Lise left Fran at the bookstore—the customer looking for

books about baseball had finally cornered her. If Fran had found out so easily that Richard had been nearby when Dyann died, why hadn't the police discovered the same? Signe had sounded sure Richard had nothing to do with her death and had shut Lise down when she'd mentioned it. What did Signe know that she didn't?

Chapter 7

The butcher shop was in an old storefront with plate glass windows trimmed in glossy black tile, and this morning customers crowded its display cases. Lise had walked past it many times in the few months she'd lived in Astoria, but she'd never gone in.

At the counter, Charlene wrapped sausages in white paper, handing them to her son to ring up. Lise waited for the customers to thin. Some were simply grabbing ready-made sandwiches for lunch, but one customer, a stocky man who kept fidgeting with his trucker cap, ordered a complicated spread of sliced meats. Charlene deftly lugged logs of various sausages to the slicer, a few fingers of her latex glove waggling empty where she had missing digits.

"Half a pound of salami cotto, half a pound of bresaola, and a quarter pound chicken liver mousse," she called to her son at the cash register. "Plus a Lebanon bologna sandwich." Then, to the customer, "Will that be all?"

Lise wandered toward the meat case. Hopefully, the customer had a good cardiologist.

"Aren't you the gal from the Lucky Lotus?" Charlene asked as she pulled a tray of chicken thighs from the case. "You helped me when I bought that book on astrology."

"Yes." She hadn't been sure Charlene would remember her, but Lise certainly remembered Charlene. She'd smelled of happiness and smoked meat.

"Four chicken thighs and a pound of bacon ends," she shouted toward her son. She turned to Lise again. "What'll you have?"

"Nothing, thank you." Lise was vegetarian. Her whole family was. Sometime early in their marriage, her parents had participated in research on cardiac health. Since then, they'd subsisted on beans, tofu, and whatever vegetables were on sale. Her brother Albert occasionally conducted trace nutrient studies of the family's diet, requiring them to keep detailed logs, including weighing portions and tracking meal times. Her father had sent her a blood pressure cuff after she'd moved.

Charlene stood back from the meat counter. "Then how can I help you?"

"I understand you saw Richard's Camaro down the block the night before last, the night Dyann died."

"Yes." She pulled a fat, white paper–wrapped package from the freezer behind her and deposited it on the counter in front of her son. "Pork ribs for the Satterburgs. Ben should be in to pick them up in a minute. Ah, there he is."

A man in plaid golf shorts waved at Charlene and pulled out his wallet at the cash register.

Charlene returned her attention to Lise. "Sure, I saw his car."

"After the butcher shop closed?" Dyann had returned to the Lucky Lotus after the birthday dinner for Murphy. Why, she couldn't say.

"Around nine o'clock. I closed up the shop, went home for dinner, then returned to make a batch of maple sausage for the Elks breakfast this morning." She looked wistful. Lise didn't know if it was because of the Elks or Dyann. Finally, Charlene said, "She was a fine lady, Dyann was. A little cuckoo, maybe, with all that aura reading and energy healing, but she was generous. After she won the lottery, she made a nice gift to the maritime museum in honor of my father." She slowly shook her head. "That gal could really put away a rib eye, too."

"You're sure it was Richard's car?" Fran seemed positive, but Lise wanted to hear it directly from Charlene.

"Absolutely certain. You can't miss the bumper sticker." Thoughtful, she rested her hands on the glass display. "Richard preferred the New York strip, but Dyann had it right with the rib eye. You need that marbling, especially if you plan to grill."

"Thank you, Charlene."

Charlene straightened her apron and reached into the meat display for a tray of pork chops. "Anytime, hon. You take care of yourself."

The Fort George Brewery was only a few blocks from the Lucky Lotus, so it made sense that Dyann wouldn't have moved her car for Murphy's birthday dinner. She would have returned to the Lucky Lotus, then driven home. But for whatever reason, she'd opted to go into the shop first. Her decision had been fatal.

Outside the butcher shop, Lise hesitated. Could anything that happened at Murphy's birthday dinner had led to Dyann's change of plans? Maybe someone at the brewery had seen something. It wouldn't hurt to check it out. She shifted her cardigan to her other arm and headed up the street.

The Fort George Brewery occupied a full city block and consisted of two warehouse-sized buildings with a courtyard between them. As usual, it swarmed with tourists. Some sat in the courtyard, enjoying the season's last sun, while others took lunch in the brewery's main building or the annex, on the other side of the courtyard, where a casual bistro served hamburgers and pizza. The occupants of one table consulted a map. If their *Goonies* T-shirts with skulls and crossbones were any indication, they were on the trail of movie locations.

For Murphy's birthday party, Dyann would have reserved a private room. Lise took the curved staircase to the annex's second floor. She waited her turn in line at the reception area.

"Table for one?" the host asked, one hand on an iPad, the other clutching a laminated menu.

"No, actually, I have a question about the night before last. A party," Lise said.

The host looked past her at the line of customers coming up the stairs. "I don't know anything about that. You'll have to talk to the manager. Back there." He gestured with the menu toward the bar.

Beyond the bar was a hall leading to an office with its door ajar. Lise knocked twice on the office door and pushed it open to see a man with his feet on the desk, watching something on his phone. The overheated office smelled of garlicky pizza, and a grease-smeared plate with a piece of crust on it sat on the desk. When she entered, the manager quickly swung his feet to the floor.

"Can I help you?" he said, looking at his computer screen as if his attention had never strayed.

"I hope so. I have a question about a party here the other night. They probably reserved a private room. Murphy King's birthday."

He looked away from his computer screen and gave her an expression to indicate that his time was valuable and she was wasting it. "And?"

"I was wondering what time they left," Lise said.

"I can't tell you that."

"You weren't here? Maybe you could point me to the server working that night."

"You don't understand," the manager said. "I can't tell you that because it's none of your business. Who rented what and ate and drank and why and when they left is none of your business."

She hadn't expected that tone. "I was just—"

"Would you want someone reporting on you?" He switched to a falsetto. " 'She had the crab salad and picked out the peas. She drank two pinot grigios, and the man with her wore a wedding ring.' Is that what you'd want?"

Wow. "Sorry to bother you." Lise backed from the room.

She'd certainly struck out here. She walked down the curved staircase. A small blonde with a broad pink streak through her pixie haircut cleared a table near the exit. "Lise?" She was a Lucky Lotus customer with a staggering collection of tarot cards. Lise couldn't remember her name.

"Nice to see you again," Lise said. "How did you like the Cat People deck?"

"Phoebe," the woman said. "Hang tight a second, if you don't mind." Phoebe crossed the room to dump her armload of dirty plates and returned. "I heard about Dyann. Shocking."

"No kidding," Lise said. News sure traveled quickly in this town.

"What makes it even weirder is that I was working that night. I bet I was one of the last people to see her alive. I wouldn't have even paid much attention to them if they weren't so bizarre." She stepped closer. "What's even weirder is I'd drawn the Ten of Swords before I came on my shift." She dragged a finger across her neck to drive the point home.

What luck. "Do you have a minute to talk?"

Phoebe glanced toward the bus tubs, then back to Lise. "Sure. I'll tell my boss I need a quick break. Meet me in the courtyard."

Lise found a spot in the courtyard to lean on the garden wall. She'd barely settled when Phoebe hurried over.

"I only have a second," she said.

"You said they were 'bizarre,' " Lise said. "What do you mean?"

"First of all, it was a strange collection of people." Phoebe eyed a table that a family had just left, undoubtedly mentally measuring the space their dishes would take up on a tray. "Dyann and her son were there, of course—Dyann had ordered a birthday cake to be delivered—and Richard King. It totally made sense that Murphy's dad would be there. But his girlfriend, too?"

"Sylvia Borlotti, the singer," Lise said.

"Yes," Phoebe said. "She was dressed for her set at Amato's. All sequins, neck cut down to here." Her finger dropped low on her chest. "So that was odd. Then there was this tattooed guy. Tons of tattoos, mostly snakes." Her expression softened. "Actually, he was kind of cute. I hope he comes back."

Murphy's friend. "Who else?"

Phoebe's attention snapped to the present. "Another weirdo. Some old lady with a walker. She was actually wearing a turban with a rhinestone brooch pinned on it. Although . . ."

"Although what?"

"When I refilled her water, she whispered to me to hide my purse." Phoebe toyed with her amethyst ring, a Lucky Lotus purchase purported to enhance intuition. "So I did. I took it out of the employees' locker room and hid it in the coffee cupboard." Phoebe looked at her with wide eyes. "This morning I heard Regan's wallet was stolen that night. The lady was right."

"No kidding?" Undoubtedly the palm reader from Blavatsky Manor. "Did you happen to hear what they were talking about?"

She shrugged. "I was there to refill water glasses and clear plates. You know how people usually shut up when restaurant staff appear. I wouldn't say it was a happy group, though, for a birthday party."

"What do you mean?"

"Not exactly a party vibe. Dyann was looking daggers at her ex and his girlfriend. She seemed to be ignoring the cute guy with the tattoos, and she was making kind of a production about the lady with the turban. Dyann's son—"

"Murphy," Lise said.

"—seemed totally oblivious. He sure could put away the pizza, though." Her attention drifted again for a second. "The lady with the turban has quite a voice. She belted out 'Happy Birthday' like she was calling for a life raft." She leaned forward and lowered her voice. "When I came in to check on beverages, there was beer all over the place. Dyann said there'd been an accident, but accidents don't usually end up with a pint glass on the floor in pieces."

"I see what you mean about bizarre." So far, everything lined up with what Dyann had predicted, down to Richard bringing his new girlfriend. "Did you notice what time they left?"

"They didn't stick around long. Two pizzas, a pitcher of soda, a couple of beers, and cake. I bet they were out of there by eight o'clock. Sylvia left before the rest of them. She gave Richard a long kiss good-bye."

Lise bet he liked that. Anything to irritate Dyann. As for the precise time they left, the police could check when Dyann or Richard—or whoever paid for dinner—ran their credit card. That, combined with when Dyann was composing her response to Lise's resignation email, would give a rough timeline of events.

However, the big question wasn't *when* but *why* Dyann had returned to the office at all.

CHAPTER 8

Dyann's house was a twenty minute walk uphill. Astoria was compactly built, and at fewer than ten thousand residents, small. However, due to the hills rising from the Columbia River, aside from a narrow strip of downtown built on pilings over the river, the town climbed up, with a collection of Victorian working class homes in various states of repair mixed with more solid, newer homes.

Dyann's house was one of the newer homes, with an English basement and attached garage. The basement's entrance was on the side of the house, and two mailboxes were posted by the front door. The basement must be Murphy's apartment. Lise wondered what, if anything, he'd inherit from Dyann's estate now that she'd changed her will—that is, if she'd succeeded in getting the second signature.

Lise climbed the stairs and rang the doorbell. She couldn't hear anything inside—doorbells were so often broken—so she knocked. No response. She prepared to drop the key into Dyann's mailbox, then hesitated. Was this really safe? What if someone learned Dyann had died, then came by to break in? All they'd have to do is check the mailbox, and they'd have free entry.

She retraced her steps and went around the side of the

house to knock on the basement door. Murphy answered right away.

"Hi, uh . . ." Murphy said. Behind him, a mammoth TV screen portrayed a paused video game showing a winged dragon suspended over a jagged red canyon. A man sat on the leather couch facing the screen. Snake tattoos sheathed his arms. This must be the man Phoebe had seen at the brewery.

"Lise," she reminded him. "I'm sorry to interrupt you while you're"—she glanced at the video game frozen on the screen—"grieving, but I wanted to return the key to the shop."

Murphy shared his mother's blond coloring, but that's where the resemblance ended. He struggled with acne, and his sartorial choices leaned heavily on sweatpants and T-shirts. Instead of Dyann's wide, expressive eyes, his were remarkably small and nearly swallowed by his cheeks.

Dyann had seemed to both adore and be repulsed by her son. She couldn't help squeezing him in hugs, and she smiled broadly when he showed up at the shop, but when Murphy left, she mumbled ominously about his aura and commented that he might shower a little more often.

Trailing from him this afternoon was a dry scent, almost like old hay. Not grief, strangely enough. It was boredom.

"I'm really sorry about your mother," Lise said. "I can't even imagine how awful you must feel. And to think she died on your birthday, too. Terrible."

"Yeah." Did Murphy ever blink? He didn't move to take the key.

The man on the couch rose. "I'm Ornette Cassell, Murphy's friend. I'm afraid Murphy's in shock. You must be the woman who found Dyann. I'd heard it was someone who worked there."

"Shock is understandable," Lise said.

Ornette. Dyann had made a note in her calendar to call him the day she'd died. His skin crawled with tattoos of jewel-toned reptiles, but instead of being creepy, they were mesmerizing. As was Ornette's friendly smile and otherwise clean-cut air. Phoebe had been right. There was something alluring about him. He gave her a feeling of complicity, as if they were both the adults in the room and Murphy was their charge.

Lise was preparing to reply when motion to the right of the TV screen caught her eye and froze the words in her throat. It was a snake as thick as a rolling pin, an eerie pale orange color, slithering in a lit aquarium.

Ornette's words seemed to rouse Murphy. He took the key Lise still held toward him, and his features came to life. "Ornette runs the reptile refuge where I volunteer."

Ornette nodded toward the aquarium. "We met when Murphy adopted Tangerine Dream."

Lise gave a weak smile, and they all stared at the aquarium. The snake glided behind a chunk of driftwood and seemed to draw into itself, compacting into a tight orange bundle.

Murphy's bizarrely detached attitude sparked an idea. "I wouldn't mind putting a few things from the shop—you know, papers, etcetera—upstairs," she said.

She patted her tote bag, which contained nothing more than her coffee mug and cardigan, handy for when Dyann boosted the shop's AC to counter a hot flash. She held her breath. There was no reason he wouldn't simply ask her to leave the papers with him.

"Okay," Murphy said, his prior expression of indifference returning. He rummaged through a pile of junk mail and handed her a key.

"Let me give you my number, in case I can help with the shop somehow." She recited it aloud. Murphy typed it into his phone, more out of duty than interest, Lise guessed. "Thank you. It was nice to meet you, Ornette."

Murphy settled on the sofa and picked up the game controller. "Leave the key on the kitchen counter. The door will lock behind you by itself."

* * *

Lise let herself in Dyann's house. She'd expected a variation on the Lucky Lotus's New Age vibe, but other than a single crystal hanging from each window, her home's decor was more Barbie Dream House than spiritual mom. A powder-pink leather sectional sofa wrapped around one corner of the living room, with a frilled lampshade on the table lamp and chintz-covered pillows tossed here and there. A silk ficus in a rattan basket anchored the couch's opposite end. Near the sofa sat a plush baby-blue recliner. She must have bought everything at once when she'd won the lottery.

The couch faced a gas fireplace, its mantel crowded with framed photos: Murphy as a baby, Murphy as a plump grade-schooler, Dyann as a Miss Oregon runner-up, even a wedding photo of Richard and Dyann. Lise picked up a porcelain-framed photo on the end table nearest her. It was of a younger Dyann and Richard in Hawaii, maybe on their honeymoon. Richard's arm wrapped Dyann's shoulders, and she leaned against him. They glowed with happiness.

Lise replaced the photo. She was in. If Fran were here, she'd tell her to hurry, that Murphy would unleash his snake on her or that Signe would arrive with handcuffs, ready to cart her off for fibbing to get inside.

Between the dining and living rooms ran a hall to the house's rear. Lise passed a bathroom, a guest room with an exercise bike heaped with clothes in the corner, and another bedroom that looked to be Dyann's office. She poked her head in the third bedroom. Yes, this was the master bedroom. Dyann's sheets—lavender satin—were still rumpled from her last night's sleep there. Lise corrected herself: her last night's sleep anywhere.

She couldn't help crossing the apricot-carpeted floor to get a closer look at the perfume bottle on the dresser. It was Alien by Thierry Mugler, now turned amber with age. She sniffed its lid. It smelled of shrieking jasmine, sharp enough to hatchet a path through a warehouse rave. She dabbed some on the back of her hand to remember Dyann by.

Keenly aware of Murphy and his friend downstairs, Lise retreated to Dyann's office. The thick carpeting muffled her steps. A table near the window held a desktop computer. Lise shook its mouse to wake it, and a demand for a password appeared.

Could Fran be right? Lise tapped *Richard is an asshole* at the prompt. The box shook twice. Invalid.

Hmm. Lise typed *Murphy* with the same result. What else could it be?

Then she tried *Richard is an asshole!* with the added exclamation point. The screen woke all at once, sending Lise back a step. Damn, Fran was good.

With luck, Dyann had synced her computers in the cloud, and her reply to Lise's resignation would appear here. Lise clicked the email icon, and an unfinished email popped up—*bingo.* Lise read over it quickly. Dyann had not been happy about Lise giving notice, but the overall message was mixed. First, she'd written that Lise was letting her down and breaking a commitment and that her aura was blackening by the minute. A sentence later, she was telling Lise how lucky she'd been to work in such an uplifting shop and how dozens of other people aspired to her position. Then, in an about face, she wrote about the joy of helping Lise explore clairalience. The email was date-stamped eight-forty-three the night she died. Did her death halt the email, or had she simply set it aside while she dreamed up a zinger to sign off with?

The computer's desktop was remarkably clear: no invoices needing attention, no correspondence untended. Dyann's background in admin at King Cars had served her well. One envelope from a law firm, its top neatly slit, rested against a cup of pens. Lise looked over her shoulder, slid the letter from its envelope, and scanned it. It was from an attorney retained by

Sylvia Borlotti and demanded that Dyann "cease and desist her harassing overtures" toward their client. She replaced the letter.

Lise turned to the computer and clicked to Dyann's sent mail box in the hopes of finding a copy of her will. Perhaps she'd emailed revisions to her attorney. She was in luck. She opened an email to Preston Morningsun at Cox and Morningsun. "See the attached revision to will," Dyann had written. "Please prepare papers immediately. I'll bring the signed codicil tomorrow afternoon." Dyann's automatic signature included rainbow and mandala emojis with the words "*Manifest your dreams.*" And on the next line, "*Creator of the world famous Magnet Oil.*" She wondered what the attorneys had thought of that.

Dyann clearly believed her codicil would be completed the day after Murphy's birthday, but Lise still didn't know if she'd gotten the second signature.

She reached for the mouse to forward the email to herself, then thought again. What if the police searched Dyann's computer? They'd see Lise had been here. Instead, she opened the attached codicil and photographed it with her phone.

Two minutes later, she had left the key on the kitchen counter and was out the front door. No snakes, no arrest, no interruption. How easy was that?

CHAPTER 9

Teddy had experienced some exceptional evenings. She'd sipped martinis on the terrace of a billionaire's penthouse in Manhattan with the streets below her streaming with sparks of traffic like a roman candle tipped on its side. She'd dined on the Eiffel Tower—this was just the sort of thing Bernard had loved, an expensive, clichéd luxury—as the sun set, with waiters in crisp black jackets setting plates before her. She'd meditated in Nepal with Tibetan monks and rock stars, back in the sixties, when enlightenment was all the rage.

But for sheer contentment, tonight topped them all. She sat in Corrie House's backyard in an Adirondack chair. Burt was in the chair next to her, clutching the neck of a bottle of beer, well deserved after his afternoon spent tinkering with the furnace. Crickets chirped, and the stars appeared in the sky as if an interstellar fairy turned them on one by one.

She glanced at Burt and frowned. "Darling, are you all right?"

His momentary wince became a smile. The color returned to his face. "Better than all right. How could I not be, here with you?"

"As long as you didn't overexert yourself." She'd noticed when, in the basement, Burt had paused. For a moment, he'd seemed almost frail. Then he'd lifted the screwdriver and again became the hearty Burt she knew.

"A few adjustments here, that's all," he'd said. "My Band-Aid repairs won't keep her going much longer. You're looking at a new furnace, Teddy."

She had suspected this was coming. Tomorrow she'd put up an ad at the Blue Scorcher café for another housemate. The front bedroom was empty, and although four people were a lot for a house with just one bathroom, it had to be done.

However, that was tomorrow; this was now. Teddy relaxed back into her chair. Yes, a remarkable evening. There weren't too many of these left. Swallows circled overhead, preparing to nest in the rafters, and the sun set orange, bruising to purple near the horizon. What was it A. E. Housman wrote?

Now, of my threescore years and ten,
Twenty will not come again,
And take from seventy springs a score,
It only leaves me fifty more.

And since to look at things in bloom
Fifty springs are little room,
About the woodlands I will go
To see the cherry hung with snow.

She had already cheated Housman's calculations by a decade. It was good to be here, to be herself, to feel comfortable in her skin. It had taken a lot of years to arrive at this place.

"How'd you stumble on this old house, anyway?" Burt asked.

Strange that they'd never talked about it. Yet there had been so much else to catch up on, and her connection to Corrie House was deeply personal. "I've owned it for a long time—

let's see, almost forty years now. But I only moved here a year ago last spring, a few months before we met."

"How's that?"

"Ready to settle in for a story?"

He swirled the beer remaining in his bottle. "I like your stories."

"I inherited it."

"You're a Corrie?"

"No, I'm not a Corrie, but I fell in love with one. Marcus, the last of the Corries. We were best friends since grade school out east. As close as two people could be."

Closer, even. Teddy swore their thoughts flowed freely from one head to the other. When he was hungry, she had a tuna salad sandwich already prepared for him. When she wanted to see a particular movie, he'd already bought tickets. She knew every millimeter of his face—the ears that stuck out from his black curly hair, the beard that grew in red before he shaved it away, the conical shape of his hands, an artist's hands.

"You never married him, that is, unless you're keeping something from me," Burt said.

Teddy rested back in her chair and faced the garden shed across the expanse of shaggy weeds they called the lawn. "No, we didn't marry." She hadn't told Burt this story yet, either, as important as it was to her. "We weren't even romantic—at least, not in the traditional sense. He was gay. Died from complications of AIDS. This was back before the good meds." Deep grief never vanishes. It simply becomes wrapped in life and rocks painfully back and forth until it finds its home. Sometimes Teddy felt grief, still, and it pinched.

Burt granted her the respect of not responding with words. He briefly laid a callused palm on her arm.

"His family had disowned him. They left him Corrie House, anyway, almost as a curse, was my guess. Marcus's life was on the East Coast, so he let the house out to roomers, and when he died he left the house to me. He used to tell me stories about how he played here as a boy with his imaginary friend."

"No kidding?"

"Not the kind of friend you'd expect, either. His was a young woman. She wore a long dress and talked with a soft voice, as if she wasn't used to being listened to. He told me she was sad, but she read him stories in bed at night."

"Makes sense," Burt said. "A boy who felt apart would have an imaginary friend who felt the same."

For a moment, Teddy and Burt listened to the swallows chirp overhead. Teddy set her empty beer bottle on the ground.

"You didn't move here right away," Burt said.

"No. By then I was involved with someone in New York."

Burt knew about Bernard. She'd been "involved" with him as his mistress. He'd paid her rent and given her a healthy allowance. She'd slipped on her Louboutins and charm to accompany him on business trips, and she occupied herself when he was with his family. He'd tried to convince her to sell Corrie House, saying he could invest the proceeds for her. He was good at that. Maybe she would have been rich. But for Marcus's sake, she wouldn't.

When Bernard had died, Corrie House was all she had left. On the airplane coming west, she'd reluctantly made plans to sell the house and settle somewhere warm to wait out her remaining years. What other choice did she have? However, as she'd exited the rental car in Astoria, pulling her suitcase behind her, and gazed up at the Gothic Victorian with its peeling paint and weedy trees of heaven sprouting from its foundation, she'd felt instantly at peace. *Be with me,* the house seemed to say. It pulled her toward the door and up the steps. *Come in. Come home.*

She'd once compromised on her life big time. She would not do it again.

As she sat beside Burt, lost in thoughts, the kitchen door

burst open, and Lise rushed down the steps like a filly on new legs. She stopped short. “Oh, hi, Burt. Am I interrupting you?”

“No, darling,” Teddy said.

“What’s going on?” Burt asked.

“I’ve got it.” Lise lifted her phone. “I know more about Dyann’s will.”

Lise lowered herself to the weed-dense lawn to face Teddy and Burt. Burt had a comforting solidity about him, but he trailed the scent of stones and musty cardboard boxes. He was lost in thought, and . . . something else. Ill, maybe?

Underneath each of their chairs lay a twin cat. Lise extended fingers for Charm to sniff. “I went to Dyann’s to give back my key to the shop, and I found her email to her lawyers with the changes she wanted to her will.”

A face briefly appeared in the kitchen window. Fran. She emerged from the back door and lingered at the top of the steps.

“Come join us, Fran,” Teddy said, without even turning to see who it was.

Fran scampered down the steps and plopped next to Lise on the grass. “What happened?”

“What’s all this about?” Burt asked.

Lise cast a questioning glance at Teddy.

“He knows,” she said.

“I heard a bit about it at lunch at the Labor Temple, too,” Burt said. “Please, continue.”

Lise kept her eyes on Burt. “The afternoon Dyann died, she’d told me her ex-husband would kill her when he found out how she’d changed her will.”

“Who’s to say he’d find out?” Burt asked.

“She made sure he did,” Lise said. “She announced it at her son’s birthday party. The detective thinks she was poisoned.”

“You told all this to the detective, of course,” Burt said.

"Yes," Lise replied. "She said it couldn't have been him, but she wouldn't say why."

"Was the thinking that she was poisoned from something she drank?" Burt asked.

"That would be my guess. She'd been into the Mayan ceremonial liqueur."

"He could have put poison in her beverage at any point," Fran said.

"True. If he'd had access to the shop." Richard had come in a handful of times while Lise had been working, but as far as she could tell, only to argue with Dyann. He had a habit of slamming the door, setting off the chime, when he left. Lise found it hard to believe he'd have had time between shouting sessions to poison bottles and hide them on her shelf. "However, it was only the day before yesterday that he found out about the change in her will, and he hadn't been in the shop during business hours. That much I know."

"Meaning the poisoning probably happened that night," Fran said. "If Richard had put something in her liqueur earlier, why would he bother slashing her tires?"

Lise marveled at how different Fran looked when she was drawn into a topic. Lise had been so used to Fran skulking around with her hair flopped over her glasses. Now, with a murder to talk over, she was a different person.

Burt nodded slowly. "You found her will. I won't ask how."

"I went into her house," Lise said. "Her son okayed it." Maybe he didn't tell her to nose around on Dyann's computer, but he hadn't said not to.

"Fine," Fran said. "So, what did you find?"

"I took a photo of the email. Let me read it to you." Lise tapped her phone's screen. "The subject line is '*Immediate Attention Required*.'" She looked up to make sure everyone was listening. They were. "This is the codicil attached to the email. It must be what she asked me to sign. 'Please change my will as follows'—here it's numbered—'One: Add the Blavatsky Manor, Home for Retired Psychic Mediums. Two: Leave the entirety of my estate to the new legatee, except for a monthly allowance of the current amount to my son, Murphy King, until he reaches the age of thirty, at which point the allowance will cease.' Besides that, she included a provision that if Richard marries Sylvia, her attorneys will take out a weekly notice in the *Astorian* saying that Richard has persistent halitosis."

"Wow," Fran said. "That must be why she didn't want you to read it, Lise."

"Let me get this straight. She was going to leave her money to her son and now is giving it to a bunch of psychics?" Burt asked. "How much money are we talking about?"

"I'm not sure exactly. Millions, is my guess," Lise said.

"That's something," Burt said. He seemed to light up as she talked.

"Any idea what her original will said?" Teddy asked.

"Dyann told me her son would have received it all."

"So, we have three murder suspects now," Fran said. "Richard, Murphy, and the psychics." She rested back on her palms.

"Because they were psychic? Just kidding." Burt laughed at his own joke. Teddy laughed, too.

"They didn't have to be psychic to know they were in the new will," Lise said. "Dyann met with them last week."

Fran sat up. "Let's examine motive. How desperate were any of them for money?"

"We know Richard has a motive," Teddy said. "It sounds like he and Dyann had it in for each other. As for his financial situation, who knows?"

"Her son had a motive, too," Lise said. "Money. And let's not forget Sylvia Borlotti. When I was at Dyann's house, I found a letter from her attorney threatening to sue Dyann."

"Remember? Sylvia Borlotti was Richard's lover," Teddy

told Burt. "The bartender told us she saw them at the Labor Temple. They were all over each other."

"Sue her about what?" Fran asked.

"I don't know."

"So that's"—Teddy looked toward the treetops; the stars were graying over with clouds—"Four suspects, right? Richard, her son, the psychics, and Sylvia Borlotti."

Fran looked strangely satisfied. "Not bad. Plus, there might be more."

Lise hesitated to say the words, but they had to be said. "You forgot about me."

For some reason, Burt was smiling. "You're a suspect?"

"I'd emailed Dyann my resignation the night she died, and she had started a pretty nasty reply that she'd never sent. The detective made a point of letting me know."

"Darling, give me a break," Teddy said.

Fran's only reply was to roll her eyes.

"Four murder suspects." Burt shook his head. "Four entities who wanted to kill Dyann King."

"That's an aside," Fran said. "All signs point to Richard as the killer. He threatened her, remember? Plus, he lied about where he was. What else do we need to know?"

Burt chuckled.

The wind had picked up. They were in for rain.

"What?" Lise asked Burt. "What's so funny?"

"All of this, everything we've been talking about, assumes Ms. King was actually murdered."

"Signe—that's the detective—said she was poisoned," Lise said. "I'd call that murder."

"I mentioned I had lunch at the Labor Temple today, right?" Burt said.

"Meatloaf platter," Teddy said.

"Turkey loaf today," Burt said. "Green beans on the side."

"Continue, please, Burt," Fran said.

"Marty from the police station was picking up his BLT at the same time. The waitress asked him about the case, and he said the medical examiner found no trace of poison in Dyann, her glass, or her liquor bottle." Having secured his triumph, Burt leaned back and hooked his thumbs in his belt loops. "You know what that means."

Teddy nodded. "No poison, no murder."

CHAPTER 10

Lise sure was handy with a wrench, Fran thought. What an odd duck. She was so gawky, but she smelled like a pasha's harem.

They'd turned off the water to the toilet, and Lise was loosening the tank's innards. A blister pack of toilet parts was open next to them, and a dim lightbulb lit the space. Fran clicked on the table lamp on the cabinet—Teddy had little lamps all over the house; this one was plaster and shaped like a branch with yellow birds perched on it—but it didn't do much to counter the night pressing against the windows with its threat of rain.

"I bet it's the shut-off valve," Lise said. "If it's not the flapper, it's the valve."

Fran sat cross-legged on the bath mat and ignored the baby's whimpers she heard. There was no use pointing them out to Lise. Like everyone else, she'd just tell her she had too wild an imagination. "Where did you learn to fix a toilet?"

"My father and brother are scientists." Lise twisted something inside the tank. "They could tell you the chemical composition of every bottle of lotion in the cabinet, but they can barely operate a stove. If something went wrong, it was up to me to figure it out. It doesn't make a lot of sense to drop a hundred bucks–plus for a plumber when the fix is five dollars in parts. Would you hand me that screwdriver?"

"Here."

Music from a jazz trio drifted up from Teddy's sitting room. It was oddly comforting chatting with Lise around the toilet.

"How did you get so interested in perfume?" Fran asked. "It doesn't sound like something your family would have been into."

"They weren't. Oh, I suppose my father would have a passing interest in the dispersal rates of its molecular materials, but that's it. I discovered perfume by accident." She pulled a black rubber disk from the toilet tank. "I was at a sleepover at a friend's house in second grade, and my friend's mom gave us each a spritz of perfume before she went out. I think it was Jungle Gardenia."

"Is that a fancy one?" Fran asked.

"No. But it certainly opened my eyes. In that one spritz, I smelled not just a creamy knockout of a tropical flower, but green notes, sweetness, and something skin-like and as magical to scent as salt is to food. I later discovered it was musk. All that night, I kept smelling my wrist as the fragrance changed."

"What did your family think of that?" Fran had seen a family photo in Lise's room. Lise was tall and awkward, and her father and brother looked short and intense. "Did your mom wear perfume?"

"My mother died when I was five. I don't remember any particular perfume on her, but I do remember her warm, milky scent." Lise stopped fussing in the toilet tank for a moment and took a lung-filling breath, as if she was smelling something in her head.

"Maybe your biological parents were perfumers." Fran imagined a grand salon, something like she'd created in the thriller she was writing, *Dead Bolt*, with gilded moldings, velvet curtains, and a woman wielding a test tube as she stuck her nose into a bouquet of tropical flowers.

"That would explain a few things, like why I . . ." She shook her head. "Never mind."

Fran sat back on her heels. "What perfume did Dyann wear?"

"A showy jasmine," Lise replied. Then, "Do you think Burt was right and Dyann wasn't poisoned? Signe had stated it like it was a fact."

"Dyann could have had a stroke or something," Fran said.

"Could be. The medical examiner should be able to tell that." The toilet's innards now lay spread on a towel on the cheap linoleum, a leftover from when bathrooms were avocado green and harvest gold. This house was a hodgepodge of eras.

"But if nothing fishy happened, why did her ex lie about where he was?" Fran asked. "I mean, I assume he told the detective he was nowhere near the Lucky Lotus when Dyann died. Why else would she give him a pass?"

"Maybe he had something else to hide."

"Like what? It sounds like everyone knows about his affair with the bean lady."

"Sylvia Borlotti," Lise said.

"Yeah."

"Dyann's tires were slashed. Maybe he wanted to hide that."

Fran scooted back until she leaned against a cabinet. "If that was true, he'd want to own up to it to help pinpoint the time the murderer showed up. No, he's hiding something, and the biggest thing to hide here is murder. You need to tell the detective everything you know."

Above them, footsteps sounded and stopped. Fran and Lise looked at each other. "That came from the attic. It's just the old house settling, right?" Lise asked.

"Sure." Let her think what she wanted.

"I've heard noises up there before and mentioned it to Teddy. She says maybe raccoons are living up in the attic. If so, they're big ones."

"I wouldn't worry about it."

Lise returned her attention to the toilet and tightened something in its tank. "There. Just about done." She reached over to turn on the water supply, and the tank slowly filled. "What's this?" She peeled back a corner of painted-over wallpaper near the spigot on the wall.

Fran leaned forward to look. The peeled-back paper revealed another wallpaper, something from a much earlier time. Fran yanked the paper further.

"Watch out. Teddy might not be so crazy about us ripping up the bathroom walls," Lise said. At the same time, the water switched off. The toilet tank had filled.

"Who cares? This place is a wreck. She's probably going to paint it red in here, anyway, and nail up a bunch of paintings of ladies' heads."

The baby's crying rose a notch. Lise clearly didn't hear it, although she did give another short sniff. "Do you smell powder?"

Fran was too absorbed by the revealed wallpaper to respond. "Look at that."

The wallpaper, faded and worn, showed children hand in hand in Victorian dress, with prancing dogs and wreaths of tiny flowers. The baby's crying dulled to a whimper, then quieted.

"This must have been the nursery," Lise said. "Before indoor plumbing. It makes sense someone chose this room for the bathroom, since it's right above the kitchen. Easier to plumb."

A baby had been here, likely the baby Fran heard some nights. What was the deal with the crying woman? "Do you ever wonder who lived in this house?"

Lise slowly nodded. "I do."

"Yeah, me too." Both women stared at the toilet. "Do you ever, you know . . . ?"

"Know what?" Lise asked.

"Get the sense that . . . I don't know." Fran shoved her

hands in the front pockets of her jeans. "They say Corrie House is haunted." She watched Lise for a reaction.

At her words, the light switched off. Fran reflexively listened for the baby and the sobbing woman, but they were silent. However, the room's temperature dropped. She rubbed her arms to keep warm.

"Okay, that's weird." Lise moved toward the door, but before she arrived at the switch, the lights came back on. She startled, then sucked in a breath. "Electrical problems? That's all we need."

"Must be." Fran didn't point out that while the bathroom light was out, Teddy's music had continued to play downstairs. No, it was the house. The house wanted them to know something. Margie at the bookstore had a connection to Astoria's historical society. Fran vowed to find out more about Corrie House. Something had happened here, and its ghosts wouldn't rest until they'd told their story.

Lise inhaled again, as if she were smelling something, but if she did, she didn't say anything about it. "Yeah, this place is haunted all right." She wiped her hands on her jeans and flushed the toilet once again. It refilled. "All done."

Fran's bedroom was upstairs, wedged between Lise's and the front room, across the hall from the octagonal room formed by the house's tower. When Fran had answered the ad for a housemate, Teddy had first offered her the octagonal room. Fran didn't even step beyond its door before she said she'd take this one instead, even though it was smaller. The tower room had scary energy. She hadn't wanted the front bedroom, either. Teddy had touted its view, and that was exactly why she'd refused it.

Fran felt drawn to Corrie House. Funny, since it was the last place anyone would imagine her. She hated heights. She kept her bedroom curtains closed during the day so she wouldn't catch an accidental glimpse of the hill falling away to the river. She wasn't particularly crazy about old buildings, either. Nothing in this house worked like it should, except the locks, and that was thanks only to her and the fact that her parents had owned Kellers Lock and Key.

Still, the moment Fran had walked into the house's grand front hall, all cold and damp, with Teddy's worn-out rugs and paintings of strange ladies, the house seemed to whisper *You're home*. Even when she'd heard someone talking in the kitchen—the empty kitchen—and crying from the bedroom next door, the room that was now Lise's, she'd felt welcomed.

In a way, she liked it that no one could imagine her here. She didn't want anyone's attention. Not that she'd ever had it anyway, she reflected. "Aren't you Harry Kellers's sister?" people at the bookstore would ask. "Get a life," she wanted to tell them.

Fran opened her curtains to a view of nothing but shades of black. With the velvet pillow of night surrounding her, she could pretend she was not on a hill, not on the second floor, and not so scarily high above the ground.

By now, Teddy and Lise were in bed, and the kitchen and bathroom were free. The house would begin to talk.

She used to tell her parents when she heard voices, but they'd chalked it up to her imagination. "Remember when we took you to Disneyland, and you had dreamed up this whole world of castles and princesses? You thought Mickey Mouse was a real mouse, and you made us bring him cheese," they'd said. Yeah, she remembered it, all right. Mickey turned out to be some guy in a mouse suit. What a letdown.

Fran hung her bathrobe on the hook behind the bathroom door. The robe, a gift from Harry, dated to just after he, then her parents, moved to Los Angeles. One day her parents were happy, or so Fran had thought, running the lock and key shop, then—*boom!*—they'd announced they were moving. Harry needed them, her parents had told her.

Fran ran water in the tub. Then she heard it again, a baby crying. Not a terrified cry, but a fussy one. "Hush," Fran whispered. "You're okay." After a moment, the crying quieted.

There was a lot of baby crying in here, but it was better than in Lise's room. Some lady had been very unhappy in there, although Lise didn't seem to have a clue.

Fran eased into the hot water. Just her imagination, people always told her. If it wasn't for people's overblown ideas, she wouldn't have to worry about her imagination at all. Take hiking, for example. People made a big deal out of it: nature, birds, wildlife, etcetera. It had sounded so exciting. Maybe she'd see a deer, a buck on the hill with its antlers glinting in the sun, or maybe even a bear. The earth would be rich with moss every color of green, and birdsong would flow through the air like a symphony.

So, she went on a hike with another one of the clerks at the bookstore. It was just a walk in the woods. That was it. Dirt, trees, other people with their dogs scaring you half to death.

After her bath, Fran returned to her room, being sure to close and lock the door. She settled on the bed to work on her novel. Hers would be the first historical thriller centered on lock picking. The idea had popped into her brain seconds after learning Louis XVI was a lock fanatic. Plus, Versailles had to hold lots of great places for bodies. Imagine trying to escape a murderer in a hall of mirrors.

Fran opened her notebook to last night's scene in *Dead Bolt* and read: "*Marguerite LePonce scurried up the drainpipe with the ease of grease on a hot skillet.*" She crossed out "*grease on a hot skillet*" because a reader might think Marguerite smelled like chicken fat. Marguerite was a classy burglar. She would smell like something a princess would wear. Fran would have to ask Lise.

She read on:

"Another thief would have struggled, the bitter wind of a Parisian winter biting at his neck. Not Marguerite. Her training as an acrobat in the circus made child's play of this ascent. Soon she would be in the Comtesse de Versailles's boudoir. Thinking of the sparkling treasures within, Marguerite licked her lips."

Not "licked her lips." That was gross.

"She dreamed of donning the Comtesse's jewels for the Duke's appreciation. How they would glimmer in the moonlight as she stroked the Duke's beard. But no, these jewels would be sold to save her baby sister, slaving in the cruel orphanage."

Not bad. She'd given the duke a beard in tribute to the hot tattoo artist who came by the bookstore sometimes. "*Dead Bolt*, chapter four," she wrote.

"Marie Antoinette ducked behind a gilded doorway. She pulled her voluminous skirts to the side, but it was too late. He had seen her!

The duke was masked, but Marie Antoinette knew the powerful shape of his torso anywhere. "Alas, my queen, fear not, for I am here to protect you from the killer. Follow me to the stables. I have prepared a sumptuous bed in the hayloft where you will be safe."

Fran closed her notebook. She couldn't focus tonight. The murder was a reminder of Dyann's death—not that she'd do anything to solve it except encourage Lise to get off her butt.

That was, if her death was murder after all. The orphanage was a reminder of the nursery-slash-bathroom down the hall.

She set her pen aside. Despite the excitement on the page, she yawned. Besides, it was almost eleven o'clock. She opened her laptop and popped in her earbuds. She was just in time to catch the opening bars of the theme music to *The Harry Kellers Show*.

CHAPTER 11

Lise cradled a cup of coffee and stared through the kitchen window into the backyard, watching Charm—or was it Grace?—pounce on imaginary prey. Now that Lise didn't have to go into work at the Lucky Lotus, her day yawned before her. She had zero gardening gigs lined up for the fall. She would start paying rent by working in Teddy's garden.

But not immediately. She remembered Burt, sitting right there in his Adirondack chair—there where Charm now sharpened his claws—saying the investigation was over. The medical examiner had not found poison in Dyann's body.

That said, Fran was right. Signe needed to know about Richard's car being spotted down the block. Lise didn't want to see Signe again. She didn't want to stand before her, knowing Signe might know why she'd left Seattle in such a hurry.

Then again, did she want to be safe or did she want to do right? Lise rinsed out her empty coffee cup. She owed this to Dyann.

Upstairs, Lise opened the perfume cabinet and surveyed her collection of bottles. Which one should she wear? Perfume was a silent garment that might lend Lise a variety of qualities, from focus to allure to strength. She knew she looked like an overgrown Pippi Longstocking, but she could feel like Greta

Garbo with a dab from her half-filled bottle of Narcisse Noir *parfum*. Lise began to reach for the Bandit for its lash of leather and galbanum, but no. She didn't want a mask today, as comforting as that might be. Today she wanted to feel more like herself. She chose a drop of Fleurs de Rocailles for its old-fashioned floral innocence coupled with maternal warmth.

Half an hour later, Lise drove down the hill toward the police department. She kept a foot on the brake pedal—the last thing she needed was to screech into a pedestrian on the steep decline—and pondered why Signe was in Astoria at all. Maybe police jobs were hard to come by.

She'd considered calling Signe, but she wanted to see her reaction in person. It had been more than a decade since Lise and Signe had spent time together, and Lise could no longer read her expressions. But in person she could smell her reactions. Lies, Lise knew, were bitter as castoreum. The garden show back home, the root of her trouble, had been thick with that scent. She winced to think of it.

The Astoria Police Station occupied an indifferent one-story building not far from the riverfront, on the east side of town. Lise confidently pushed open its front door and crossed the few yards to a reception desk set off from the rest of the open room by a cubicle divider. Only a half-filled coffee mug showed that anyone had been there. She rang the bell on the counter.

A man who looked barely out of high school, with a short, curly ponytail that might have graced a pug's rear end, ambled around the divider to the desk. "May I help you?"

"I'd like to see Signe Rasmussen, please."

The man's expression didn't change. "Detective Rasmussen is busy. What's the problem?"

Astoria had its share of domestic disputes and barking dogs, but Lise had to guess it didn't generally host murder. "I want to talk to her about Dyann King's death."

If Lise had thought this would ruffle him, she was wrong.

Instead, his expression continuing placid, he tipped up his chin and yelled, "Signe!"

Signe appeared around the divider with an expectant look on her face that fell when she saw Lise. "Can I help you?" To Lise, the words read as "What do you want now?"

"You said I should get in touch if I remembered anything about the day Dyann died. I have new information."

Signe didn't exactly roll her eyes, but she might have, given her expression. "Follow me."

Her office was a windowless room at the back of the police station. Lise took a seat, and Signe settled herself at her desk. Behind Signe, on the credenza, was the photo of a smiling blonde in a wedding dress. She held a bouquet of daisies that suited her prairie-style ruffles.

Signe noted her glance and spun to the photo. "That's Adrienne. My wife. You're not married, are you?"

Signe had not changed. She couldn't resist the dig. However, the scent of fruity summer roses confirmed she'd found love. Here they sat: one woman a college-educated detective in a committed relationship, and the other an out-of-work spinster living in a group house so decrepit that kids dared each other to knock on its door on Halloween.

"What do you want to tell me?" Signe said. "I only have a minute. I'm working on another case."

The man who had shouted for Signe appeared at the door. "Detective Rasmussen? Call for you. It's the lady with the escaped goats."

"Tell her I'll get back to her."

Lise leaned forward. "I can see you're busy, all right, so I'll get to the point. Richard, Dyann's ex, was a block from the Lucky Lotus the night Dyann died. The butcher saw his car."

"His car." Signe's tone of voice made it clear this was not adequate information. "You came all this way to tell me that?"

Lise crossed her arms in front of her chest. "Dyann said he

was going to kill her, remember? No one else in town has a red Camaro like his, and it was right there, steps from the shop."

"And no one else in town drives?"

Who else would be driving Richard's car? God, Signe was irritating. Lise stared at her hands long enough to regain her cool. "I thought you should know about it."

"Richard's son drives. Also, Richard owns a car lot. I imagine he has lots of choices of vehicles and might not be glued to his Camaro." Signe picked up a pen and doodled a circle on the corner of an office memo. "However, thank you for your information." She looked up and delivered a painfully fake smile redolent of carnations and sour milk—in other words, disdain. "We'll be sure to look into it. The Astoria police bureau relies on citizens such as yourself to help us out."

Lise couldn't even muster a smile—fake or not—in return. "It is still a murder investigation, right?"

Signe's smile faltered. "We've closed no avenues."

"I heard the medical examiner didn't find poison. You told me she'd been poisoned."

Signe opened the desk drawer below her and carefully replaced the pen before looking up. "No. No poison found. Yet. That's all I can say."

"So, it is a homicide investigation. You do suspect murder."

"The case is not closed. Now, if you don't mind—"

"Don't you care at all about what I have to say?" This argument was beginning to sound painfully like their high school squabbles. Only, in high school it had fed rivalry for everything from scholarships to a position on the yearbook staff. Today, it concerned murder.

"Why should I listen to someone who committed a class C felony?"

The words pierced like scalding needles. Lise stared at Signe. When Lise regained her breath at last, she choked out, "I didn't do it."

“That’s what you say. According to my mother, you lost your landscaping license and came this close to being thrown in jail.” To demonstrate, she pinched her thumb and index finger together.

Signe knew. She knew all about what had happened, and she didn’t believe in Lise’s innocence. Why would she, with her mother’s word to go on?

Earlier in the summer, Lise had entered the garden design portion of the Madrona Park garden show. Signe’s mother, the garden club’s president, had invited her to participate. For once, Lise was grateful to have this connection with Mrs. Rasmussen.

Madrona Park was a ritzy neighborhood and a rich source of possible gardening clients. This would be Lise’s breakout moment. Her blood fizzed like champagne as she thought of the gardens she could create. What she could do with those yards, with their gazebos and greenhouses, their terraced decks and views of the lake. No chance of that now.

She had put together a surefire winning entry. She’d spent weeks designing a scent garden that was not only beautiful but also created a canvas of fragrance that evolved through the seasons just as a symphony coursed through its movements. Except these instruments grew from the earth. Grape hyacinth carpeted gently scented rhododendrons, and when they faded, lilacs, then mock orange took over, giving way in summer to roses and jasmine.

Lise set up her display the night before the judging took place. When she finished, she perused the other entries and was confident she’d earn, at a minimum, an honorable mention. Besides the plan she’d drawn up, Lise had rendered monthly paintings of the flower beds in watercolor, complemented by a tabletop diorama of the garden in June.

The garden show’s longtime winner—Signe’s mother—had

set out what Lise was sure was her usual display, a shouting match of tuberose, hothouse roses, and gardenias. Yes, they were beautiful, but they were predictable. They were the Ritz version of a floral display: the French poodle, beef Wellington, chinchilla coat equivalent of garden design.

Lise had driven home looking forward to the next day and dreaming of her career unfolding in a series of richly scented garden beds and joyful clients. Then, overnight, several of the displays had been vandalized. Someone had smashed the window on the door to get in, then they'd swiped vases and flowers to the floor, leaving a carpet of broken glass and dead blossoms. They'd even—Lise ached to summon the memory—spray-painted disgusting words across the glass cases.

Lise's entry was untouched. Worse, Signe's mother said she'd seen Lise's car at the garden club headquarters later that night. Her twenty-year-old Kia with a dent in its door would have stood out among the late model SUVs and German sedans the other contestants drove. However, Lise was home alone that night, with no one to back up her word that she was sketching garden designs, excited about her future. This is what she'd told the police the next morning when they showed up at her door.

Mrs. Rasmussen had called Lise to the garden club's headquarters and told her they would drop charges if she promised not to approach the club or any of its members in the future. Then she filed a complaint with the licensing board.

Signe's mother had set her up. All it had taken was Mrs. Rasmussen's word, and not only was Lise kicked out of the show, her reputation was decimated. Who would the other garden club members believe? An upstart designer of scent gardens or the club's president? It was infuriating, but there had been nothing she could do.

On top of all this, apparently Mrs. Rasmussen had aired the whole fiasco to Signe.

"Right." Lise rose and pulled her purse over her shoulder. Maybe Signe was being a pain in the hind end, but Lise had accomplished what she'd set out to do: she'd delivered the information about Richard. "I'll let you be. You have goats to tend to."

"Don't worry." Signe smiled, but only with her lips. "I won't tell anyone what happened in Seattle. Unless I have to."

Chapter 12

Lise burned with humiliation. She let the police bureau's front door close behind her. Worse than a dead end, her meeting with Signe had been a disaster. Naturally, Mrs. Rasmussen had told her daughter about the garden show. And, of course, Signe didn't believe in Lise's innocence. What would happen if word got out about it? Lise could kiss her chances of local garden commissions good-bye.

She hadn't learned much about the investigation into Dyann's death, either. If Burt was right, the death would be ruled as from natural causes. Signe wouldn't commit to that, but neither would she say it was a homicide investigation.

Lise wasn't ready to attribute Dyann's death to natural causes, either. Initially, yes. But she couldn't shake the idea that Richard was behind this. They'd been tormenting each other for so long, and the torment, as far as Lise could see, had snowballed. Dyann had said Richard would kill her. Richard had lied about his whereabouts that night. Signe herself had suspected Dyann had been poisoned. Lise drew a breath and let it out as steadily as she could manage. How she'd love to prove Signe wrong.

As she drove away from the police station, Lise felt the pull of a booster cup of coffee. She eyed the vegan café, but now that she was out of work, she needed to keep an eye on her budget. The Labor Temple's coffee wasn't as good, but it was half the price with unlimited refills.

She took Commercial Street through town. Shops were just beginning to open—the gift shop had set out a rack of wind chimes, and in front of the butcher shop stood a sandwich board featuring a pig eating a hotdog. She glanced across the street at the Lucky Lotus, its windows dark.

Lise parked outside the Labor Temple diner. She pushed open the front door and let her eyes adjust to the relative dimness of the café, with its row of stools at the counter on the left and booths lining the wall on the right. Beyond the café was the bar. The air smelled of pancakes and coffee.

Lise was about to take a seat at the counter when Teddy's voice drew her attention from a nearby booth.

"Darling," she said. "What are you up to this morning? Come sit with us." Across the table from Teddy sat Burt, and over them hung the scent of roses.

Lise had long associated roses with affection—and love—but that was too broad a description. Roses had a language as varied as Shakespearean sonnets. A rose could be sheer and fruity, like the rose Lise had smelled when Signe spoke of her wife. Or it could be powdery, or tart, or cold and tight. Unrequited love was dusted with violets. Painful love—love that had been betrayed or that of a lover who had been indulged in and then ghosted—smelled of roses stewed with rotting strawberries.

This rose was rich and laced with overripe peaches. It was a deep love forged by experience.

"Steph," Burt said to the server behind the counter, "get us another coffee, please." Then, to Lise, "You will have a cup with us, won't you?"

The table held two plates, one smeared with maple syrup, the other with a few crusts of toast. Burt had been reading the newspaper. He folded it and took off his reading glasses.

"Thank you," Lise said. Teddy slid over, and Lise sat next to her. "I just left the police department. Signe had zero interest in the fact that Richard's car was nearby the night Dyann died. She said anyone could have been driving it."

"Not Richard's Camaro. No way," Burt said. "He coddled that car."

"Remember when he drove it in the Fourth of July parade?" Teddy said. "You weren't here yet, Lise, but some boy threw a milkshake at his Camaro. Richard actually stopped the car and ran after the kid."

Remembering, Burt shook his head. "The Shriners were all backed up, driving their mini-cars in circles waiting for him to get back in his Camaro and go."

"And the high school band had to march in place. I couldn't get the song 'Tequila' out of my head all day. Those tubas."

Lise could see it. She wondered if Dyann had given the kid a twenty and supplied him with the milkshake. Extra large.

"Back to the detective," Burt said. "Maybe she didn't want to be shown up. Ego, you know. Or maybe they've called off the investigation, so she doesn't care. Did she say anything about the medical examiner's findings?"

Lise shook her head. "She wouldn't say the investigation was still on, but she wouldn't say it wasn't, either." Lise remembered Dyann, lifeless, on the floor, that strange acrid smell permeating the room. She thought of the framed family photos on Dyann's fireplace mantel at home. Her throat tightened. "Dyann wasn't perfect, don't get me wrong, but she didn't deserve to die."

Teddy rested a hand on her arm. "It might have been natural. Maybe she had a weak heart."

Lise let out a long breath. "Maybe."

In a skillful ballet, the server arrived with a coffee mug, set it down on the table, and filled it from the carafe in her other hand. She reached into her apron pocket for a handful of plastic creamers and dropped them on the table. Then, with a hand free, she dropped the check on the table while, seemingly at the same time, scooping up the empty plates. Amazing. If Signe decided to broadcast around town what had happened at the garden show, Lise's gardening work would never get off the ground. But whatever her future job, she guessed it would not be as a waitress.

"I'll get this," Burt said, reaching for the check.

"No, Burt. You got the dining room windows unstuck. The least I can do is buy you a short stack and bacon." Teddy pressed her credit card over the check.

Lise stirred creamer into her coffee and watched the traffic outside the front window. Strong, healthy women didn't just drop dead the night they changed their wills.

"What are you thinking about, darling?" Teddy asked. "It's Dyann, isn't it?"

"Yes." Then, because she didn't want to belabor the subject, Lise said, "And finding a job."

Teddy saw through her. "Gardening will pick up, and, as I said, you can work off your rent in our yard."

Burt slipped on his reading glasses again and opened the paper.

"As for Dyann, it sounds like you need closure," she added.

"What kind of closure?" Lise brought the coffee cup to her nose and sniffed. She added another plastic container of cream.

"You have doubts surrounding Dyann's death. Richard's car, for one."

Lise nodded. "Definitely. Something is off about it."

"Then why not follow up on your own? Why not talk to Richard and confirm his alibi? Then you can be satisfied the situation is being taken care of, and you can let it go."

True. If she knew for sure Richard was somewhere else when Dyann died, her brain might quiet. "What excuse could I use for talking to him?"

"Your car is old," Teddy said.

"Yes, but it still runs great," Lise said. "Most of the time."

"So what? Richard sells cars, right? You could look into buying a new one."

What Teddy said made sense. Lise could find out why Signe had so readily dismissed Richard's involvement in Dyann's death. And, she admitted to herself, if she could find a hole in his alibi—and Signe's work—she'd proudly bring it to the attention of the chief of police.

Burt set down his newspaper. "You said you were looking for a job, too."

"I am."

He tapped his index finger on the back page of the front section. "Right here." He pushed the paper toward Lise.

"*Help wanted,*" it read, "*Assistant at the Blavatsky Manor retirement home.*"

A wisp of pastry cream and iris-infused anise rose and then vanished. L'Heure Bleue again.

At Blavatsky Manor, Lise might learn something about the night Dyann died. One of its residents had been at Murphy's birthday party. More than that, she might learn something about herself. It was a home for retired psychics, after all. Surely, they were familiar with clairalience.

She folded the paper so the ad was front and center. "May I keep this?"

Chapter 13

Lise drove to King Cars in Warrenton, just outside of Astoria. Where Astoria was a mix of charm and grit, slotted between the coastal mountains and the Columbia River, Warrenton lay flat and suburban. Warrenton was where Astorians went to buy electronics at chain stores and stock up on bulk toilet paper at warehouses. They also came here to buy cars.

She parked outside the King Cars office, a small trailer at the back of the lot. Dyann used to work here. Lise imagined her typing up sales contracts while cars on the highway roared by.

Lise had barely turned off her engine when Richard strolled down the wooden steps from his office, a salesman's smile on his lips.

"Welcome to King Cars," he said over the traffic's steady hum.

At the sight of Lise, Richard's smile disappeared, transforming his face almost entirely. She actually liked this face better. It was more authentic. This face showed what must have attracted Dyann beyond his blandly handsome features: soft eyes with a hint of worry and a surprisingly delicate mouth.

"You worked for Dyann, didn't you?" he asked, as if she'd been sent to him to pull off one final trick.

"Yes. At the Lucky Lotus. I'm sorry"—she was going to say "for your loss" but detested the pro forma words—"this awful thing happened."

A mix of emotions seemed to race through his mind, leaving a trail of scent too muddy to read. Riding above the miasma was another fragrance, this one an actual perfume. Tabu, was Lise's guess. It had been one of the first fragrances she'd collected. Every yard sale seemed to have a half-used drugstore bottle of it on a table with cracked soap dishes and ratty towels. It was an exotic, old-school choice for whomever Richard had been mingling with when he last wore this shirt.

Richard ignored her words and smacked the Kia's side, making a hollow thud. "You're looking for a car? We might be able to squeeze a bit of trade-in value for this one. Lots of youngsters looking for these older makes."

"I'm the person who found Dyann." Lise watched her non sequitur land on Richard.

He frowned and shifted on his feet. Guilt? "A bad business, that. Now, tell me, what do you have in mind? I can see you in one of our subcompacts."

Lise supposed she'd have to play along if she wanted to get him to open up. "Dyann drove a Mercedes convertible."

"I'll be honest with you. We don't get many convertibles, because we're not a great market for them. Have you considered a small SUV?"

At this rate, she'd never be able to lead him to the topic of Dyann. "I haven't thought about it, really. Is that what you'd recommend?"

He stopped in front of a white Honda that looked like it had belonged to a party girl in a private high school. "This car is a sweet deal. Fully automatic. Air conditioning, too. A real step up from what you drive now and"—he gave her a quick head-to-toe assessment—"plenty roomy for someone of your height. Not showy, either."

Not showy if you were an NFL cheerleader, Lise thought. "I suppose the police talked to you."

He opened the driver's side door. "We just got it in, but it will be fully detailed. Check out the sound system." He turned the key partway, and the stereo came on to a woman singing a song that might have been played in a Berlin cabaret to lush orchestration. A strange choice given the car's party vibe.

"Nice," Lise said. How was she going to get him to talk?

"How about a test drive? It handles like a dream."

Richard had probably been saying these exact words for the past decade. For a moment, Lise wondered why she was here. Signe had already covered this ground. She'd ruled Richard out as a suspect. Nonetheless, a test drive meant at least ten minutes of undistracted attention, and Lise had made it this far.

"Okay." She settled in the driver's seat and adjusted the rearview mirror while Richard took the passenger seat. "Where to?"

"Take a right at the highway."

Lise pulled out of the car lot. He was correct—compared to her car, this was like driving a toy. Power steering, no clutch. For a few miles, neither of them spoke.

Richard broke the silence. "I bet they talked to you, too. I know I would have."

What was that supposed to mean? Lise glanced at him before returning her attention to the road.

"Turn here. Left." He pointed at a narrow road leading off the highway. The turn signal clicked in the silence.

Richard stared straight ahead. "You never liked Dyann, did you?"

"What makes you say that?" Lise's voice was louder than she'd intended.

"You were planning to quit."

How did he find that out? "The job wasn't a great fit. But that wasn't because of Dyann." Not completely because of her, anyway. "I'm a garden designer, and I want to develop that work. I really did appreciate Dyann, though. She was . . . she was nurturing."

Dyann's caring was the whole reason Lise had taken the job. When she'd interviewed at the Lucky Lotus, Dyann had asked her about her spiritual beliefs.

She had hesitated before responding. "I believe there's a lot we don't know, that science hasn't caught up with yet."

Dyann had nodded enthusiastically. "Intuition, spirits. Magic."

Magic. At the word, a tingle had passed through Lise.

"Do you have any gifts yourself?" Dyann asked.

"I smell emotion." Lise had never told anyone outside of her family about her gift, but she'd felt led to Dyann. Her gaze was so welcoming and attentive, and a halo of lilies of the valley surrounded her, signaling genuine curiosity. Lise knew Dyann wouldn't classify her as a freak when she heard about her ability to smell emotion. Lise had told her everything.

Now she was dead. "I liked Dyann," Lise repeated, "and she certainly didn't deserve to be killed."

"You think someone killed her," Richard said.

"I don't know," Lise said.

"But you're here, asking. You're not here to buy a car at all, are you?"

They passed a house set far back from the road. Other than that, all around them were green fields broken only by barbed wire and the occasional dairy cow. Lise realized how vulnerable she was. Getting in a car with a possible murderer? This was the stupid move girls made in slasher movies.

"Since you brought it up, where did you go after Murphy's birthday party?" Lise's voice started shaky but picked up confidence.

He nodded slowly. "You think I killed Dyann."

"Why would I—"

"What did she tell you about me?"

"Did she have to say anything?" Lise said. Their words shot like volleys in a duel. This was not the conversation she'd envisioned. "You two were always at each other's throats."

"You say she was murdered. How do I know you weren't responsible for her death?"

"Would I be here if I were?" She was beginning to understand why Dyann felt compelled to torture him.

"You want to know where I was when Dyann died, do you?"

Lise kept her focus on the road. Her palms felt sweaty on the steering wheel.

"I'll tell you what I told the detective. I was at the car lot, putting together a deal for someone who works nights. I came back to the lot after Murphy's party. It takes a while to get through the paperwork, then I had to take her to work."

"She didn't drive her new car?"

"It wasn't ready yet. In fact, this is her old vehicle. She traded it in."

Lise's gaze remained locked on the road. The car had been cleaned, but nothing could hide the patchouli-rich hint of Tabu wafting under the freesia air freshener with which Richard had doused the car. This car had belonged to Sylvia Borlotti, Richard's girlfriend.

Finally, he looked away from her and toward the road. Lise shot a glance his way and read determination in the tight set of his jaw.

She pressed her foot on the accelerator. The sooner they returned to the car lot, the better.

A soft breath escaped Richard. "You cared about her, you say."

The scent of old violets, strong enough to overpower Tabu's residue, filled the car. Richard was in mourning, reminding her that murderers could be sorry, too. Then the violets vanished, replaced by the scent of hot steel. "Dyann changed her will."

"I know." The car lot was near. All Lise wanted to do was to park and get out of there.

"Lise Bloom." Richard's voice was low and measured. "You believe someone murdered Dyann, and for some reason, you suspect me. Don't you ever repeat any of these allegations. Do you understand?"

She pursed her lips to not give him the satisfaction of a reply. The lot was now in sight.

"I asked you a question." A threat masked as a question.

Lise pulled into King Cars and shut off the engine. She yanked the emergency brake. "Here we are."

"I hope we understand each other." Slowly, like a cat that had decided to bestow mercy upon its prey, he unclipped his seatbelt and let himself out of the car.

Lise released a shaky breath and slid from the driver's seat. She refused to look back as she returned to her car at a pace she hoped appeared confident.

Once safely behind the wheel, Lise checked her phone. She had a voicemail from an unknown number. She stared at the cars whizzing by on the highway as she listened.

"Lise, this is Ornette Cassell. We met at Murphy's apartment. I hope you don't mind that I'm calling, but I'm worried about Murphy. Do you have a minute to talk?"

Time was something Lise had a lot more of these days. What did Ornette think she could do for Murphy? They barely knew each other. On the other hand, Ornette had been at Murphy's birthday party. He might have seen or overheard something linking Richard to Dyann's death. Now more than ever, Richard looked like a murderer.

She risked a glance toward the King Cars office. Richard had disappeared inside. She texted her willingness to talk, and Ornette instantly responded with a suggestion to meet at a café downtown.

If Richard had killed Dyann, as she suspected, there was no way she'd let him get away with it. No way at all.

Ornette was already sitting outside the Blue Scorcher café when Lise arrived. He waved at her to join him. "I'm having a late lunch, so I put in an order for the Reuben. Can I get you something?"

A vegan Reuben sandwich. The Blue Scorcher was known for them, and Lise hadn't eaten since breakfast. "I'd love one, too." She reached for her purse, but he waved it away.

"I've got it."

He disappeared into the café. Lise took a deep breath and stretched her arms. It had been a busy day. After lunch, she'd head home for a nap, maybe send her resume to Blavatsky Manor, and survey Corrie House's garden. She had to pay her rent somehow. Teddy had been generous in telling her she could work it off in the garden, but it was no secret that Corrie House needed a lot of expensive work—work Teddy couldn't afford.

Apparently, money wasn't as pressing an issue for Ornette Cassell. Judging from the reptile refuge bumper sticker, the car parked at the curb was his, but it wasn't the aging compact the executive director of a small nonprofit might have driven. No, it was a newer model electric SUV whose cost would probably pay three years of her living expenses.

"Order's in." Ornette sat across from her and smiled. Close up, she could see that his snake tattoos were meticulously detailed, with glinting eyes and scales. They moved with his arms.

"I don't want to mislead you. I barely know Murphy. I feel terrible for him, but I'm not sure what I can do."

"I thought that might be the case. He doesn't seem to have any friends, except me, of course, and he's getting more clingy than I'm comfortable with. So, when you left Murphy your number, I couldn't help but put it in my phone. I thought, maybe, since you knew his mother, you'd be willing to check on him."

Ornette knew right where to strike. "You think he'd want to spend time with me?"

"At least chat with him. Maybe Murphy's in shock, but I don't understand his attitude. He won't talk about his mother's death at all. He's obsessed with the sanctuary. He seems to pour all his emotion there." Anxiety wafted from him in ribbons of tarry leather.

"He works for you, right?"

Ornette nodded. "He's a great volunteer, don't get me wrong. He'd be hard to replace. But tending homeless reptiles shouldn't be the emotional center of anyone's life." At Lise's look of surprise, he held up his palms. "I know, it's my life. But not all of my life, you know what I mean? I worry about him."

Ornette was maybe fifteen years older than Murphy, but it seemed he'd taken on the role of big brother—or even father. "I couldn't help noticing in Dyann's calendar that she had a note to call you. You don't go in for aura readings, do you?"

He looked momentarily confused, then smiled. "No, not that. I wanted to talk with her about Murphy, too."

"Ornette?" A server stood on the sidewalk with two plates, surveying the café tables.

He raised a hand. "Here."

The server slid their plates on the table and set napkin-wrapped silverware next to them. "Sorry. I thought 'Ornette' would be someone else. My bad."

When she'd left, he said, "Happens all the time. She was probably looking for an elderly lady. I was named after Ornette Coleman, the jazz musician. My parents were fans."

Lise smiled. "Do you like jazz, too?"

"As it happens, I love it. I was weaned on Miles Davis. I bet our reptile refuge has the best soundtrack in the nation. We have an iguana who I swear bobs his head in time to Henry Threadgill." To illustrate, he tapped his plate in an erratic rhythm. "And that's not easy."

"How did you end up running a reptile refuge?"

Ornette laughed once. "Let me guess. You don't like reptiles, do you? Especially snakes."

"I have to admit . . ."

"The beleaguered snake." Ornette leaned back and clasped his hands over his middle, as if he'd given this speech many times. "As a kid, I always felt like the odd one out. Besides my unusual name, I was kind of quiet. One day a garter snake showed up on the playground at school. A bunch of kids were poking it with sticks. I saw myself in that snake. All the snake wanted to do was find something to eat and somewhere to hide, and now it was being picked on."

"You saved the garter snake."

"I did. Not only that, but I started learning about them." He leaned forward, resting his forearms on the table. "Snakes are fascinating creatures. If people would get to know them, they'd see that, just like cats and dogs, snakes have personalities."

Lise knew which one she'd rather cuddle in her lap. "What about getting bitten?"

"The vast majority of snakes aren't venomous. Not that the venom is so bad—"

"Getting bitten by a snake isn't bad?"

"You don't want a poisonous snake to bite you, I give you that. But their venom is prized by many cultures. By modern science, too. Researchers are looking at it for help curing cancer." At Lise's look of surprise, he added, "It's true. Snake venom is amazing stuff. Besides that, snakes are beautiful, and they play an important role in the ecosystem." He returned to his Reuben.

Lise took another bite of hers. The sandwich was exactly what she needed after an emotionally draining several hours. So much information swirled around her. "You were with Dyann not long before she died."

"True." Ornette was a fast eater. Lise was only halfway finished with her sandwich, and he was already wiping the crust through his sandwich's saucy remains.

"How did she seem? Was anything weird about the dinner?"

"You mean aside from the fact that her ex had brought a scantily clad nightclub singer and that across the table was a palm reader who looked like she'd escaped from a circus in a Depression-era movie? No, not weird at all."

"How was Richard?" Lise asked.

Ornette pushed his plate to the side and shook his head. "Those two. Murphy's told me about some of the stunts they played on each other. There was a lot of sniping back and forth that night. Dyann made a few digs at Richard's girlfriend. Richard let her know she'd be sorry. Then Dyann broke the news that she was changing her will to give money to a retirement home for psychic mediums."

"Thus the palm reader."

"Right."

"How did Richard take it?"

With his foot, Ornette nudged away an assertive pigeon pecking for scraps under the table. "He went ballistic. He swiped a pint of beer to the floor." He mimicked a broad backhand. "We didn't even get our fortunes told. Although the lady in the turban put away a lot of pizza."

"Richard didn't make any specific threats, did he?" Dyann's words, *Richard will kill me*, rang through her head.

Ornette got her drift immediately. "He did tell her she'd pay for what she'd done. That's almost a direct quote. You don't think . . . ?"

Lise blotted her mouth with her napkin and shoved it under the lip of her plate. "I don't know what to think, but you have to admit it doesn't look good for him."

"You found her, didn't you?"

She nodded. His question wasn't prurient. Instead, it actually sounded caring. Lise got why Phoebe at the brewery had hoped Ornette would return. She couldn't call him handsome—a photo would never communicate the animation, the appearance of always being on the verge of a smile, that made him so attractive.

"Do you have any idea of what the police are thinking? Are they focusing on Richard?"

Remembering Signe's dismissal that morning, she said, "I don't think so. I don't know that they're focusing on anyone. Still, who else would slash her tires? That's classic Richard."

Surprised, Ornette leaned forward. "Her tires were slashed?"

Lise nodded. "Both rear tires, plus a note under the windshield wiper. The note was too wet to read, but you can bet it said something petty and mean."

He leaned back again and folded his arms over his chest, revealing a rattlesnake, rattle raised, on his forearm. "But you're skeptical. And the police don't believe you."

How much would be different if the detective in charge didn't know Lise from another life? "Apparently not." As she pulled her purse to her lap, she caught a glimpse a few tables away of the ghostly pale woman who had bought Magnet Oil at the Lucky Lotus the day Dyann had died. Lise wondered if she was feeling more hopeful. There was so much grief and anxiety in the world.

"Thank you for lunch, Ornette, and it was nice to get to know you. I'll think about what you said about Murphy."

He stood. "It was good to talk it over with someone, anyway. Maybe you'd like to come out to visit the refuge sometime?"

Lise smiled but made no promise.

Chapter 14

"Dad?" Lise held her phone to her ear with one hand and with the other lifted aside the sheer lace curtain on her bedroom window. She sat at the bay window and looked over the darkening yard. One of the cats pounced on something below.

"Lise, honey. How are you?"

Lise imagined her father at the kitchen table, research papers scattered around him, his glasses slipping down his nose.

She and her father caught up on the usual business—the weather, her father's research project, her brother—before her father asked about her job.

"I'm not working at the Lucky Lotus anymore."

"Too much gardening work?"

"No, it's just . . ." How to say it? "My boss died, and the shop closed. I'm out of a job at the moment."

This was clearly the opening her father had been waiting for. "Why don't you come home? You can sleep in your old room. I bet I can get you a job at the lab. I know you'd rather be designing gardens, but it will hold you over until you find something better."

The offer was tempting. She'd be away from Signe, away from the questions surrounding Dyann's death. She wouldn't have to worry about money. Her father and brother would always be happy to see her, and, she noted wryly, she'd be there to get things off the higher shelves.

But in Astoria, for the first time, she truly felt she was living her own life. She'd already spent a month in Seattle licking her wounds after the garden show disaster. Plus, she'd worked so hard to smooth over her abrupt decision to abort her participation in the Stanford study and stay in Astoria.

"Thank you, Dad, but I don't know."

"Think it over, will you?"

"I will." She lifted her wrist to her nose. This morning's Fleurs de Rocailles had long worn off, and when she'd returned home, she'd searched through her perfume collection for something leathery to complement her mood. She chose an old Chanel, Cuir de Russie. Its leather scent reminded her of the inside of an expensive handbag with a smear of Florentine iris. Coco Chanel had supposedly favored Cuir de Russie and recommended that women spray it inside their coats so they'd always know which one was theirs at the coat check.

"I'm here for you, honey," her father said.

Normally, this would be the part where they would say good-bye. Her father would take his specially calibrated vitamin concoction before bed, and she would pick up a novel. Instead, he said, "Honey, you don't . . . those smells. Are you still getting those smells?"

"Yes." She didn't want to tell him that, if anything, it was more intense than ever. He would think she was losing her mind.

"Dr. Siegler is a respected researcher. I'm certain he could map the synesthetic—"

"Dad, I smell more than feelings now."

Silence was his response. She'd stymied him.

"I can smell history."

"Honey."

She knew what that meant. He already viewed her as something "other," and he treated her flushes of emotion as if she were a wild animal and he was a zookeeper, taking notes. "I can't explain it. If I clear my mind, sometimes I smell things that have happened in the past. Maybe they were events surrounded by emotion and that's why they're coming through. I don't understand it."

"When did this happen?"

"I noticed it about a month ago." After her stay in Wilfred to meet Josie, the witch.

"Lise, I don't want you to take this wrong, but we don't know anything about your genetic history, and it's possible . . . well, it's possible there's some mental—"

"Mental illness," Lise finished. The yard was now dark. She clicked on a nearby lamp.

"It's possible," her father repeated.

"Dad, I'm perfectly sane. I promise you. What do you know about my birth parents, anyway?"

She'd asked before, of course, but it had been years. She'd first learned she was adopted at her mother's funeral. Lise was five, and her brother Albert a mere two years old. Already, the differences between Lise and the rest of her family had become apparent. A stranger—all Lise remembered was a dry hand on her back and a cologne rich in what she now recognized as orange blossom—had knelt beside her at the church. "Poor little girl," the stranger had said. "To have lost your mom. She may not have been your real mother, but I'm sure it still hurts."

The stranger's words had puzzled Lise. Not her real mother? Of course she was her real mother. Who else read her stories in bed and kissed her scraped knees to make them better? Who walked her to school every morning and taught her the names of the birds and plants they passed?

Later that day, their house had swarmed with relatives, but her father had retreated to his study to be alone. She'd pushed open the door, and her father had invited her into his lap. She'd leaned against him, inhaling the scent of cotton and sandalwood that was particularly his.

"Why is it dark in here?" she asked. She'd long before given up her blanket, but when her mother had gone to the hospital, Lise had unearthed it from her closet. Now she hoisted it to her belly.

"I'm thinking," he said, "that's all. Sometimes I think better in the dark."

"Mama died."

Her father rested his hand on her head. "Yes, honey."

"A lady said she's not my real mom."

Lise, her head against her father's chest, had felt him tense beneath her. "Of course she's your real mom, just like I'm your real dad. But you came to us in a different way than Albert did. You were a special gift."

That had been all her father would tell her. Nothing else. In her teens, when the differences between her and her family had become more stark, she'd registered with the state's reunion registry to find her birth mother. No match had surfaced.

Her father loved her—she'd always felt cared for. But she was so different from him and from her brother Albert. They were scientists, each of them strangely logical yet impractical, and she was the opposite: practical yet intuitive. They'd named her Lise Meitner for a famous German physicist, but she had no head for science. Their home was functional but unadorned, with Rube Goldberg–type mechanisms to feed the cat and make the morning coffee.

Lise was the cuckoo in the nest. In family photos, she towered above both her father and Albert, and her freckled face smiled widely while they appeared to be calculating the camera's shutter speed. She picked dandelions and put them on the kitchen table in a cup of water so she could enjoy their sharp, green scent and watch the flowers transform into globes of wishes ready to be released into the wind. Her family indulged her with lessons on photosynthesis. She left peaches on the counter to ripen to the moment of peak scent, while her father and brother were content to open a can. She could smell anxiety or frustration when her family didn't even seem to be able to tune into their own emotions. She craved to know more about herself.

Tonight, Lise tried again. "Where did I come from?" she asked her father. She looked into the night as her father contemplated his response. Maybe he'd ignore her. He did that sometimes, not out of malice but from a seeming inability to recognize his feelings.

This time, he replied with a poignancy Lise had never before heard. "I don't know."

She turned away from the window and drew the curtains. "I didn't simply appear in my crib at home. I mean, you must have gone to an adoption agency. Surely, you remember that." There were whole processes to interview a family, collect references, inspect a home. It's not as if a stork had dropped her off.

"No, Lise. I truly don't know. Your mother brought you home one day. That was it."

"Did you ask her about it? No one simply shows up with an infant."

"I did, of course. I gathered she had a research assistant who had become pregnant, then disappeared."

Pressing the phone even closer, Lise stood. This was more than she'd ever before learned. "Tell me about that day. Tell me everything. I know you remember—your memory is legendary." It was, especially with regard to formulae. His coworkers at the lab constantly stopped by to ask him everything from the phase transition temperatures of a particular element to a former colleague's phone number.

She heard a creak and knew her father was standing, too, perhaps pacing, with the phone to his ear. His sigh traveled the phone lines. "Your birth mother asked your mother to care for you, and she promised. She'd handed you over with a blanket and a sealed note. You should have seen your mother's face when she unwrapped the blanket and showed you to me. Your pink lips, those arms waving tiny hands and fingers . . ."

She'd never heard her father so emotional. Perhaps some of it was from missing Mom. She'd been gone almost twenty-five years, but the grief—both of theirs—lingered. "The research assistant was my birth mother? Who was she?"

"I don't know anything about her. I really don't."

She wouldn't have predicted it, but her biological mother may have been a budding scientist. Might still be, Lise corrected. "Why didn't you tell me this earlier?"

"I couldn't. It wasn't a legal adoption. We couldn't give you up to some agency who would peddle you between strangers until you found a home. Your mother bonded with you so intensely and completely. I'd never seen her that way. Even when Albert was born. She loved him, of course, but you . . ."

Lise gave her father time to collect himself.

He cleared his throat. "We'd broken the law. We couldn't tell anyone."

This explained why she never had a birth certificate. Her father had made an excuse about losing it years ago. Still, with this information, she could dig a bit further. The university must keep records of past employees. Perhaps she'd find a name. In the meantime, there was one thing she could do. "The letter. Is it still around?"

"We kept it, but I'm not sure where it is."

"Do you remember what it said?"

"I never read it. It was sealed up, addressed to 'baby,' to give to you when the time came."

When exactly would that be? "The time is now, Dad. I'm ready."

"I'll look for it and send it on."

The thought of her father trying to find anything with his logical yet impractical methods discouraged Lise. "Maybe Albert could help?" Albert, although gifted with his own scientific bent, was more able to navigate daily life.

"I'll ask him," Lise's father said. "I'm making a note right here."

He'd said that to reassure Lise. For him, a note was a commitment. "Thank you."

"You're welcome, honey. One more thing before you go. Are you sure things are all right there?"

Her father had sensed something was troubling her. *Well, well,* Lise thought. People could change.

"No, Dad. I'm fine."

"You're okay for money?"

She squeezed her eyes shut, willing him not to pry further. Her father might operate like an old IBM mainframe, but there was a heart under his analytical thinking. "I'm doing fine here, Dad. It's late. You'd better get to bed."

Then came a pause as her father searched for the right words, words that didn't spring naturally to his lips. "I love you, Lise. No matter what. Remember that, will you?"

Teddy put a kettle on to boil. One of her indulgences lately had been to take a small pot of chamomile tea to bed as she read. Grace and Charm would snuggle in the blankets—Grace, especially, loved the velvet crazy quilt—and she would turn off all but the opaline glass lamp at her bedside. When Captain Corrie had built this house, she was sure he hadn't anticipated the parlor becoming a bedroom, but it was a comfortable one with its chipping plaster moldings and parquet floor.

Tonight she'd sort through the responses to her ad for a housemate. She didn't anticipate it being easy. When she'd first put up notices for housemates earlier this summer, three applicants had never made it past the front door before they'd backed away. One candidate was a young man with black-painted fingernails and plucked eyebrows who'd announced he'd heard Corrie House was haunted and couldn't wait to move in. He'd halted in the entry hall and said the place was freezing cold, that an evil entity occupied it, and he'd hastily left. In fact, that day it had been so warm that Teddy had worn a sleeveless dress. Clearly, the house hadn't wanted him. Other candidates suddenly changed plans or simply never showed up for their appointments.

"Hi, Teddy." Lise came into the kitchen. From the way her gaze wandered through the room without landing anywhere, it was clear something preoccupied her. Perhaps it was the job search. Teddy didn't want to bring it up, because she didn't want Lise to feel pressured. Or, more likely, Dyann's death continued to weigh on her.

"Would you like some tea?" Teddy asked.

"No, thank you. I'm going to toss together a salad." Lise went to the refrigerator to rummage on her shelf.

"What's wrong, darling?"

Lise stood clutching a bag of mesclun mix to her chest. "Do you think I'm making a mistake by staying here?"

"What makes you say that?"

"Maybe Dyann's death is a sign I shouldn't be in Astoria. I just got off the phone with my dad. He wants me to come home."

Teddy drew a steadying breath. She sprinkled chamomile blossoms into the teapot. They sat like golden tufts on the white porcelain. "If you go home, you're going back to an old life. Is that what you want?"

"You're right. It's just . . ."

"Honey." When Lise didn't respond, Teddy said, "Did you make it to the car lot?"

Fran, as was her wont, appeared unexpectedly in the doorway. She took a seat at the kitchen table. "You went to see Richard? Why didn't you tell me?"

Lise set the makings of a salad on the counter. "At Teddy's suggestion, I went to his car lot and pretended I needed a new car. I wanted to find out what he was doing the night Dyann died."

Teddy poured boiling water into the tea kettle. Almost at once, Lise tipped up her face to smell the weedy tea. That girl sure had a nose on her.

"And did you?" Teddy asked. "Do you feel confident that Richard had nothing to do with her death?"

Fran watched earnestly.

"Richard told me where he was that night, but I don't know." She set the paring knife on the counter. "He said he was at the car lot doing the paperwork to sell a car. His client"—here Lise looked up to catch Teddy's eye—"was busy during the day. I'm sure it was Sylvia Borlotti."

"That makes no sense. She's a nightclub singer," Teddy said. "By definition she works at night. She should have plenty of time during the day to buy a car."

"Yes, and more than that, according to someone at the brewery, Sylvia was dressed to perform that night. You don't squeeze into a sequined dress to buy a car."

"Of course she'd cover for him," Fran said. "Duh. They're lovers. Maybe she helped him do the deed." Fran rose and pulled a packet of tortillas and cheese from the refrigerator.

"I had the same thought," Lise said. "Besides the Richard angle, she wasn't a fan of Dyann. She came into the Lucky Lotus once and demanded to see Dyann, but she was out. She said, 'You tell your boss that no one makes a fool of Sylvia Borlotti,' and she left."

"Dyann must have pulled some kind of stunt with her to get Richard riled up," Teddy said. She set the teapot on the table.

Tonight she'd have her tisane here. "So you don't feel any more settled about Richard's innocence?"

Lise resumed chopping vegetables. "I'm not convinced. If it turns out Dyann was murdered, Richard has to be at the top of the list of suspects." Again, she set down the knife. "But the investigation is over. Or not. Signe wouldn't tell me."

"Something is wrong," Fran said. "A woman was killed—"

"Or died naturally," Teddy said.

"And you found the body. She was in the process of sending you a nasty email. Plus, the detective in charge of the case hates you." The burner rattled as Fran nearly slammed a cast-iron skillet on it. "You are being set up as a murderer. You should be finding the real killer yourself."

Fran was a sweet girl, but her imagination was out of control, Teddy thought. "Perhaps we should reframe this. It's possible—"

"You're right." Fran spun toward Lise and Teddy. "Once Lise starts asking questions, she's a target. Now she has Richard suspicious of her. We could wake up one day to find Lise dead. Strangled." Fran waved the spatula toward Teddy. "Right in that chair."

"Darling," Teddy said, "calm down. I'd like to point out, again, that we don't even know that Dyann was killed. Isn't that right, Lise? You saw the detective this morning."

"You saw the detective and didn't say anything?" Fran asked.

"We need to cut you off reading crime novels," Teddy said.

"I did see Signe," Lise replied calmly. "I wanted to pass on what we learned about Richard's car. In short, she didn't care. She said Richard was accounted for and someone else might have been driving his car."

"Like who?" Fran demanded.

"His son, perhaps," Teddy said. The tea was warm and so calming, unlike this conversation. "Fran, how would you like a relaxing cup of chamomile tea?"

Fran ignored her. "You're telling me her son is a murder

suspect, is that it? Not to mention that Richard's alibi is totally lame. Is the murder investigation over, then?"

"No," Lise said. "I mean, maybe. As I said, Signe wouldn't commit to it being over, but she wouldn't say it was continuing, either."

"Perhaps she and her boss have different ideas," Teddy said. She knew the police chief by reputation from chatter at the Labor Temple. Burt knew him better than that. The chief was an "evidence only" man and wouldn't likely pursue hunches or nurture ambitious detectives. Besides that, he liked to brag about Astoria's lack of violent crime under his watch.

Fran abandoned her quesadilla on the counter in uncooked pieces and pulled a screwdriver and oil from a drawer. She set to unscrewing the back door lock with unusual vigor.

"Is it a good idea to start that now?" Teddy said.

"This lock has been bothering me. It desperately needs to be cleaned. That's why it won't bolt half the time." She sprayed oil on the old brass hardware.

Apparently, this was meditative work for the girl. Teddy refreshed her tea. If that was so, there was plenty of meditating to be done in the house. She wondered if Fran fixed window locks, too.

"There's more," Lise said. "I had lunch with the guy who runs the reptile sanctuary. He texted because he's worried about Murphy. He was at Murphy's birthday dinner and said Richard threatened Dyann."

"Surprise, surprise," Fran muttered as she jiggled the screwdriver.

Lise's phone dinged, and she glanced at the screen.

"So, you're going to give it up?" Fran asked. "Just like that? Richard tells you he was busy with his girlfriend—who also hated Dyann, by the way—and you're letting it go?"

"I know," Lise said. "I see your point. All signs point to Richard."

Poor Lise, Teddy thought. She was lost, but she would find

her way. Perhaps Teddy could help—she and Burt—with a trip to Sylvia's nightclub. Plus, they might be able to leverage Burt's connection with the police chief. She wondered what Burt was up to the next day.

Lise took her bowl of salad to the table and sat across from Teddy. "I guess I haven't completely given it up yet. That email? Tomorrow I have a job interview at Blavatsky Manor."

Fran settled in bed with her laptop. Just a few more minutes until *The Harry Kellers Show*. Thankfully, tonight the house's ghosts were quiet.

Earlier, it hadn't been as peaceful. The piano played on its own—Lise seemed to think she played the piano, which was hilarious—and spirits stomped all over the attic.

Fran got it. They were probably worked up that Lise was being so wishy-washy about investigating Dyann's murder. Richard's alibi was so full of holes it made Swiss cheese look like cheddar. "Swiss cheese look like cheddar"—that was good. Fran made a note to use it in *Dead Bolt*. That is, if the French ate cheddar cheese in the eighteenth century.

Lise needed to nail Richard; that was all there was to it.

Fran had once seen danger and let it ride, and it had nearly resulted in fatal consequences. Lise should not do the same.

CHAPTER 15

Lise parked her car outside what had once been a sprawling midcentury house. It was now Blavatsky Manor, home for retired psychic mediums. She was five minutes early for her job interview. She'd made a deal with herself: if she didn't get the job, she was going home to Seattle. She knew that despite her reassurance, Teddy needed a boarder with a paycheck. Not to mention Lise's own needs for things like, for instance, groceries.

Yes, Lise wanted a job, but she also saw this as an opportunity for more information about Dyann's bequest. Dyann had invited a retired psychic from the manor to give palm readings at Murphy's birthday party. Besides her turban, walker, and appetite for pizza, there was little Lise knew about the person. However, the psychic may have overheard something more specific than Phoebe and Ornette had, something that could convict Richard—something Lise could lay on Signe's desk with a satisfied smile.

Dahlias circled the dogwoods in front of the manor. The trees weren't in bloom now, of course, but they'd be lovely in spring. A neatly trimmed hedge led her to the front door. If it were her garden, she'd add a carpet of white sweet william for its slightly spicy fragrance and the way it glowed at night.

Lise got out of her car and smoothed her shirt. On the path to the front door, she passed a pedestal holding a stone-hewn bust of a doughy-faced woman with her hair parted in the center and pulled back severely into a bun. A plaque read HELENA BLAVATSKY, SPIRITUALIST, 1831–1891. Again, Lise wondered if any of the residents were familiar with clairalience. The Lucky Lotus had been a bust, but perhaps this is where she was meant to be when she'd had such a strong and unexpected compulsion to stay in Astoria.

The manor's front door opened to an entry hall giving into the house's former living room, now a lobby. Floor-to-ceiling windows lined its far wall, revealing a shady terrace with small tables, a few occupied by elderly people sipping coffee.

On the leather couches and Barcelona chairs in the lobby sat more of the home's residents. One woman read a magazine, a Pekingese in her lap. Lise did a double take. The well-worn magazine was titled *"Locks, Safes, and Security."* Across from her, a man shuffled playing cards like a Vegas pit boss. A stack of financial journals and a jeweler's loupe sat on one end table, and, oddly, a tall man wearing a newsboy's cap appeared to be taking apart a carburetor.

"Lise?" asked an efficient-looking woman in a greige tunic and pants. "Maxine Marvel. Pleased to meet you. I'm the manager here at Blavatsky Manor."

When they'd concluded their greetings, Maxine gestured toward a table in the corner of the lobby. "Please. Have a seat. Before I ask you about yourself, I'd like to tell you a little about the manor."

That suited Lise fine. A few of the people in the lobby turned to check her out. Maybe this was part of the interview process and they had say on whether she was hired.

"We currently have fourteen residents, not including myself." Maxine placed a brochure in front of Lise with a picture of a smiling older woman with denture-perfect teeth and the words BLAVATSKY MANOR! in large font, tarot cards floating around them. "We draw people from throughout the nation. We're not an assisted living community, but many of our residents need a little extra help."

One resident of an age too venerable for Lise to estimate was settled two chairs away. He tapped his phone—adjusting a hearing aid?—and said, "Or mixing a Manhattan. How are your bartending skills?"

"Johnny, get lost," Maxine said.

The man named Johnny cackled and wandered toward the patio.

Maxine stood. "Come with me, and I'll show you around." Maxine led her to the right, through an arch, to a large room with dining tables and a TV and couches in the corner. "You've seen the lobby. This is our other primary common area."

A bald man with a face etched with wrinkles nodded at Lise.

"Lise, meet the Kid," Maxine said.

The Kid? Lise might have guessed "the Grandpa." At that moment, the Kid smiled, and his face lost several decades and gained a boyish innocence. "Pleased to make your acquaintance," he said.

Another man, this one small with a tidy round belly and wearing a Hawaiian shirt, rose from a table where he was doing a crossword puzzle with a woman dressed in a similar Hawaiian print. The man offered his hand. "Arthur." His voice was businesslike for a former psychic. "This is my wife, Jean."

Or perhaps Jean was the psychic who'd merited them a place at Blavatsky Manor. Lise followed Maxine back toward the lobby.

"We'll take the elevator to the basement."

"Are all of the residents psychics?" Lise asked.

Maxine didn't answer. In the basement, she pointed down a hall. "Down there we have three bedrooms. Upstairs is another five." A dried floral wreath hung on one door. "That's my suite. And here"—she opened a door—"is the exercise room."

Lise stepped in, expecting to see an exercise bike, maybe, or a weight bench. Instead, a silver-haired woman in a black leotard hung upside down from a sling. The woman quickly righted herself and leapt from the sling like a cat.

"Is this the one from the Lucky Lotus?" she asked.

Lise remembered the police officer who'd accompanied Signe as describing the manor as a "freak show." He wasn't wrong.

"Let's go upstairs," Maxine told Lise.

In the elevator, Lise asked, "The position you're hiring for, what are its responsibilities?"

"Gal Friday," Maxine said.

Lise knew this as a movie, not a job title. "What might be some examples of the duties?"

Maxine shrugged. "Whatever we need. Help putting on shoes, picking up prescriptions, reading aloud. Light housekeeping. You know, this and that." They returned to the dining room, and Maxine pulled out a chair for her.

"Thank you for responding so quickly to my application," Lise said. "I haven't done work exactly like this, but as you can see from my resume, I have broad experience. Dealing with a wide variety of people is my specialty."

Besides landscape gardening and being shop girl at the Lucky Lotus, while everyone else was at college, she'd worked at a perfume counter at a department store. As much as she loved fragrance, the constant miasma of synthetic musk, amber, and new "accords" left her not able to parse scent for hours after each shift. Frankly, given her lack of caregiving experience, Lise was surprised, but grateful, Maxine had called her for an interview.

"I'm sure you're very capable," Maxine said. "Did you know Dyann King well?"

"She was in the shop most days." Lise chose her words carefully. "I understand you knew her, too, and that one of the residents went to her son's birthday party."

"I met her once, but that's it," Maxine said. "Last week she stopped by and asked about us. She brought crystals."

The man Maxine had called Johnny had returned and snorted at the mention of crystals.

"And, yes," Maxine continued, "she asked for a palm reader for the party." Maxine scrutinized Lise as if she were a crystal ball herself. "She hinted about leaving the manor money in her estate. Then she died."

A few more people had settled around Johnny, including the card player she'd seen in the lobby. They didn't hide the fact that they were listening. Lise had the strange sensation she was on trial.

"The police were here," a woman with short platinum hair said. Instead of curiosity, Lise heard antagonism in her voice. She had a walker parked near her chair, but no turban. Could this be the palm reader they'd sent?

"They wanted to know about our relationship with the deceased," another woman said, this one wearing a Kansas City Chiefs sweatshirt.

"I see," Lise said. Perhaps Signe was actually investigating the case, not just herding goats. "Was that recently?"

"The day after she died," another resident said.

Not recently, then. "She talked with me, too."

"What did she want to know?" Maxine said, almost before Lise had finished her sentence.

"I found the body. When I came into work that morning. She wanted details."

The handful of residents within hearing made no secret of their interest. Johnny again adjusted his hearing aid.

"Did she say anything?" Maxine asked. "Do they have a suspect?"

Then Lise understood. They weren't interested in her as an employee at all. They wanted the scoop on Dyann's death. When they saw on her resume that she'd worked at the Lucky Lotus, they couldn't make an appointment with her fast enough.

As she pondered, five people continued to watch her with the intensity of an owl locked on a field mouse. "When the detective first talked to me, she assumed Dyann was poisoned. But apparently the medical examiner couldn't find anything."

"Does that mean it's not homicide?" the Chiefs fan asked, her shoulders relaxing.

"They're not looking for anyone?" Johnny asked.

"Honestly, I don't know."

No one responded, but the tension she'd formerly felt building had seeped from the atmosphere. Two of the residents who had stood when Lise came in now sat. However, the woman with the walker continued to stare at Lise.

"I don't like it," Maxine said, but she didn't specify what, exactly, she objected to.

"She was planning to leave the bulk of her estate to you," Lise said. "I signed the codicil."

Sounds of disappointment—murmurs, groans, one "dear God"—swept the room.

"But Dyann's new will might not be legal," Lise said. "She never made it to the lawyer's office to finish the paperwork. Yes, I signed the codicil, but she had to get one more signature. I'm not sure she ever did."

"Good news," Maxine said.

"If you'll excuse me, I'll tell the others," said the Chiefs fan.

This was without a doubt the strangest job interview Lise had ever had. "Anything else I can tell you about my experience? Would you like to see my references?"

"Never mind that," Maxine said. "You're hired."

The front door closed behind Lise, leaving the puzzling world of Blavatsky Manor behind. Too bad she hadn't been able to talk with the psychic Dyann had hired for Murphy's birthday, but there was still time. She'd be back in a few days to start work.

She took a moment to enjoy the view of the river from the home's veranda before heading toward the stairs to her car.

Before she'd made it more than two steps, she heard someone say, "She's passed."

"I'm sorry," Lise said, puzzled. She looked around her. The voice seemed to have come from nowhere.

"Over here." Behind a camellia, next to a potted gardenia, the platinum-haired woman with the walker basked in the sun reflecting from the house's walls. "Your mother. She's passed."

Lise circled the shrub to where the woman sat on a bench. "I know. When I was in kindergarten."

"No, I mean the other one."

Lise could only stare in astonishment. "You mean my birth mother?"

The woman pointed to the cast-iron chair next to her. Its molded vines and flowers were freshly painted white. "Have a seat. I'm Bea, by the way. Bea Marvel. Maxine's mother."

Lise took the chair, warm from the sun. Perhaps this was a trick. Psychics might work like comedians. If you threw them a curveball, they didn't fold, they lobbed it back at you.

"How did you know I was adopted?" she asked.

"There's something special about you, isn't there?"

Again, a trick. Just about anyone would think there was something special about them. Besides, she hadn't answered Lise's question. "What do you mean?"

Bea examined her the way she had earlier, in the dining room. "Yes. I see it. You're one of the special ones, like me."

"I don't understand."

The morning's warmth lifted a perfume of lilies of the valley from Bea's skin and clothing and mingled with the creamy scent of potted gardenias. Diorissimo, maybe. Lise inhaled. Correction: probably a drugstore bottle of Muguet des Bois. Bea's emotional scent aura was serene. No drama, no deception.

Bea locked eyes with her and smiled. "Did you feel anything the night Dyann King died?"

"No. Why?"

"It may not work that way for you. I can't say."

Lise scooted forward in her chair. "You were there, at Murphy's birthday party. What happened?"

"I didn't want to go. I told Maxine it was a bad idea."

"But you did go."

"In the end, I said I would. People love having their fortunes told. I read palms." Bea's voice drifted from the dreamy to the practical. "It's an old trick. People betray information about themselves without even knowing it. All I have to do is pick up a clue or two, say something vague, and, presto, they think you're a genius."

Lise felt more comfortable now. This was stable ground. Blavatsky Manor was likely nothing more than a retirement home for old folks who had worked at suspect storefronts back in the day. "What can you tell about me?"

"Besides your gift?" She gave Lise a quick once-over. "You're dressed secondhand, but not just used—old."

Lise would call it vintage, but she got the drift. "And?"

Bea nodded toward the street below. "You drive a clunker. Combined with your wardrobe, I'd say you don't have much money, but you have an artist's eye. No makeup, unfashionable hairdo—you don't follow trends."

The warmth of the sun reflecting from the building lulled Lise into a near trance. She inhaled honeysuckle from somewhere deep in the garden. "Yes?"

"You've always felt apart, is my guess. Put it all together, and you're the picture of someone who's had to prove herself but hasn't given up." She squinted. "And you keep smelling things. Is that your gift?"

Lise looked at Bea in wonder. "How did you know?"

"It's a strange one, true," Bea said. When she tipped back her head, the sun caught the rhinestones in the bee-shaped brooch on her blouse and sparkled. "But we don't get to choose our gifts, only if we're going to use them."

"Am I a witch?"

"'Am I a witch?'" Bea repeated. "What kind of a question is that? Of course you are. We all are. It's like—it's like running. The vast majority of us can run." She glanced toward her walker. "Not me, but you know what I mean. Some people are genetically predisposed to be better runners than others, but none of them are going to win gold medals unless they practice."

"Is magic hereditary?"

"Yes and no," she said. "You met Maxine. She's a wizard with a spreadsheet, but I'd hardly call her magical."

Lise rested her head against the wall. Instinctively, she trusted Bea. "I can smell emotion and, sometimes, history. I want to learn more about it—where it came from, how to use it. But I'm frustrated at every turn."

"Maybe you're not meant to know it now," Bea said. "I can't say. But I can answer questions about the boy's birthday party. That's one of the reasons you're here, isn't it?"

Lise turned to Bea. "Yes. You truly are psychic."

"Have at it, then. What do you want to know?"

"What did you see that night? Anything unusual with Richard King?"

"I'm not a fan of pizza and beer," Bea said. Lise had heard otherwise but didn't press the point. "Fortunately, Cook had left me a serving of chicken à la king."

"People here seem concerned about Dyann's death, but it doesn't look like you're hurting for money. I'd almost guess you'd be happy if it turned out you didn't inherit at all."

Bea lifted a penciled eyebrow. "Indeed."

Lise forced herself to slow down. Bea would take her own time getting to the reveal. "What can you tell me?"

Bea's eyes lowered halfway. Whether this was some form of psychic meditation or simply defense against the sun, Lise couldn't say. "Richard King. In love. In a big, messy, painful love affair. It will not end well."

"Sylvia Borlotti," Lise said. "I heard she was there, too, dressed for her show."

"The gal in the sequins? Yes, she was there, but he wasn't in love with her. Oh, no." Bea swatted at the air as if to dismiss the thought. "She'll be all right. The son is drifting, poor boy. Clung to his friend like he was a life preserver and sharks were circling."

"Did Richard threaten Dyann at all?"

"Most certainly. When she announced she was changing her will, he swung an arm and knocked over a pint of beer. He told Dyann she'd pay for it. Not for the beer, honey."

"I get it." Lise could picture the scene—Murphy clinging to Ornette, Sylvia mopping beer from her lap, Dyann's look of victory, Richard's rage. Meanwhile, Bea would have placidly looked on, perhaps adjusting her turban. "You weren't worried for yourself, were you?"

"No, hon. I had the impression those two went at it all the time, that Richard never really took the change of will seriously."

"Did you notice what time Richard left?"

"He left right then. Got up and walked out, leaving his sweetheart to gather up her purse and follow. Not what I'd call a gentleman." She mused on this a few seconds before her expression darkened. "No, it wasn't Richard I was worried about, it was Dyann."

Monday morning quarterbacking must be a rewarding sport for psychics. "I'll bet."

Bea tossed her a sharp look. "Coming from you, that's rich. You have a lot to learn."

She was right. Lise had been rude. “I’m sorry. Please continue.”

Bea looked into the distance. A hummingbird landed on the trellis behind her. Finally, she spoke. “Dyann’s palm.”

Lise remembered Dyann’s hands—her French manicure, the rings of various stones embodying special spiritual qualities, the long fingers. “Yes?”

“I couldn’t see a future there at all.”

CHAPTER 16

"Blavatsky Manor was something else," Lise told Teddy. "I'm sure they only wanted me to come in because of Dyann's death. They kept asking what I knew."

"Retired psychic mediums," Teddy said. "I wonder where they worked? Maybe at a 900 line? The Psychic Friends Network?"

"A what?"

"Never mind, darling. That was before your time. You took the job?"

They were back in the kitchen at Corrie House. Conversations always seemed to happen in its cozy warmth. It was crazy, but Lise often felt like a motherly housekeeper was here, chopping vegetables on the counter or stepping to the back door to check on the laundry drying on the line. Sometimes she swore she could smell the coffee and baking bread.

"Yes. You can expect a rent check soon."

"Am I that obvious?" Teddy said.

"It's not you, it's this house. It can't be cheap to keep everything running."

Teddy sighed. "I won't lie. Except for the locks—and that's thanks to Fran—this place is falling apart. Burt says the furnace doesn't have another winter left in it, and I'm looking at a minimum of ten thousand dollars, not counting duct work."

Poor Teddy. "You had some nice jewelry."

"'Had' being the operative word. I sold the Bulgari ring when the refrigerator shorted out and scorched the wall. That was before you came. I had a nice Patek Philippe watch, too, that went to repair the dry rot in the conservatory. I tried to trim the jasmine and discovered it was the only thing holding it together." She put a hand on her chest as if to calm herself. "I'm so sorry, darling. I shouldn't be troubling you with this."

"Any luck with new housemates?"

"Plenty of applicants, but four out of the five phone numbers I called were wrong."

The house. For some reason, the house hadn't wanted them, Lise thought.

Teddy sat back. "I've always taken the approach that something would come along when I needed it, and something usually did—an unexpected gift, a man."

Lise watched Teddy and waited. She was going somewhere with this.

"You know how I've been encouraging you to stay in Astoria?"

Lise nodded. "I've noticed. You need housemates."

"It's not just that, darling. Not just the money or your wonderful company. It's that I know what it's like to give up a dream and take the easy route. I did it, and I don't recommend it. It's easy only in the short term." She placed a hand on Lise's arm. "Enough about me. Tell me about your new job."

The fragrance of regret, full of dried lavender and hot tar paper, suffused the room. There was more to Teddy's story, Lise was sure, and she hoped to hear it one day. "I took the job. I need the paycheck. But wow. I wonder what those people are up to. It's not a typical retirement home. Maxine didn't even ask me if I know how to operate a vacuum cleaner. All she cared about was gleaning info about Dyann. The others, too."

"The others? You mean you think Blavatsky Manor might somehow be involved with Dyann's death?" The blue in Teddy's eyes lightened a few shades when she turned her head and they caught in the light.

"I can't say. A group of residents gathered to listen while Maxine and I were talking. I have the feeling they want to keep me around just so they can keep tabs on the investigation."

"Are they hoping the codicil is legal? They'd stand to receive a lot of money."

"That's the thing. They seemed relieved that it might not be legal. I don't understand."

"Maybe they're simply snoops," Teddy said. "Maybe they don't have a lot going on."

"Possibly." But not probably.

"How about the palm reader? Did you happen to see her?"

"I did. We talked for a minute. She didn't have anything new to offer about Richard. In any case, I start the day after tomorrow." She leaned back in her chair. "Here I go, complaining at you, and I haven't even asked how you're doing. You said four out of five numbers were wrong. Any luck with the fifth?"

Teddy nodded. "We have one gentleman coming tomorrow to look at the house."

Lise pivoted to stare out the back window, and, with a *thunk*, her foot hit a box wrapped in Kraft paper. "What's this?"

"Oh, it was on the stoop. A package for Fran. Grace was sleeping on it."

The mail carrier was already irritated that he had to climb the path from the cul-de-sac for mail delivery to Corrie House. As a sign of his displeasure, he often didn't ring for packages but dumped them on the front steps.

Lise lifted the box to the table and gave it a little shake. Its contents didn't budge. "Look. The return address is 'H. Kellers, Los Angeles.' Isn't it strange that Fran refuses to talk about her brother?"

"There was a letter for you, too, darling. Just a moment."

Teddy disappeared and returned with a business-sized envelope. "Certified mail."

Lise took the envelope. She hadn't been expecting anything, and it was too soon for her father to have forwarded the letter from her birth mother. She ripped it open and let her hands drop to her lap after reading only a few lines. "You have got to be kidding." Lise handed the letter to Teddy. "Take a look at this."

Teddy slipped on a pair of mother-of-pearl reading glasses. "Darling . . . Oh, my . . . Richard King will sue you if you ask any more questions about Dyann's death. Defamation, he says." She set the letter aside and removed her glasses. "That's an admission of guilt if I've ever heard one."

"He clearly believes in the old saying that the best defense is a good offense." Lise tucked the letter into its envelope and sighed. If Signe found out about this, she'd run wild.

"It's time to make a plan," Teddy said. "Fran is right. We need to gather more evidence, real evidence, to counter Richard. Secondhand word that his car was down the block is not enough."

"What good does evidence do if the detective in charge won't listen to me?"

"It will do exactly zero good if we don't have evidence at all," Teddy said firmly.

Lise had already accepted the job at Blavatsky Manor. She'd promised herself she'd stay. She owed it to Dyann—and herself. "You'd do that for me?"

"It's easy, darling. We collect evidence, we present it to the detective, and Richard is confirmed as suspect number one. Presto. No grounds to sue. Burt knows the police chief, and I've already talked to him about arranging a visit." When Lise opened her mouth to reply, Teddy rested a hand on her arm. "I didn't want to say anything in case you'd decided to move on."

"Thank you, Teddy."

"Besides that, Burt wants to take me out tonight. Dinner and music would be nice, and I know where there's a good nightclub singer." She stood. "I'll go get my phone."

Although her ownership of Corrie House had drawn Teddy to Astoria, it was the town itself—the river views, the nearby ocean, the forested hills—that had sealed the deal. She was reminded of this once again as she and Burt walked down a dock in the Columbia River with boats bobbing and sea lions barking. The breeze tousled her hair. Gulls the size of chihuahuas waddled by on the prowl for dropped french fries.

"Crime Pays is in a slip not too far from the end," Burt said. "Ah, there it is. And there he is." Burt stopped near a vintage boat that looked as if it had sailed in from a Katharine Hepburn movie. He extended a hand to a small man with a ruddy face and mop of white hair sticking out from under a baseball cap. "Chief. I'd like you to meet Teddy Bright."

The chief of police doffed his hat, and white hair sprang everywhere. He smoothed his hair with one hand and replaced his hat with the other. "Call me Merrill. Welcome aboard."

They stepped onto the boat's deck, Burt lending a stabilizing arm to Teddy. Merrill led them to low lawn chairs on the bow. He let out an "oomph" as he lowered himself into one.

"Thank you for meeting with us," Teddy said.

"No problem at all, not for a pal like Burt. If I can ease a lady's mind, so much the better."

Burt and Teddy had already worked out their roles. Burt would be the protector and Teddy the fearful woman. She would have no problem playing her role. Hell, until a little over a year ago, her whole life had been theater.

"If it weren't for Lise," Teddy said, "I wouldn't be so concerned. But what if Dyann King was murdered?"

"Nope," Merrill said instantly.

"Are you certain?" Teddy said. "Lise is my boarder, and our

house is on the hill, separate from the rest of the neighborhood. If anyone was after her . . ." As she let her words trail off, she looked into the distance, as if imagining the worst. It wasn't a difficult expression to put on. Richard's threat to sue Lise was no joke. "I have a motherly feeling for the poor girl."

Merrill patted her knee. "Don't you worry. This isn't official, so don't go spreading it around, but the medical examiner is preparing to rule her death as from natural causes."

"A heart attack, for instance?" Burt said.

"She definitely had heart failure and some sort of seizure, to boot."

Teddy shielded her eyes from the sun with one hand. "The detective—"

"Signe Rasmussen," Merrill said.

"—hinted that it might have been poison."

"Nope," Merrill repeated. "The medical examiner ran a tox screen for the usual suspects and found nothing."

"What do you mean by 'the usual suspects'?" Teddy asked.

"Recreational drugs, medication, the sort of things that do in ninety percent of folks who die from poisoning."

Leaving a clear ten percent unaccounted for, Teddy thought. "I suppose you tested the cup she drank from, too, and the Mayan ceremonial liqueur?"

Merrill chuckled. "She's a smart one, that lady," he said to Burt. Then, to Teddy, "We certainly did and found nothing but doctored booze. The toxicologist wagered it was Benedictine with cinnamon sticks."

"Could some other sort of poison have killed her?" Burt asked, echoing Teddy's thoughts.

"Look. I understand your concern, but there's little to no violent crime in Astoria, and that's how I like to keep it." Merrill's gaze strayed past them, toward the river, where a barge trundled upstream. "I'm not saying law enforcement is unnecessary. We've got federal agents here looking into a case right now. But murder? Rare to vanishing."

"You'd say there's no chance Dyann was poisoned," Teddy said.

"People drop dead from heart attacks all the time." Merrill shook his head. "Nope. Poison didn't kill her."

Nope. His favorite word, Teddy thought.

"Nope. It was a tragedy. Such an attractive lady, too. You know she was a runner-up for Miss Oregon?"

"You don't say?" Burt said.

"Attractive lady, unstable ticker," Merrill concluded. "The alcohol likely didn't help. Plus, I hear she was stirring up trouble with her ex-husband, Richard King. Add stress to the mix, and you have a recipe for cardiac failure."

"I imagine the medical examiner had access to Dyann King's medical history," Teddy said. "They would know if she was susceptible to heart problems."

Merrill had a blank look. "Of course. Why not?"

In other words, he had no idea. "Do you know Richard King well?" Teddy asked innocently. The chief was feeling expansive. Maybe he'd be willing to reveal a police record, if it existed.

"Sure do. He's been out with me on the boat a few times. Bought my Chevy from him. More of a golfer than a boater, though." His expression told Teddy he figured he'd explained everything one needed to know about Richard King.

"I understand he'd harassed Dyann," Teddy said. "Plus, her tires were slashed."

"I know what you're thinking," Merrill said. "You think Richard King killed his ex-wife some tricky way with a nondetectable poison. Nope. Think of it like this: if she died, who would he torment? Besides, he was just in my office, asking the same questions you are. I don't know why people are so convinced the poor lady was murdered."

Teddy shot a glance at Burt. Of course Richard went to the chief of police. If he was guilty, he'd want to know from his friend what the evidence was against him. "It's just that the detective was so certain."

"Detective Rasmussen is a smart gal, no doubt about it. But she's young and perhaps a bit overeager. She's from the big city. Sees a killer behind every jay walker. Plus, she's ambitious."

"And you're close to retirement," Burt said.

"Indeed, I am," Merrill said. "That's why we took on a detective in the first place. Signe might be more than we bargained for." His look of focus relaxed, and he smiled. "But that's none of your worry. She'll understand what Astoria is about soon, and it's not about murder, that's certain."

Teddy looked at the chief, holding a mug of coffee, gazing toward the river's almost impossibly blue surface. "Nope."

Chapter 17

Fran rarely heard voices—voices no one else could hear—at the bookstore. For this, she was grateful. She had enough to do to keep the customers happy without that kind of distraction.

That said, occasionally, a girl came to visit the back room. From the *scrape-scrape* sound Fran heard, the girl was busy doing something with dishes. The bookstore's pug growled at the ghost but didn't seem overly threatened. Fran figured the store had been a restaurant at one point, or maybe a bar. Astoria's main drag had been loaded with them when the canneries were in full swing. Men had worked long shifts processing salmon and wanted somewhere to blow their earnings. Now the space was filled with light and books.

Fran prepared to shove her purse into the cubbyhole assigned to her when she found a fat manila envelope lying in it. "For Fran—Info on Corrie House" it read. Excellent.

A few minutes later, she was in the cookbook section replacing a volume on Szechuan cooking a customer had left in the self-help section when someone tapped her shoulder. She stood abruptly. Who had the nerve to touch her without her permission?

She swiveled to see Murphy King, mouth breather and son of a wife killer. His beady eyes scanned her. He'd been in the store once or twice, but Margie had dealt with him. Frankly, Fran was surprised he read.

"I'm here to pick up my book," he said.

She pasted on a smile and rubbed her shoulder where he'd touched. "Let me check if it's in. Follow me."

She went behind the cashier's counter to check the "will call" books lined up on the shelf against the wall. As she ducked into her safety zone—no customers were allowed here—she realized that she might be able to turn the misfortune of having to deal with Murphy to her favor. "Name, please?"

"Murphy King." His voice was adenoidal. She bet he always sounded like he had to blow his nose.

"Here it is." She pulled a fat volume from the shelf. *The Ultimate Ball Python: Morph Maker Guide*, the title read. The cover alone spiked her cortisol. When she turned again to face Murphy, she wore what she hoped was a sympathetic smile. "I heard about your mother. I'm so sorry."

"That's okay." Murphy reached for the book, which Fran held just out of reach.

"You must feel terrible," she said.

"Yeah," was his only reply.

"Losing your mom like that."

He sniffed. "Yeah. My dad's super bummed."

This was going nowhere, fast. She set the book face down on the counter, happy to let go of the snakes but reluctant to let Murphy get away. "I bet you like driving your dad's Camaro." She glanced up. How would he react?

"Uh, I don't drive it. My dad is touchy about his car. Hey, is your brother Harry Kellers?"

She pursed her lips firmly. She would not respond to this. "You never drive the Camaro at all? Like, not even on your birthday?" If Murphy didn't drive it and Richard was at his car lot that night, as he'd claimed, how did the car get down the street from the Lucky Lotus? Unless, as she'd suspected all along, Richard had lied.

"I mean, sometimes I do. I could drive it anytime, if I asked him really nicely," he amended.

Margie's pug waddled over and sniffed at Murphy's pant legs. The dog growled.

Fran acknowledged defeat. "That'll be forty dollars." She held out a hand for his credit card.

The pug barked and backed away from Murphy.

"Geronimo," Fran said, "Hush. What's your deal?"

"I bet he smells my snake Tangie."

"Tangie?"

"Tangerine Dream is her full name." Murphy smiled, and his tiny eyes nearly disappeared into his cheeks. "Good boy." He knelt to pet the pug, and to Fran's surprise Geronimo came closer, tail wagging. "Animals love me."

Wasn't it always like this in books? Fran thought. A character gave off one vibe, then showed another one to trick the reader. That's exactly what a murderer would do. You'd think he was a big animal lover, then he'd turn out to have poisoned his own mother.

"Do you like cars?" Murphy asked.

Fran shrugged.

"Do you want a ride in my dad's Camaro? You asked about it."

"What?"

"I could borrow it if I promised to be careful. We could go somewhere. Out to Fort Stevens Park, maybe," he said. "Take a walk on the beach."

A walk on the beach? With Murphy? Her horror grew. All by herself? Visions swept through her mind of body parts washed up on the surf. Plus, what if there was a tsunami? "That's not why I asked about the car."

"Then why did you?"

"I'm very busy," she said.

"Would you rather go for a ride in a Mercedes convertible? I'll be getting my mom's car once the police are through with it and my dad has fixed the tires."

She'd made a mistake by probing into his alibi. He was getting entirely the wrong idea. "No, thanks."

Murphy's expression shut down, and he handed over his credit card at last. "I didn't mean anything. I just wanted to talk to someone about what I should do with my money." A snide smile crept over his face. "I'm rich now. Or I will be once probate is sorted out."

Geronimo lay belly-up at his feet, panting. Murphy bent to scratch his tummy.

"No offense, I hope," Fran said. Lise and Teddy needed to hear all about how Murphy was parading his wealth.

"None taken." Murphy tucked the book under an arm and left.

Geronimo trotted to the front window to watch him walk away.

Chapter 18

Moonlight splashed ivory-gold over the calm Columbia River. Burt enclosed Teddy's hands in his on the linen tablecloth. "You look lovely tonight, Teddy."

"Thank you."

She certainly felt lovely. It wasn't the dab of Shalimar that Lise had insisted she wear, or the dusting of rose-tinted blush, or the linen gown that brushed at her calves. She had been to fancier restaurants with fancier views in fancier clothing—La Tour d'Argent in Yves Saint Laurent with a view of the Seine and Notre Dame; the bar at the Savoy in London, all shiny wood and Deco styling to the music of cocktail shakers. Bernard had liked her in Rive Gauche perfume and couture.

Again she mused how glamour and money didn't guarantee happiness. This was something more—something better. A small Italian restaurant on the river with surprisingly delicious ravioli and a man with whom she could be herself. She took in the crinkles around Burt's eyes and the gray hair that escaped from the neckline of his button-down shirt, and she was happy.

Teddy and Burt had first met at a restaurant, only it was the Labor Temple, not a place as snazzy as Amato's. Teddy had been antsy that night, restless, and Corrie House itself had seemed to eject her onto the street.

As she had strolled downtown, she'd considered stopping at the rooftop bar at the Hotel Elliott. There, among the gimlet-sipping tourists, she could play the part of a moneyed woman. She'd find someone—a vacationing businessman, maybe—drawn to her bohemian yet worldly style. She knew how to interest a man, even at her age. Not just Bernard but a few of his so-called friends had let her know subtly and not-so-subtly how she intrigued them.

Night had been falling, and lights were being switched on in the houses she passed. In one, a dinner table was being cleared and a baby lifted from a high chair.

The Labor Temple was about as far style-wise from the Hotel Elliott as you could get. Here, blue collar workers grabbed a quick one on the way home. In the back, beyond the diner where regulars tucked into chicken-fried steak and chili, was the bar. She had taken a seat at its counter.

"Teddy, hello," Sabrina, the bartender, had said. Sabrina looked barely old enough to tend bar, let alone accumulate an ex-husband and young daughter. "What can I get you?"

"Chamomile tea, please." An unusual order in a bar, but thanks to Teddy, tea bags were always at hand. "How's Hazel? Liking kindergarten?"

"She loves it, thank you." Sabrina slid a crayoned paper across the bar. It showed a woman with a triangular body and arms like sticks terminating in suns. "She gave me this yesterday."

Teddy returned the drawing. "Adorable."

"Herbal tea in a bar?" came a masculine voice with a rough edge.

Teddy turned to see a man two stools down. His buzz-cut hair—he had lots of it for his age, which had to be near hers—was as gray as the cutting edge of a well-worn shovel, and something in the way he held himself said "military." She instantly clocked his casual but well-cut jacket and expensive watch.

For a moment, Teddy's features drew themselves into those of someone more conservative. She could match him whiskey for whiskey, rail about kids these days, lament the lack of discipline in society. Then she relaxed. She wanted nothing from him.

"Chamomile," Teddy replied.

"I'll get one of those, too. Sabrina, bring me a tea?" the man said. He extended a hand. "Burt Wilkinson."

"Theodora Bright. Call me Teddy. Pleased to meet you."

In the past, a meeting like this would have served as a sort of job interview. Did she have what this man wanted? Did he have what she needed? Bernard had been the last of those. It had taken too long, but she was free of mercenary love affairs.

"May I?" He lifted his highball, now mostly ice, and took the stool next to her.

Teddy nodded. They chatted for a while, and she said, "Veteran. Navy is my guess."

"Got it in one. Career navy. I saw time in Vietnam, but the military life was too much for my family. I settled here and became a bar pilot."

Bar pilots were near celebrities in Astoria. The mouth of the Columbia River was hazardous, with shifting shoals. Before a ship set to sea, bar pilots were lowered by helicopter, or—more likely in this man's time—ferried by motorboats. They boarded ships on rope ladders, often in roiling storms, to pilot them to the open ocean. The job was glamorous, highly skilled, and occasionally deadly.

Teddy had known celebrities. Bar pilots might be a big deal here, but George Harrison was a big deal everywhere.

"I was involved with the Vietnam war, too," Teddy said. "As a protester." She watched Burt keenly for a tightened expression, a shutting down of interest.

For a moment, his face was still. Then he laughed. "Of course you were. Sabrina, get this lady more hot water. Her teapot has run dry."

It had. Teddy was surprised he'd noticed. She felt herself relax. Someone put a Patsy Cline song on the jukebox and sang along about walking after midnight. "I'm surprised I haven't seen you around."

"I settled with my family over the hill in Hammond." Burt looked into the depths of his mug. "Stayed there a while after my wife died. The kids were gone, and I rattled around without much to do but work on the boat and watch TV. I thought, what the hell, and sold the place. Bought a condo a few blocks from here. How about you?"

"I have a Victorian up Eighth."

"Corrie House," Sabrina said, returning to refill Teddy's teapot.

"The haunted mansion?" Burt said. "Sure, I've heard of it."

"Haunted by the desperate need for a new roof. And more."

She must have betrayed some anxiety, because Burt asked, "A lot of work, huh?"

"Right now, it's the furnace."

"What kind of heat? Gas? A boiler, maybe? Lots of those old houses had boilers."

"Oil." The furnace drank more greedily than W. C. Fields during Prohibition.

"Maybe I could have a look at it," Burt said. "I've worked in a few engine rooms in my time. At least I could tell you if it's worth saving."

At rest, Burt's face had little to recommend it—a nose maybe a little too large, nondescript eyes, thin lips. But when he talked, it radiated warmth. In the center of the animation was a pillar of calm. Teddy's anxiety waned.

"You just met me," she said.

"I volunteered to look at your furnace, not move in with you."

She smiled at the flirtation in his eyes. "That's so kind."

"Life is short, Theodora. We should both know that by now."

Getting old was crazy. Inside, she was still in her twenties and the world was limitless. Every once in a while, she would catch herself in a mirror and not recognize the woman with the long white hair. Or she'd see a hand and be momentarily surprised at its age spots and raised blue veins. The elderly had always been "other," yet here she was.

Later, when they had left the Labor Temple after a late dinner in the diner and hours of conversation, she had almost forgotten those elapsed decades. She'd remembered again when Burt had clutched his cane and hesitated as he stood.

Yet, somehow, life was beginning to seem richer than ever. Tonight was another example.

"Do you really think Sylvia will tell us anything?" Burt asked.

"Hard to say. Either way, we get a nice meal." Teddy squeezed Burt's fingers and released them.

"Barbara and I came here once," Burt said. "She loved the pasta carbonara."

On a stage no bigger than a dining room table, Sylvia Borlotti took the microphone for her second set. She filled a bead-splattered gown, nearly, but not quite, spilling from its neckline. She was all brunette pulchritude. Richard had a type. It was as if she and Dyann had come from the same line of dolls, but Dyann was the New Age Socialite and Sylvia was the Mature Starlet.

The pianist played the first notes of "Melancholy Baby," and Sylvia began to sing in a surprisingly rich alto. The woman had genuine talent.

Burt gazed toward the river. "It's calm tonight."

"Yes. You're thinking of your work, aren't you?"

A server came to collect their plates and offered dessert menus. Burt had a sweet tooth. He ordered tiramisu to share, plus two decaf coffees.

When she left, Burt said, "Some nights it was so stormy the helicopters couldn't take us out." He nodded up the pier. "The pilot boat had to do it. Let me tell you, it's no joke to look at a flimsy nylon rope ladder swinging against a massive tanker, slick with icy water and bobbing like a rubber duckie."

Such a gentle man and such a violent job. "How did you do it?"

"I had no choice. I didn't think about it. I counted on fate to see me through, and I guess I got lucky."

Kind of like life, Teddy reflected. She was healthy and had a decade, maybe more, on Earth if fate was on her side. He hadn't said anything, but Teddy's guess was that Burt wouldn't be as lucky. He'd scheduled a doctor's appointment and follow-up lab work, but it didn't take a doctor to notice how short of breath he'd become and how his complexion had grayed. He refused to talk about it.

An hour later, from her spot next to the baby grand piano, Sylvia Borlotti wound up a sultry version of "Wild as the Wind" and found a seat at the polished oak bar. The restaurant was small enough that she was easily in Teddy's view. The bartender handed Sylvia a flute of champagne.

This was Teddy's chance. She raised an eyebrow at Burt. He nodded.

Teddy slipped onto the stool next to Sylvia. Her decades of training locked into place. She felt like an interpreter who could switch languages without a second thought.

"That was marvelous. You have a gift."

Sylvia gave Teddy a quick once-over and returned dismissively to her glass. "Thank you."

Teddy wasn't a man, and even if she were, she wouldn't be a wealthy man. No matter. Many roads lead to Rome. "Not only is your voice a dream, you have simply remarkable skin. Just gorgeous."

This brought more attention—a tilt of the head and a quarter turn toward Teddy. "Thank you."

"Bartender," Teddy said. "Will you bring me a bottle of Veuve Clicquot? You don't happen to have the Grande Dame 2008, do you?"

Now she'd captured Sylvia's attention, the snob. Sylvia turned fully to Teddy.

"No?" Teddy said to the bartender. "How about the 2002 Taittinger, or the 2006, in a pinch?" This would cost her a pretty penny, but the information gained might be worth it. She cast a glance at Burt, who watched with an indulgent smile. He'd foot the bill, anyway. She'd make it up to him.

"What table, ma'am?" the bartender asked, already filling a silver urn with ice.

"There, near the window," Teddy said. Then, to Sylvia, "Will you join us? It would be an honor."

Sylvia's shoulders raised in a barely perceptible shrug. "I guess that would be fine. Thank you."

At the table, Burt stood and held Sylvia's chair. "Just lovely, your voice. Wonderful."

As Teddy had predicted, Sylvia responded more warmly to a man. She took the seat next to Burt's. She smiled and, cupping her chin in her hand, leaned toward him. "Which song was your favorite?"

Burt, bless him, was up to the challenge. "So hard to choose. Perhaps 'It Never Entered My Mind.' I've always liked that song." He filled her glass.

Teddy caught Burt's eye. "We were just talking about the death of the woman who owned the Lucky Lotus. Terrible."

Sylvia coughed on her sip of champagne. "Did you know her?"

"No," Teddy said truthfully.

"I did. Frankly, she's no loss."

"Oh my." Aging presented certain perks, and one was being

perceived as below suspicion. Few people viewed you as a threat, no matter how scheming you were, if you had white hair and a pleasant demeanor.

Sylvia looked from Teddy to Burt. "She used to be married to Richard King. Of King Cars?" Once she'd determined they knew who Richard was, she continued. "She made his life a living hell. Every chance she got, she'd needle him."

"You don't say?" Burt said.

"She was awful. She reported his business for environmental violations because of runoff from washing the cars, and once she even put Limburger cheese in the trunks of some of the high-value vehicles."

"How'd she do that?" Teddy didn't have to pretend to be interested.

"Used to work there and still had a key to the office." Sylvia held out her glass for a refill. A demilune of hot pink lipstick marked its rim. "Richard changed that, of course."

"Sounds like you and Mr. King are close," Burt said.

Sylvia smiled and leaned back. "He's one of the area's leading businessmen." She lowered her lashes. "We're practically engaged."

Teddy couldn't blame her. After all, she'd done the same in her time. "A fine man, I'm sure, and didn't deserve his ex's treatment."

Sylvia's expression darkened. "Once she got wind that he and I were involved, she made trouble for me, too." She lifted her chin. "My looks are vital to my success."

"Indeed," Burt said and glanced at Teddy.

"She didn't"—Teddy placed a hand on her chest to express shock—"she didn't try to disfigure you, did she?"

"She did."

This wasn't the response Teddy had expected. From what she'd heard, Dyann was a menace, but not criminally so. "I can't believe it."

"I'd gone into the shop to buy a small bottle of Magnet Oil. You've heard of it?"

"Sure." Heard Lise complain about it, at least, Teddy thought. "It's supposed to be something else."

"Maybe it is. I have no idea. It was stupid, I know, but I wanted to bring more attention to my career." She held her glass for a refill. "I know I'm meant for more than singing in a tiny Italian joint like this." She drank deeply.

A pity to gulp it, Teddy thought. This was superlative champagne.

Sylvia continued, "When I went to the Lucky Lotus and asked for Magnet Oil, Dyann said she had a special batch with unusual powers. She brought a bottle from the back and gave it to me. She said someone with my talent should be rewarded by the universe. She told me to rub it on my body, liberally."

"Uh oh."

"Welts," Sylvia said. "All over. I had to cancel a full weekend of shows."

Teddy exchanged glances with Burt. His face was sympathetic, but his eyes told her they'd be smiling about this later.

"Clearly, she was jealous of you, both for your beauty and your relationship with her ex," he said. "I wonder how she found out about you and Richard King?"

He was good, that Burt.

"I have no idea," Sylvia said, again holding out her empty glass. Burt complied.

Teddy had an idea, and his name started with a capital *R*. From what Lise had said, those two lived to torture each other. "How dare she take out her jealousy on you. Richard must have been furious."

Sylvia toyed with the stem of her champagne flute. Teddy translated that move as frustration that Richard was not as angry as she'd hoped. Perhaps he'd even laughed.

"We're practically engaged," Sylvia repeated, her voice faltering.

Teddy and Burt again exchanged glances, but this time they communicated pity. Sylvia Borlotti was not a happy woman.

Then Sylvia sat up straight. "That . . . that *cow.*" The champagne had taken effect, and she stumbled on her words. The face of the sultry nightclub singer was gone, replaced by naked anger. "If someone hadn't killed her first, I might have been tempted myself."

Chapter 19

Fran carefully set the teapot on the coffee table in Teddy's sitting room. The clock on the marble mantel chimed ten o'clock, its little golden cherubs spinning.

"It's working again," she said.

"It started up again not long after you left that night." Teddy stifled a yawn.

It was late for oldsters like Teddy and Burt, Fran thought, especially after a big meal, and Lise tended to turn in early, too. As for Fran, she was wide awake and still had an hour to kill before Harry's show. "We're all here, the complete investigative team. Let's give our reports." She set out a teacup for each of them: Lise, Teddy, Burt, and herself.

Burt reached for his cup, then withdrew his hand and placed it on his chest.

Teddy instantly set her hand on his arm. "Are you all right?"

He took a moment to regain his breath. His brief grimace became a smile. "Just fine, hon."

Night pressed on the windows, and a soft moan crept down the chimney, flickering the candles Teddy had lit and scattered here and there—two on the marble mantel, one on the table next to the chaise longue, one on the coffee table next to a plate of shortbread cookies.

"The song of an old house," Burt said.

Teddy's gaze swept the ceiling's cracked plaster moldings. "Everyone says Corrie House is haunted, but I think it's more than that. This house feels alive, like it has a soul."

"It does," said Fran promptly. As if surprised by her exclamation, she dipped her head, letting her hair fall over her eyes.

"What do you mean?" Lise asked.

Fran wouldn't look at them. They weren't up late when the crying began. Not that they could hear it, even if they were. They couldn't know how the house made its will known by drawing them in, giving each of them a little of itself. To Teddy, it released its feminine charm, letting orchids and a jasmine vine thrive in the conservatory off her parlor bedroom, even with the north wind rattling its windows. To Lise, it gave up scented flowers and shrubs—Fran didn't know their names—strangely blooming after all these years. Plus, there was that little bottle of perfume she'd found in her room. That wasn't normal. No, this house had a mind all its own.

Fran took the lid off the teapot and stirred the leaves. "Just that I feel it, too."

"I did," Teddy said. "The moment I stepped into the hall, I knew I belonged here. But it wasn't that I thought, 'What a lovely house.' The place was a wreck." She shook her head. "There wasn't a window that wasn't cracked, and I feared even to plug in the toaster. You should have seen the yard. Weeds up to here." She lifted a hand above her head.

The clock on the mantel tinged. Fran looked again. It was seven minutes after the hour.

"That's odd. Didn't it just chime the hour?" Teddy said. "It usually keeps good time."

"I felt it, too," Fran said. "About the house, that is." She'd seen herself somewhere modern, with beige carpeting and a sparkling bathroom. Somewhere on the ground floor. "If it's haunted"—and it was, no "if" about it—"it's a friendly haunting. Mostly."

"Sometimes I think the house has an agenda," Teddy said. "Besides keeping us here."

Lise took a shortbread cookie from the plate. "Don't you wonder about the history of this place?"

"Margie at the bookstore set me up with someone at the historical society who gave me a packet of info about the house, including the original floor plans," Fran said.

"No kidding?" Teddy said.

"I'll show you. The room across from mine, in the tower? The one we all avoid?" Fran looked around the room at the nodding heads. "That was the library."

"I imagine the top floor was servants' quarters?" Burt said.

Teddy nodded. "It holds a couple of rooms, plus an open attic. Right now it's empty, except for boxes and broken furniture. It has a stupendous view. I need to do something about the loose handrail."

No way Fran would go up there.

Burt rested a hand on Teddy's knee. "I'll help you fix it."

Fran watched Teddy place her hand on his. She wore a date night outfit of a flowing black dress and shoulder-dusting earrings, plus she'd put on lipstick. Fran wondered if the two of them were getting it on. It wasn't impossible. Not that she wanted to dwell on that image.

"Maybe the old place really is haunted," Burt said. "It happens."

Duh, Fran thought.

Teddy smiled. "What makes you say that?"

"When I was in the navy, I did service in a haunted battleship. Lights went off and on in the engine room at odd times."

"Did you hear voices?" Fran ventured.

"Just the lights. They weren't the engine room lights, either. They looked like lanterns, bobbing here and there, but there were no lanterns."

"I haven't seen lights—" Lise began.

"What about when the bathroom light turned off by itself?" Fran said. "Then on again?"

"True. That was strange. I've also heard footsteps in the attic. Sometimes my things move around, too."

"You've seen them move?" Burt asked.

"No, but I'll swear I've set something in one place, and I find it somewhere else. For instance, the other day I put a bottle of Femme perfume on the dresser, then went to brush my teeth. When I came back, the Femme was gone, and Joy was there, instead," Lise said.

"Could you have confused them?" Teddy asked.

Lise shook her head. "No way. The bottles look nothing like each other, and the perfumes themselves are as different as Marlene Dietrich and Jackie O."

That would be the ghost, all right, Fran thought. Whoever Marlene Dietrich was.

"What else did you find out about the house's history?" Lise asked Fran.

"Not much. Let me run upstairs and get the envelope. I haven't had the chance to give it a good look yet." She'd thought she'd put the envelope on top of her dresser, with her purse and lunch bag on top, but when she arrived at her room, it was waiting for her in the center of her bed. A moment later, she was back in Teddy's sitting room, sliding the envelope's contents onto the coffee table.

Teddy pulled two pages from the pile. "Here are the floor plans. It looks like they're from an old book. *Sloan's Victorian Buildings*," she read. "'Gothic Villa.' Amazing." She placed a finger on the room labeled SITTING R. "That's where we are now."

"What else do you have?" Lise asked.

Teddy poured more tea for each of them. A chamomile bud had escaped the pot's strainer and swirled in Fran's cup.

"Census records. Plus copies of old photos, but they're hard to make out. And an obituary for Captain Corrie."

They all leaned over the photos. Fran had already examined them, so she sat back. One photo showed the front of Corrie House with an old, bearded guy and a young woman in a top with puffy shoulders and a long skirt. The other was taken, perhaps on the same day, in Corrie House's back garden and was of the same woman standing among blurry roses and other flowers Fran couldn't name.

Lise picked up the garden photo, and her eyes widened. "Look at that. Roses, honeysuckle, and loads of peonies." She inhaled. "Jasmine, too. Gorgeous."

"How do you figure all that?" Burt said. "I can barely make out the gal's face."

Teddy held one of the census sheets. "The woman must be Ayla, Harris Corrie's daughter. He was a sea captain—we knew that—from Scotland. Presbyterian." She picked up the other census sheet. "In nineteen-ten, none of them lived here." She replaced the sheet on the table. "I wonder what happened?"

No mention of a baby, Fran noted. She liked watching Teddy and Burt together. They seemed almost too comfortable to be in love, but maybe that's how love was. Her parents were that way. Her father would be at the lock shop and would open his mouth to say something to her mom, and her mom would already have in hand the key blank he needed. "Margie says her friend at the historical society can get more, but she didn't have much time."

Lise read from the obituary. "'Captain Harris Corrie died Sunday, March fourteenth, nineteen-oh-nine, at the age of fifty-four.' Young."

"They didn't last long in those days," Burt said.

"'His wife Selma Corrie, née Douglas, and daughter Ayla Janette predeceased him.' That's it, except for information about services."

"What do you know about the house, Teddy?" Fran asked.

"Not much. I inherited it from a friend. Corrie was a family name on his mother's side, but I don't think the house came to him through a straight succession."

The baby cried again upstairs. This time Fran heard its mother shush it. The mother then sang, softly, but she was too far away for Fran to make out the words.

"I can tell you Corrie House was built in eighteen-eighty-five," Burt said.

"How do you know that?" Teddy asked.

"It's chiseled into a stone in the basement behind the furnace. I saw it the other day."

"I wonder what it is about this old house that draws us in? It's drafty, the plumbing needs serious work, and the furnace . . . the less said, the better," Teddy said.

Fran replaced her teacup on its saucer. Chamomile wasn't really her thing. "I wonder."

"Wonder what?"

"You said the house felt like a mother." The baby upstairs had quieted now. "Maybe it likes orphans."

The lights in the house flickered as if there was a storm, but the night was calm. Fran wouldn't be surprised if the electrical system, like everything else, was on the fritz.

"I'm an orphan," Teddy said.

This was news to Fran. She really didn't know much about Teddy, except that she had something to do with rock stars in the olden days and carried herself like impoverished royalty.

Lise set down her cup. "Technically, I'm not an orphan. I mean, my father and brother are alive. But I was adopted into my family, and as much as I love them, I've always felt like the square peg. Maybe I'm an orphan of another kind. What about you, Fran?"

She was not going there. She owed no one the story of what had wrenched her family from her. "We're not here to talk about the house. Anyone learn anything new about Dyann's death? I can start."

* * *

Lise smiled. Fran loved the intrigue surrounding Dyann's death. "Okay. What have you got for us?"

"I saw Murphy at the bookstore this afternoon," Fran said. "Trigger warning. He was picking up a book about snakes."

Lise remembered the eerily orange snake in his apartment. Creepy, maybe, but not a murder motive, and from Burt and Teddy's calm expressions, Fran was the only one freaked out. "Did he say anything about Dyann? Maybe the police have told him something?"

"No, but listen to this: Richard doesn't like him driving his car, which points even more to Richard being at the Lucky Lotus when Dyann died."

"Just because he's not supposed to drive his father's car doesn't mean he doesn't," Burt said.

"True. In fact, he asked me to go on a drive with him in Richard's Camaro."

"He has a thing for you," Teddy said.

"No, he doesn't." Fran said this so fast that the syllables practically piled on top of each other to form one word. "He was just showing off." She swooped away her long bangs, revealing those startling eyes. "Plus, he expressed exactly zero emotion that his mother was dead." She leaned back, her coup de grâce delivered.

"You think it's teamwork, then?" Lise asked. "He and Richard ganged up to do her in?"

"They have the motive," Fran said.

"Money," Teddy said. "I wonder what was really in that will, the original one?"

"Speaking of teamwork," Burt said, "the Richard and Sylvia Borlotti team is a possibility, too. Sylvia is not a fan of Dyann. Apparently, Dyann gave a bottle of some kind of potion with something in it that made her break out in a rash. She was peeved."

"Magnet Oil," Lise said. She could still feel its stench in her nostrils.

"'Peeved' is an understatement," Teddy affirmed.

"Okay," Fran said, "that's two strikes against Richard. What about you, Lise? What did you learn at the Blavatsky Manor?"

"They're an odd bunch over there," Lise said.

Fran snorted. "No kidding. Retired psychic mediums? Not exactly your usual retirement home. What's your job? Polishing crystal balls?"

"I start tomorrow, so I don't have much to report. Yet. But they wanted to know all about Dyann's death."

Teddy placed her hand on Burt's palm, and he lifted fingers to encircle hers. The scent of roses deepened. "They're curious," Teddy said. "It's drama."

Lise shook her head and remembered the leather and tarry vetiver fragrance in the manor's lobby. "It was more than that. It was as if they were afraid."

"Afraid they'd be nailed as killers, you mean." Fran said this as a statement, not a question. "There's a bunch of them. They might have planned some sort of group action to knock off Dyann. I bet lots of them take meds. Skim a pill or two from each resident's medicine cabinet and *boom*! Poison cocktail."

Lise wasn't the only one staring, jaw agape, at Fran.

"That said, my money's still on Richard," Fran concluded.

"Not to mention his letter threatening to sue me," Lise said.

"He threatened to sue you?" Fran said.

"His attorney says I must 'cease and desist' spreading lies about Dyann's death or he'll sue for defamation."

Fran mimicked pushing a button. "Ding, ding—guilty!"

"We have something to report, too," Teddy said. "This afternoon, Burt and I paid a visit to the chief of police. He confirmed they tested both Dyann and the liqueur—no poison."

Lise leaned forward. "But Signe—"

"He told us Signe is ambitious and sees crime everywhere.

As far as he's concerned, unless new evidence comes up, Dyann died of natural causes, and the case is closed."

"Is that what the medical examiner ruled?"

"There's no official ruling yet, but the chief told us, informally, that her heart had stopped."

"Which could have been caused by poison," Lise said. "What about everything we just talked about? Dyann was sure Richard would be furious when he found out about the change in her will. She even used the words 'he'll kill me.' Plus the rest—Richard's lies, the scene at the brewery, his threat to sue me . . ."

"You aren't happy it's not murder?" Teddy asked gently.

"It's not that. Only—"

"Justice must be served," Fran said.

CHAPTER 20

At least she had a job, Lise thought as she pulled up to Blavatsky Manor. Even if she wasn't one hundred percent clear on what it was. She'd dressed this morning in one of her favorite men's button-downs, a well-worn vintage Arrow with thick blue stripes, and she'd applied a grounding-yet-refreshing spritz of Silences, a 1970s mossy green fragrance that made her think of what it might feel like to sit in a velvet chair in a jungle on a cool morning. She was prepared for anything from reading aloud to cleaning toilets.

Maxine was waiting for her in the lobby—as were another dozen of the home's residents. Lise scanned the group. They were a quiet bunch, but they watched her intently. Perhaps this was the way of the psychic medium.

Lise barely had time for a "good morning" when Maxine led her to the chairs in the lobby. "Everyone, meet Lise Bloom. She's our new gal Friday. Lise, I won't introduce you to everyone now. Too many names to remember all at once."

Lise smiled. "Hello. I'm looking forward to getting to know you."

"We may know more about you than you suspect," Bea said.

"Mother, leave the poor girl alone." She gestured to a Barcelona chair that must have been kept empty just for her. "Please, take a seat."

Lise was about to ask about the job when Maxine said, "Before we talk about the day's work, tell me, have you heard anything new about Dyann King's death? Maybe the detective came around again?"

Again, she suspected her primary job was as an informant, not an assistant. "Nothing to speak of." Evasive, but not a lie. The information about the medical examiner's impending findings wasn't public.

Maxine let out a snort of frustration. "Can you handle a van?"

"Sure." When she'd worked for a landscaping company—where she got her start in designing scent gardens—she often drove the van full of shrubs and potted plants.

"Good, because your first task will be to take me and Arthur to meet with our attorney. Bitsy usually drives, but his lumbago is acting up again. Arthur, you ready? If so, let's go."

"Ready, all right."

Arthur was the man Lise had met who'd worn a Hawaiian shirt that matched his wife's. Today, he was in a well-pressed suit. He made up for the scarcity of hair on top of his head with a thin skirt of white hair at his neck. Was he a retired psychic, too? He looked more like a CPA.

In the van, Maxine directed Lise toward Seaside, a coastal town a half hour away known for fudge shops and spring break shenanigans. Lise attempted to start a few conversations, asking about Maxine's background and about the residents of the home, but each time Maxine changed the conversation. Eventually, they fell silent. The ocean came into view on their right, sparkling in the sun, then was obscured by hills and fir trees.

Finally, they arrived at the outskirts of Seaside. They approached a strip mall, and Maxine said, "Pull in here."

"I thought we were going to see an attorney?" Lise asked.

"We are. Take that place in front of the tanning salon."

Lise pulled into the open spot and cut the engine. Even an ambulance chaser could find better digs than these. A breeze off the ocean sent a crushed fast food bag skittering past, and seagulls pecked at spilled popcorn near a dumpster.

"Come with us," Maxine said. "We may need you."

Looking at the strip mall's storefronts, Arthur shook his head. "Remember when you had to cruise the lot to find parking? Those were the days. The pizza parlor went out of business. The coin shop, kaput."

They approached a modest office next to the darkened Mr. Scotty's School of Hair Design.

Maxine pushed open the office's glass door. "Willie?"

"Back here, Maxine."

They crossed a small, dark lobby and entered an office with a wide window behind the desk. Lise had expected to see, maybe, the back exit of a taqueria or a tire shop, but from here the view of the ocean stretched into the horizon. It would be glorious when the sun set.

"Who's this?" the man named Willie asked.

"This is our new helper, Lise. Lise, meet Willie Blount. We go back a long way," Maxine said.

"Should I wait outside?" Lise asked.

Willie looked from Maxine to Arthur and, apparently getting their okay for Lise's presence, pointed to a chair in the corner.

Willie was nearly Arthur's double, down to the small stature, tidy suit, and thinning hair arranged in a similar style. They might have been brothers.

"You two really resemble each other," Lise said.

"Willie and I are brothers," Arthur said.

"Like I said, we go way back," Maxine said.

There was seriously something off kilter about this group. It briefly crossed Lise's mind that they planned to kidnap her.

But why? For what? Besides, she bet she could take them all and dash to the tanning salon for safety before they even got off the floor.

"Here's the letter." Arthur handed his brother an envelope that looked familiar. Lise craned her neck for a better view. Yes, very much like the one Lise had received—same envelope, same stamp.

Willie opened the letter and cleared his throat, even though he wasn't reading aloud. He made a few "Mmm" and "Aha" sounds and drummed his fingers. "May I make a copy?"

"Of course," Maxine said.

They all turned to look at Lise.

She got the hint. "Where's the copier?"

She took the letter to the lobby, where a combo printer/photocopier rested on a credenza. While the copier moved over the letter, she took a look around. A sink was mounted on the far wall. She closed her eyes and breathed in, and the scent rose of wet dog and soap. Former dog grooming parlor, was Lise's assessment.

When the copy emerged, her guess was confirmed. This, too, was from Richard King's attorney. The letter notified the retirement home that the codicil changing Dyann's will was not legal, and if they thought otherwise, Richard would sue.

With the letter and the copy in hand, Lise stood in Willie's office doorway. "I got one of these letters."

"You were named in Dyann's will?" Arthur said.

"No. He . . ." How much should she tell them?

"Spit it out, hon," Arthur said.

"He said I defamed him by asking a few questions about where he was when Dyann died."

Once again, the three looked at each other. Maxine said, "See? I told you this was the right move."

Lise couldn't take it any longer. "What's going on? You're so secretive." What did they do, anyway? Launder money?

Run an illegal gambling operation? "A home for retired psychic mediums is strange enough, but something else is going on here."

Maxine's expression firmed, and she stood. "I will give you that we're not all psychics."

"Bea is," Arthur said.

"That's what she says, anyway." Maxine sat again. "Our pasts are none of your business. However, as far as Dyann's death goes, we're on the same page. We all have our own reasons for wanting to learn more about her murder."

"How do you know it was murder?"

"A woman in the prime of her life falls dead, and the medical examiner can't find a physical reason for her death other than vague words about seizures and heart trouble? Tomfoolery is involved, guaranteed," Arthur said.

"Remember that fellow who ran the insurance scams in Florida?" Willie asked.

Arthur chuckled. "See how that turned out."

"How what turned out?" Lise asked.

Willie and Arthur turned to Maxine for direction. She nodded. "Go ahead."

Arthur took up the thread. "We knew this fellow, see, who arranged to have items stolen for a cut of insurance proceeds."

They had to be kidding. "Stolen?"

"Oh, don't worry, he returned the items to their owners."

"Naturally," Willie added.

"You're telling me the owners hired him to steal their items," Lise said.

"Isn't that what I said?" Arthur looked at her like she was slow. "Anyway, he was loaded."

"Cash up the wazoo," Willie confirmed.

"So he tricked out his house and office with every gadget you could imagine to make sure no one knocked him off. He'd provided generously for his family, see."

"In other words, his family had a reason to do him in," Maxine said.

"He set up alarms, dogs, firearms, booby traps. You get the picture," Willie said.

Lise was beginning to get the picture, all right. She glanced at Willie's framed law school diploma. Could he have earned it in prison?

"Then he got hit by a falling piano." Arthur leaned back, arms crossed over his chest.

"A what?" Had she heard right?

"Just like in the cartoons," Arthur said. "He was walking down the street, and, *whammo*, a piano lands on his head. Killed him instantly."

"Goes to show that even the tightest of plans can only go so far," Willie said.

"All right, boys," Maxine said. "Back to the matter at hand. Dyann planned to change her will. She met with me a few days earlier, then announced it at her son's party. Mom told me. Then she dies that night? The timing isn't a coincidence."

Willie steepled his fingers and half-closed his eyes. "Walk me through your meeting."

Lise wanted to hear this, too.

"Last week—" Maxine began.

"When last week?" Willie said.

"Let's see, a week ago yesterday, it was. Dyann King called and said she wanted to see me right away, that afternoon. She told me she had something important to say that had to do with Blavatsky Manor, so I agreed. I thought maybe she wanted to hold a psychic fair or whatnot at the Lucky Lotus. I was ready to tell her we didn't do that sort of thing."

"She came over that afternoon," Arthur said.

"Let Maxine tell it, Art."

"She came over that afternoon," Maxine said. "She was obviously very excited about something—angry, too, somehow. You know how some people break into laughter in a way that's almost nasty?"

Lise knew. She'd witnessed that of Dyann more than once. That and bursting into tears.

"She said she owed her success to a fortune she got in a cookie, and she wanted to repay soothsayers," Maxine said.

"Soothsayers, eh?" Willie said, eyes still at half-mast.

"Direct quote. She said she planned to amend her will so we were the beneficiaries."

"All of it?" Willie said.

"I honestly don't know. She collected some information from us, then left. She looked healthy to me, and if her attitude was any indication, she had plenty of fighting spirit in her. Next thing I know, she's dead."

"I signed the codicil," Lise said. The memory was so clear: the laughter, the honey smell of the liqueur, the triumphant announcement that Richard would kill her.

"What did it say?" Maxine asked.

"I didn't read it." This was, strictly speaking, true. She hadn't read it at the time. "She even went so far as to cover it with an arm. She just asked me to sign. But what she told me was that it reduced Murphy's payout to an allowance and left the balance to you."

"That's it, and that's what Mom says she announced at the party," Maxine said. "The whole story."

"There's more, or you wouldn't be here." Willie had now opened his eyes. He leaned forward, his forearms on the desk.

"He's right, Maxine," Arthur said. "We learned Ms. King had died when her ex-husband came roaring up in his red sports car and barged in, telling us we'd never get away with it."

"When did this happen?" Lise asked.

"The day after Mom went to the boy's party."

"He accused you of killing her?" Willie asked.

"He was very upset," Maxine said. "Outraged. Kept saying 'You'll never get away with it.' "

"He would be, if he killed her," Lise said. She pulled her chair into the circle of discussion. "Think about it. It's the perfect way to throw suspicion elsewhere."

"It would be very helpful to know what was in Ms. King's will before she changed it—or before she attempted to change it," Willie said. "Specifically, I'd like to know how much this Richard character stood to inherit."

"Is the codicil legal?" Lise asked. "When I signed it, no one else had. Dyann said she'd get someone at the party to sign it, too, but I don't know if she ever did. The hard copy seems to have vanished."

"Depends," Willie said. "Estate planning isn't my area, but I'd guess it could go either way. First, we'd need to know if she'd succeeded in getting her second witness. However, even if she hadn't, she'd made her intentions known by having you sign the codicil and by announcing it at a gathering that evening."

"You aren't planning to contest the will, are you?" Lise asked.

"Oh, good Lord, no," Arthur said at the same time Maxine said, "Not at all."

"You could," Willie said. "You have standing. You might be kissing good-bye to a hell of a lot of moolah."

"Not interested," Maxine said firmly.

More and more curious. "Then why are you going to all this trouble? All you have to do is tell Richard you have no claim on the will, and he'll leave you alone."

"You forget," Willie said. "In saying, 'You'll never get away with it,' he implied they had something to do with Dyann's death."

"But you didn't kill her," Lise said. She smiled but was serious. "Did you?"

"Absolutely not," Maxine said while Arthur said, "Are you nuts?" at the same time.

"Then what are you worried about?"

"The police detective has already visited once," Maxine said.

"Richard is threatening to stir up more trouble," Arthur added.

Lise didn't respond, but her unspoken "and so?" hung in the air.

Willie opened a fresh file folder and slipped the photocopied letter inside. "You don't need anyone rooting around in your business."

"That," Maxine said, "is for damned sure."

CHAPTER 21

"I don't see what difference this will make." Fran struggled to sit still as Teddy applied a smudge of eyeliner. Teddy had opened a full cigar box of makeup on the bathroom cabinet—lipsticks, pots of color, and brushes of various shapes—and was applying bits to Fran's face.

"Darling, you're an attractive girl. We're simply giving Mother Nature a boost. Nothing obvious, just a hint of color here and there," Teddy said. "All you have to do is smile at Murphy and find out if he was driving his father's Camaro the night Dyann died. No wishy-washy answer this time."

Easy for her to say, Fran thought. "What's that?" she asked as Teddy approached her with a silver contraption.

"You've never seen one of these? It's an eyelash curler," Teddy said. "You have the most lovely eyes. This will help open them up."

"Do we really have to do this?" Fran asked. She knew the answer, but it was worth another ask, if only to register her discontent one more time.

Teddy straightened. "Darling, we've been over it. It was your idea, after all. Who else would Murphy talk to? All you have to do is spend an hour or two with him." Eyelash curler in hand, she again bent over Fran's face. "I've done worse in my time."

Fran begrudgingly nodded. "Okay, but don't mess with my hair."

"I know better than that." Teddy finished with the eyelash curler and stepped back to survey her work. "Very nice."

The old house seemed to agree, and Fran heard the baby again, but this time it was gurgling. Ever since she and Lise had uncovered the nursery wallpaper in the bathroom, the house had seemed to relax. The baby's crying still woke her some nights, but it came less frequently, and the woman's weeping had nearly stopped. Plus, a jammed window in Fran's room had become unstuck, and now morning air full of birdsong flowed into her room.

"I didn't think Murphy would respond so fast. I'm not ready," Fran said.

"Nonsense," Teddy said. "You ask him if he had his father's car that night, maybe feel him out about his parents' relationship, and that's it."

Easy for her to say. Fran could easily imagine Murphy, his beady eyes darting over her, hatching a plan to dispose of her body. That was, if she survived the drive at all. She'd only agreed to go to Fort Stevens Park because it beat going to his apartment where the snake was. Besides that, she didn't want anyone in town to see them together.

"He's here," Lise shouted from downstairs. "I see him coming up the hill."

Fran suppressed a groan. She imagined Murphy huffing his way to the door.

"I'll get it," Fran said, Teddy right behind her.

Fran arrived at the front door at the same time Murphy did. Just behind him was a slender, bearded man with a serious expression. Fran's heart stopped. It was the man from the tattoo shop, the one who sometimes came into the bookstore.

The man stopped a mesmerizing three feet from her. His hair flopped over his eyes. "Hi. I'm Sid Cassidy. You have a room for rent?"

Fortunately, Teddy stepped in, because Fran couldn't speak. "Sid, come in. I'm glad you could make it."

His name was Sid. Sid Cassidy. She watched him disappear into the hall behind Teddy. With Sid gone, Fran pulled herself together. "Are you ready?"

"Wow," Murphy said. "This is a big house." He made to come in, but Fran blocked the door.

"No duh," she said. "Where are you parked?"

Jangling keys in one hand, Murphy led the way down the path to the cul-de-sac. They stopped before a red car that might have featured in an action movie starring Bruce Willis.

"Like it?" he asked. In a surprisingly gentlemanlike move, he held the passenger door open for her. "It's an eighty-six Camaro IROC."

"Nice," Fran said without feeling. She wasn't a car expert, but she wondered why they would make a Camaro that wasn't a stick shift. She slid into the seat. At least it wasn't a bench seat, and a gear shift separated her from Murphy. No airbags, either, on a car this old. *Great.* She would be riding in a death trap.

"Ready?" Murphy started the Camaro's engine.

"I guess," Fran said.

In another surprise, Murphy was a skillful driver. He gracefully maneuvered the car through downtown traffic, and minutes later, they were crossing the Youngs Bay Bridge headed toward the coast.

Fort Stevens Park stretched along the Pacific Ocean. Murphy pulled into a parking lot and popped the trunk. Fran stepped out, the wind off the ocean rustling her hair.

"I brought snacks." He lifted a bag of cheese puffs and a six-pack of lemon-lime soda. "There's a spot under the cliff I like. No wind there. We can sit on a log and watch the waves."

That Murphy had a particular place he liked to go to watch the ocean told Fran he was a loner, like she was. His mother had just died, poor guy. Maybe he wasn't so bad. Fran followed him along the beach, her bare feet digging into the sand. On one side rose beach-grass-topped dunes, and on the other the ocean rumbled.

"I lost my mom, too, not long ago," she found herself saying.

"Oh."

"Kind of, that is."

This captured his attention. "What do you mean, 'kind of'?"

"I mean she and my dad left town and pretty much forgot about me."

"What about your brother?" Murphy turned to face her full-on. "I'm an only child, but you have a brother. A famous one."

"He lives in L.A.," she said, as if this explained it all.

Murphy seemed to accept this response. "How did he get in a wheelchair, anyway?"

Harry was known for his wheelchair. He was the genius comedian, the great interviewer, and the paraplegic. Considering he was an adult when he lost the use of his legs, he'd adapted quickly, and besides hosting *The Harry Kellers Show*, he was a terrific rugby player. At least, that's what her parents said.

"Accident," Fran said. Her throat tightened. Why was she telling him this?

"Wow. I bet the guy driving the car was really bummed."

Harry's injury didn't come from being hit by a car. Fran had been there. She could have prevented it. She could have stopped him from stepping on that rung, the one so clearly rotted through, when he was coming down the ladder. Harry was always the popular guy at school—smart, athletic, star of *The Music Man* that year—and beloved by her parents. She had been angry at him for teasing her, so she deliberately threw the Frisbee on the roof.

"Stop calling me Freaky Fran," she'd said.

"Ha, ha," he'd replied. "There's a ladder in the garage. Besides, I always wanted to go up on the roof." And he did. He'd stood on the roof like a figure in a movie, with the sun setting behind him. He pounded his chest and let out Tarzan's signature howl.

It was on his way down the ladder that Fran spotted the cracked rung. "Harry, watch out," she'd warned just as his foot hit the top rung.

"What?"

At the same time, a thin garter snake had slithered through the grass at the ladder's base, and Fran stiffened in fear. She couldn't move, couldn't speak.

Then Harry's foot fell through the rotted rung. When he hit the ground, he had been motionless.

Fran dug her hands into the warm sand and reoriented herself to the present. "It was a bummer, all right."

Murphy's gaze dropped to his feet, and he nodded slowly but said nothing.

"I'm surprised you feel alone. Your mom lived right upstairs," Fran said, remembering too late she wasn't supposed to know about Murphy's living arrangements. A side glance showed he hadn't noticed the slip. To her relief, neither did he mention her brother Harry.

"Mom was too busy with my dad to take time for me," Murphy said. "That's okay, though. I get along fine."

"I heard your dad is engaged to a nightclub singer."

Murphy laughed in a series of snorts. "Sylvia? No way. You're funny, Fran."

Once they were settled on the log, an open bag of cheese puffs between them, she asked, "Is there going to be a memorial service for your mom?"

Murphy seemed unfazed. "Probably. My dad will fix something up. First, they've got to release her body."

The ocean reared its waves and sent them noisily crashing,

leaving a scrim of white froth. As violent as it was, it was also hypnotic. It was easy to imagine wooden ships over the centuries collapsing in the frigid water after thousands of miles voyaging from Asia. The ocean floor must be littered with treasure, she thought: crates of golden coins, maybe, or jeweled chalices or Chinese porcelain. She pictured rainbow-hued fish flitting through the skeleton of an old ship.

"Do you have a boyfriend?" Murphy asked.

"Yes," Fran lied.

"Really?"

"Is that so surprising?" Fran examined the cheese puff she'd just bit into. She wasn't used to leaving lipstick on her food. "He thinks I'm wonderful. Plus"—she thought quickly—"he's really handsome. He has a beard."

"I bet he doesn't drive a Camaro."

"That's for sure," Fran said. Time to get things over with. "Did you have your dad's car the night your mom died?"

"What time?"

Fran hadn't expected this question. A vague response was probably best. "After the party."

"No. I didn't borrow it at all that day."

Then why did he want to know what time? "Do you know what's in your mom's will?"

Murphy shrugged. "Dad says I almost lost everything, but now I'm rich." His eyes nearly disappeared as he squinted into the sun. "My dad says I should be grateful to him."

"For what?" Fran asked quickly.

He turned a beady eye toward her but didn't respond.

"What are you going to do with the money?" she tried next.

"Dad says he can invest it for me, but I don't care. Money can't buy happiness. Besides"—he gave Fran a mysterious glance—"I have other prospects."

Watching his parents squabble had probably taught him that trite little saying about money. As for "other prospects," who cared? She stood. She'd done her job and had the information she needed. "Ready to leave?"

"We only just got here." Murphy's surprise was evident in his eyes, which were now open widely enough that Fran could make out their entire circumference.

"I need to get home to do some stuff." Fran wiped the sand from the seat of her pants.

"Want to meet Tangerine Dream? You'd love her."

"That's your snake, right?"

Murphy nodded. "Tangie's a ball python. She has a lot of personality."

She didn't bother to tell him she'd rather be dangled from a cliff with tigers prowling below. "No, thanks."

He reluctantly rose and jammed the remaining snacks into a backpack. "You're missing out. Snakes are misunderstood. Ornette says they're the most maligned animal on Earth. Even rats get more respect."

"Who's Ornette?" The sand was warm under Fran's feet as they walked back to the car. If it were another day with another person—that possible housemate, for instance—she'd want to stay until dark. She rolled the name Sid Cassidy through her mind.

"He runs the reptile refuge where I volunteer. He's the guy who got me Tangie. She was a foster, but she was so great that I had to adopt her. She's beautiful, too. About this color." Murphy held up a cheese puff–stained finger. "Maybe a little paler."

"I didn't know that snakes came in different colors," Fran said. "I thought they were all green or black or something."

"Oh, no. Even in the wild, snakes are all kinds of colors. And patterns." This was the most excited Murphy had sounded all afternoon. "Tangie was bred for her color, though. Some loser bought her and had to surrender her. Snakes play an important role in nature, and they can even help cure cancer. That's what Ornette says."

"You don't say?" He could cut the snake talk right away, as far as she was concerned.

"Not everyone knows how to care for snakes."

"Hmm," Fran said.

"I do," Murphy said.

"No kidding?"

"Want to drive out to the reptile refuge? I can introduce you to Ornette. He'd love to meet you."

"Thanks, but I need to get home." When they were back in the car, Fran threw out one last question. "Do you think your mom was murdered?"

Again, Murphy didn't seem distressed. He shrugged. "Could be. I'm not sure who'd do it, though."

"Maybe your father?"

The Camaro engine roared to life just as Murphy burst into laughter. "They hated each other too much to kill each other. What would they do with their lives if one of them died?"

"Teddy Bright." Teddy held out her hand to the potential housemate.

"Sidney Cassidy. Call me Sid."

Teddy took in his quiet demeanor and the smudges of blue and white paint on his pants. An artist, she thought. She hoped the house liked him. It had already driven off the other three prospects. For one, the front door had refused to open. Crows had attacked another prospect as she walked up the path.

A third woman had sounded very interested in the ad. Her already alarmingly pale skin and hair—seriously, she might have been a phantom—blanched further when she approached the house, and she didn't even make it to the entry hall before smiling apologetically and leaving.

"Come this way." Teddy led Sid to the hall and pointed to the curtained French doors closing off the sitting room and parlor. "Those are my private rooms. Back here, the kitchen and dining room, are common areas."

Sid followed her and listened without commenting.

"Out back is the garden, and you're free to use that, too, of course. Lise, one of the housemates, is a garden designer. She's taken the yard on as a project." Charm appeared from nowhere and wound through Teddy's calves. "Are you allergic to cats? I forgot to mention that we have two of them."

He knelt to scratch Charm's ears. "I adore them."

So far, so good. The house hadn't delivered any cold spots or slammed any doors in their faces.

"Follow me upstairs, and I'll show you our two open rooms. You'd have your choice of them."

They climbed the stairs, and Sid turned his head to look at the portraits up the rose-papered walls. "Don't you wonder about their lives?" he asked.

"I do. I wonder about the artists, too. Take this one, for example." She pointed to a midcentury portrait of a woman in a green dress with cats'-eye glasses and a drawn mouth. Her forehead was unnaturally short and her chin bizarrely angled, but her mouth was sensitively rendered, with pillowy lips a lot of women would pay plastic surgeons to attain. "Can't you picture the artist, maybe this woman's sister, in a room with barkcloth curtains, a TV with a rabbit ears antenna, and maybe a dachshund running around?"

"I like your style," Sid said.

"Here's one of the bedrooms."

Teddy stopped at the head of the stairs and opened the door to the front bedroom. Sunlight from a bank of windows facing town illuminated the walls, which were covered with a faded wallpaper of pinecones on an aqua background. On one wall, a marble-topped fireplace held a jar with a few dried branches. Otherwise, the room was empty.

In Teddy's opinion, this was the house's prime bedroom. Fran hadn't wanted it, saying she'd rather not be forced to look so far down. She'd taken the cozier middle bedroom. Lise had glommed onto the back bedroom with the garden view the moment she'd discovered the little bottle of perfume. Teddy hadn't forced the issue, since this bedroom was directly above the parlor, where she slept, and she was fine not having someone walking above her.

"What do you think?" Teddy asked.

"You said there was another room?" Sid said.

"Yes. It's an interesting space. Octagonal, part of the tower on the other side of the house. I just saw the house's original drawings and learned it was originally a library." They retreated down the hall, and Teddy opened the door across from Fran's room. She stayed in the hall. Something about the library raised the hairs on the nape of her neck.

Sid clearly felt it too and quickly backed out of the room. He pointed at the stairwell rising next to the library. "Where does that go?"

"To the attic, the old servants' quarters, then to the tower's top level. It's a mess up there."

For the first time, she saw animation in Sid's features. "Could I have a look?"

Teddy closed the library door, and they mounted the steps to the attic. She hadn't been up here in months—not since they had to patch the roof and replace a front window that had blown out in a storm.

In the intervening months, dust had again coated the attic floor. Despite the footsteps Fran and Lise claimed to hear, the dust was undisturbed. The cast-offs of decades—broken chairs, trunks, a few objects Teddy couldn't even identify—plus dirt-smeared windows and walls open to the old house's fir sheathing, gave the attic a Dickensian feeling.

And yet, the light. Light filled the attic, and the sun's warmth pulled the smell of wood from its joists. If Teddy wasn't mistaken, the house was showing off for him.

Sid slowly turned, taking in the space. "It's wonderful. Would you consider renting this?"

The thought had never crossed her mind. "It would be cold up here in the winter."

"I could have it insulated," Sid said. "That is, if you don't mind." He poked his head into the two rooms built into the attic's rear. "There's power in here. That's good. And a secret staircase to the kitchen."

"From when there were servants." Those were the days. "It's boarded off now on the second floor." She hesitated, then continued. "Insulation could get expensive, and I'm afraid I'm not in a position to afford it."

"That's all right. I could take care of it." Sid was in the corner, rooting through some of the junk that had accumulated. "I'm a painter, and the light here is ideal. What's this?" He pulled small piece of broken furniture from the pile.

"It looks like a cradle missing one of its rockers."

"Solid walnut. Nice." He dusted the top of a trunk. "It's monogrammed. S V C."

" 'C' is probably for Corrie." Teddy had to do it, had to ask. It was only fair. "I have an odd question for you."

Sid stood and hooked his fingers in his beard. "Yes?"

"How do you feel about ghosts? Corrie House has some odd phenomena. Nothing dangerous—just strange."

Apparently unconcerned, he returned to the junk pile and opened the trunk. Empty. "It's an old house. No biggie."

"You wouldn't mind if, say"—here, Teddy pretended to search her imagination—"oh, I don't know, lights went off and on or you heard footsteps?" She wanted to add the bit about piano music, but that might be pushing it.

"Footsteps? No kidding? Cool."

The house had chosen him. How and why, Teddy didn't know. "Are you by chance an orphan?"

"A what?" He laughed. It looked good on his normally solemn face. "No. At least, not really."

In other words, yes. Fran was right. The house had a yen for people who felt removed from their families.

Sid straightened. "If you rent me the attic, I'll understand if you need to charge more. It's a big space."

"Sold," Teddy said before he could change his mind. She surveyed the space once again. It would cost something to get it livable. "What do you do for work?"

"Tattoo artist."

Sid's skin, as far as Teddy could tell, was ink free. Plus, she'd never known tattoo artists to make more than a nominal living. Still, appearances could be deceiving. Some of the musicians she'd known had banked hundreds of thousands of dollars but lived in bedbug-ridden hotels.

He'd noted her assessment. "No, I don't have tattoos. All my art goes on my clients."

This prompted a thought. "I don't suppose you do many snake tattoos?"

"Sure. Why? You thinking of getting one? We could do a Cleopatra-like asp up your arm."

"Oh, no." Teddy actually already had a silver dollar–sized tattoo of a mandala on her pelvis, but that was none of his business. "One of the women who lives here worked for Dyann King at the Lucky Lotus. Her son is into snakes. He volunteers at the reptile refuge for a man with a number of snake tattoos."

"Yes, Murphy King. He came to the shop a few months ago to ask about getting a tat of an orange python. I did the art, but once he got a look at the tattoo machine, he backed out. I did some of Ornette Cassell's ink—an iguana and a copperhead snake—and I guess Murphy wanted one for himself."

"I hear Murphy worships him."

"Ornette's an interesting guy." Sid crossed to the front window and looked down at the town. "He has money from somewhere."

"Tattoos aren't inexpensive, I'd guess," Teddy said.

"You're right, but it's more than that. It's more than his BMW SUV. You can tell he was raised with it."

How Sid knew about what it was like to be raised with money, Teddy had no idea, although there was something well-bred in Sid's manners. Teddy had seen it often enough to recognize it. "I guess you'd need money to start a reptile refuge."

"Definitely." He turned to face Teddy. "There's lots of room for canvases here—big ones." He looked at the ceiling rafters and again to the windows. "Insulation, no need to drywall. Maybe work on the electrical. I'd run any contractors' bids past you, of course." His chest rose as he breathed deeply. "This place already feels like home."

Chapter 22

That evening, Lise plunged her fingers into the soil. Day was slipping into night like a poured glass of water, slowly and then quickly. The air smelled moist, and crickets chirped. She'd work just a bit longer before going in for dinner.

The dirt felt good under her hands. She'd abandoned her gloves and threw her whole weight into Corrie House's back garden. Sure, the ground would be better worked in spring, but now was when she needed the distraction. The last time she'd done this, it had been to siphon off the shock of finding Dyann's body. This time, it was to work through Richard's threat of devastating both her reputation and bank account. All she needed was the garden show fiasco dragged to light before a judge.

This patch of soil had clearly once been a bed of roses. Now only the knotty trunks of three bushes remained, two of them sprouting the long runners of rootstock. One of the bushes, however, still bloomed with deep pink Louise Odier roses, ruffled like camellia blossoms and unusually fragrant.

Too fragrant, in fact. Lise sat up and inhaled through her nose. The scent of roses and something else—yes, honeysuckle and stock—thickened in the gloaming. The lemon cream fragrance of a nonexistent magnolia with flowers as big as cabbages mingled with them. However, it couldn't be emotion she smelled, because she was alone, and there was no way the few roses on the old bush could produce this much or this kind of fragrance. It was as if she were smelling the garden of a century earlier.

The light over the kitchen stoop clicked on, and Teddy, barefoot, crossed the weedy lawn. She wore an ankle-length dress of well-worn indigo-dyed cotton. Her white hair shone in the waning light. "I brought you a glass of iced herbal tea, darling."

Lise wiped her hands together and took the glass. "Thank you." The tea tasted of lavender and—there it was again—rose.

Fran emerged from the house with her own glass. Lise hadn't seen her since her outing with Murphy. When she'd returned, she'd gone straight to her room. She plopped cross-legged onto the grass near Lise.

"Since you're both here," Teddy said, "I have an announcement. We have a new housemate. His name is Sid, and he's a tattoo artist. He's taking the attic."

The attic? How could anyone live up there? "Is he really—"

Fran cut in. "The guy I saw when I left with Murphy?" She sounded breathless.

"That's him. He's moving in at the start of the month. I think you'll like him."

Lise glanced at Fran. From the waft of rose—not from the Louise Odier bush, either—it was clear she already did. "How did things go this afternoon?" Lise gingerly lifted a mat of bindweed roots from the soil. It was so satisfying when a tangle of them came out whole. If only the mystery surrounding Dyann's death could be so easily unearthed.

"Those two—Dyann and Richard—couldn't leave each other alone," Fran said. "According to Murphy, they were at each other's throats all the time." Charm crawled into her lap, and she absently stroked between his ears.

"Poor child." Teddy had settled into one of the Adirondack

chairs. Lise glanced at the other chair. It felt empty without Burt. Something was up with him, something Teddy didn't want to talk about.

As for Murphy, Lise agreed with Fran. He would never have been first with Dyann and Richard always squabbling. Lise might have felt like an outsider in her family in some ways, but she always knew she was loved. "Did he tell you anything else—anything useful about Dyann?"

The scent of a summer garden was more intense than ever now. Lise looked first at Teddy, who gazed toward the house, then at Fran, still petting Charm. The scent wasn't coming from either of them. She definitely smelled Corrie House's past.

"Not much. Just that he says he didn't have Richard's car that night and that his parents were obsessed with each other. Also, he likes snakes." She wrinkled her nose. "Gross. And he doesn't know what's in the will, just that he'll be rich."

"Do you two smell anything?" Lise asked.

Fran shook her head, and Teddy said, "Just dirt and night."

Lise returned again to the rose bed. Only half an hour of work to go, and the stretch would be clear of weeds and ready for a good layer of mulch. The kitchen stoop light was just bright enough to allow her to see.

Teddy pulled up her legs and tucked them beside her as gracefully as a teenager. She was an advertisement for the benefits of yoga. "It's strange."

"I know," Lise said. "How can there be honeysuckle in the air when there's no vine in sight?"

"I mean about Richard," Teddy said. "I'm not saying it was the most healthy relationship, but he was clearly in love with Dyann. Couldn't let her go. Why would he kill her? But, if he didn't, why would he lie about where he was?"

"Maybe he had another lover, not just Sylvia," Fran said. "Or maybe Dyann had a lover, and he was jealous."

"If Dyann was seeing someone, she certainly never let on to

me about it, and I have no doubt she would have flaunted it." Lise grabbed the spade and plunged it into a hardened section of earth.

"Is there anything we're missing?" Fran asked. "Let's walk through that night as far as we know. Lise, you start."

Lise paused weeding and left her trowel in the soil. "I can tell you again, but don't have anything new to add."

"Tell us, anyway," Fran said.

"I closed the shop at six o'clock, as usual. When I left, Dyann was still there. I turned off the lights and got my purse from the back."

"What was Dyann doing?" Teddy asked.

"Laughing about how Richard was going to kill her"—Lise couldn't help repeating what had been running through her mind again and again—"because of the changes she was making to her will."

"Was anything weird? Not usual?" Fran said.

Lise sat back. "Not that I remember. The back door was closed—I'm pretty sure it was, anyway. Even on hot days, she tended to keep it closed. The fan was going—"

"Was the fan still on when you came in the next morning?" Teddy asked.

"No. It was off."

"Go on."

Lise closed her eyes to better picture the shop. "Dyann was at her desk, and she had the bottle of Mayan ceremonial liqueur next to her." She opened her eyes. "Not unusual. Her laptop was open." She shook her head. "I can't think of anything else out of place. Of course, I wasn't looking for anything."

"The codicil wasn't there?" Fran asked. "The one you signed?"

"No. I didn't see it."

"Okay," Fran said. "What about the next morning?"

"Let's see." Again, she closed her eyes. "I was kind of apprehensive about going to the shop that morning. I knew Dyann would have received my email, and I didn't know how she'd take it."

"I would have been apprehensive, too," Teddy said. "But you were doing the right thing, darling."

"The Lucky Lotus seemed the same as always when I arrived." The dark shop, smelling of cheap incense and Magnet Oil, the still wind chimes, the stacks of tarot cards, and the display of Buddha statues. "I locked the door behind me—I always do that while I'm getting the shop ready—and flipped on the lights to the right of the front door. I made sure the credit card reader was charged up, and I turned on the music."

"Where's Burt?" Fran asked out of the blue.

"He's not feeling well. Go on, Lise."

"I know my Lucky Lotus routine isn't very exciting, but you asked me to be complete," Lise said.

"Yes," Teddy said. "Fran won't interrupt again."

"Next, I went to the back room." Lise had parted the wooden beads. She could still hear them clatter. "The lights were on, and the back door was off its latch. My first thought was that someone had broken in, but the shop was dead quiet. If someone had robbed the shop, they'd already left. So I went to close the door and saw Dyann's Mercedes in the alley."

"Is it usually there?" Fran asked.

"It's never there. At least, not in the morning. When she comes in, rarely before noon, she parks it next to the door, nose up to the dumpster. Anyway, I saw right away that her rear tires had been slashed. Both of them."

"Then what?" As the moment of reveal grew closer, Fran's attention was sharp.

"It crossed my mind that a burglar might have done that. I closed the back door. My plan was to call Dyann. When I turned around, I saw her, face up on the floor by her desk."

"As if she'd collapsed?" Teddy asked.

"She didn't look pushed?" Fran added.

Lise nodded. She pulled the spade from the ground and laid it in front of her. "Say this is Dyann's desk. It floats in the room so that the stock shelf is behind her, along with a minifridge. The other side of the back room is where she makes her oils and does aura readings. Dyann was lying here." Lise pointed behind the spade. "I called 9-1-1."

"Think," Teddy said. "What was on her desk? Anything different from the evening before?"

"The glass, of course. The bottle of liqueur was on the ground. It might have toppled when Dyann fell."

"No marks on Dyann? Nothing unusual with her clothes?"

Lise again pictured the scene. "No, she was wearing what she'd had on the night before. Just a really weird smell. Not perfume, not from the oils." Not emotion, as far as she knew.

Teddy shifted in her chair. "The smell. Did the police say anything about it?"

"One of them sneezed. Probably the incense," Lise said.

Charm crawled off Fran's lap to chase a moth, and Fran leaned back on her palms. "What I don't get is why Dyann's tires were slashed. If you were planning to kill someone, why would you slash their tires, too?"

"A crime of passion," Teddy said. "Say Dyann called Richard after the party and taunted him about the will. Richard got angry and hightailed it to the Lucky Lotus. He slipped a knife into his pocket."

Lise again turned to the dirt. She was so close to finishing this bed. "Dyann wasn't stabbed."

"Maybe he put poison in his pocket, too."

"Who has poison hanging around?" Fran asked. "No, it's too weird. Poison points to premeditation. Slashed tires point to violent emotion."

"We don't even know for sure she was poisoned," Lise said. "Remember, the medical examiner didn't find anything. Maybe

Richard threatened her with a knife and she had a heart attack and died."

"Then he slashed her tires?" Teddy said.

"He slashed them on the way in." Fran chewed on her lower lip. "There's too much we don't know. For instance, what was in that will. The old one, that is. What was it that someone was so desperate to protect?"

Lise's fingers hit something hard in the dirt, something smooth and flat. Not just another rock. She grabbed the spade.

"What about this?" Teddy said. "What if Richard confronted Dyann, slashed her tires, and left. He was so angry that he went to the pharmacy and bought poison. Then he returned and slipped it in her liqueur."

"She drinks the liqueur every night, right, Lise?" Fran asked.

"Uh-huh. She has a couple of backup bottles." Lise jammed the spade under the object and used it as a lever.

"So the poison could have been put there at any time," Fran said.

"You already brought that up." Lise jiggled the spade. "We're going in circles. And I know what you're thinking." This conclusion didn't make things better for her. Lise and no one else had nearly unfettered access to Dyann's liqueur stash.

"This is getting ridiculous," Fran said. "What more do you have to do to prove that Richard killed Dyann?"

"I know. But Signe won't listen to me, and if Richard ever finds out I'm asking around about him . . ." She let out a long breath.

"I'll visit Sylvia again," Teddy said. "I bet she knows more than she's letting on. Besides, Richard didn't send *me* a letter."

"Thank you, Teddy." Lise wrenched the trowel into the soil once more. The object was a box—a dirty metal box, maybe tin, perhaps once meant to hold gloves. Its hinged lid was rusted shut. "I found something." A bit more digging, and she had wrested the box free.

"Maybe it's money," Teddy said.

Lise knew Teddy needed cash right now, but the box felt too light. Again using the trowel, she pried it open. "Whoa."

Fran crowded near. "What is it?"

"Not what I expected," Lise said.

It was now dark enough that Fran and Teddy had to lean in close to see its contents.

Fran lifted the deteriorating bundle from the box, and they stared at it.

"Baby shoes. Who buries baby shoes?" Fran said.

The leather booties, small as mice, had once been white with leather laces. Now they were cracked, brown, and crumbling.

In the house's second floor, a lamp came on, casting a pane of pale light on the grass.

"That's funny," Teddy said. "We're all out here."

The house again, Lise thought. "The bathroom. The house's former nursery. That's where the light is."

Then the light winked out.

CHAPTER 23

Teddy lay awake, staring at the chandelier, which was missing so many of its crystals. Years ago, someone had converted the gas fixture to electricity, perhaps at the same time they put up the wallpaper with its hypnotic pattern of urns and acanthus leaves, now faded to pearl gray. In houses of this age, the parlor was a room rarely used by the family. This room, the parlor, had been kept for entertaining guests or housing the dead in their coffins with black cloths over the room's mirrors. She doubted anyone had anticipated the room would ever hold a bed and an eighty-year-old woman still as baffled by her life as she had been at sixteen.

She should be somewhere else. Women her age aspired to condos in Palm Springs and Scottsdale, not Victorian mansions falling to splinters. Yet the house wanted her here—even wanted her sleeping in its parlor. The pocket doors between the sitting room and the parlor had almost magically loosened when she first tugged at them, and the conservatory—moonlight illuminated it now, jadeite green—had tantalized her with dreams of tropical flowers.

She couldn't walk through the house that first day without images of her life materializing at almost every turn. There, in the front hall, she saw her yoga mat laid out and a thread of smoke rising from a stick of incense on the hall table. In the kitchen, her treasured hand-thrown coffee mugs, a gift from an old lover, seemed to fill the cupboard. In the sitting room, the walls nearly painted themselves Bordeaux red, and visions of anonymous portraits of women with nineteen-forties hairdos and wistful expressions covered the walls in her imagination.

More than that, at Corrie House she felt at peace. Despite her long-ago life as a hippie, Teddy wasn't usually given to the woo, but it was as if Corrie House had eased her into its orbit with soothing words of protection, like she was a toddler folded into a loving woman's apron. Although, she had to admit, the house wasn't all sweetness and light. It had an agenda, an agenda Teddy didn't yet understand. And there was definitely something very off about the library.

Burt had told her stories of his life as a bar pilot and about how the shifting bars deep under the river could topple ships. This, she reflected, was a good metaphor for life—for her life, at least. The shifting bars were finances and, now, Lise's predicament with Dyann's murder. Burt's failing health lurked beneath the surface, as well. When she'd asked him about it, Burt simply told her he loved her and smiled. Teddy had seen enough of life to know she would have to trust the process. She'd pilot the craft the best she could.

Why she was at Corrie House, she had no idea, but she was sure more than ever that here was where she was meant to be.

Lise, too, was wakeful. She'd dabbed Jean Patou's Moment Suprême on each wrist so its lavender and amber could ease her to sleep, but tonight it didn't work. She rolled onto her back, disturbing Grace, who'd padded to the pillow next to Lise's head and curled up to dream of things cats did: moths flickering a paw's reach away, maybe, or bowls heaped with chicken livers.

To ease into sleep, Lise played a familiar mental game. She

thought of a famous woman—tonight she'd try Audrey Hepburn—then imagined what she might have in her purse. First, Lise pictured the purse itself. For Audrey, she chose a black calfskin handbag that opened with a snap of its clasp and revealed an emerald-green leather lining.

Imagining the green leather led to the green of Dyann's eyes. Fran was right—someone could have put poison in Dyann's liqueur bottle any time after its wax seal was broken. Lise tried to remember how full the bottle was. With the rate that Dyann drained them, this bottle must have been opened sometime that week. Which meant that anyone who'd visited Dyann in the back room, either for an aura reading or something else, could have slipped poison into the bottle. Of course, Lise herself could have uncorked the bottle at nearly any time, and she was sure Signe had noted that.

Lise wrenched her thoughts back to Audrey Hepburn's purse. What was inside? A purse spray of L'Interdit, her signature perfume. The old L'Interdit, that was, not the newer version tarted up with strawberry. She might carry a monogrammed handkerchief, too, never used yet replaced daily.

Lise's thoughts drifted again. Richard had come by that week, she remembered. Why, she didn't know, but Dyann had been furious afterward. Sylvia had visited, too, to brag about her engagement. Murphy had stopped in to ask for cash. Then, of course, someone might have broken in anytime when the Lucky Lotus was closed. The shop didn't have a security system apart from the bolts on the doors and the evil eyes Dyann had hung in the windows.

Signe cared about none of this. She had Sylvia's and Richard's statements that they were together when Dyann died, and the medical examiner had found no evidence of homicide. It wasn't right to let a murderer go free. That is, if Dyann's death was the murder that Lise suspected.

Richard thought he could bully his way out of suspicion by

instructing his attorneys to send threatening letters. She loathed the idea of having the police show up at her door again, but worse was the chance that he would escape justice.

If Lise's thoughts kept drifting to Dyann's death, she'd never get to sleep. Back to Audrey Hepburn's purse. She'd certainly carry a lipstick. Perhaps a pink-tinged nude in a refillable gold case. Did she smoke? Lise wasn't sure, so she added a cigarette case to match the purse's green lining.

As far as Signe was concerned, Lise was a sad underperformer and an unprosecuted felon. If only there was a way Lise could see Dyann's original will, but she had no access to either the shop or Dyann's house. That window had closed.

Forget it. The purse game wasn't going to work tonight. She slipped from bed and went to the bay window to stare down at the garden. The baby shoes in their box now sat on the kitchen table. While she'd dug them out, it was as if she were smelling a whole summer's garden of fragrant plants—a garden at the peak of a July afternoon—yet it was September.

Lise lifted her wrist to her nose and inhaled. So good. If she were a perfumer, she'd craft fragrances that were complex and moody, like this one. These days, people simply didn't know how to smell. Perfumes were "old lady" or "powdery" to people, no matter their actual notes. She'd teach people to appreciate scent, just as they learned to love Mahler or savor Burgundy or appreciate Jackson Pollock.

The old house creaked like an arthritic woman as the cooler night air cushioned its bones. Fran was up, too, Lise noted, judging from the rustling next door. Fran often wandered the house at night and probably thought no one noticed when she made midnight sandwiches or watched shows on her laptop. Lise did.

Too many unanswered questions jostled in Lise's head to make sleep come easily, but she had better try, anyway. Tomorrow was another day at the Blavatsky Manor, and God only knew what they'd have cooked up for her then.

* * *

That night, the voices were too insistent for Fran to ignore.

Lise was in her room next door, undoubtedly dreaming of fancy perfumes. Teddy, too, was likely asleep in the house's old parlor downstairs. Her lights tended to turn off early.

Fran set aside her notebook. She was trying to write a scene where the master burglar in *Dead Bolt* breaks into the duke's castle, but her mind kept straying. The baby shoes in the garden had to be attached to the baby she heard crying sometimes. But why would anyone bury shoes? Unless there was a body there, too. Maybe a bunch of bodies.

They didn't know anything about Captain Corrie. He might have plotted murders in the library, and that's why it felt so dire in there. She pictured a sea captain with a pipe and a red beard shot through with gray. He tested a rope between his hands. Sailors worked a lot with rope, right? They might have had a serial killer right here in the house.

Fran pulled back the blanket and got out of bed. For a moment, she considered slipping into the robe her brother had sent. Teddy would probably *ooh* and *ahh* over its craftsmanship, if not the Gucci label, but instead, she pulled a T-shirt over her nightgown. Her love was not for sale.

She stood in the hall and listened. The voice—a woman's—sounded from upstairs. The new housemate, the cute one, would have the entire attic, but the tower, which rose through it and up another story, was open to all of them. Fran had never been up that high. There was no way she'd look out from the tower and way down the hill during the day, and what was the point in the dark? But tonight it called to her.

She glanced across the hall at the library. Its door was closed. The room's nasty energy could stay locked behind it.

Fran looked up the stairs and bravely plunged ahead. The moon was bright enough through the landing's narrow window that there was no need to turn on a light. The woman's voice was louder here, but she couldn't quite make out the words. She continued to climb.

Fran was afraid of many things. Heights, for sure. Crowds, people she didn't know well who wanted to hug her, rats, snakes, and enclosed spaces were at the top of the list. But for reasons she couldn't explain, the voices had never bothered her. Maybe it was because they kept to themselves. She felt a kinship with them.

At the third floor, she came to the attic door. What was on the other side? She glanced at the lock. No bolt. It took a skeleton key, like the other original locks in the house. She could pick it in seconds.

As she contemplated this, the door opened a few inches. All on its own.

The ghost voice continued, without pausing to respond. From the doorway, Fran thought she heard, "Where are you? Come home. Stephen."

Fran whispered up the stairs, to the top of the tower, up from where the voice had come, "Hang on, I'll be with you in a moment."

Then she pushed the attic door open further. Fran had expected a cavernous open space, but the attic was divided. Ahead, three rooms with doors occupied the southern part of the house—the former servants' quarters and maybe a storeroom. A pile of junk sat against one wall. She wondered what the new housemate would do with the space. Teddy had said that besides working in a tattoo shop, he was an artist. She imagined large canvases and the smell of turpentine.

She closed the attic door and returned to the hall. One flight up was the top of the tower, where she heard the woman's voice.

Fran forged ahead. A stair creaked, but it didn't stop the words of the woman. "Where are you?" came the plaintive voice. "Come home."

Heart pounding, she edged open the door at the top of the stairs. Windows encircled the tower, and moonlight made it easy for Fran to maneuver, but it was still dark enough to hide the frightening drop to the ground. A bare swirl of light stood near the tower's far opening, but Fran couldn't make out any of the ghost's features, couldn't see if she was the woman in the photographs Margie's friend had gotten for Fran from the historical society.

"What do you want?" she whispered to the woman.

"Where are you?" the woman said in a low voice. She couldn't hear Fran. Yet the house knew Fran was here. The house had welcomed her up here. "Come home," the voice said.

She wondered if the woman whose voice she heard had been married to the captain and was waiting for him to return. Given her constant moaning about it, it seemed likely he never did. Yet something dramatic had happened in this house. Fran's imagination could churn out a dozen stories, ranging from pirates to femme fatales to serial-killing marauders, but the feeling she had from the woman's voice was longing and sadness, not terror. Corrie House itself felt melancholic. As if in response to Fran's thoughts, the house shifted and let out a sigh.

What had happened here? Fran thought she might like to find out.

She hovered a moment at the doorway, then returned to bed.

Chapter 24

Lise had shown up at Blavatsky Manor in a repeat of yesterday's outfit of a denim skirt and men's button-down shirt. If she'd known what they'd intended for her, she might have worn the cat burglar's getup of a black leotard and stocking cap.

When she'd stepped into the lobby, the air had buzzed with the scent of cedar: excitement.

"You're going to do *what*?" Lise had asked. "There's no way I'm going to be part of this. I'll quit first."

Maxine rose and smiled widely with a look Lise instantly suspected meant trouble. Near Maxine, Bea sat clutching a cane. She was dressed uncharacteristically severely—no makeup and all in black. However, she had a honking giant diamond ring and a brooch with a bowling green of emeralds on it. Two of the home's other residents, Arthur and Gerald, occupied the chairs next to her. They wore work overalls and caps.

"Calm down, Lise," Maxine said. "All you're doing is driving and minding your own business. We'll take care of the rest."

"Besides, hon, you have a vested interest," Bea said.

"If we're caught, this won't make it any easier," Lise replied. "Not for me, not for you."

"We might see our way to a small bonus for your service," Maxine said.

"What? A file in the cake you'll bring me in prison? You're talking burglary. Besides, how does stealing Dyann's will help you?"

Maxine slung her purse over a shoulder. "We need to see if they have the codicil, and if it has both signatures. Also, we'll have a better idea of her ex's interest in her estate. We'll know what we're up against."

"This is a big deal," Lise said. The Blavatsky Manor wasn't a memory facility, but she was beginning to suspect dementia may have set in among its residents. Sheer craziness.

Arthur's wife, Jean, wandered in and kissed him absently on his forehead before taking a seat. "Nice jewels, Bea. Are those from the Arndt job?"

"Don't you love them?" Bea said. "Margaret cracked the safe this morning to get them out."

Gerald chuckled. "I knew she still had it in her. The Kid said he'd changed the combo to something she'd never get."

Lise glanced from Gerald to Bea. The Arndt job?

Bea, catching her look, said, "We tried to give them back."

"But Arndt had already been thrown in the cooler," Jean said.

"Still there, as far as I know," Gerald added.

Lise set down her purse. "What is this all about?"

For a moment, no one responded. Bea broke the silence. "You've got to tell her."

"She deserves to know," Jean said.

"Know what?" Lise asked.

Maxine set her purse on an end table. "Our appointment's at ten. I guess we have a few minutes before we have to leave. Mom?"

Bea cleared her throat. "Lise, hon, we're not actually psychics. Well, I am, but not the others."

Lise relaxed. Was that all? "I'd wondered if that was the case. Why, though? Why tell people you're retired psychics? It seems like a strange thing to pretend to be."

"It started with me," Bea said. "The home was my idea, so we decided to work the psychic angle."

"We wanted to make it exclusive, you know?" Gerald said, and took a pack of cards from a pocket in his overalls.

"We didn't want just anyone thinking they could settle here. We wanted a sort of brotherhood—"

"Sisterhood, too," Bea said.

There was more they weren't telling her. Lise knew it. "Because?"

Again, silence.

Maxine sighed. "Because they're a bunch of crooks."

Say, what? Lise looked at the people gathered in the lobby. One woman in black, with a walker; a man in work overalls, nervously shuffling cards; another man, also in overalls, fiddling with his hearing aid; a cheerful woman in a Hawaiian shirt. Not what she'd call a criminally dangerous group.

"I'm not, though," Maxine said.

"As my daughter," Bea said, "she's here on a family waiver, to help manage the place."

Lise had to sit. She took one of the Barcelona chairs. "Crooks? Like what?"

"Nothing serious," Arthur said. "Mostly misdemeanors and clean felonies."

What was a "clean" felony? Lise wondered.

"Financial crimes," Bea answered, as if reading her mind. "No violence."

"Be more specific, please," Lise said.

"Embezzlement, insurance fraud, burglary—" Arthur began.

"—numbers, a bit of forgery," Jean said, finishing. "My specialty. I'm artistic. Plus we've got a getaway driver."

"Bitsy suffers from lumbago, so his driving is spotty," Bea said.

"You must be joking," Lise said.

Arthur lifted a hand to tick off other residents. "Safe cracker, slip-and-fall artist, two confidence men, pickpocket, forger, card shark—"

"I was an executive secretary," Maxine said.

"We've paid our dues to society," Bea said, her emerald brooch glimmering. "To live at Blavatsky Manor, we agree to a life on the straight and narrow."

"Except for stealing from a law office," Lise pointed out. "That's what you're planning, right?"

"To prevent a larger crime," Maxine said. "You know about Richard's threats—you got a letter, too. We find out who benefited from Dyann's old will, and we steer attention away from ourselves."

Bea wasn't finished. "When you've led the kind of life we have, you want to be around other people who get it. That's what the Blavatsky Manor is about. Arthur—"

He raised a palm. "Six years for embezzlement."

"—is good with money. Bob Ellsley, an associate in the south of France, helps us with investments."

"The home is well funded," Maxine said. "We don't need Dyann King's money."

"And we certainly don't need the police poking around in our affairs," Bea added.

It was all starting to come together. They'd hired her because of her inside knowledge of Dyann's death. Their goal was to get themselves off the hook for her murder as soon as they could and avoid any further digging into their pasts. Incredible.

She looked at the group in the lobby. Another resident wandered through, with a chihuahua under an arm. Lise wondered what her crimes had been. If you weren't privy to their rap sheets, the crowd certainly looked harmless enough.

"You don't know anything about what we're up to this morning," Maxine said. "I'd swear to that, and so would they."

Everyone nodded and murmured agreement.

They were right. Anything they found could help Lise's case, too. As far as anyone knew, she was simply a caregiver at Blavatsky Manor. But there was just one thing . . .

"Before we go any further, I need to tell you something about myself," Lise said.

"All ears," Maxine said, and the others looked on, smiling calmly.

"There was a situation a few months ago in Seattle," Lise continued.

"Oh, that." Bea swatted the air.

"Is that all?" Arthur said.

"A total setup," Gerald added.

"You know?"

"We checked your references," Maxine said.

"I hadn't listed any. You never asked for references."

"You have them whether you know or not. There's a home outside Seattle—" Maxine began.

"—Blondin Tower, a retirement home for acrobats," Jean said.

Right, acrobats, Lise thought.

"—where one of the Kid's old gang lives. He's gifted with computers, and he did a background check for us. Deep background," Maxine said. "We figured your situation might make you a little more sympathetic to ours."

Lise looked at the residents gathered in the lobby. The saying that "truth is stranger than fiction"? It didn't even touch this situation.

"Okay," she said. "I guess we'd better get moving."

* * *

The Cox and Morningsun offices were in a new, one-story building not far from the courthouse. As instructed, Lise first pulled up a block away to let out Arthur and Gerald. Their overalls were meant to camouflage them as gardeners.

"This is a real change from Willie's place," Arthur noted, looking up the block to the law offices.

Obviously, Lise thought, Willie had some kind of criminal background, too.

Arthur and Gerald left the building plans they'd been examining in the back seat and, as Lise idled, pulled pruners and a spade from the trunk. "Don't forget the gloves," Lise had told them when they'd left the manor. "Gardeners wear gloves."

"Ha. We're professionals, remember?" Arthur had said. "Gloves are de rigueur for the job."

Once they were out of the car, Lise drove up the block to the office building.

Maxine put a handicapped parking permit on the rearview mirror. "Take the spot up front, there."

The placard appeared convincing, Lise thought, but now she wouldn't be surprised if it were counterfeit. Jean's work, perhaps.

"Don't look like that," Maxine said. "It's real, I swear."

Maxine helped her mother from the back seat and unfolded the walker in front of her. "Come on, Lise, if you want. You're her caregiver."

Lise hesitated only a moment before joining Bea and Maxine. She helped Bea edge up the few stairs to the building's lobby, then held the glass front door open for her. Cox and Morningsun's offices were directly to the right. Lise held the door open here, as well.

"Mrs. Marvel here to see Preston Cox, please," Maxine said. Bea, focusing on looking wealthy, stood by her side.

A red-faced man in a golf shirt and khakis came from the

back and clutched Bea's hand in both of his. "Mrs. Marvel. So pleased to meet you. Won't you come back to my office?"

"No," Bea said.

Preston Cox looked momentarily befuddled, then his jovial smile returned. "Is it my casual dress? We're informal around here." He chuckled, but it didn't show in his eyes.

"Mother doesn't like enclosed spaces," Maxine said. "Perhaps you have an open area. A conference room, maybe?"

"Yes, yes, of course." Preston Cox glanced at Lise with curiosity. Again, the chuckle.

"Caregiver," Lise said.

"Of course, of course." Now his gaze lit on Bea's brooch before lowering to her ring, which, if Lise wasn't mistaken, Bea was turning to catch the light. "Come this way."

The conference room was unremarkable in the way of so many conference rooms: a long table stained mahogany, chairs padded in dark green leather, portraits of old white men on the walls.

"Will this do?" Preston Cox asked.

Bea nodded once, and Maxine said, "Yes. Thank you. That's your office across the hall?"

"Yes. You're sure you wouldn't be more comfortable there? There are plenty of windows."

"I like it here," Bea said.

Eccentricity was a privilege of the elderly, Lise thought. Maxine checked her watch, undoubtedly calculating how long it would take Arthur and Gerald to carry out their task. The door to Preston Cox's office was open to the hall, but with only two attorneys it was unlikely someone would stroll by and see anything fishy. At least, Lise thought, this was surely their hope.

Preston Cox launched into a speech about estate planning he'd probably given many times over the years. ". . . your legacy being the mark you leave upon future generations. At

Cox and Morningsun, we strive to ensure this legacy is legally sound, from the first to last words." He punctuated this with an unconvincing chortle.

The scent of hay grew, informing Lise she wasn't the only one in the room slipping into boredom.

Maxine glanced again at her watch. A quarter of an hour had passed. Not long enough.

"Do you have any questions?" he asked. "If not, I'll grab a few forms from my office."

"Yes," Maxine said quickly. "I have a question. Can the executor and main beneficiary be the same person?"

"Ha, ha, ha," Preston laughed. It was beginning to be irritating. "Yes. In fact, it happens more often than not when the person drawing up an estate plan is the head of a family. Now, about those forms—"

"What about a caregiver?" Lise asked. Why not get in on the fun? "Can a caregiver be included in a will?"

"If that's what Mrs. Marvel wants, of course. I—"

A crash from Preston Cox's office drew their attention. *Uh oh.* Maxine squeezed her eyes shut while Bea's lips moved in a silent prayer. The attorney's habitual smile flattened.

"A question, Mr. Cox—" Maxine's attempt to stall Preston Cox didn't work. He was across the hall in two long steps. Lise followed, Maxine and Bea behind her.

"What are you doing in here?" he said.

Arthur and Gerald stood next to a broken vase spilling lilies and water over a Chippendale-style chair. Gerald crossed the room and shook Preston Cox's hand and slapped him on the back. The attorney jerked his hand free. "I asked you what you were doing in my office."

"Are you Preston Cox?" Gerald asked.

"Isn't that my name on the door?"

"We were doing some work on the side of the building and

found your wallet." Gerald proffered a fat leather wallet, shiny from use.

Wow, Lise thought, he's good.

Behind them, the window was open but not especially wide. No wonder they'd knocked over the flowers. It must have been quite a squeeze, especially for Arthur.

Preston Cox opened the wallet and thumbed through its contents. "It's mine. Everything's here. I could have sworn it was in my pocket." He patted his rear pants pocket as if the wallet would still be there. "Curious."

"Accidents happen, sir," Arthur said. "Now, if you'll excuse us, those shrubs won't trim themselves."

"The forms, Mr. Cox?" Maxine asked.

His attention was clearly split between the "gardeners" and Bea. Bea tilted so her brooch sparkled in the morning light, and Preston Cox once again smiled. "Yes, Mrs. Marvel. Let me get them for you."

A few minutes later, when they had all returned to the car and were a few blocks away, Bea said, "That was close. Why did you have to knock over the vase? I don't suppose we'll be able to try it again."

"Never fear," Arthur said and produced a file folder. "*Ta-da!* Snatched it just before Gerald busted the posies."

From her seat on the passenger side, Maxine took the file. She opened it, glanced, and, sighing, stuffed it into her bag. "You weren't wearing your reading glasses, were you?"

"What? Gardeners don't wear reading glasses. It's not like we're hanging out in the tulips flipping the pages of *Peyton Place*."

"This isn't Dyann King's file, you dummy. It's for Murphy King. Her son."

Lise's disappointment was only momentary. This might actually work to their advantage. She pulled over and turned from the driver's seat. "May I see that?"

Maxine handed the papers to her, and she scanned their contents. She closed the file and used it to gesture toward Maxine. "This might be more useful than we'd thought. It says here that in the case of Dyann's death, Richard King will manage his son's money until he turns twenty-one."

"He's eighteen now," Bea said.

"Gotcha, Richard King," Gerald said.

It looked worse and worse for Richard, Lise reflected. And better for her.

CHAPTER 25

Teddy glanced around Sylvia Borlotti's condo. It was in a new building that looked over the tall arch of the Megler Bridge spanning the Columbia River. From Sylvia's living room window, cars whizzed like sparkling ants across its span. The setting sun frosted the water with orange and pink light.

"Breathtaking, isn't it?" Sylvia said.

"Absolutely," Teddy said. Corrie House had amazing views, too, but from Corrie House, Astoria spilled forth like an offering. Here the town was behind you, and you felt alone. Alone and suspended above the world, not part of it.

Yes, the view was wonderful, but the decor of Sylvia's condo didn't inspire much in Teddy, unless it was an acknowledgement of how a bland interior didn't compete with Mother Nature. Somehow, Teddy doubted that had been Sylvia's intention when she'd bought the white couch and matching white armchair with velvet throw pillows, each sporting evidence of a karate chop down its middle. Blond wood side tables held lamps with white ceramic bases. A white sheepskin throw lay before a gas fireplace with brass trim and, yes, white tile. The whole decor begged for a spilled glass of cabernet.

"You really think Marvin Sholes would be interested in my work?" Sylvia asked. She wore white jeans and a T-shirt. If she sat on the couch, she'd vanish.

"Oh, I know it," Teddy said. "Your voice is pure magic. When I heard you sing, I was tempted to tell you right away I thought you would be a great fit for his new project, but I wanted to check with him first."

Teddy had first met the producer Marvin Sholes when she was a bassist's girlfriend and he a roadie. He'd had a gift for suggesting adjustments in playlists and instrumentation that had quickly promoted him from stringing speakers to producing concerts. In his retirement, he'd shifted from organizing arena concerts to hosting small-venue, intimate shows. Sylvia was perfect for him, not to mention the perfect opportunity for her, and the perfect excuse for Teddy.

"I have to get ready for tonight's gig." Despite that, Sylvia sank into an armchair. Teddy had to admit that with her dark hair and fair skin, she looked good against white upholstery. "I hope you're right about Mr. Sholes's interest. If so, this would be the first piece of good news I've had in a long time."

This was Teddy's opening. "Dyann's death was a shock, I imagine. Even with the horrible trick with the oil she played on you."

Sylvia looked toward the living room window. "Yes." When she returned her gaze to Teddy, her eyes and her cheeks bore splotches of red. "It was my fault."

"What was, darling?"

"If it weren't for me, Dyann might still be alive."

What was this? Teddy patted the cushion next to hers. "Sit here. Tell me about it."

There were a lot of disadvantages to age. Words occasionally slipped your mind, your bones protested when rising from bed, and the world as you knew it was so far away that kids couldn't even figure out how to operate rotary phones. But there were advantages, too, and one of them was that you simply didn't appear to be a threat. Some people might clock this as a disadvantage, but Teddy loved it. Let them underestimate her and see how far it got them.

"I feel awful," Sylvia said. She drew a tissue from the box on the coffee table—white, of course—and honked into it before settling next to Teddy on the sofa.

"I was so angry about the oil that when I felt better I went back to the store and gave her a piece of my mind."

"I don't blame you."

She toyed with the tissue. "I might have told her we were getting married, Richard and I."

"I see." The logic was clear, but Teddy wanted to be sure. "So you think she was angry about your engagement, changed her will, and that led to her death."

Sylvia nodded.

"Is it true?" Teddy asked. "Are you and Richard planning to marry?"

"Good God, no." Sylvia's voice boomed. "Not now. How could I?"

Teddy let the emotion settle. Sylvia's tears were drying, although her face remained splotchy. "You changed your mind about him."

Sylvia tossed the mangled tissue on the coffee table. "He never let go of Dyann. Everywhere I looked, there were photos of them together. His bedroom was a freaking shrine. You ever try having sex under a collage of photos of your lover kissing another woman?"

Although Teddy recognized this as a rhetorical question, she didn't need to reflect for long. Yes, in fact, she had, when Bernard's wife was in Europe. She shared Sylvia's feelings about the situation.

"That must have been distressing." Coupled with the rash, it certainly might lead someone to be impetuous.

"Those two deserved each other," Sylvia said. "Always finding ways to make fresh hell for the other. And to think of what I did for him."

They were getting close to a reveal, Teddy knew. She held her breath and affected her most sympathetic expression.

Sylvia merely shook her head.

"You gave him so much," Teddy prompted.

"I lied for him," Sylvia said.

This lie wasn't about an engagement, Teddy felt sure. She chose her next words carefully. "You told the police he was with you when Dyann died." Waiting for the response, she barely breathed.

"I told her I was at King Cars buying a new car. I wasn't. I'd bought it earlier in the day." Her face had cleared now. It was good to see healthy indignation replace grief, Teddy thought. "I returned that car yesterday and got my old Honda back." Sylvia shook her head. "The interest rates he tried to charge me were outrageous."

Gently, Teddy drew her attention back to Dyann for confirmation. "Richard wasn't with you that night."

"Nope. Not at all. A hundred to one he was at the Lucky Lotus." Her voice rose. "You should have heard him when Dyann announced she was changing her will. He was furious."

"Did he say anything in particular?"

"He couldn't even finish a sentence, he was so outraged, but he did manage to choke out something about her paying for her actions. And Dyann sat there, smiling the whole time like she'd won the lottery." Sylvia wrinkled her brow. "Actually, she did win the lottery, but that was a while ago."

This was it, then, the clincher of Richard's guilt. Teddy watched Sylvia stare, unseeing, toward the setting sun. Sylvia turned to Teddy with decisiveness, inhaled deeply, and went to the kitchen. She withdrew an envelope from a drawer.

"There's something else," she said. "This. I saw it when I went to return the car. I thought it might be something I could . . . use, but now I just want to be through with him."

She handed the envelope to Teddy.

Chapter 26

Lise was in her room when she heard the front door slam. Teddy's voice rose from the hall. "Lise, Fran. Are you home?"

Lise arrived in the front hall just as Fran emerged from the kitchen, holding a sandwich. She swallowed the bite she was chewing and said, "What?"

"You're never going to believe this," Teddy said. "Come into my sitting room."

A moment later, they were once again seated around Teddy's coffee table, Fran wiping her mouth after her last crust of sandwich and Lise resting next to Charm and Grace, who were giving each other an enthusiastic bath.

Teddy flattened a sheet of paper on the table. "I just got back from seeing Sylvia Borlotti. Not only did she admit she lied to cover up where Richard was when Dyann died, she gave me this."

Lise's jaw dropped. "The actual codicil! Sylvia took it?"

"Look here." Teddy placed her finger at the bottom of the page. "Dyann signed it and you signed it. There's an empty space for the last witness."

"Where did she get it?" Lise asked. She could imagine Dyann willingly letting her into the Lucky Lotus after hours.

"At Richard's office at King Cars. She caught a glimpse of

the codicil when she went to return her car. She said Richard denied ever seeing it. He made a big production, saying someone must have planted it there."

"Of course he would," Fran said.

"Not only that," Teddy continued, "but she admitted to lying about Richard's whereabouts to cover for him."

Fran's eyes were wide. "What?"

"I think Sylvia finally reached the end of her rope where Richard is concerned. It didn't take a lot of convincing to get her to tell me she only pretended to be at the car lot with Richard that night. She doesn't even have the new car anymore."

"I knew it." Lise rose and paced the room, circling Teddy's and Fran's chairs before standing behind the sofa. "Where was he when Dyann died?"

"She doesn't know, but she guessed he was at the Lucky Lotus."

"We should tell the detective," Fran said.

Lise fingered the rosettes carved into the sofa's frame. "Richard stole the codicil. He didn't want to lose control over the money Dyann left Murphy in her original will."

Fran cocked her head. "How do you know Richard had charge of Murphy's money?"

Whoops. Lise wasn't sure how much she should reveal about Blavatsky Manor or this morning's activities. The manor's residents had told her their pasts in confidence, but Fran and Teddy deserved to know as much as she did.

"I've seen notes on Murphy's will." Lise described the visit to the Cox and Morningsun office but glossed over why they were there. Neither did she tell about the true backgrounds of the Blavatsky Manor residents.

"Murphy's will was just lying around?" Fran said.

"In a manner of speaking."

Teddy clasped her hands. "So Richard was angry he was cut

out of managing his son's money. It didn't have to be the money itself that motivated him."

"If he managed Murphy's money, he might invest it in anything he wanted—say, a used car lot," Fran pointed out.

"He went to the Lucky Lotus that night, slashed her tires, and killed her." Lise returned to her seat.

"And in the meantime got hold of some kind of untraceable poison?" Fran asked.

"Maybe it's something automotive. A cleaner or brake fluid or something," Teddy said. "Something the medical examiner wouldn't test for."

"Richard would have to be an expert in poisons." Lise knew what she had to do, and she didn't like it. But what were the alternatives? They had evidence—not lots of it and not any that anyone would swear to, but evidence nonetheless—that Richard had killed Dyann. Plus, they'd found the actual signed codicil, the one she'd signed. The police needed to know. "I'll tell Signe."

"She's going to tear you apart," Fran said. "Sylvia won't cop to lying to her or to taking the codicil. Richard already swears he doesn't know anything about it. He'll say you had it all along. Charlene at the butcher shop was distracted with work when she saw Richard's Camaro."

Fran was right. "Okay, the evidence is weak. But there's so much of it."

"Lise knows what she's talking about, darling. Telling the detective is the right thing to do. Let her decide."

"I get it, and I agree, but I think you're opening the door to a whole lot of trouble," Fran said.

Lise nodded slowly. "Maybe. I hope I'm simply handing off the trouble to someone whose job it is to manage it."

"Lise," Teddy said suddenly, "in my excitement about Sylvia, I forgot to tell you that I brought in a letter for you. Looks like it's from home."

"Left at the bottom of the walk, no doubt," Fran said.

"Under a bush," Teddy said. "It's on the table in the entry hall."

It had to be from her father. At last he'd forwarded the envelope from her birth mother. Lise hurried to the entry hall and stopped short. The envelope was opened, its flap severed neatly, and its contents lay in shreds over the rug.

Fran was right behind her. "Did the cats do that?"

As if in reply, the entry hall windows shivered like a small earthquake had rumbled through. Both Lise and Fran inhaled sharply.

Lise stooped to pick up the yellowed paper. It was torn in dime-sized pieces, some marked with faded blue ink. She struggled to hold back tears. "I don't know." Maybe if she gathered the pieces she could tape them back together.

"The cats have never done it before," Fran said.

"It was a letter my birth mother had written to me. It had been sealed up this whole time. My father finally sent it to me, and . . ."

"And now this." Fran stooped to help her gather the pieces. "I'm so sorry." She looked at Lise, and her bangs fell away to reveal compassionate eyes. "Your luck has to change sometime. Let's hope it's soon."

Hours later, after her nightly viewing of her brother's show, Fran closed her laptop. As it clicked shut, her bedroom door opened.

"Hello?" Fran said.

No one responded. Neither was the ghost lady worrying nor the baby crying. Fran crept to the hall and looked out. Lise's door was ajar so the cats could get in and out, but all was quiet there. No, Fran corrected herself, she heard footsteps, and not the ghostly steps in the attic, either. Despite the late hour, Lise was awake.

Poor Lise. To be so close to learning about your mom, then have it literally torn into pieces.

Fran shut the door again, but before she'd reached her bed, a creaking told her the door had reopened. The old house sure was bossy.

"What do you want?" Fran whispered.

From upstairs came the creaking of steps on the attic's floorboards. The ghost.

She got up again to close the door and found herself face-to-face with Lise.

"Hey, Fran," she said. "You're up, too."

"I heard footsteps."

They both looked toward the ceiling. "Me, too. I'm getting used to them," Lise said. "I couldn't sleep. I can't stop thinking about the letter."

"You think the house did it?"

"Does that sound crazy?" Lise asked. "I don't know anymore. Usually, the house feels protective—except for the library. What if, for some reason, it doesn't want me to know my biological family?" She shook her head slowly. "I'm going to the kitchen to make a sandwich. Thought I'd take it to the tower to eat. Care to join me?"

The tower was alarmingly high, but it was dark outside. Fran thought of her journey up the stairs the other night to follow the ghost voice. She'd survived that. "Okay."

"I'll fix us something. Better bring a sweater or a blanket."

While Lise was downstairs, Fran contemplated the letter. Why would the house turn to vandalizing mail? Could it be jealous? Unless the cats really did do it. Grace could get wild with a rubber band, but Fran had never seen either cat shred paper.

Lise returned with two plates. Fran drew a deep breath and followed her.

Up one floor was the attic level. She'd been this high just the other night, but she hadn't looked out the window. They continued to the top of the tower and closed the door behind them. A cool breeze blew through the openings.

Fran stayed close to the wall and kept her eyes closed.

"There are two chairs here—Fran?"

She heard the clink of plates being set on a table. "Yes?"

"Have a seat. The view is amazing."

The knowledge that they were four stories above the ground kept Fran's pulse pounding. There was no way she'd open her eyes. "I'm fine here." Her voice sounded like a chipmunk's. Now she was both terrified and humiliated.

"Your grilled cheese is getting cold."

She was already feeling her way toward the door. She'd tell Lise she had a sudden headache and go to her room.

"You're afraid, aren't you?" Lise's voice was calm and low. "You're neurotic, and your imagination is running wild."

"Neurotic?" For a moment, Fran forgot her fear and stepped away from the wall. "You think I'm neurotic?"

"That's more like it." Lise led her to an armchair. Fran smelled of something sweet and herbal, undoubtedly from some crusty bottle she'd scored at a thrift store. Lise gently tapped her shoulders, and Fran sat.

She instantly closed her eyes. "I just don't like heights. That's not unusual. Lots of people don't like them."

"Okay," Lise said. She lifted Fran's hand and placed it on the toasted top of a sandwich. "Can you eat with your eyes shut?"

Fran's response was to lift the sandwich and take a bite. "Did you put horseradish on this?"

"Like it?"

"Yes." The chewing motion calmed her. The house sighed and creaked as if resting its old joints. Fran grasped Lise's arm in panic, then, horrified at what she'd done, snatched back her fingers.

"Relax," she said. "Corrie House has stood for almost a hundred and fifty years. Chances are good it will make it through tonight."

"Have you been able to piece together what was in the letter you got today?" Distraction would be good. Distraction and deep breaths.

"A tiny bit, but I think some of it is missing. Maybe it blew under the bureau. I'll look in the morning."

"You registered at one of those places that hooks you up with your birth parents, right?"

With her eyes closed, Fran felt rather than saw Lise nod. "It was, well, it was an untraditional adoption."

Fran heard a sigh. She felt around her plate and found a pickle. "Are you really going to see the detective tomorrow?"

Lise didn't reply for so long that Fran wondered if she'd heard her. Finally, Lise said, "Yes. It's the right thing to do. Still nervous about being up here?"

Fran didn't respond. What was the point?

"How about this?" Lise said. "You keep your eyes closed and finish your sandwich, and I'll tell you what I see."

That sounded okay. She could do that. With the damp breeze, she'd pretend she was on a pier by the river, not suspended above the town, although the pier wouldn't have an ancient armchair on it with ratty upholstery and a seat hollowed to a long-dead someone's hind end. "Fine."

Lise's chair apparently had a sprung seat, too, because it creaked as she relaxed. "There's half a moon in the sky and only a smattering of clouds, so it's just barely light enough to see the shape of the monkey puzzle tree to the house's right."

Fran knew that tree. It was gigantic, with heavy branches curled like articulated robot arms. It must have been planted soon after the house was built. "What else do you see?"

"Streetlights—not as many of them as you'd think—making pools of yellow light. Lots of dark spots where the houses are.

But I can see a couple of tankers on the river and cars passing through downtown."

Although Fran's eyes were fastened shut, the vision suddenly became too much for her.

Lise must have noticed, because she said, "Enough of that. We've never really talked much about you. I know about your brother, of course, and I know you don't want to talk about him," she added quickly. "Are you originally from Astoria?"

"Yes. Born and raised. I like it here," she said, almost before she knew the words had left her mouth. "I mean the house," she added quickly. "Astoria, too, but I like the house."

"I like the house, too. I didn't think I'd be living someplace like this, but here I am."

"Do you . . . I know we talked about this the other day, but do you really think Corrie House is haunted?" Fran knew the answer. Did Lise?

"Scientists raised me. I never thought I'd say this, but yes. I've never seen ghosts, but too many weird things happen here. The footsteps, the piano playing by itself. Lights going off and on. Stuff moving around on its own. Teddy's clock stopping and starting by itself. I smell things, too, things that aren't there. Like the other night, when the garden smelled like a summer a century ago."

Of course she did. She smelled ghosts, and Fran heard them. Here, in the dark, so late, Fran took the risk and asked. "Do you ever hear voices?"

"No." No judgment. "You asked Burt about that, too. Why? Do you?"

"Yes. A woman moaning about someone named Stephen. I hear a baby crying sometimes, too. The lady spends a lot of time in your room, by the way." Fran held her breath, waiting to see if Lise would call her crazy.

"I think she wears heliotrope cologne" is all Lise said. From far off, a boat's horn sounded. "Get this. One day I came upstairs to find 'S V C' smudged on my window. I thought one of you guys had done it—"

"No way," Fran said.

"Way."

"Okay, that's really weird. The 'C' probably stands for Corrie."

"Maybe the 'S' is for the Stephen you keep hearing about? Or Selma, Captain Corrie's wife."

Fran considered this. "My next day off, I'm going to the county historical society for more information." There was definitely an uneasy presence in the house. Besides the mother and baby, something borderline evil lurked across the hall from their rooms. Perhaps that was what had shredded Lise's letter.

"Fran?"

"What?" Was she going to tell her that her imagination was running away with her? That her brother—damn him—was right about her neurosis?"

"Your eyes. They're open now."

Chapter 27

When Lise came down the stairs the next morning, Teddy stood in the kitchen. She wore a phoenix-ornamented kimono and had a cup of coffee in hand. Charm wove through her ankles. “Do you want me to go with you?” she asked.

“No,” Lise said. “Seeing Signe is something I need to do alone.”

The codicil was in her bag. Lise had hesitated when she’d called the police department, but to her surprise, Signe didn’t fight Lise’s request to see her—she’d even scheduled the appointment right away, for eleven o’clock. Maxine had given Lise the green light to skip work, saying that arresting Richard King would put the matter of Dyann’s death to rest and give the residents of Blavatsky Manor peace once again.

Teddy motioned toward the refrigerator. “What’s with this list?”

Lise laughed. “Fran must have done that.” A sheet of paper was stuck to refrigerator with a black cat magnet. On its top was written “S V C.” Below that was “Señor Victor Cranston” and “Super Volatile Cupcake.” “Fran and I were talking about these initials last night.”

Teddy set down her coffee and picked up the nearby pen. “Sweet Vigorous Cockroach,” she wrote.

Half an hour later, Lise was in her car, nervous but resolute. At the police department, the same employee who'd yelled for Signe's last week was at the reception desk. He looked up, his curly ponytail bobbing, when Lise pushed through the glass door. "Signe is waiting for you. You remember where her office is?"

As promised, Signe was at her desk. She didn't stand or bother with superficial greetings. "You wanted to see me?"

"Yes." Despite the lack of invitation, Lise took the chair across from her and pulled it closer to the desk. "You need to reopen the investigation into Dyann King's death."

Signe fidgeted with a notebook. "How do you know it's closed?" When Lise didn't reply, she added, "Why?"

Lise took the codicil from her bag and slid it toward Signe.

Signe only glanced at it for a second. "Where did you get this?"

She had considered refusing to reveal its source, but homicide wasn't the place to fool around. "It came from Sylvia Borlotti. She found it in Richard King's office at the car lot."

"She gave it to you?"

"My housemate Teddy went to visit her, and she handed it over. Sylvia said she found it when she went to return the car Richard had sold her."

Signe's eyebrows drew together. "The car she said she bought the night of Dyann's death."

Lise nodded. "Truth is, she'd bought it earlier in the day. She said she lied about where she was that night, that she and Richard weren't together that evening. They never went to King Cars. They split up after Murphy's party. She doesn't know what Richard was doing that night."

Signe fidgeted with a paperclip, but ribbons of excitement flowed from her in a bouquet of cedar tinged with lemon.

"Why didn't she bring this to the police?" Signe asked. "If I go to her, what will she tell me?"

This was the tricky part. "She'll deny it." Before Signe could reply, Lise added, "Think about it. She lied to you. Plus, she's making her boyfriend look bad." Possibly soon-to-be former boyfriend, Lise corrected silently. It sounded like she'd reached the end of her rope with Richard.

"How do I know you didn't have this codicil all along?"

"You don't," Lise conceded. "But I have more to tell you that might convince you."

Signe leaned back and folded her arms over her chest. "Really?"

"The night Dyann died, the owner of the butcher shop saw Richard's car parked down the block. I've already told you that much, and it backs up what Sylvia told Teddy. One more thing. It's possible that if Murphy inherits, Richard will manage his money. That's a pretty strong motive to want to prevent the codicil from taking effect."

"How do you know about Dyann's will?"

Describing the break-in at the law office would not help Lise's case. "Just a thought, but it bears following up."

"You have no reason to lie to me," Signe said, as if she were talking to herself and not Lise. "You didn't even like Dyann King very much."

She was wrong—Lise had indeed liked Dyann. She'd just irritated the hell out of her. Nevertheless, Lise gave Signe a faint smile.

"Dyann's death isn't even officially a homicide." Now the truth was coming out, and Signe's office filled once again with the scent of warm steel. "But I know it is."

"You thought Dyann had been poisoned, but the medical examiner didn't find anything."

Signe tossed her pen, and it skittered across the desk. "Yes and no."

"What does that mean?"

She looked over Lise's shoulder and lowered her voice. "She

didn't find anything in Dyann King's system that could have killed her. I've been working under the assumption that Dyann had ingested some kind of toxin. When that didn't pan out, I had the medical examiner do a thorough check for needle marks. I haven't yet heard back."

The thought of Richard confronting Dyann, jabbing her with a needle . . . Lise suppressed a shiver. "Wouldn't they have already looked for that? Besides, whether poison was in her liqueur or injected, it would have shown up in the toxicology results, wouldn't it?" She began to understand. "Unless the investigation was called off because Dyann's death was determined to be from natural causes, because the initial tests came back negative." As the police chief had wanted. Lise sat back. Signe was going rogue on this one.

Signe's expression settled into a combination of obstinacy and focus that Lise remembered from high school. She was ambitious, and herding goats had probably ceased to satisfy her a long time ago. She wanted to dig into a homicide.

"The chief told me . . ." Signe tapped the codicil with her pen. "I don't know what good this is unless Sylvia Borlotti is willing to testify to having found it, but it confirms something I've suspected."

"There's more." Lise drew from her bag the letter from Richard's lawyer. "Richard King threatened to sue me if I asked questions about Dyann's death. He sent a letter to Blavatsky Manor, too, warning them not to pursue the codicil."

"How do you know about Blavatsky Manor?"

"I'm working there now." At Signe's incredulous look, she added, "What? Obviously it was over at the Lucky Lotus. I have to earn my living somehow."

Signe turned Richard's letter over, then back again. "Richard would sue if he knew you were here."

"Probably."

"But you're pursuing this, anyway."

Lise didn't respond.

Then Signe looked at Lise with a warmth that surprised her. "Thank you for bringing the codicil to me and for sharing the information you have. I . . ." A moment passed, then two. Lise was beginning to suspect Signe would leave her thought hanging, when she drew a long breath. "The garden show."

"What about it?" Lise asked, her voice low.

"I know the truth about the garden show."

"We talked about this. I told you—"

Signe held up a palm. "Hear me out. I said I know the truth about it." She lowered her hand. "I know all about my mother. I have no doubt she saw you as a threat and sabotaged your chances of winning by framing you for vandalizing her display, and I'm sorry."

Whatever Lise had been expecting to hear, it wasn't this.

"I'm really sorry," Signe repeated. "Mom can be awful."

"The incident at the garden show is in the past," Lise finally said.

"That's generous of you," Signe said. "You moved here because she ruined your business, right?"

"I like Astoria." Lise forced her gaze away from Signe. *Keep your cool*, she willed herself.

"And you liked being a cashier at a shop specializing in coffee mugs shaped like leprechauns?"

So much for the play at nonchalance. Lise locked eyes with Signe. "Your mother lied about me. She drove me from my home and destroyed my chances of future work, all because she wasn't going to win a blue ribbon." Lise stood. Her lips trembled. She needed to leave before she did something she'd regret.

Signe remained seated. "I understand." Her chest rose and fell with a deep breath.

"Then why are you needling me?"

"I'm really sorry. I am." Signe said. "I'm handling this all wrong. Please sit down."

Lise slowly lowered herself again into the chair.

"I know my mother screwed you over."

Lise wouldn't respond. If Signe was going to explain and apologize, Lise was not going to help.

"I've no doubt she staged the whole debacle—the graffiti, lying to the police, everything. She's like that, my mother." Signe's discomfort showed in how she arranged and rearranged her paperclips. "Remember in high school how you were offered the spot of yearbook editor and it was taken away?"

She remembered, all right. One day Lise was jubilant, planning articles, and the next she'd received a call telling her she was demoted to production, with Signe as the editor.

"That was Mom," Signe said. "She called the superintendent of schools and made him give me the position."

"How did she do that?"

"She knew he was fooling around on his wife and blackmailed him."

"She did?" Lise mourned both of her mothers, but she'd take two dead moms over one living Mrs. Rasmussen any day. "And the scholarship?" The scholarship that would have paid her way to a nice university out east?

"Same." Signe let go of a long sigh. "I'm so, so sorry. She's the reason I left Seattle. I couldn't bear to be in the same city as her. She's also the reason I got into law enforcement. I figured if I could bring some kind of justice into the world . . ."

As Signe's words trailed off, compassion began to replace Lise's anger. "I had no idea."

Silence rested between them for a minute. In the distance, a phone rang and was answered. A police radio sounded with muffled words. A strand of verveine and lavender rose between them. Peace.

Signe pushed the paperclips to the side. "There's something else I want to tell you. You're right. The chief called off Dyann King's homicide investigation, but I haven't closed the books."

This was a big admission, Lise knew.

"The evidence you've brought me? I'm really grateful. There's enough here to request a warrant for Richard King's arrest."

Lise felt the anger draining from her. Signe had said she was sorry for her mother's actions, and she'd actually listened to Lise's information about Richard. Signe had to deal with visiting her mother at holidays and living up to her likely unreasonable standards. On top of that, Signe's boss had dismissed her recommendation to pursue a murder case. For the first time, Lise looked at Signe and felt sympathy.

Signe stood. When she spoke, it was as if the last few minutes of their conversation hadn't happened at all. "Thank you. Richard King has some explaining to do."

As she left the police station, Lise was gratified to know that sometimes you take a risk and it works out. Justice would be done for Dyann. Everything would be fine. At last.

Lise drove a few blocks up and parked near the Bowpicker, a shack-sized wooden ship fitted as a fish-and-chips food cart. It was lunchtime, and she had a hankering for a basket of fries.

She took her fries to a bench near the river. The wind off the water felt soft, and the sound of sea lions playing by the docks was less plaintive than usual and more joyful. Maybe Lise's life wasn't figured out, but today she'd accomplished something important. For a moment, she even entertained the idea of asking Signe what a detective's life was like, but she nixed that idea almost as soon as it crossed her mind. She was better suited as a gardener than a detective.

Maxine and the rest of the residents of Blavatsky Manor would be happy to know their pasts would stay under wraps. She'd call when she got home. Right now she'd do what Teddy always urged and be in the moment. She'd simply enjoy the sun and the feeling of accomplishment.

Fries eaten, Lise left her car on the street and turned toward town. She slowed as she came to the dark windows of the Lucky Lotus. She cupped her hands around her eyes and peered through the window. She used to be behind that counter, surreptitiously reading about psychic abilities and clairalience and counting the hours to quitting time. Now the counter was empty, but the rest of the store looked as it always had. What would Murphy do with it?

Lise crossed the street and walked up the block to Margie's Books. Fran would want to know about Richard's pending arrest.

The bell at the door jingled as Lise entered. Fran wasn't behind the counter or anywhere Lise could see from the entrance.

Margie, holding a stack of cookbooks, emerged from the back. "Hello, Lise. Looking for Fran?"

"I am, in fact."

"She's at lunch, but I'm glad you came in." She set the cookbooks on the floor. "I have something I think you'd like. Follow me."

Margie, the pug on her heels, led Lise to a waist-high bookcase. She pulled a large book from the top shelf. "A customer sold this to me. It's in French, but I thought you'd be interested."

Arts et Parfums, the cover read. Lise opened a page at random to a photo of a bottle of Rose de Rosine by Paul Poiret. "How much?" She had to have it, budget be damned.

Transaction concluded, Lise backtracked, the book under an arm, to return to her car. Yes, it was a good day.

The sound of screeching and people shouting drew her attention. Ahead, vehicles honked as a red sports car barreled down Fourteenth Street, through the intersection against the traffic light. This wasn't just any car. It was Richard's Camaro. It hurtled by so quickly that Lise couldn't make out who was inside.

Then she realized the car wasn't speeding, it was out of control. Fourteenth Street sloped at a dangerously steep pitch straight from the hills to the river. A car would gain momentum like a boulder tumbling down a mountain until it was unstoppable.

Lise ran to the corner amidst the chaos of shrieking tires and honking as the Camaro intersected Astoria's two main commercial streets, narrowly avoiding being hit by a semitrailer.

The next moments seemed to play in slow motion. Her heart stopped and breath lodged in her chest as she watched the Camaro hurtle off the riverfront and bounce with a hollow thud from the weather-worn posts that had once supported a long-demolished pier.

"No!" She ran toward the river's edge. The back of Richard's head, jerking from side to side, showed through the Camaro's rear window. "Open the door! Open it!" She willed the door to open, for Richard to swim to the shore, but although he seemed to throw his body weight toward the door, it remained shut.

Then she smelled it, the earthy-yet-frantic scent she'd smelled when she found Dyann. Now she recognized it for what it was: the smell of death.

The Camaro bobbed only a moment until it was sucked under.

CHAPTER 28

Lise closed the casement windows in Corrie House's dining room. Nights were getting colder. Soon they wouldn't open the windows at all, and they'd draw the curtains against the chill.

"I'm sorry, darling," Teddy said. "It couldn't have been easy, seeing what you did."

Fran's eyes were wide behind her wire-rimmed glasses. "No joke."

"By the time I got to the river, it was clear there was no way he could have survived."

Lise returned to her chair at the round mahogany table. Although Teddy had designated the dining room for the whole house, they didn't use it much. The leaded glass built-ins and heavy molding made the room feel imposing. In the corner, the piano, which Teddy had moved from the parlor, collected dust.

This evening the dining room's cold mood suited Lise's state of mind. The smell of death clung to her nostrils, and she couldn't even think about food. "I don't understand it. Could it have been suicide?"

"He was obsessed with Dyann," Teddy said. "I understood—not condoned, mind you—but understood why he tortured her, and vice versa. But I was startled to think he killed her. It wouldn't surprise me at all if he found he couldn't live with himself."

Fran's chair creaked as she shifted on its seat. "Isn't it kind of a coincidence he died so soon after Dyann? Something is wrong there. Ten to one it was murder."

Fran had an imagination, true, but she also had a point.

Lise caught a whiff of her mental state before she saw her. The scent of frenzy—clove-tinged carnations and burning paper—invaded the dining room's fragrance of lemon wood polish.

"The door was open," Signe said, standing at the dining room's entrance. "I rang the bell, but no one answered."

"I fixed those latches," Fran said. "And locked the front door."

Lise exchanged glances with Fran. Clearly, the house had other ideas.

Teddy stood and rested a hand on the back of one of the heavy oak chairs. "Can we help you?"

Lise didn't miss Signe's glance toward her. She gave Signe a barely perceptible nod. How strange to be the one now granting permission.

"Lise told you about Richard King," Signe said. When Teddy and Fran nodded, she continued. "I believe he was killed."

"Told you," Fran said.

"What makes you say so?" Lise asked.

Teddy pulled out a chair. "Please, sit."

Signe took the seat. She seemed smaller, somehow, than she had this morning. "We towed the car from the river." Her gaze settled on a tarnished teapot on the buffet, and her expression became grim. "It's at the garage being examined, and I wouldn't be surprised if we find the brake line was cut."

"You said you think it's murder," Lise said. "You haven't even checked out the car yet. You must have more reason than that."

Signe pulled her phone from a pocket. The sun had nearly set, and the room was dark enough that Lise briefly considered turning on the light, but whatever it was Signe had to share kept her in her seat.

"His call to 9-1-1." Signe tapped the screen. "Listen."

First came static, then, "You've got to help me. I lost control and my car is in the river. Help!" It was Richard, and the bald terror in his voice clawed at Lise's chest. A calm female voice responded. "Remove your seatbelt and open the window. Leave the car immediately." Again, Richard, this time in a higher register: "I'm trying. I can't!"

Signe shut off her phone.

Lise's heart raced, and she was surprised to find her breath so shallow and quick. Across the table, Fran swallowed. Only Teddy remained calm, but Lise had the feeling Teddy was rarely ruffled—or rarely let herself appear to be.

"He couldn't get his window to open," Signe said. "It was tampered with."

Teddy tapped the table. "The car was submerged. The electrical system might have shorted out."

"Not yet," Signe said. "He would have had a few minutes. Besides, the car wasn't fully underwater. Richard was able to use his phone, remember."

The sickening image flashed through Lise's mind of Richard trapped in his water-filled Camaro, pressed against the driver's side window.

"What does this have to do with us?" Lise asked.

Signe stood, leaving her phone face down on the table. It looked so benign after its horrifying message. She wandered to the window and looked out. It was completely dark now. She could have seen nothing but the black humps of shrubs.

Teddy turned on the table lamps on the buffet. The dining room was now enveloped in a warm glow, and the room's shabbiness receded to show some of its former grandeur. This house had layers upon layers.

Signe faced the room. "I want you to help me."

"Sorry?" Lise said.

"The chief isn't interested in Dyann or Richard. Dyann's death isn't conclusively a homicide, and nothing has been proven about Richard's death. Even if we do discover his car was tampered with, that's one homicide, not two."

Lise raised a hand. "What about a suicide note? Did you find one?"

"Nothing. Nothing in the car, nothing at home."

Fran flipped back her bangs. "They won't let you investigate this. Is that what you're saying?"

"I know it's murder. I can feel it." Signe paced the dining room. "It's wrong. Every hour that goes by, the trail gets weaker."

"But you aren't allowed to investigate," Fran repeated.

Signe let out a sigh of exasperation. "No. I went to him with the evidence Lise had provided—"

Both Teddy and Fran nodded.

"—and minutes later we got the call about Richard. The chief told me to lay off the case. He said I was 'overreaching.'"

"Why us, darling?" Teddy said. That she called Signe "darling" was an indication to Lise that Teddy was warming up to her.

"You're already involved. You care. I don't know why, but you do." She dropped into a chair. Lise was glad, because her pacing was distracting. "You've already talked with some of the people involved. You know what the case is about." She fastened her eyes on Lise, the first time since she'd arrived that she let herself look fully on her, Lise noted. "You found Dyann's body."

"If we agree, are you going to designate us official deputies?" Fran asked with hope in her voice.

"No. But I can help with information from the medical examiner, police records, things like that. It won't be much you'll need to do. Just ask a few questions, double-check a few alibis."

Lise could tell Fran was antsy to say yes. Teddy's expression betrayed no emotion.

"Can you be more specific?" Teddy asked.

"Each of you has relationships with the main suspects," Signe said. "Lise told me about Sylvia Borlotti giving you Dyann's codicil, not to mention lying about Richard's whereabouts."

"But he didn't kill Dyann," Fran pointed out. "Someone else did, probably the same person who killed him."

"Richard still might have done it," Lise said.

"It's true," Signe said. "We still don't know if he's in the clear. But Sylvia Borlotti has opened up to you, and she might have more to say. Fran, you've spent time with Murphy King."

"How do you know?" she asked warily.

"You know him, and you might be able to get more information from him if you know what questions to ask. Richard lost control of his car on Fourteenth Street, not far from where Murphy lives. You, Lise, have a relationship with Blavatsky Manor. There may be more to learn there, too."

If only Signe knew exactly how much, Lise thought.

"I'm not asking you to do anything that would put you at risk. Just ask a few questions, see if you can gather any information we can use."

"I remind you that two people are dead, likely murdered," Teddy said.

"I know that all too well." Signe laid her palms flat on the table. "We'll play this safe. No risks. Just justice. You want to see a murderer caught, right?"

Lise understood Signe's drive for justice and even got some of her hunch about homicide. As she knew, the world was far from purely logical. However, she suspected Signe wanted glory, too, the glory of apprehending a murderer.

"What do you think, Lise?" Teddy asked.

"Yes," Fran said. "We'll do it."

"Honey, let Lise answer. She's the one closest to this, and we need to respect what she wants."

Lise examined Signe. What a change from only a week ago. And how strange to be—sort of—on the same side. Then there were Teddy and Fran, invested in helping her for reasons ranging from curiosity to keeping steady rental income to sisterhood.

"Okay," Lise said. She drew a deep breath. "What's the plan?"

CHAPTER 29

After Signe left, Lise, Teddy, and Fran remained at the table to rough out their plan. Fran would talk with Murphy to determine who had access to Richard's car, besides Richard. Teddy would follow up with Sylvia Borlotti to see if she'd detected any hints that someone was out to kill Richard—or if Sylvia had done him in herself. Lise would check in with the residents of Blavatsky Manor to feel out if they would go so far as to tamper with the Camaro. She doubted it but agreed to ask about their movements this morning and last night.

Eventually, Fran went upstairs and Teddy went to the kitchen, but Lise remained at the table, staring toward the night-black window. There was nothing to see but a wavering reflection of the room.

How had she gotten herself into this mess? It was all her sense of smell. If she hadn't caught hints of L'Heure Bleue in the air that afternoon, she never would have stayed in Astoria. If her magical ability to smell emotion hadn't arisen, she wouldn't have applied for the job at the Lucky Lotus. If none of this had happened, she wouldn't know the smell of death. At least, not yet, and not this way.

"Darling." Teddy stood in the doorway. "Are you all right? You've had yet another shock."

"I don't know."

Teddy rested her hands on her hips. Finally, she said, "Burt is coming over soon. Until then, why don't you keep me company?"

Lise followed her through the pocket doors to the sitting room. She felt good in this room, with its moody colors and thrifted decor. The chandelier twelve feet above them was missing a few crystals, but it was right at home above the brass candlesticks, threadbare upholstery, and fringed textiles. It was as if an impoverished princess with a yen for the Far East had settled here—the opposite of the practical, logical, yet unconventional home she'd been raised in.

Teddy clicked on a table lamp with a red glass globe and faceted dangling crystals. Again, Lise admired her grace and ease.

"Now, darling, tell me what's wrong."

If anyone might understand, it would be Teddy. If Teddy thought she was nuts, she wouldn't show it. "I smell things."

"You say when you found Dyann you smelled something out of place," Teddy said without skipping a beat. "Is that it? What was it?"

"I didn't know. I'd never smelled it before. It wasn't a happy smell. Then, when I saw Richard's car . . ."

"You smelled it again." Teddy stretched her legs forward and pointed her toes, painted, Lise noted, gold. "You like to smell things. I've noticed that. You sniff your tea before you drink it, but calling a scent 'unhappy' is something new to me."

How would Lise's life have been different if Teddy were her mother? Again, she wondered who her birth parents were.

"I smell emotion," she said, then clammed up. She'd already told Fran, but somehow Fran's imagination and neuroses made it easier, as if she'd better understand.

She didn't need to regret it. Teddy was unfazed. "Fascinating, darling. Tell me more."

"It's kind of weird."

"My favorite kind of story."

Charm watched from the chair nearest the hearth. His tail flicked across the velvet seat.

Lise pulled at the fringe of the shawl covering her chair. "This is going to sound strange, but I can smell when someone's sad or afraid or happy, for instance. Sometimes . . . this is really bizarre, but lately, if I focus, I swear I smell things that have happened in the past. The other night in the backyard, for instance, I smelled a garden that doesn't exist anymore."

"Sounds like synesthesia. You sense an emotion, and it translates into a smell. It happens," Teddy said. "I knew a guitarist who had it. He heard music in color."

"Not Jimi Hendrix?" Lise had heard of "Purple Haze."

"Maybe he had it, too."

"My father thinks it's synesthesia, too. But what about past events?" Lise's voice picked up speed. "If I focus, really calm myself, I swear I can smell things that happened decades ago. Just last week, I was walking to work and thinking about Astoria's past. You know, how the town was built on wooden pilings and burned down."

"A few times," Teddy said.

"I could smell the smoke. It was a clear morning, but I could smell smoke. And fear." Lise watched Teddy. Would she think she was unbalanced? "That's not synesthesia. I think it's clairalience—a sort of psychic smell."

"The mind is marvelous, isn't it?" was all Teddy said.

Charm was now asleep, belly to the ceiling, with his paws folded over his eyes, snoring gently.

"In the Lucky Lotus's back room, before I found Dyann, I

smelled something I'd never smelled before. If it was emotion, it was an emotion I'd never encountered. Then, when I saw Richard's car plunge into the river . . . I smelled it again. Death." Her breath caught in her throat. "I can smell death."

If Lise had shocked her, Teddy didn't show it. "Have you encountered death before?"

Her mother had died, but it had been at a hospital, and Lise was too young to visit her. They'd never had pets who'd died—animals hadn't fit into her family's home. When Lise had asked for a kitten, her father told her he'd investigate studies of the costs and benefits of pet ownership. What would Teddy think if she could see the contraption her father had rigged up to do laundry?

"No. Not firsthand."

"What do you smell now?" Teddy's voice was low, soothing.

Lise sat back and calmed her racing mind. The murky scent of the river rode the night air through the open window, carrying with it hints of conifers and dry earth, plus the warm asphalt of the street below. Teddy wasn't wearing perfume right now, but hints of Shalimar clung throughout her rooms in wispy pools. The hearth was still redolent of last spring's fires.

"I smell everything, but nothing in particular," she said finally.

"You must have a keen sense of smell."

"My sense of smell isn't sharper than anyone else's, really. The difference is that I pay attention. I can . . ." She searched for the right word. "I can dissect scent. That, and the emotion thing." As if in response, an aroma of lilies of the valley unfurled from Teddy. Curiosity. "It's like a painter. A painter doesn't have to be able to have x-ray vision to be able to distinguish many shades of blue and create a work of art."

"How do you go through your day with so many odors around you?"

"I tune them out. Everybody does. Think about sound. If you really paid attention right now, you'd hear everything from the traffic down Eighth Street to the refrigerator humming." Lise cocked her head. It was true. The wind, a faraway helicopter, Charm's gentle snoring, the creak of the floorboards above them. "My brain puts them on mute. Sometimes I really need to clear my head, though. The wind off the ocean is good for that."

Lise let out a long breath. To say she was tired was an understatement—she was worn out both physically and emotionally. "I took the job at the Lucky Lotus hoping I could figure out this strange . . . magic. Dyann said she could help, but I think she wanted someone to complain to about Richard more than anything else. That said, I did learn about clairalience." She brushed nonexistent dust from her jeans. "Do you think I'm crazy?"

"No. Not at all. But I do think you're tired, darling." Teddy stacked the teacups and saucers from earlier on a silver tray.

She was. Wrung dry of energy. "Sometimes I wish I couldn't smell anything at all." No death, no emotion that didn't stem from her own drama. "If I were normal, I wouldn't be in this mess."

"Don't say that." Teddy's voice was unusually stern. "You are normal. You're simply not average. You're exceptional. The world is full of gifts we know nothing about. You are blessed with one of them, and it's your job to make the most of it. Like any gift, it comes with a cost, but I believe, Lise, you are more than its match."

The doorbell rang, a tinkling rendition of the Westminster chimes. Hadn't Signe said the doorbell wasn't working?

Teddy rose and kissed the top of Lise's head. "That must be Burt. Would you let him in? Tell him I need a few minutes to get ready."

Lise welcomed Burt into the entry hall. "Come into the kitchen. Teddy will be out soon. Can I get you something to drink?"

"If it's not too much trouble." Burt had made an effort on his appearance tonight. His slacks were pressed, and his steely hair carefully tamed. He held a paper cone of scarlet dahlias with petals that curled at their ends. "Could you put these in water? They reminded me of Teddy."

As she arranged the flowers in a chipped vase Teddy had harvested from an estate sale, the memory of her words soothed Lise. Maybe she wasn't such a freak after all. This was a bump in the road, but, in the end, everything would be all right.

She poured a finger of scotch into a tumbler for Burt. Something about him warmed Lise's heart. He looked so awkward in Teddy's kitchen, rough and masculine, like a broken-off oak bough in a vase of roses, but friendly, too. "You heard about Richard King?"

"Everyone has. I told Teddy I'd take her for a drink at the Elliott after all the drama. You want to come along?"

"No, thank you." Lise sat across from him. Tonight she smelled the scent of a well-used kitchen—coffee grounds and Burt's whiskey—complemented by the sound of crickets through the screen door and, of course, Burt's love for Teddy, which settled comfortably on him like a wreath of high-summer roses.

"I have news you'll want to hear, but let's wait for Teddy." He leaned back and examined Lise. "You look pensive. What's on your mind?"

Lise toyed with the salt and pepper shakers, antique porcelain cylinders edged in gold. “All this death has me thoughtful, I guess. It’s got me thinking about my family and home. Is your family around here?”

Burt continued to look at her, as if to let her know he was on to her game, but he responded to her question, anyway. “I have two sons, and they’ve both settled elsewhere for work, one back East and one in Chicago. How about you?”

“My family’s in Seattle. My mother died. I was adopted into my family as a baby.”

Burt nodded slowly. Lise dropped her hands to her lap and looked at them. Finally, he spoke. “In my experience, the best family is the one you make. This house, for example.”

Lise raised her gaze to his. “What do you mean?”

“You all have formed a nice group. You like each other. I feel comfortable with you, as if I’ve always been here.” His chair creaked as he leaned back, and the house seemed to sigh at his compliment. “Don’t get caught in the trap I did, Lise. Life is shorter than you think.”

Burt had said this very thing when she was considering leaving the Lucky Lotus. “What trap is that?”

“Spending too much time mourning what could have been. You’ve got to stay open to what might be, even if you didn’t expect it and don’t understand it. Teddy, for instance.”

Lise smiled. “Yes?”

“My wife, Barbara, was a wonderful woman and a good mother. We went through a lot, Barbara and I. Practically grew up together. We saw things the same way. I couldn’t have asked for better.”

“And?” From the burgeoning scent of roses, Lise knew what was coming.

“Teddy is like no other woman I’ve met. It’s a cliché to call someone a free spirit, but I’m not a fancy guy, and I can’t think of any other way to describe it.”

"It wasn't always that way," Teddy said. She'd appeared at the kitchen door in a caftan with a tasseled drawstring at the neck and artful gathers down the middle. Instead of looking like an escapee from the 1970s, she looked like an Indian goddess. She moved closer, her earrings swaying against her shoulders. "I spent a lot of time being a woman who could please a particular man. Now I please myself."

"Among others," Burt said.

As he turned toward Teddy, the light hit the side of his face, setting the crags under his eyes into relief. Lise caught a whiff of something interfering with the fragrance of roses. Burt was freshly showered and shaved and had rubbed Bay Rum on his face. She smelled it. But the faraway scent of dissipation, like wet cardboard, that was Burt, too. He was ill.

"The detective stopped by here tonight, Burt," Teddy said.

"She had more questions for you?"

"No, that is, yes. She wants us to help."

"No kidding?"

"Apparently, the police chief is ready to dismiss both Dyann's and Richard's deaths as from natural causes and bad luck. Signe's not convinced, but she can't do anything about it."

His military bearing came to the fore. "She wants you to investigate? Are you sure that's a good idea?"

"Not investigate exactly, but to keep our eyes open for anything that might lead to the case being reopened," Lise said. "I don't want to overstate it."

Burt raised a bushy eyebrow. "An unusual request."

"She knows we're interested. That's all."

He stood, as strong and solid as he always was. Maybe Lise had imagined the smell of illness. She hoped so.

"An unusual request," Burt repeated, "but not unfounded. I told you I had something to share? Apparently, the medical examiner found marks at the base of Dyann King's scalp. Merrill—

that's the police chief—says they bear more investigation, that they might be bug bites."

"But they might not be," Lise said. So, Signe may have been right.

"Good night, Lise," Teddy said. "Don't stay up too late. We have a lot to do tomorrow."

Chapter 30

Fran sat on her bed and opened her laptop. A woman's mournful murmuring floated from the bathroom. Wailing Mary again, thought Fran. Probably stirring up a fuss about the baby shoes.

She popped in her earbuds to the familiar theme song of *The Harry Kellers Show*. There he was, her older brother, smiling and gesturing toward the audience as he rolled his way behind the desk. He never used to wear a suit—he always said suits were too stuffy for him. But he wore them now, probably tailored in Italy and bought at some boutique on Rodeo Drive. You didn't find that kind of pizzazz at the mall.

Despite herself, she enjoyed watching him deliver his opening patter. That smile still made her smile, too. He had always known how to get her to laugh. She sighed. It wasn't his fault, really, that their parents had given up the lock shop and abandoned her for a life near Harry. Harry needed them, they told her, what with his disability. Surely, she understood.

She thought maybe she did understand. He was fine, Fran knew that, but his parents were hers, too, and she knew what worrywarts they were. She might call him tomorrow and tell him she was involved with a murder investigation.

Harry interviewed his guests, a Broadway actress and a thriller author. Harry knew a lot of people. Maybe he could introduce her to someone to give her a leg up on *Dead Bolt*. For the first time, the dread that usually tainted her enjoyment of the show was absent.

Now came the segment she liked best, where Harry talked about his own life, not riffing on politics or current events, but telling stories about life in a small Oregon town. In the past, he'd mentioned to the audience he had a sister, but—thank goodness—he never revealed her name, and her role in his stories was always incidental. She loved his goofy tales of growing up: the time he was pushed off a fishing boat, camping in the rain, getting stuck high up a Douglas fir.

"It's taken me a while to unpack my things from Oregon," he said. It didn't surprise Fran that Harry was slow to move in, even though he'd been in L.A. for at least a year. He never did care much about his surroundings, only about people and his career. She'd refused to visit him, but maybe she'd reconsider. "A few days ago, I opened a box to find this." He held up a dirt-smudged pink notebook with a reflective sticker of a unicorn on it.

Fran's heart stopped. He wouldn't.

He did. Harry opened the notebook, turning the pages back on their spiral rings. A cold sweat covered her face and chest. "It's my sister's diary from middle school. She had a lot more imagination than I'd thought. Listen to this."

No, no, no. He couldn't do this. In private, it would be horrifying enough. But on national TV?

Harry gave a goofy smile, and the audience, primed for something hilarious, laughed. He hadn't even started, and they were laughing at her. " 'Harry is rude!' " He held the diary to the camera. "See that? She'd finished that sentence with a hollow exclamation point. 'He thinks he's perfect in every way. I hate him.' "

"Don't do it, Harry," she pleaded to the screen.

"'If a space ship came and aliens were killing everyone, I'd push him out the door and lock it so he'd be taken into space, and they'd do experiments on him.'"

The audience laughed so hard, some people were bent over, squeezing tears from their eyes.

Harry had ignored her when she was a kid, and he'd amused her, but he'd never been blatantly cruel. Until now.

Before the monologue ended, Fran slammed her laptop shut. Her cheeks burned with humiliation. She was ruined.

She could never show her face in public again.

The next morning, Lise rapped on Fran's door. "Are you in there?"

"I'm not coming out," Fran said.

Lise shook her head at Teddy, standing beside her in the hall. "I don't know what got into her. She was fine last night."

Teddy clutched her kimono closer. "Some kind of bad news, maybe?"

"I can hear you, you know." Fran's voice was muffled from behind her door.

"Then come out and get your flowers," Lise said. Behind her stood an enormous bouquet of garden roses, peonies, and cattleya orchids. The whole hall smelled of a florist's cooler.

"Put them in the trash," Fran said.

Lise looked at Teddy, who raised an eyebrow. She was definitely not throwing away this gorgeous bouquet—not the flowers nor the silver urn they came in. Besides, what about Fran's assignment today? She'd agreed to meet with Murphy.

"What's wrong, Fran?" Lise asked.

"I don't want to talk about it." A pause. "One more thing."

"Yes?"

"Could you bring me some coffee and a peanut butter sandwich? Just leave it outside my door."

Lise peered at Teddy through the profusion of flowers before turning again to Fran's bedroom door. "You've got to tell us what's wrong."

"No, I don't. Go away."

Teddy shrugged, and she and Lise went downstairs to the kitchen. Lise set the flowers on the kitchen table, where they took over the entire space. Teddy refilled her mug from the teapot on the counter. She opened the kitchen window, and Grace jumped to its sill to breathe in the morning air.

"Maybe set those in the dining room?" Teddy said.

Lise did as she was asked and returned with a small card. "The envelope isn't sealed. What do you think?"

Teddy lifted the card from Lise's fingers and opened it. "For Fran's own good," she said, and read aloud, "Thank you for the inspiration. You were a hit! Love, Harry." Frowning, Teddy dropped the card on the table. "Does Fran have a beau? I don't remember seeing a Harry around here."

"Her brother," Lise said. Now it was coming together. "You know how she's so secretive about her family? Her brother is Harry Kellers."

"That's right," Teddy said. "Her famous brother."

"A late night TV host. You must be the last person in town not to know who he is," Lise said.

"I can tell you about Ed Sullivan," she said. "He wasn't the mild-mannered TV host you'd expect."

"Who?" Lise said.

Teddy sat and arranged her kimono around her. With her long white hair in a braid, wisps escaping, she might have stepped from a pre-Raphaelite painting. "Never mind."

Lise pulled her phone from the counter and tapped. "Here it is."

"What happened?" Teddy asked.

"He read an entry from her middle school diary," Lise replied, her eyes still on her phone. "Over ten thousand views, and it isn't even noon."

"Not with darling Fran." Teddy shook her head. "I don't blame her for being upset. That's awfully intrusive, and she's a sensitive girl."

"Fran was supposed to talk to Murphy today." Lise set down her phone. She leaned against the counter and cradled her mug in both hands. "That's the prime piece of information. Murphy may have had keys to his father's Camaro. If so, it would have been a cinch for him to mess with it."

"I don't see him talking to me about the car," Teddy said. "You met him, though, right?"

"Yes, but what excuse do I have for talking with him now? And what am I supposed to say? 'Hey, did you sabotage your dad's car?' "

"You can stop by to offer your condolences." She glanced toward the dining room. "You could even bring him flowers."

The orchids gave off a faint green scent with a touch of honeyed sweetness. "I guess I could. I don't have his phone number, so that's an excuse for showing up unannounced."

Teddy crossed her legs. Her gold toenails should have looked Palm Beach tacky, but on her they were chic. "You do that, and I'll call on Sylvia again. I wonder if I could convince Burt to come along? Sylvia responds well to men."

Lise turned toward the refrigerator and pulled out the bread. "Meanwhile, I guess I'd better make a peanut butter sandwich."

"Better leave her the whole loaf, darling."

CHAPTER 31

One of Teddy's skills was to listen. People thought that to be a seductress you had to look good: keep a curvy yet firm figure, have a dewy complexion, wear clothes that hinted at midnight and rumpled sheets. Teddy knew this was a bare ten percent of the package. A real seductress listened, really listened. Few men could resist a woman who paid them genuine attention. Women appreciated a good listener, too.

That's how she found herself again in Sylvia's apartment that morning with a weak cup of tea and a box of tissues. Given Sylvia's love of men, Teddy had hoped to bring Burt along, but he'd had another doctor's appointment. Teddy was increasingly worried about him.

Sylvia drank bourbon from a tumbler that, judging from the smudged layers of lipstick on its rim, had been in heavy use the night before, as well.

"He told me he loved me," Sylvia said. Daylight and booze-broken sleep had done her no favors.

"Men are complicated creatures," Teddy replied. This, in fact, was false. In her experience, men were quite straightforward—more so than women. Both what they said and didn't say might as well be written in neon.

"He told me he loved me, but all he could talk about was

Dyann. Dyann this, Dyann that. I'd order a poached egg, and he'd tell me Dyann liked hers scrambled. I'd change the sheets to a nice white set, and he'd say Dyann slept in lavender sheets."

Teddy wasn't surprised about the white sheets. Only Sylvia's red sateen robe, mussed brunette bob, and circles under her eyes gave color to the room. "So frustrating."

"Yes." Sylvia nodded, then shook her head. She poured another slug of bourbon. "I was angry at him, and I let him know it. But I never thought he'd kill himself."

Teddy kept her tone gentle. "You think that was it? Suicide?"

"What else would it be?" Sylvia leaned over to place her tumbler on a coaster and missed the first time. "He was distraught. His ex dies, then I tell him to go to hell. He couldn't take it." At this, she burst into tears. "I have nothing left of him."

Poor girl. Teddy handed her the box of tissues. She gave Sylvia a moment to blow her nose before saying, "There was talk that Richard might have been murdered, that someone tampered with his car."

Sylvia's voice went from mournful to dismissive in a second. She flipped her wrist in a "pshaw" gesture. "If anyone was going to kill Richard, it would be Dyann. Obviously, she didn't do it."

"Some people might have thought you'd kill him. You certainly had grounds to."

Sylvia's response to this was a high-pitched laugh. Her roller-coaster show of emotion put *What Ever Happened to Baby Jane* to shame. "I'm not going to lie. I was mad. I thought about it. A night last week he was here, snoring in bed. I looked at my pillow, looked at his face, thought about how easy it would be . . . but he wasn't worth the trouble." Tears again. She lifted the whiskey bottle and, finding it empty, tossed it aside. "Those two deserved each other. Now they'll be together forever."

Teddy braced herself for another volley of noisy tears, but Sylvia laid her head back on the armchair and quietly stared toward the river. Teddy examined her. Sylvia seemed more the type for an impulsive display of emotion than something calculated. If she were going to kill Richard, it would either be the smothering method she'd mentioned or in public with a few choice insults and a chair to the back of his head.

"Do you know much about cars?" Teddy asked.

Sylvia lifted her head. "Do I know what?"

"Never mind, darling." Teddy kept her voice gentle. "You are a passionate, talented woman. Today is painful, but life is full of surprises, and some of them are quite good. I understand Marvin Sholes was quite taken with your voice audition."

Sylvia looked at Teddy like she was speaking Swahili. Her eyes couldn't quite focus.

"I'll leave you to rest," Teddy said. Her visit had convinced her that Sylvia couldn't have sabotaged Richard's car. Besides, why would she? She had no motive other than hurt, and lovers had been hurting each other for millennia.

Sylvia's phone chimed with a message. She reached for it, then lay back again. "Would you get that? I can't deal right now."

Teddy handed Sylvia her phone, but Sylvia pushed it away. "You read it. Tell me what it says."

"It's private, darling."

"Read it. I have nothing to hide." She pulled Teddy's hand holding the phone to her face, and its screened unlocked. She collapsed again on the chair.

"An email," Teddy said. She pulled a pair of mother-of-pearl reading glasses from her embroidered tote. "From Cox and Morningsun, the law offices. Are you sure you want me to read this to you?" Teddy looked up. "Sylvia?"

Sylvia was asleep. At last the poor girl looked at peace. She might as well enjoy some rest now, because she'd have a sonofabitch of a hangover when she awoke.

Teddy adjusted her glasses and read. Her jaw dropped, and she glanced again at Sylvia.

Richard had amended his will immediately after Dyann had changed hers, and Cox and Morningsun had recorded it. He had divided his estate in two parts: half to his son, Murphy, and the rest to Sylvia.

As Lise drove to Blavatsky Manor that morning, she pondered the possibility that its residents had anything to do with Richard's death. Motive was easy. Richard had threatened to sue them, and they were adamant their pasts not be exposed. Means wasn't too hard, either. Bitsy was presumably handy with cars, and, as long as his lumbago wasn't acting up, he could have tampered with the Camaro.

That said, she couldn't see it. Stealing a will was one thing, but murder was quite another. Besides that, the residents of Blavatsky Manor wanted to exist under the radar, not find themselves on the witness stand. They'd built too valuable a community to risk losing it.

Maxine met Lise in the manor's lobby, where Maxine gestured for her to sit. Through the window, Lise saw Bea sleeping in an easy chair in the sun, her walker at her side. "It's all so unreal." Maxine said. "One day Richard King is threatening to sue, and the next he's dead."

Lise winced at the memory of the stench of death that permeated the beautiful late summer afternoon.

"Have you heard anything more from the detective?"

"A little bit." Lise filled her in on what Signe had told them about Richard's death. "The detective in charge, Signe, wants to follow up the deaths, but her chief is slow-walking it."

"Why is that?"

Lise shook her head. "For one, the medical examiner found no proof that Dyann was poisoned, although I've heard secondhand that they did find what might be needle marks."

"Needle marks!"

"Or bug bites. Or something. But it does make it more likely she was poisoned. The trouble is that they still haven't identified a poison."

"What about the slashed tires and the note? Anything new there?"

"I don't know. I wonder . . ."

"Wonder what?"

"What if Richard slashed her tires, but someone else killed her?"

"There might be a third party, you're saying." Maxine leaned back and nodded slowly. "Not good news. Bad news."

"Yes?"

"For one, we're not completely in the clear about the law office." Maxine let out a long breath. "There weren't so damned many cameras in our day."

"What? We were filmed?" For a bunch of ex-criminals, they had certainly soured that caper.

"Once the police determine Dyann was poisoned—and it sounds like it's only a matter of time that they do—they'll be at our doorstep again," Maxine said.

"The detective thinks Richard's death was intentional, that someone cut his brake line."

Maxine groaned. She took the chair next to Lise's. "That's what I was afraid of. What if they decide we had something to do with it? Or what about the son? What if he wants to carry out his father's lawsuit?"

Lise doubted Murphy cared enough to sue. "Do you have alibis for last night?"

"Yes—"

"Then you don't have to worry about it."

"—and no. We were in all night. All of us. Cook made beef bourguignon, and a plate of that is better than taking a valium. We weren't going anywhere, but all we have is each other's word."

"You have cameras on the building's perimeter," Lise said. "Surely, those would have caught anyone coming or going."

Maxine sat straighter at this revelation, then sank again. "It erases every twenty-four hours." She sighed. "The residents aren't taking it well. Jean was up all night long. I found her this morning, collapsed over a table in the dining room with a list next to her titled 'prison essentials.' Bitsy is talking about taking to the road, which is problematic."

"How's that?"

"For one, the only vehicle we have is the van, and we need it here. Besides that, he gets forgetful. I could just see him pulling into a roadside motel in Nebraska and completely neglecting to take his heart pills."

Lise glanced toward the patio, where Bea still dozed. "How about your mom?"

"We've all been after her, asking if she had premonitions about the situation, but she won't say a word." Maxine also looked toward her mother, who now swatted away a bumblebee. "I wouldn't say she's serene. Something is definitely bothering her, but she's not frantic, either. That's something, I suppose."

"I believe you," Lise said. "I know you had nothing to do with Richard's accident." She'd swear so to Signe. Signe could cross the residents of Blavatsky Manor off of her list.

Maxine reached over and placed her hand on Lise's. "Thank you. That means a lot. It might not hold up in court, but I appreciate it." She rose and smoothed the trousers of her pale green pantsuit. "Enough of that. Let's get to work."

Lise stood, too. "What's on the agenda today?"

"The residents are worked up. Let's do what we can do to

calm them." Maxine started toward the dining room. "I'll meet with Cook, see if we can get a carb-heavy lunch on the menu. You sort through the DVDs and find some comforting movies."

While Maxine was in the kitchen, Lise went to the corner of the dining room, where two couches and a large TV were set up next to a bookcase of DVDs. She pondered the shelf a moment, then pulled out the BBC *Pride and Prejudice* collection, a boxed set of *The Andy Griffith Show*, and a couple of romantic comedies featuring maids, called-off weddings, and surprise inheritances.

Maxine arrived and sorted through her choices. "No, no, and no."

"What's wrong with them?" Lise asked.

"The sheriff's department in *The Andy Griffith Show*. Really? Remember, this crowd knows jails, and they've never seen a cell fitted up like Otis's drunk tank." She made a dismissive noise and went to the shelf. She quickly selected a handful of discs. "Here we go. Set these by the TV, will you?"

Lise glanced at the titles. *Ocean's Eleven*, *The Italian Job*, and *To Catch a Thief*. All movies about heists.

"What?" Maxine said. "The folks here find it relaxing to watch stories about crime. Especially if they have happy endings." She sank to one of the sofas and sighed. "I wish there was something we could do. It's torture to feel so helpless, to sit back and wait for the police to arrive. If only we could find the real murderer. Now that Richard King is out of the way, the son is the logical suspect."

"He definitely stands to gain the most."

Maxine stood suddenly. "Hold tight." She disappeared from the dining room.

While she was gone, Johnny wandered in and walked purposefully, if slowly, into the kitchen. Lise heard him trying to wheedle a cocktail from the cook. "This could be my last drink before prison," he pleaded. "The police are going to stick us with murder. Couldn't you make me something easy? A gin and tonic?"

A moment later, Maxine returned with the file they'd erroneously stolen from Cox and Morningsun. "Remember this?"

"Murphy's file from the law office," Lise said.

"I nearly put it through the shredder. I figured we had the information we needed, and I didn't want to get caught with it." Maxine flipped the file open and slid on reading glasses. "Looks like a few different documents." She set aside one stapled bundle. "Murphy's will."

Lise picked it up and flipped through the pages. "His estate, such as it is, goes to his mother. If she predeceases him"—she turned the page—"everything goes to the reptile sanctuary." Lise looked up. "Not much of a surprise there."

"But it makes the reptile sanctuary a possible suspect," Maxine said.

"Then why were Murphy's parents killed and not him?"

"Not him first," Maxine emphasized. "With his parents dead, Murphy has real money."

"I don't see it." Lise shook her head. "Kill two people—with Murphy next up—for money? It would be screamingly obvious. Plus, I've talked with the man who runs the refuge. As far as I can tell, he's not short of cash."

Maxine turned her attention to the remaining document. "Look here. Notes on his mother's and father's wills with references to their files." Files Arthur and Gerald had failed to collect. "Could this be useful somehow? Just a few bullet points, not the actual documents. From his mother's estate, Murphy would be paid a regular income from a trust, with the trust under Richard King's control until Murphy reaches twenty-one years of age, at which point he inherits it all." She slipped off her glasses and used them to gesture. "We knew that. This was before the codicil, of course." Again, on with the glasses. "As for his father's estate, Murphy inherits half plus the car lot." Maxine looked up. "Huh. This is a new change. Just last week."

Lise did mental calculations and came up with a figure large enough to grant Murphy the freedom to do little more with the rest of his life than tend his snake.

"You tell me," Maxine said. "Is that a motive for murder, or what?"

Behind Maxine, Johnny emerged from the kitchen holding a martini glass and looking pleased with himself.

Maxine focused on Lise. "We've worked hard to make Blavatsky Manor a place where we can live peacefully. We don't need the police or anyone else disturbing our lives. Isn't there something we can do to make this all go away?"

After her shift at Blavatsky Manor, Lise parked in Dyann's—now Murphy's—driveway and pulled Fran's bouquet from the passenger side door. She re-fluffed the flowers and made her way around the house's side to Murphy's apartment and knocked on the door. No response. As she waited, she mentally rehearsed her lines.

Shifting the bouquet to her other hip, she knocked again, and this time Murphy responded from the house's front porch. "What do you want?"

Lise returned to the front of the house. "I heard about your father. I'm so sorry."

"Are those for me?" Murphy's BB-sized eyes were wide. A second later, they disappeared into his cheeks again.

"Yes. May I come in?"

He hesitated at the door, then moved aside. "Okay. Watch out for Tangie."

"For what?"

"My python. I just moved in up here, and she got loose when I was fixing her tank. I've got to find her before she gets into trouble."

The snake. Now she remembered. Lise set the vase on a side table and scanned the room. "Where is she?"

"I don't know. That's the problem. Snakes like to hide. She might be in a piece of furniture or curled up in a corner. I covered the heating grate and shut the bedroom doors. She's got to be out here somewhere."

Lise had never had a fear of snakes—at least, she didn't think so; she hadn't been around enough of them to be sure—but she did not like the idea of a giant orange snake slithering loose.

She steadied her breath. "Like I said, I'm so sorry about your father. Losing both your parents, and within a week of each other, must be really hard."

"Yeah," Murphy replied, his expression bland.

He wasn't distraught in the least. "Do you have any idea of what happened?"

"He crashed into the river and drowned." Murphy pulled the cushions from the couch. No snake.

"That's what the papers say," Lise said, only half paying attention. Where was that snake? "Do the police think it was an accident?"

"I don't know. How's Fran? You live with her, right?"

Lise drew her attention back to Murphy. "Sure. She's fine, I guess."

"I saw her brother talking about her last night on his show. I think Fran is nice. You can tell her I said so."

Both of his parents just died, and he was talking about TV? "Murphy, where were you when your father got in his car yesterday? He lost control of his car just a few blocks away. Was he here?"

"Yeah. I was using the Camaro while he worked on Mom's Mercedes. I took it to the refuge. He brought back Mom's car yesterday around noon and picked up his."

Murphy's expression was hard to read. Sure, he might have been overlooked as a child while his parents reenacted *The War of the Roses*, but he'd lived in his mother's basement apartment. Wouldn't he at least have some kind of feeling about her?

Murphy froze and listened. Then, in a surprisingly nimble move, he darted toward the armchair and grabbed a yard-long stick with a pincers at its end. "Got you!" He pulled back the chair's cushion and jammed the stick behind it. When he removed it, holding on with both hands, a large orange snake dangled from its end. "Tangie, you stinker, you're going back in the tank." The snake drooped on the stick, its tongue flickering. Five feet of snake muscle twisted and waved. Murphy turned to face Lise. "Are you scared?"

"Why do you ask?"

"Some people are afraid of snakes." Tangerine Dream lifted her head and stared at Lise. Her eyes were almost as beady as Murphy's.

"I like cats better," was all Lise said.

Murphy laughed and started down the hall toward Dyann's office. Lise followed at a respectful distance. He lifted the lid off a large aquarium, and the snake dropped to its bottom and compacted itself under a ledge until only a coil of its mottled orange scales showed.

With the snake found, Murphy relaxed. He shut the door to the snake's den and returned to the living room. He wasn't going to ask her to sit—he wasn't the type to think of it—so she helped herself to a place on the sofa while he plopped into a blue plush recliner that had been Dyann's, judging from the crystal and the book on reincarnation next to it. "Last night Harry Kellers read from Fran's diary from when she was a kid. Did you see it? It was hilarious." At this, he smiled and his cheeks once again obscured his eyes. "Fran is cool."

Never mind about Fran. "So, you're saying you had the Camaro, then your dad picked it up, and that's when it sped down the hill into the river."

Murphy was expressionless again. "Yeah, I guess so. Why do you care, anyway?"

Lise looked at the grade school photos of Murphy on the mantel, then at the real thing, sitting in the recliner. Murphy leaned back, and the footstool kicked up.

"Fran wants to know," she said finally.

"She does?"

What the hell. It wasn't like Fran planned on leaving her room anytime soon. What she didn't know couldn't hurt her. "Fran's concerned someone might have tampered with the car, and that you won't have an alibi."

"She's worried about me?" Murphy looked so surprised that for a moment Lise thought he might be on to her.

She kept a straight face. "That's what she said."

"I didn't do anything."

"Sure, but can you prove it? I mean, if the police came and asked, would you be able to say where you were and what you were doing?"

"I told you. I went to the reptile refuge." He took the crystal from the side table and rolled it in a palm. "I always do that on Tuesdays. It's my day. If you don't believe me, you can ask Ornette." He set the crystal aside and smiled. "I'll be taking care of the entire refuge tomorrow. Ornette's going out of town and left me in charge."

"The police would want to know if you had any reason to hurt your father. If you had some kind of fight with him." Say, if he were concerned that Richard killed his mother, for instance.

Murphy stared at her, his mouth slightly agape. "No."

"Your mom and dad fought a lot."

"So what? Mom's dead."

Lise had no ready response. She'd discovered he'd had the

opportunity to tamper with the car. That was valuable information. He'd apparently driven the Camaro to the reptile refuge and back again without a problem. The next morning, Richard had dropped off Dyann's car for Murphy, gotten into the Camaro, and plunged to his death.

Even if Signe could fingerprint the Camaro, Murphy would be all over it. Fran's fingerprints, too, she reflected, thanks to their drive to the beach. They needed better evidence.

Blank-faced, Murphy sat in the recliner as if he were watching a particularly dull TV show. Maybe this was how psychopaths acted. They killed and felt no emotion. Or, a more generous take, this was how the emotionally wounded acted. Their parents died, and they were in shock.

When her own mother had died, Lise had responded bizarrely, too, but there had been no doubt about her heartbreak. This was according to her father, who had taken her and Albert to a family therapist. To a scientist like her father, surely a therapist—to him, a technician of emotions—could fix whatever ills they had. Lise's chief grief symptom was that she wouldn't sleep. She had a fear that if she did, she would miss her mother's return. Lise didn't remember any of this, but she recalled the wisps of perfume she began to smell when no one else was around. She now recognized that scent as L'Heure Bleue.

Lise didn't exactly know the contents of Richard's will, just bullet points from Murphy's file, but chances were that Murphy was now a very rich man. Somehow, she doubted he gave a damn.

"Murphy," Lise said, "did your father kill your mother?"

Murphy stared at her a moment, his eyes practically hidden in his plump cheeks, his lips parted. Then he burst into laughter. When he could finally speak, his face had reddened in splotches. "Did Dad kill Mom? You're hilarious. Fran asked me that, too."

She willed the anger rising in her to calm. He had more to say. She'd wait him out. "No, he didn't kill her, but he thought someone else did. He told me he'd find out who killed her if it was the last thing he did."

Murphy's phone rang from his pocket. He withdrew it and glanced at the screen. "Ornette. I need to take this."

"I'll see myself out."

As she returned home, her visit with Murphy replayed in her mind. He was either completely shut down emotionally or incapable of feeling. Either way, it was the affect of a murderer.

CHAPTER 32

Fran's phone rang. Again. She rolled over and pulled the sheet over her head.

She'd drawn her curtains tight, and only a slice of sunlight lay across her bedroom floor. Teddy had come upstairs twice to try to persuade her to come downstairs, but there was no way Fran was going to leave her room, not for Teddy, not for work, not for anything. As long as someone brought the occasional sandwich, she was staying put. The humiliation from showing her face in public would stop her heart cold.

Fran's phone rang yet again. She relented and glanced at her phone's screen. She'd had a number of calls she'd ignored from her parents and one from her brother Harry, plus a volley of texts. No doubt they begged her forgiveness—or made excuses.

This call was the third from Murphy. The other two he'd ended when she hadn't answered, but this time he left a voicemail. What did he want from her, anyway? Just because they'd hung out one afternoon didn't make them best friends. She didn't have time for his boo-hooing about his parents or more talk about his freaky snake. Worse, he might be calling to make fun of her.

She flopped over in her bed. She was too worked up even to focus on *Dead Bolt*. After last night, she might never write again. Her life was over.

While she waited for night to fall, she pulled to her lap the envelope of history about Corrie House. With a closer examination, maybe she'd be able to figure out who SVC was.

The envelope held half a dozen or so photocopied sheets. She spread them on the bed. Fran closed her eyes and imagined the big old house at the turn of the last century. It would have been full of dark furniture, gaslight fixtures, parlor palms in brass pots, and paintings—regular ones, not amateur portraits of sad-looking ladies. All the locks would have worked great. One crusty old ship's captain had lived here by himself, probably reading his Bible, while a mantel clock *tick-tick-tick*ed behind him.

In the darkness, her door creaked open. No one was there. This had already happened once today, even though she'd closed and locked it. She heard faraway noises of a baby gurgling.

"Stop it," Fran said firmly. "I'm not leaving my room, and that's final." She closed the door and double-checked its latch.

Back to the papers. Ayla's obituary was not among them. What had happened with her? Had she married and died in childbirth? Those days, it happened a lot. The moaning, the baby's crying, the scary energy in the library—Ayla's death might have been more nefarious than that.

With a creak, the bedroom door opened again, this time widely, letting in sunlight from the library's windows across the hall. Someone had opened its door, too, and Fran's room's temperature dropped several degrees. Fran's neck tingled as she got up to slam shut the library door. She re-closed her own door and moved a chair in front of it.

As Margie had it, Corrie House had been considered haunted forever. Fran wondered what that was about and what the baby shoes had to do with it. Despite Fran's ability—curse?—of hearing ghosts speak, she'd rarely tried talking to one.

She cleared her throat. "Ayla?" Her voice was wobbly. "Is that you I hear at night?"

Her bedroom door remained closed, but the library door across the hall must have drifted open again because it slammed shut. A chill settled over her. Yes, Fran decided. Ayla had indeed died here, and she'd never left.

Her phone chimed again with a text, and she turned it off.

Chapter 33

Lise took the stack of dirty plates to the kitchen sink. Teddy had made ratatouille, and Lise, Burt, and she had shared it at the kitchen table. "We need one more piece of solid evidence to prove Dyann's and possibly Richard's murders," Lise said. "That's all. Everything else lines up."

"You mean the motive lines up," Burt said.

He folded his napkin so the edges matched perfectly and set it aside. Military habits must die hard. To Lise, tonight seemed almost like old times, but not quite. Burt's face was paler than usual, and she didn't miss the concern in Teddy's eyes.

"Definitely the motive," Lise said. That was simple: money. Murphy stood to gain a lot from his parents' deaths. "But also opportunity. Murphy had Richard's Camaro all night, and he was definitely near the Lucky Lotus the night Dyann died. The brewery is only a few blocks away."

"'Means' is the last factor, right?" Teddy said. "Fran would love this discussion."

True. Fran would be sorry she missed this, Lise reflected. But she still refused to come downstairs. Lise had left a tray outside her door with jars of peanut butter and jelly and the rest of the loaf of bread.

"Murphy probably knows a lot about cars," Lise said. "He grew up working on his dad's car lot."

"That covers tinkering with the Camaro. But what about Dyann's death?" Teddy said.

"Poison. Some kind of poison, injected." Lise returned to her place at the kitchen table. Teddy had turned off the overhead light in favor of a small lamp and a candle, and the soft light was comforting. "The problem is that the medical examiner can't figure out what the poison is."

"That would be your last piece of evidence, then," Burt said.

"The poison." Teddy placed her hand on his forearm. "We need to find a poison so that Dyann can be tested specifically for it. Maybe a hypodermic needle, too. Is that right?"

"It seems backward, but I'm not sure how else to make a direct link between Murphy and his mother's death," Lise said. "But, yes, if Murphy is the killer, he would have the poison."

"Unless he tossed it," Burt said. "That's what a smart person would do."

Lise wasn't sure if Murphy qualified as a smart person. Here again, Fran would be the best judge. Lise raised her gaze to the ceiling. If only she would come out.

"The next logical step, then, is to search Murphy's house," Teddy said. "The police could get a search warrant."

"Except that Signe's boss has shut down the investigation," Lise said.

"What Signe doesn't know won't hurt her," Burt pointed out. If his smile was an indication, he was enjoying himself.

"Burt, you're suggesting we break in?" Teddy said.

"Not a break-in. Not exactly. We get him to let us in."

"Let us in so we can search his house." Teddy raised an eyebrow. "Really?"

"We might be city inspectors or something like that."

"What if he's not home?" Lise asked.

"Think about it," Burt said. "You see people crawling all over houses all the time. Gardeners, cable installers, you name it. There's always a way."

"Honey, that's awfully risky," Teddy said.

A waft of late summer roses drifted in with the word *honey*. Love. "Too bad Fran has shut herself away. Murphy would let her in, no problem."

"Plus, she knows her way around locks," Teddy said.

"Enough of this 'what if,'" Burt said. "Someone has killed two people, and all signs point to Murphy. Right?"

Lise and Teddy looked at each other. Teddy said, "Okay."

"One of them was likely poisoned, and we don't know what that poison is. Correct?"

"Yes," Lise said.

"To catch a murderer, we need to find that poison and match it to the victim. It's a straightforward task."

It probably did sound straightforward to someone who had made his living doing something as hairy as piloting ships through stormy seas. To Lise, it sounded foolhardy. "I couldn't do it. Murphy knows me, plus the neighbors might have seen me."

"I could help," Teddy said. "I have the advantage of being older. No one notices an elderly lady."

In Lise's opinion, Teddy was very noticeable. "Are you sure you want to risk it? You've already been so much help with Sylvia Borlotti."

Teddy rested her forearms on the table and leaned forward. "Darling, I'm having more fun than I have since I smuggled hashish across the Turkish border in my bra." Then, to Burt, "That was nearly sixty years ago. I'm not so foolish now."

Burt smiled. "I would have liked to see that. In any case, I'll help."

"No," Teddy said firmly. "You will not." Their glance

communicated something further between them not meant for Lise.

"Somehow," Lise said, "we figure out how to get in the house. We look for a poison. We take it to Signe to test against Dyann."

"We need more than a plan. We need people," Teddy said. "Lise, you've been to Murphy's place twice, so you're out. It's a nice idea, I just don't see us pulling it off. We don't have the resources."

Lise picked up her phone. "I think I know who can help."

At the sound of Lise's feet on the stairs, Fran lifted her head from the brass grate set into the bathroom floor and hurried across the hall to her bedroom. The house was so old that it didn't have heating ducts—heat simply rose from the furnace in the basement up through grates punched into the floors. With her ear to the grate in the bathroom, conversation in the kitchen was as clear as if they'd held a confab in the bathtub.

She closed her bedroom door behind her. Once again, her phone lay on the coverlet. Honestly, this house was so bossy. She'd hidden the phone out of sight on her dresser three times already tonight, but when she'd turned her head the phone had reappeared on her bed.

"Fran?" Lise called from the hall.

"I'm asleep," she said.

"Ha, ha." A pause. "I know you're embarrassed, but we're all friends here. You can come out anytime."

Fran remained silent.

"We're planning something big. Don't you want to hear about it?"

Again, she didn't respond. Besides, thanks to the bathroom grate, she was up to date.

The hall floor creaked as Lise stepped back. Finally. "Sleep well. I hope in the morning you're ready to join the world."

The sound of Lise's door closing told Fran she was settling in for the night. As she should. It was getting late. Burt had left and Teddy would soon be coming upstairs to brush her teeth. In half an hour, they'd all be asleep.

Maybe Lise was right. Harry should have never read from her diary, but what he'd made public wasn't super incriminating. He'd simply read that she detested him. Was that so bad? Practically every kid detests their older brother.

She glanced at her laptop. She'd do it. She'd see what Harry had planned for tonight. It had better be a public apology. Flowers were not enough.

As Fran had predicted, Corrie House was soon silent. While she waited for *The Harry Kellers Show*, she scrolled through the "recent calls" log on her phone, but there was no way she'd listen to the messages. She had calls from her mom, Margie at the bookstore, and a few from Murphy, plus his voicemail. Nothing new from Harry. She tossed the phone on the nightstand.

Really, it could be worse, she told herself. Some people might even say Harry was making fun of himself. All he had to do was tell the audience that the diary entry was a fake. That's all. Surely, her parents had chastised him. He knew better. Otherwise, why would he have sent flowers? He'd laugh at last night's show and say it was all a joke.

On this hopeful note, Fran popped in her earbuds and opened her laptop. At last *The Harry Kellers Show* was on.

First, the opening with his cheesy band. Then seemingly interminable interviews with some old starlet and a guy who wrote a book about the history of curtains, like anyone would ever want to read that.

However, Harry was funny and engaging, and she found herself beginning to relax. He had always been a decent older brother. He used to pick her up sometimes from middle school when he was in high school, and her friends would run to the parking lot to say hi to him. She'd roll down the window and wave good-bye, like a dairy princess on the Cattlemen's Association parade float.

Now they were at the end of the show, the part where Harry talked about his life. She turned up the volume.

"Last night I read from my sister's middle school diary," Harry said. He was seated behind his desk with a fake skyline behind him. The studio's light blurred to black, except for an ivory nimbus around him. "It was a hit. My team says we've never had so many comments, even when we had the singing geese." The audience laughed.

Please say it was all phony, Fran willed him. *Please, please, please.*

"So we're making 'My Sister's Diary' a regular feature." Harry drew her diary from a drawer. "You're going to love today's entry. 'My list of secret boyfriends.' " And he read.

" 'After fifth period I saw Mark Carruthers in the hall!' She drew three hearts here." He showed the audience the page and the hearts in pink felt-tip marker before flipping the notebook back to continue reading. " 'I put another checkmark on my notebook. It's the sixty-fourth time I've seen him this year. (It might be sixty-five, but I can't tell if that mark is one I made when I saw him or is from when my pen broke.)' "

Hot tears stung Fran's eyes, and her throat felt thick.

The audience roared. Harry held up a palm to indicate he wasn't finished.

" 'I feel sure we met in another life. Maybe he was a cowboy and I was a pioneer lady alone on the prairie, and he saved me when my cabin was on fire. Or, I was in a dungeon, chained to the wall. He busted in and smashed my chains and took me to his castle.' " Harry lifted his eyebrows in a sweet but mocking way. " 'His horse really liked me. His name was Precious Fairy.' " He paused for dramatic effect, and laughter rolled through the audience.

Fran wiped away the tears. She had been completely, utterly betrayed. She shut her laptop.

That was it. There was no way she could show her face in this town again. She didn't know where she'd go, but it would be somewhere no one knew her.

First thing in the morning, she would be out of here.

CHAPTER 34

Teddy closed the car door behind her and glanced up the walk. Lise had told her Blavatsky Manor was—what did she call it?—"unusual," but from here, in the morning light, it certainly looked conventional: a lovely, large midcentury home with Asian touches; lots of windows; tidy landscaping; and a neat silver-tone placard reading BLAVATSKY MANOR. NO SOLICITORS.

Teddy mounted the stairs, taking note of the ramp winding the longer but safer route. At the front door, she wasn't quite sure what to do. Should she knock, as if this were a private home, or was it more like an institution where you walked right in?

The decision was made for Teddy when the door opened. A woman surely too young to be a resident welcomed her, dressed in a lavender suit with a scalloped lapel Teddy pegged as 1990s Bill Blass. It had been popular in the ladies-who-lunch set when she'd first met Bernard.

"Welcome," the woman said. "You must be Teddy. I'm Maxine. Come in."

Teddy entered a lobby with a terra-cotta tile entrance and the wide, cool feel of a 1960s spread in *Architectural Digest*. Floor-to-ceiling windows at the lobby's rear showed a sun-dappled patio where residents might linger with coffee or a book, but no one was there. Everyone was right here, at least a dozen of them, watching her.

"Lise has been a godsend," Maxine said, as if Teddy were Lise's mother. "We've been so pleased to have her."

"She's a good housemate, too," Teddy said. "How about you? Are you ready?"

All their preparation had been done by phone. She, Lise, and Burt had stayed up late planning their approach. Once they had an idea of the direction the plan was taking, the residents of Blavatsky Manor went into action. In the end, the plan belonged more to them than to Lise, Teddy, and Burt.

"I don't have a good feeling about this," a white-haired woman holding a walker said. The woman looked to be a decade or so older than Teddy, and her years showed in the furrows in her cheeks and watery eyes. Teddy was reminded of the advantages of her posh former life, even if the facials and personal training sessions had cost her in other ways. This woman, on the other hand, had the air of having maximized every one of her rotations around the sun. She had stories to tell.

To Teddy's surprise, Maxine looked concerned. "What do you see, Mom?"

"It's not what I see, but what I feel. It feels . . . confusing." She drew her eyebrows together. "Useless, and"—she winced—"terrifying."

"But we should go ahead?" Maxine pressed.

Teddy watched intently.

Bea shrugged. "We'll be all right. I think so, anyway. Maybe?"

Maxine faced Teddy. "I'll take that as a go. Mother can get confused. If she were serious, we'd know it." Then, to the others, "Arthur, Bitsy, Kid, come into my office with Teddy. The rest of you can get back to your business. I'll fill you in later."

Teddy followed Maxine and the others into a roomy office

off the lobby. The man called Arthur wore a suit and a lanyard with credentials that looked impressively real, although Teddy knew they couldn't be. The Kid's eyes darted around the room, and he couldn't seem to settle. The other man jingled keys in his pocket. Maxine handed Teddy a clipboard and a lanyard.

They were really going to do it. Teddy wished Burt could see this.

"Have a seat," Maxine said. "We'll run through the plan once again. Then it's go time."

At Corrie House, Lise paced a loop through the entry hall, into the dining room and around the table, to the kitchen, where she glanced out the window, then back to the entry hall.

Teddy should be at Blavatsky Manor by now, she figured. It would be a while before they arrived at Dyann's—now Murphy's—house, and a while longer still before she'd know if they'd found anything.

All morning long, thumps and sounds of things being dragged had come from Fran's room. At Fran's request, Lise had left coffee and a bowl of cereal outside her door, but she continued to refuse to come out.

Again, Lise climbed the stairs. "Fran? Are you sure you don't want to know what's happening?"

"I don't want to talk to anyone." Fran's door clicked open by itself, and Fran leapt off the bed to slam it shut with a "*Stop it!*"

What Teddy and the others were doing would be risky only if Murphy found them out. He might call the police, which would be awkward, but not fatal. However, he was supposed to be at the reptile refuge all day. She had to hope everything would go smoothly.

Remembering the failed attempt to pinch Dyann's will, she wasn't completely confident. Still, they'd run through the plan several times last night, and the residents of Blavatsky Manor had seemed surprisingly excited. Maxine had even remarked she hadn't seen them this upbeat since they plotted the capture of a neighborhood porch pirate, a caper involving a cop uniform and an exploding package.

Down the stairs Lise went, to the entry hall, where Charm and Grace napped on Teddy's yoga mat, interlocked like a yin-yang symbol, to the dining room, to the kitchen.

Soon she'd know more. Soon.

Fran had just about everything packed. A suitcase and three boxes—snuck from the basement when everyone was asleep—ranged around her, each crammed with her things. Her laptop and draft of *Dead Bolt* were in the Margie's Books tote bag Margie had given her when she'd made her six-month anniversary at the bookstore. She left the envelope with the house history on her nightstand.

All that remained was to pack up her few things in the bathroom and kitchen, but with Lise constantly knocking on her door and pacing through the house, she was stuck. Lise was circling the mansion like a shark that had to keep swimming or die.

Fran sat on the stripped bed, and her hand knocked against her phone. There it was again. At the same time, the door snicked open, and a cold breeze drifted from the library across the hall.

"Leave me alone," she said through clenched teeth.

She pushed the door closed and shoved her phone into a drawer. There were a lot of things she'd miss about Corrie House, but the domineering ghosts weren't among them.

She smoothed her hand over the mattress ticking. Yes, she would miss certain things. And people. Lise, for all her perfume bottles and sniffing everything, was okay. Teddy was nice, too, and surprisingly easy to talk to for someone so old. You'd think you'd have to be polite and bland with her because you'd have nothing in common, then she'd come out with some crazy story about getting stuck on a tour bus in the middle of the night in Kansas with a dog having puppies in the bunk next to hers. Fran would also miss the cute new guy who was supposed to move in upstairs. Sid Cassidy. Not that he'd ever look at her once he discovered she was Harry Kellers's sister.

Outside Fran's room, Lise's steps echoed in the hallway. Down the stairs, circling the hall, into the dining room and kitchen, and up the stairs again. She must really be worked up.

Then the steps ceased. A minute passed, then two. What was going on? Fran cracked the door open to listen. From the corner of her eye, she noticed that her phone had reappeared again, this time on her nightstand.

Then, from the kitchen, Lise shouted. "No! Murphy!"

Her steps rushed up the stairs. Fran followed their pounding as they went into Lise's room. Then down the stairs again and out the front door.

CHAPTER 35

The tall man they called Bitsy was behind the wheel. They were lucky his lumbago had cleared for the moment, Maxine had told Teddy, because he was unmatched as a getaway driver. He parked the van in front of Dyann's house—Murphy's house now, Teddy corrected herself. Next door, someone mowed the lawn, and the motor's steady buzz filled the air.

Bitsy pulled the emergency brake. Maxine had told Teddy he used to work for the mob in New Jersey. "No blood on his hands," she'd said, neatly sidestepping the implication he'd been nearby when it was on someone else's hands.

This morning, Bitsy was all focus: white news cap pulled low, eyes on the street. It was unlikely they'd encounter machine gun fire, but it was nice to know he took his job seriously. Arthur and someone they called the Kid—a seriously old gentleman—were with them.

"No car in the driveway," Teddy said. Good. Murphy must indeed be at the reptile refuge. She glanced toward the neighbor. A hedge partially blocked his view.

"The garage," Bitsy pointed out. "The smart driver garages his car."

"Murphy was clear to Lise that he'd be gone this morning," Maxine said. "We need to go with that. Ready?"

"Ready," replied Teddy, Arthur, and the Kid simultaneously.

Arthur and Teddy, clipboards in hand, approached the front door. Kid slipped around the side. The neighbor cut his mower's engine.

Teddy hadn't lived all her years above the law. There was the time she and the Purse Dogs—that band never did make it big—snuck across the border from Mexico. She couldn't remember exactly why, but it might have had something to do with the bass player losing his passport in a poker game. At a really low point, she'd squatted in a London warehouse. That was a cold winter, she recalled. However, it had been a while since she'd as much as strayed over the speed limit. Arthur, by contrast, might have been playing pinochle for all the nerves he showed.

They rang the bell. No one responded.

"Inspector," Arthur said loud enough to be heard at the sidewalk.

Again, nothing.

"What do we do now?" Teddy whispered.

"Stand straight and look toward the door. This will only take a moment. When the door opens, pretend someone has let us in."

Arthur took something from his pocket and stuck it in the deadbolt. Following instructions, Teddy plastered an officious look on her face and stared at the door.

With a click, the door opened. Teddy smiled widely and stared into the empty living room. "Mr. King? We're from the state. We understand there's wildlife on the property?"

They stepped inside and shut the door behind them. Teddy glanced back through the living room window. The neighbor couldn't see them here.

"You take the bathroom and bedrooms," Arthur said, all business. "I'll get the kitchen and main rooms. Be quick about it. We don't know when he's coming back."

Teddy made for the back of the house. They were looking for anything that might contain poison: small, unmarked bottles; paper packets; vials. At Blavatsky Manor, Gerald, who seemed to know what he was talking about, said Murphy would want to keep the poison close. He'd suggested looking in drawers of bedside tables, medicine cabinets, corners of underwear drawers, and inside any larger bottles or boxes that seemed out of place. He'd said amateurs weren't usually very creative at hiding things. He'd then launched into an involved story about a job where emeralds were hidden in a jar of cat treats, but Maxine had cut him off.

Teddy opened the bathroom door. Murphy had not yet fully moved in here. A pair of pajamas with laser guns and spaceships on them lay wadded near the shower, and a ratty toothbrush was by the sink, but otherwise the bathroom was a fantasy land of makeup and skin care regimes. Teddy slipped on a pair of latex gloves and quickly sorted the vanity's contents. Dyann preferred makeup with a frosty sheen, she noted, and had enough potions for the eyes—smoothing, de-redding, de-puffing, moisturizing—to treat the Rockettes. But no sign of poison. No sign even that Murphy had ever opened the vanity's drawer and cabinet.

Arthur was amazingly quiet. Not a whisper came from the front of the house.

On to the master bedroom. Dyann favored mauve satin textures and gold-edged French Provincial furniture—the dream furniture of a twelve-year-old girl. The sheets were messy, and jeans and T-shirts littered the floor next to the dresser. She did a quick search of the places Gerald had recommended. Nothing here.

She moved on to the second bedroom. Judging from the desk and filing cabinet, it was now an office. Teddy was about to conclude Murphy had changed nothing here, either, when she saw it: a large aquarium against the wall. At first, she thought it was empty. But who would have a heat lamp going in an empty aquarium?

She stepped closer. A thick orange coil moved from behind a branch of driftwood. A snake. It lifted its head, and a tiny tongue flickered in her direction. The thing must have been five feet long and was as fat as her arm. Teddy backed against the wall.

"Anything in here?" Arthur said. "The kitchen's clean." Then, "Holy sheist."

They stared at the snake.

"Come on. They're waiting on us," Arthur said finally. "I'll help you toss this room. The Kid should be wrapping up the basement apartment."

Five minutes later, the room had been searched. They'd found nothing but a few paperbacks on shamanism and a vial of Magnet Oil. It truly was as smelly as Lise had said.

Arthur shook his head. "If the Kid comes up empty, Murphy must have dumped the poison."

"Assuming he had it at all," Teddy said. Although, who else could it have been?

"Let's blow this joint."

She was happy to close the bedroom door behind her. They'd made it.

Then the doorbell rang.

Arthur's blank look told Teddy he might be aces at picking locks and searching a home, but wasn't a genius at dealing with people. Fortunately, this was Teddy's specialty.

"Let me handle this." She strode to the living room. She paused only a moment to fall into character before opening the front door.

"Who are you?" the neighbor asked. He wore a baseball cap and had a businessman's trim hair and shaved jaw along with a gym rat's buff arms. "I was mowing next door and heard you."

Teddy lifted her lanyard, displaying her fake credentials. “And you are?”

“Call me a concerned citizen.” Concerned Citizen glanced past her to Arthur then back to Teddy. “What are you doing here? Murphy’s not home.”

Teddy put on her best “don’t mess with me” air. “Clearly, we’re aware of that.”

The man squared his shoulders. Perhaps she hadn’t taken the correct approach. “You haven’t answered my question. We look after each other in this neighborhood. The owner of this house died. Burglars have been known to scope out obituaries for houses to break into.”

Behind her, Arthur snorted.

Teddy sighed as if burdened by yet another clueless pest. “As state employees, we pledge an oath to maintain the privacy of Astoria’s citizens. Suffice it to say we’re carrying out a public function that has to do with health and safety.”

The man parked his fists on his hips. “It’s about the snake, isn’t it?” He nodded toward her hands. “That’s why you’re wearing the gloves.”

Shoot. She’d forgotten about the gloves. Teddy averted her gaze a moment. “As I said, we’re not at liberty to say.”

The man adjusted the bill on his cap. “You understand my concern? I’ve never heard about state inspections like this.”

“I’m sorry you don’t believe me.” She slipped her phone from her tote and turned it in her hand.

The neighbor glanced at the phone, then her face. “I’d like to speak to your supervisor.”

“Are you sure?” Teddy said. She glanced at Arthur.

The man folded his arms over his chest. “Isn’t that what I said?”

She held out her phone. “I can dial the number for you, if you’d like.”

He smiled as if he was on to her. “No chance of it. How am

I supposed to know you won't call an accomplice? I'll make the call myself." He removed his phone from his rear pocket.

Teddy exchanged glances with Arthur before facing the neighbor again. She drew a long breath. "If you insist."

Teddy held out her lanyard, and he tapped in the number listed at the bottom. He cleared his throat. "I need to speak to whoever is in charge."

Even with the phone pressed to the neighbor's ear, the rumble of Burt's voice was clear. "What seems to be the problem?"

"There are two people here claiming to be from your office and saying something about a wildlife inspection."

"I see," Burt said. "What is the street number, please?"

Keeping his gaze on Teddy and Arthur, the neighbor smugly recited the address. Teddy kept her smile steady.

"Just a moment" Burt said. "Yes. I notice you have an extension on your garage. Is that licensed? While the inspectors are on the site, I might have them—"

Concerned Citizen pressed END and returned the phone to Teddy. "Looks good. Sorry to bother you."

"No problem." It had been Burt's brilliant idea to look for unpermitted structures by comparing the aerial view of the neighborhood to the city's permit database. Motion in the corner of her vision showed the Kid darting around the corner from the basement apartment and into the bushes to hide. "We should all have responsible neighbors like you."

Teddy ostentatiously peeled off her gloves and turned to Arthur. "We're finished here. We'll write up the certificate back at the office."

The neighbor returned to his yard, and a moment later, she heard the buzz of a weed trimmer. Teddy mimicked wiping sweat from her brow. "Close one."

The Kid slipped in the front door. "Find anything?"

"Nothing," Teddy said. "Murphy's still moving in. He may never unpack some of those boxes." It wasn't hard to imagine the boy passing years among his mother's belongings without doing much more than installing a big screen TV and maybe another python.

"Did a search," Arthur said. "The usual spots. No time for a deep clean. Did the freezer and vents, places like that, but stopped short at going through jars. The gent has a big, fat snake. A creepy orange son-of-a-gun."

Teddy hadn't thought to look in the vents. Lise hadn't been joking—these guys knew what they were doing.

"You ever need a place in a home," Arthur told her, "I bet we can find a bed at the Manor. Kid, you should have seen her handle the neighbor. She's a born con."

"As a woman, it's an easy route to get stuck on, if you're not careful," Teddy said. "Although I don't recommend making it your livelihood."

"I'll say," came a voice from behind them. A stranger stepped from the hall's recesses. Her white skin and phantom-pale hair glowed in the dim light.

The Kid and Arthur looked at each other and turned to Teddy. She realized they counted on her to get them out of this.

Teddy began to speak, then, bewildered, stopped. "Wait. I recognize you. Didn't you apply for a room? You asked a lot of questions about who lived at the house, and then left."

The woman held up a badge. "Special inspector, U.S. Fish and Wildlife Service."

CHAPTER 36

Snake venom, Lise thought as she shifted the Kia to a higher gear. That's what the poison was—snake venom. And it was Ornette, not Murphy, who administered it.

On her last perambulation of the house, she'd landed in front of the refrigerator, planning to get something to drink, and she'd caught sight of the list Fran had posted with takes on "SVC." Teddy must have added to it. A few names—Serena Vesper Corrie, Sigmund Vaughn Corrie—were followed by freer interpretations, including Super Valuable Cushion and Satin Vortex Convertible.

Then it surfaced. *Snake Venom*. Ornette had mentioned the value of snake venom, and Murphy had bragged about something only he was privileged to know. Ornette didn't need Dyann's or Murphy's money, because he made plenty of it on his own. What he needed was for Murphy to keep quiet about his operation selling snake venom. Somehow, Dyann must have found out about it. It explained the meeting with him noted in her calendar. Lise had smelled anxiety on Ornette but had wrongly attributed it to concern about Murphy. And Richard's death? The tampered Camaro had been meant for his son.

Murphy had told her Ornette was out of town today and he

was in charge of the reptile refuge. She wondered if Ornette had left for good. Her fear was that he'd left Murphy "gone for good," too.

Gravel crunched as she pulled into the parking lot outside the reptile refuge. She drew her cardigan close. The only other car in the lot was Dyann's Mercedes convertible, now Murphy's.

She pulled open the refuge's front door to see a minuscule waiting room with a counter and no one behind it. Heart in her throat, she dinged the bell and waited only a moment for the response she knew wasn't coming.

"Murphy?"

Nothing. Lise went around the counter and opened the door to the refuge's heart. Music—some kind of jazz—came from a Bluetooth speaker on a table in the room's center, but no one was around.

"Murphy?" she called again, this time more quietly.

On her left was a row of aquariums, some giving onto caged-in patios. From one, a rough-skinned lizard with horny protrusions stared at her. When it jerked forward, she sucked in a breath. Water trickled in one aquarium, a big one, holding an alligator. And it was warm in here. Warm and moist and smelling of bleach and animal.

Among the aquariums on one wall were two long rooms with windowed doors. Gathering her courage, Lise looked through the window into the first one. This room, too, was lined in aquariums, each holding a snake. Most hid behind rocks or pieces of wood or were curled up, and they ranged in appearance from lemon-yellows to vibrant reds to sharp black-and-white patterns. She felt as if she'd wandered into a sci-fi movie. She wondered if they missed the trees and smells of landscapes they might have never known.

On the speaker, a four-note tune was plucked on a bass, then a voice sang, "A love supreme, a love supreme." Eerie.

Music, yet no one was here. Was she crazy for coming down here by herself?

If Ornette knew that Murphy was hinting to others that something illegal was happening here, he would never let Murphy get away with it. Worse, if Murphy had blackmailed Ornette somehow . . .

She had to find him. His car was in the parking lot, so he was here somewhere. Lise peered in the windows of the three rooms on the opposite wall before she found him. A red bandana covered Murphy's mouth, and his ankles were tied and his hands bound behind his back. He lay on his side under a table holding an aquarium with two thin coral-tinted snakes.

Lise thrust open the door. It closed softly behind her. Murphy's eyes were wide, as if he had something urgent to say. She knelt beside him and worked at the gag. Its knot was loose enough to untie with her fingers.

Murphy gasped and said, low, "Stay still. If you don't move, it won't strike." His gaze flashed across the closet-sized room.

She turned her head, and she saw it: a khaki-green snake, longer than a man, lying against the opposite wall. It raised its head, and the flesh on its neck swelled into a hood.

Fran turned back toward her suitcase, open on her bed. What had Lise been in such a hurry about? All that pacing, and then—*boom!*—she shot out of here like there was a sale on Chanel No. 5.

Fran left the bedroom door open. It didn't matter now, since Lise was gone and no one else was home. Finally, she'd be able to grab the few things she had in the bathroom and make a sandwich for the road. She had enough in savings to rent a room in Portland. It was a real city, not like Astoria, and there were plenty of bookstores there. She'd be able to find a job, and no one would ever know she was Harry Kellers's sister.

Both Charm and Grace slinked in and nosed at Fran's boxes on the floor. Grace leapt to the bed to sniff the suitcase. Instantly, she yowled and pawed at something. Charm leapt next to her to check out whatever it was that had interested his sister.

"What is it, kitty?"

Grace stepped back to reveal Fran's phone in her suitcase.

Fran wanted to scream. Would the freaking house cut it out? "Okay. All right. I'll listen. Just leave me alone."

She turned on her phone and scrolled through the notifications. Margie had texted to see if she was feeling better. No mention of Harry, which was nice. Two voicemail messages from her mom, both of them congratulating her for her hilarious diary entries. Fran punched DELETE before the second message was over. A text from Harry asking if she'd seen his show, and another from Harry's assistant. Screw them. She deleted those, too.

Three texts from Murphy, plus a lengthy voice mail. Warily, she glanced at the first text and saw nothing about Harry's show, just a plaintive request for her to get in touch. The next two were the same, only with increasing urgency.

Now curious, Fran tapped the "play" arrow on her voicemail.

"Fran, you've got to call me. You're my only friend." Murphy's voice broke, and he sniffed. He was actually crying. "Ornette is leaving. For good."

It took Fran a moment to remember that Ornette was the guy who ran the reptile refuge. Murphy had seemed really attached to him. Funny—but maybe not unexpected—that after losing both parents, Murphy would only finally get emotional when his boss at his volunteer gig was leaving.

There was more to the message. "I really messed up. I told him I knew he was selling snake venom, and I threatened to go to the police if he didn't let me help him. It was so stupid. I wouldn't have done it. Now he's leaving me. Call me, please, Fran."

She stared at the phone as her thoughts fell into place. Snake venom. That's what had poisoned Dyann King. Murphy hadn't killed his parents, Ornette had. Fran wasn't one hundred percent sure why, but of one thing she was certain: Murphy was at risk. Not only that, but Lise must have somehow figured it out, too, and gone after him.

He was at the reptile refuge. Fran had overheard this fact last night.

Long ago, she had the chance to help Harry by warning him about the rotted ladder. She had frozen, and look what had happened. This time, she wouldn't hesitate.

Fran grabbed her purse and made for the door, then returned to fetch one more item.

Then she ran for her car.

Chapter 37

"Don't move," Murphy repeated. "It'll strike if you move."

Lise was frozen. She couldn't have moved if she'd wanted to. The cliché was that fear inspired "fight or flight." Whoever had made that up had left out the paralysis of sheer terror.

The snake's hood retreated slightly, and it partially dropped its head, but it still watched her.

"It's the black mamba," Murphy whispered. "Without antivenom, you're dead, and there's no antivenom for hundreds of miles. Or more. We had some, but Ornette took it with him."

Lise edged toward the door. She'd heard it click, but had it locked behind her?

"I said, don't move!" Murphy said, this time more loudly.

The black mamba raised its head again and inflamed its hood.

Lise again froze. Her heart pounded so violently she was sure her body vibrated from it. The snake's mouth parted, showing small, deadly teeth and a jaw like a bear trap. She smelled it again, the acrid scent of death: earthy, sharp, and dizzying.

She glanced at Murphy, hoping the movement of her eyes didn't set off the snake. Murphy lay still, his eyes closed.

With Ornette gone, they could be stuck here for hours—or, more likely, days. There was no way they'd survive that long shut into a ten-by-ten room with a poisonous viper. She edged toward the door, holding one hand close to her cardigan and reaching the other one ever so slowly toward the doorknob.

The black mamba watched but kept its distance.

Her extended hand felt ridiculously exposed. If she could just get out, she could find some kind of weapon to subdue the snake. Then she'd drag Murphy from the room and undo his ties there.

From outside, the radio continued to play. "A love supreme, a love supreme."

She grasped the doorknob and turned. And pushed. *Damn.* Locked.

The motion had roused the black mamba again, and it rose further, chest high, only a few feet away. At the same time, Lise smelled something. It wasn't fear, nor death, but—could it be?—the jasmine of Dyann's perfume.

Lise flattened her back against the door, and her hand fell into her sweater pocket in an urge to protect it. Something was in the pocket, not a weapon, but—a sample vial of Magnet Oil. The snake's hood widened further, and it reared as if to strike. She grasped the vial and sprayed it in the viper's face.

The snake rocked and backed off, but Lise had only seconds. She couldn't grab the snake with her bare hands, could she? The black mamba fell to the ground, then waved again to rise.

"The snake stick," Murphy croaked and nodded toward a stick contraption with a pincers on one end and a lever handle on the other. She remembered the one she'd seen at Dyann's house when Murphy'd found his snake under the chair cushion.

Lise grabbed the stick, and on her second try managed to snag the mamba at its throat. Its long body thrashed and wrapped at the stick. She held it at arm's length.

"Into that empty aquarium. The lid's on the floor next to it," Murphy said.

She dumped the snake stick into the aquarium, and with

one hand firmly holding its handle closed, she reached for the lid. She crammed the lid over the aquarium with half the black mamba's body wriggling outside. In seconds, it had pulled its body inside and struck blindly at the aquarium's glass walls. Lise secured the lid.

Gasping, she knelt to untie Murphy's hands, then leaned back to catch her breath as he worked at the knots binding his feet.

"You should have made sure his whole body was in the aquarium before you put on the lid," Murphy said.

"Shut up," Lise replied. The mamba might be secured, but they were still stuck in this hot room full of snakes and now reeking of Magnet Oil, too. She flattened a hand to her stomach, hoping she wouldn't throw up.

"That was my mom's potion, wasn't it?"

Lise nodded.

"I guess it worked to magnetize help," he said. "Look."

Fran stood at the window to the snake room, her face blanching. She yelled something to the side, and Signe joined her.

At last, the door opened to cool, fresh air.

Chapter 38

Corrie House was quiet tonight, Fran noted. No baby crying, no lady fretting. They had gathered in Teddy's sitting room, but, unlike the last time a few weeks earlier, tonight they were discussing murders solved, not how to find a killer. Teddy had made a fire, and the cats lay like beans, side by side on the tile hearth. Burt's bottle of scotch rested on the coffee table, but there was no Burt.

The new housemate, Sid, sat quietly on a chair he'd pulled in from the dining room. Fran put fingers to her hair. Late last night, she and Sid had formally met in the kitchen. She had gone downstairs to cut her hair with the kitchen scissors, and he was looking for a sandwich to eat while he unpacked. He'd helped trim her bangs. If he knew about her brother's betrayal, he hadn't mentioned it.

Fortunately, she'd made sure that Harry publicly announced the glory of her rescue of Lise and Murphy. Fueled by her success at the reptile refuge, she'd called Harry that night and demanded he return her diary by overnight mail. Then she let him know she was a heroine and hinted he might want to share the details on national TV. She had to admit, she was something else—nearly as brave as the heroine in *Dead Bolt*.

Teddy and Lise were here, too, of course, Lise on the couch and Teddy tending the fire. All at once, the nights had become cool, and the fire felt good on the outside with the whiskey warming her on the inside.

Finally, Signe, cross-legged near the couch, nursed her scotch.

"Fran saved you," Sid said. With his beard and thick hair, only his eyes and nose showed to express his surprise.

"When I heard Murphy's phone message, I figured out what had happened. Lise had run off to the reptile refuge to see if Murphy was milking the snakes for venom. Murphy had said Ornette was leaving Astoria, but who knew if he was gone yet? So I called Signe, grabbed my picklocks, and took off."

Sid's expression hadn't changed, but Fran sensed his amazement all the same. "You picked the locks?"

"I didn't want to be seen, so I didn't go in the front. Remember, Ornette might have still been hanging out, maybe with a gun to Lise and Murphy's heads. So I came in the back. The lock was a simple deadbolt. Ten seconds max to crack."

She stole a glance at Sid. She could imagine the duke in *Dead Bolt* looking something like him. Sid watched without saying a word. Later, she'd tell him how she'd rehabilitated the locks around the house, too. He'd surely be impressed.

"What happened to Murphy?" he asked.

"He knew about Ornette selling snake venom illegally, and he didn't report it, which makes him an accessory to the crime," Fran said.

"Worse," Lise said, "he blackmailed Ornette about it. He saw Ornette as a father figure and assumed they'd work together. When Ornette backed off, Murphy said he'd tell the police unless he could be part of the business, too."

Teddy nudged a log with the poker. "Poor boy. He just wanted to be loved. His parents were so obsessed with each other that they didn't have time for him."

"The case is complicated," Signe said. Charm had crawled

into her lap and was submitting to a belly rub. "Ornette Cassell tried to kill Murphy. Not just by locking him in with the black mamba, but by sabotaging Richard's Camaro."

"Richard King, who died when his car went into the river," Sid said.

"Right," Lise said. "You know about that? Ornette cut the brake line and glued the electric window button in place, thinking Murphy would be the victim. He didn't know that the next morning Richard was dropping off Dyann's car for Murphy and taking back the Camaro. But it worked to his advantage. Richard was onto him for killing Dyann and for planting the hard copy of the codicil in his office at King Cars. Richard had been doing his own investigating."

"Murphy's out on bail," Fran said. He'd been pestering her with regular phone calls, begging her to take in Tangerine Dream if he went to prison. Fortunately, with his inheritance, he could afford a good criminal defense attorney and, presumably, a home for his snake, should it come to that.

"Let me get this straight," Sid said. "Ornette killed Dyann because she had found out about his illegal business through her son."

"We believe he brought the black mamba to the Lucky Lotus the night Dyann died," Signe said. "He must have waited until her back was turned to unleash it. The medical examiner has confirmed the marks at the base of her scalp were from a snakebite."

Fran hoped Dyann had been looking away. She'd only seen the mamba in its aquarium, but that room of snakes—thinking of it, she almost upchucked the quesadilla she'd had for dinner. Hopefully, Sid hadn't heard how she'd fainted the moment they'd opened the door to the snake room. Signe had to call the paramedics.

"He likely thought the venom would mimic a natural death and not be picked up by the medical examiner," Lise said. "He would have been right if Richard hadn't slashed her tires, making her death look suspicious."

"Ornette decided to skip town. He bought a ticket to Ecuador, and Murphy found out about it by accident at the refuge," Fran said. He'd told her all about it in the ambulance from the reptile refuge.

"When Murphy put more pressure on Ornette, he tossed him in the snake pit," Sid concluded.

Sid had such a way with words, Fran thought. And he knew about Harry and hadn't teased her once. He caught her gaze and smiled.

Teddy put another log on the fire and turned toward the gathering. Colder weather was ahead, and she couldn't invite everyone in the house to her sitting room every night. Although tonight was nice. Luckily, a new furnace was in their future. Burt had seen to that.

The house seemed content with the company, too, sighing and creaking in the night. Teddy could have sworn even the wallpaper glowed richer and warmer. A stiff wind might blow the shingles from the roof, but for the moment they were safe—better than that, happy. She and Fran had a date at the county historical society later in the week. Corrie House had a story, and she was determined to know it.

"When the real wildlife inspector showed up, I called Signe," Teddy said.

"The inspector—I'd seen her on my last day at the Lucky Lotus, and I'd had no idea," Lise said. "She was asking about potions, maybe trying to figure out if Ornette had distributed any of the venom locally. Dyann sold her a couple of bottles of Magnet Oil."

"I never wanted you to risk your lives like that—just ask a few questions, that's all," Signe said.

Teddy returned to her place on the couch. "We had no choice, darling."

"I sat in on Ornette's interviews with the Fish and Wildlife inspectors," Signe said. "He was so earnest about the benefits of snake venom. I think he's a true believer."

"As if the money he'd made from it didn't matter," Teddy said.

Fran picked up a postcard on the side table. "What's this? Looks like Manhattan."

"It's from Sylvia Borlotti. She plans to settle in New York. My friend Marvin got her a gig singing at the Ophelia," Teddy said. "I filled her in on the happenings here. She says hello."

When Teddy had come back from Blavatsky Manor the day of Murphy's rescue, no one was home. Fran's belongings had covered her bed, and her suitcases lay, open and empty, on the floor. Fran later had sworn she'd packed them.

Fran replaced the postcard and turned to Signe. "You managed to get Ornette arrested before he got on his plane."

"Thanks to your tip," Signe said.

"How did your boss react to the arrest?" Lise asked Signe. "He was so sure Dyann's death was natural and Richard's an accident."

"He's taking full credit for solving a double homicide, of course, and I spent most of yesterday drafting a press release detailing how he uncovered a web of illegal snake venom traders."

Yes, it was nice to have everyone here. Teddy only wished Burt were among them. He would have loved being part of tonight's conversation, and she would have loved his solid, kind presence on the couch next to her. With a bone-deep ache, she remembered their call that afternoon. Tonight he was in the cardiac care unit at the hospital with his sons and their families surrounding him.

Her heart was broken. And yet, her heart was full.

* * *

Lise was also content. Firelight illuminated the mismatched crystal glasses of whiskey on the coffee table, making amber pools of light on the wood. She closed her eyes and inhaled. The new housemate, Sid, trailed ribbons of grounding sandalwood, answered by a faint rose from Fran. *Well, well.* Lise turned toward Teddy and smelled a sadness of aged patchouli and violet, under the spicy vanilla of her wisdom. Together, it was a heady bouquet of joy and pathos.

Teddy proffered the scotch bottle. "More, Lise?"

She shook her head. "No, thanks. I have to get up early tomorrow." Maxine had hinted of a cat burglar they knew in the south of France who had ties to a perfumer's family, and Lise was eager to hear more.

Signe rose and stretched her legs. "I'd better be going. I don't want Adrienne to wait up for me."

Grace reached a soft paw to tap Lise's wrist and pressed her head into Lise's palm for pets. Lise still felt like an oddball with her bizarre abilities, but as she sat in Teddy's sitting room, she remembered Burt's words from not long ago. *The best family is the one you make.*

She was not finished searching for her magical roots, but she'd found a kind of family here.

Then she smelled it. There it was, then gone again. A haunting wisp of L'Heure Bleue.

Afterword

This is the first outing for Lise, Teddy, and Fran, and you wouldn't be reading it if it weren't for the faith and support of the team at Kensington Books, chief among them editor-in-chief John Scognamiglio and PR and marketing mistress extraordinaire Larissa Ackerman. They believed in me enough to ask me to introduce Lise in *Witch and Tell*, the final installment in the Witch Way Librarian mysteries, and carry her forward here. (Canny readers will have noticed the reference to Josie Way.)

My agent John Talbot's encouragement led me to further develop the idea of a retirement home for petty criminals. I would be mortified if I so much as accidentally knocked an unpaid pack of gum into my purse, but I wouldn't mind a room in a place like Blavatsky Manor.

My love of perfume was deepened by a decade-plus writing weekly articles for *Now Smell This*, a blog run by the talented Robin Krug. I hope Lise's fascination with fragrance will spur some of you to tune in to what must be one of our least appreciated and most rewarding senses.

Tracy Tsefalas, owner of Fumerie, the best perfume shop on the West Coast, once told me, "I can imagine feelings unfurling like ribbons of scent from someone's head." Every author knows that *ding, ding, ding* sensation when a story's puzzle piece snaps into place.

Brainstorming is at the root of any good novel, and Susan and Pete are founts of imagination. On an overcast New Year's Day on the Oregon Coast, Pete set aside his guitar and Susan hand-stitched buttonholes as they helped me lay out *Whiff*'s characters. We spent an afternoon speaking mostly in sentences beginning with "What if . . . ?"

JD Horn (you may have read his terrific novels) and his husband Rich are also terrific brainstormers, and it's to them I owe the idea of Harry's "My Sister's Diary" segment.

Mary Alyce Blume is exactly the kind of no-nonsense writer pal an author needs. When I was stuck and handed to her a tangled mess of a beginning with a plea for help, she shattered the morass with a few well-placed comments, and the story began to flow. Thank you, MAB. Christine Finlayson was another supportive writer friend who endured talk of plots, motivation, and character during our hours-long walks. This story is stronger because of her.

Thank you, too, to Pomegranate Doyle. As we pulled early spring weeds in my garden, Pomegranate, artist and priestess, described what death should smell like. "Buzzing and earthy," she said. We need to have a good talk soon about haunted houses.

My sweetheart David was fundamental to this story. He lent me his couch as a daily workspace, and he was always ready to cheer word count gains and plot breakthroughs. He filled my belly with noodles, tea, and orange cake and my heart with contentment. I am lucky to have him in my life.

Finally, I thank you, the reader. I'm constantly blown away by you, wherever I encounter you—bookstores, conferences, readings, social media, and in my inbox. Thank you, and don't be a stranger.

Love a Comeback

Ruthie Knox & Annie Mare

kensingtonbooks.com

KENSINGTON BOOKS are published by

Kensington Publishing Corp.
900 Third Avenue
New York, NY 10022

Library of Congress Control Number on file

ISBN: 978-1-4967-5134-8

First Kensington Hardcover Edition: March 2026

ISBN: 978-1-4967-5129-4 (ebook)

10 9 8 7 6 5 4 3 2 1

Printed in the United States of America

The authorized representative in the EU for product safety and compliance
is eucomply OU, Parnu mnt 139b-14, Apt 123
Tallinn, Berlin 11317, hello@eucompliancepartner.com

For Los Angeles, the original comeback town. We love you.

Cast of Characters

(in order of appearance)

Samantha Farmer (Sam)	TV detective
Chad Bevington	Former Ice Crew; Sam's *Theomina* costar; guest star on *The Howling*
Bexley Simon (Bex)	TV detective
Bradley Wilhite	Well-known actor; may costar with Sam in *Theomina and the Dragon of Shadows*
Sloan Lennox	Former Ice Crew; guest star on *The Howling*
Fergus Farmer	One of Sam's four brothers
Victoria Simon (Vic)	UCLA student and youngest sister of Bex Simon
Franklynn Simon (Frankie)	Stage manager and middle sister of Bex Simon
Ramona Watts	Former Ice Crew; star of *The Howling*
Macie Finn	Former Ice Crew
Juliette Draper	Former Ice Crew (deceased)
April Feinstein	Ramona Watts's agent
Haris Ahmadi	Cineline production assistant; Frankie's boyfriend
Colin Worth	Well-known Broadway composer; Ramona Watts's friend

Christian Stanstedt	Former Ice Crew; heir to the Brinley Downs fortune
Piper Redwood	Supporting actor on *The Howling*; part of Vic's "nepo baby" entourage
Archie Blasingame	Ice Crew documentarian
Ashleigh Chambers	The other Hollywood detective
Tom Kessler	Director famous for making multiple movies in the 1990s starring the Ice Crew
Logan Widi	Former production assistant for *The Howling*

Love a Comeback

Back in the Leather Corset Again

Crouching on a dirty soundstage, Sam Farmer tried to find the place inside herself where she had invited her character, Theomina, to live.

Small bits of grit dug into her naked kneecaps. When she adjusted her position, the boning of her leather corset caught painfully against her rib cage. Ignoring the discomfort, Sam listened for the voice of the dragon rider inside her.

Theomina had lost everything she loved. Her father. The witch who was the only mother she'd ever known. Her beloved dragon. She was tough, but she'd reached her limit. She was tired. Her heart *hurt*.

A tear raced down Sam's cheek as she stared up into the ice-blue eyes of her costar, Chad Bevington. His eyes were the only part of him she could see clearly, since his face was covered in the green fabric of his chroma-key suit. The evenly spaced markers sewn into it would allow the CGI people to do their postproduction digital magic and turn him into the soul-sucking beast that Theomina was fighting.

It wasn't hard for Sam to access the part of herself that believed Chad made a credible soul-sucking beast.

"Cut!"

Sam relaxed her body as much as she could in the dragon-riding leathers of her costume. She looked past the lights pointed at the studio stage. "Did we get it?"

"Your nose is running every time you cry." The assistant director sighed at her clipboard. "Take five while we decide."

Goddamnit. Sam had wrapped this movie almost two months ago. She'd wrapped it so hard, thrilled beyond description to be finished in Vancouver and finally able to unpack her suitcases at home in the Hollywood Hills. But compositing issues with some of the green-screen shots meant she'd been called to a borrowed L.A. soundstage at StudioHonor for reshoots at five a.m. on the same day her former costar, recent sleuthing partner, and current long-distance girlfriend, Bex, was finally coming home.

"When I need to cry on camera, I like to remember when my dog died," Chad said, stretching his arms above his head. "Nice clean tears." He winked at her.

Ugh. Sam didn't mind so much that Chad was vain and entitled. Vain entitlement came preinstalled in this town. What she did mind was his tendency to try to control everyone and everything that happened on set. This was a man who'd threatened to call his "legal team" so often that it became an inside joke among the cast and crew.

Sam had said nothing about Chad's behavior. Like the character she played, she was tough. She'd grown up with four older brothers and knew how to fight hard and dirty to maintain her ego under the attack of entitled boys.

Though Chad was not a boy. He'd begun his career as an icon of nineties cinema, and he remained as familiar to movie and TV audiences as popcorn.

Still. Not worth the energy.

After a long stretch of lights going on and off, crew yelling directions, and conversations between the director and his assistants, the main bank of lights went down. "Thank you, everybody, that's a wrap!" the director yelled. "Get the fuck out of here, and stay out of my face until I see you at the premiere."

Sam blew out a breath in relief.

"Except for you, my queen." The director turned to point at Sam. "I'll see *you* in a week."

Sam gave him the wide, affable smile that was her trademark, most recently reproduced on the plastic face of her Theomina action figure. "Looking forward to it."

She was not.

Making movies about magic was not a magical experience. Sam had adored *Theomina* when it was a postapocalyptic fantasy novel. She'd given copies to her nieces and nephews, and they'd been the first ones she called when she was offered the part in the film. *I'm going to play Theomina!* she'd told them over Zoom, and everyone had cheered.

Then she'd spent most of the shoot grateful beyond words that the novel's author had promised to only ever write *one* Theomina book. No more books meant no sequels. Sam would never have to play Theomina again.

Or so she'd thought.

The author's artistic convictions, it turned out, hadn't stopped her from licensing the IP to Howell Motion Pictures. Just yesterday afternoon, Sam had received an excited phone call from her manager letting her know that blockbuster-maker Bradley Wilhite had attached himself to a *Theomina and the Dragon of Shadows* limited series in the role of Theomina's romantic interest.

The one and only novel characterized Theomina as ascetic, with no other love than for her kingdom, and definitely not for a giant creep of a man who was more than twenty years older than Sam and didn't believe in intimacy coordinators. But Theomina and her fictional principles were no match for heteronormative Hollywood.

Bradley Wilhite wanted Sam to report to his ranch in Telluride in seven days for a chemistry read, and she was expected to pack lip balm, drink plenty of water, and smile.

The director gave her a wave on his way out. Soon, Sam was

surrounded by costume assistants who unbuckled her from the leathers down to the singlet and bike shorts she wore underneath. Chad was still being freed from his suit when she booked it to a dressing room to remove her makeup and fake blood. She brushed the special effects dirt out of her hair and slammed on a pair of jeans, a T-shirt, and a ball cap. They were her comfy clothes, designed for utility and escaping the set quickly. In her bedroom at home, Sam had something a lot more special laid out for when she saw Bex.

On the open-air top deck of the studio's parking garage, she unlocked her Audi and flung her hat onto the passenger seat. The first thing she did after a long, desperately needed exhalation was dig her phone out of her bag, swipe past three million notifications, and tap the only name in her saved contacts that she'd marked with a star.

Bexley Simon.

"Hello?"

Sam winced. The familiar voice sounded distracted and like there were a lot of people around. "Bex?"

"Sam? Fuck! Hold on—*I've got it, for Christ's sake!*" Bex said this last to someone else. *"It's a carry-on. I'll carry it!"*

Sam's girlfriend was a small woman, short, curvy, and deceptively cute, with a face that could make a person fall in love or weep from across an entire theater and into the cheap seats, but she was not quiet. A Broadway theater critic had once admiringly mused that given the pair of lungs on Bex, her body couldn't possibly contain much else besides her artist's heart—and what's more, she needed nothing but that heart and those lungs to keep herself upright, dancing, and singing.

Sam put the phone on speaker and turned down the volume.

"Okay. My *god.* Sam? Are you still there?"

"I am."

Bex gusted a breath out into the phone. "Give me one second, I'm at the entrance of the VIP lounge." The background noise dropped away. The sound of Bex breathing into her phone became all-encompassing, then inaudible. "Now I can hear you. Can you hear me?"

Sam laughed. "I can hear you. You must be at the airport."

"Indeed."

"LAX, I hope?"

"I *should* be at LAX, but my flight out of JFK was diverted to Denver because apparently it's hard to fly through something called—a *derecho*?"

"Sounds fake." Sam made her voice as loose as her hands, which she laid palms up on her thighs to keep from squeezing the steering wheel in bloodless fists.

"Doesn't it? They made us get off the plane. I'm supposed to stay in this room they are calling a VIP lounge. At some point there will be a new crew, and I will get back on the plane." Sam heard a loud rustling that she recognized as the sound of Bex digging through her bag for whatever gross nutrition bar she currently believed would solve her problems. "I should've taken Frankie up on her offer to drive cross-country with her, but I feel like I'm not made for road trips."

"Absolutely, you are not." Bex was a lot of things, but a woman satisfied with any kind of passenger seat was not one of them.

Sam loved that about her.

It was a helpful reminder. She held onto it and made herself take a few beats to recenter. She'd been looking forward to Bex's return more than was good for her. Possibly, a little bit, Sam had been clinging to a fantasy of what Bex's return would be like. Daydreaming about surprising Bex at the baggage carousel. Flipping through a mental carousel of potential outfits and imagining how Bex would react. Thinking up menus for a romantic evening meal they would share poolside, just the two of them.

None of that was going to happen, or at least not tonight.

Even so, it was a perfect May afternoon in Los Angeles. Hot, but with a nice breeze. The sky was clear. She'd been released from the clutches of *Theomina.* Nothing was fucked here, as her brother Fergus liked to say. No one had abandoned her. Sam would see Bex soon.

Six months, though. It had been six whole, entire months since they'd been in the same room. Their work had pulled them apart, throwing their relationship into the kind of long-distance, not-quite-there-yet limbo that made Sam worry, sleepless in the middle of the night, that she'd left it too long and missed her one cosmic chance at love.

She and Bex had been together almost every day of the six years they spent costarring on *Craven's Daughter,* a TV procedural about a kindergarten teacher (Bex's character, Cora Banks) who takes over her dead father's detective agency and teams up with a disgraced former FBI agent (Sam's character, Henri Shannon) to solve one murder per week. Those were heady years for Sam, with an undercurrent of doomed pining for her fellow TV detective.

Then, after she confessed her feelings and Bex didn't instantly admit to feeling the same way, Sam had fled, quit the show, and spent half a decade accepting any role she was offered, so long as it enabled her to avoid her quiet house and her own company (Sam's stipulation) and moved her up another rung on the ladder of Hollywood celebrity (her management's).

The result was that Sam had reached a fuck-you level of stardom, with the money to match. She was very rich and very, very famous, but without Bex, she hadn't been happy.

They'd figured it out. Their reunion six months ago had turned out to be the most delicious do-over Sam could have asked for, and it wasn't her fault *or* Bex's that their schedules had been packed ever since. The commitments that kept them apart had been made long ago. Sam was a patient person. Level-headed. Extremely chill. Everyone said so.

"You're doing the thing where you go silent," Bex said. "So I'm doing the thing where I panic."

"Right. Sorry." She wasn't brilliant over the phone. They'd suffered through a lot of calls at weird or inconvenient times over bad connections. They texted constantly at first, but small issues blew up too easily into big misunderstandings, and they'd been relying heavily on voice memos for the past few months. Sam had started to feel like she was sending letters by carrier pigeon from the warfront to her fiancée back home.

"I am disappointed. I miss you." Sam delivered this line with, she thought, enough affability to hide her vulnerable yearning. "But we can't control the weather. When do you think you'll get in?"

"They seem pretty confident a fresh flight crew will be here in a couple of hours." Bex sounded as crushed as Sam felt. "And by then, the storm will be past. With the time difference, I could be in L.A. in time for a very late dinner at Tatsu Ramen."

"Perfect." Sam bit her lower lip. She could feel every place her stiff costume had dug into her ribs, leaving injuries that would bloom into bruises tonight while she slept. Alone, most likely.

She rolled her eyes at herself. Give a girl a mom who wasn't cut out for parenthood and a dad with multiple marriages, and she'd be stuck with abandonment issues forever.

"This is what we're going to do." Bex's voice had gotten crisp, exactly like an older sister who'd had to raise her two younger sisters with literally nothing but pure faith and terrifying ambition.

"Tell me."

"This plane is pulling away from the gate in two hours or less, or I am calling Kevin Costner, who happens to owe me a favor, and who I know is at his place in Denver right now, and he will get me to L.A. in his plane."

Sam smiled at this pronouncement. At its heart, Hollywood was a small town, which meant it did a brisk commerce in favors, boons, and handshake agreements. One of the things that made Bex so delightfully *Bex* was that she kept track of every single one in a secret notebook she kept in a zippered pocket of her bag. "Why not call him this instant?"

"I have to be judicious about how I use my IOUs. But in ninety minutes or less, I want you at my house. I know you wanted to pick me up from the airport, but I'm assigning you to another mission." Bex's voice had become formidable. "Turn on the pool lights. Make sure there is a lot of food. Nothing vegetarian. Frankie's taken me to every plant-based deli, café, and bar in Manhattan, and I am getting frail. Tonight, we're going to eat a devastating amount of something extremely bad for us and listen to all of Vic's major and minor dramas, and then we will curl up together on the big pool chaise and talk until we fall asleep, or a drone camera catches a picture of my thigh between your legs and my mouth welded to yours"—Bex paused to take a breath—"and the rest of us, you and me, will start early tomorrow."

Hearing Bex's description of their bodies intertwined had Sam blushing. She pulled at her lip, acknowledging a pang of misery that she and Bex couldn't be immediately alone. Fortunately, it was a small pang. Bex and her sisters, Frankie and Vic, were a package deal. It didn't bother Sam, who'd grown up in a family where privacy was scarce.

Sam's dad had been married seven times. The longest romantic relationship ever embarked upon by Caesar Polonius Farmer, Oakland periodontist, lasted thirty-six months, and it was on supplemental oxygen by the end. In defiance of these familial odds, Sam had always hoped to find her person—her *one* person—and pair-bond until death. This meant that while the press liked to paint a picture of her dating habits that featured a revolving door of women, the truth was considerably more . . . governesslike. Proper. "That is a *plan*," she said. "No contingencies?"

"No. This is the only plan. It is a good plan, and what's more, it's the plan we deserve."

"It is a Bex plan." Sam could easily imagine Bex in plan-making mode, her cloud of unruly auburn curls bent over one of her notebooks as she made a list.

"Yes. Which means it will happen—or something else equally remarkable will—and then I'll make a new plan. But get ready. Once I'm back, we'll have six weeks. A week for every month we spent apart."

Except that I'm going to Telluride.

Sam pushed the thought and everything it represented down somewhere deep inside herself. At thirty-five, she was a couple of years younger than Bex. She didn't feel ancient yet, and her paychecks told her she was far from irrelevant, but in this industry, everyone balanced on the knife's edge of celebrity. The bigger her team got in response to Sam's prestige projects and growing stature, the more that team depended on her work bringing in the kind of money and attention that fed the beast. It was why she hadn't found a way yet to tell them that taking time off from her six weeks with Bex to schmooze with studio people, talking at and around another Theomina project, was not something she wanted to do.

No one had asked if Sam wanted to. *Bradley* wanted her to.

Sam didn't doubt that after she showed up at his rustic abode there would be other things he wanted from her, one after the next until her six weeks with Bex had broken up and disappeared like the surf when it hit the sand. But if she even attempted to refuse the meeting, her team would be thrown into a panic. Bradley's people would either start planting shit in the media about her or assume she was playing hardball and offer more money, which she wouldn't be able to refuse once her people saw all the zeroes.

Sam had to go to Telluride. But she didn't have to think about it, much less mention it, until after she'd indulged in at least a few days' worth of quality time alone with the woman she loved.

"Sam?" Bex spoke her name with a hint of concern. "You're acting—I don't know. You're *acting*. What's up with you?"

She was staring through her car's windshield at the studio building, trying to figure out a way to answer this question, when the exit door opened and her costar, Chad Bevington, walked through it. He'd changed into plaid board shorts and a loose tank that showed off his waxed muscles. His luxurious blond hair system was styled in the same tousled waves he'd sported since he was twenty.

A second man followed him out. He wore sunglasses and a black fedora that combined with the man's slight, dancerlike stature to give Sam an instant sense memory of the Juicy Couture perfume samples shoved inside the celebrity magazines she'd pored over as a preteen.

That was Sloan Lennox.

Sloan Lennox, walking out of the studio with Chad Bevington.

Sloan Lennox *talking* to Chad Bevington, with one of his signature unfiltered Lucky Strike cigarettes pinched between his first finger and thumb (on a strictly no-smoking lot), gesturing to Chad with a trail of smoke fading in his wake.

"I'll be damned." Sam couldn't believe her eyes. Seeing the two of them together was like watching a long shot from the classic film *The Lights of Marfa*, which had made both of these men legendary.

Together, Chad and Sloan had anchored Hollywood's Ice Crew, a six-pack of gorgeous young celebrities who held court in the nineties from the Velvet Chair Lounge on Sunset Boulevard. Chad, Sloan, and a third leading man, Christian Stanstedt, became famous for their roles in various Tom Kessler productions opposite Ramona Watts, Macie Finn, and Juliette Draper.

But Chad and Sloan hadn't been photographed together for at least twenty years, and probably closer to thirty.

Not since Juliette drowned.

"You'll never guess what I'm looking at," Sam whispered. She didn't have to whisper—she was encased in an Audi Q8 with the air-conditioning on full blast—but the gossip value of what she was staring at made whispering feel necessary.

Or maybe it was Chad and Sloan's body language. There was something furtive in the way Sloan kept scanning the parked cars.

"What? What are you looking at?" Bex's impatience burned through the phone line.

"The Ice Crew, if you can believe it. Chad Bevington is in this very parking lot with Sloan Lennox. They're striding across the pavement like it's *Lights of Marfa* all over again. Sloan just flicked the butt of his cigarette at the pavement, skipping it like a goddamn stone on a pond."

"Oh my God!" Bex was not whispering. "I need a picture!"

Chad and Sloan stopped in the middle of the lot to talk to each other. There was a lot of gesturing. Sam shot off a quick series of photos and sent them to Bex.

"Unreal! Chad and Sloan *together*? They loathe each other! Their feud is legend! I was obsessed with the Ice Crew in high school. I watched *Karma Revisited* so many times, I wore it out. They were my moody teen ideal."

"I don't think they were teenagers when they did those movies. They're at least ten years older than us, and that's only if they're not lying about their ages, which Chad definitely is."

"But wasn't that the appeal? Depressive twentysomethings wearing too much eyeliner, pretending to be my age. I went through a phase where I wore brocade vests with leotards exactly like Macie Finn. I *so* should've known I was queer. No one who was obsessed with Macie Finn turned out straight, that's for sure."

"I worked with Macie." Sam said this distractedly, absorbed with watching what was now a heated conversation. She took a few more pictures.

"Wha-a-at? How do I not know this?"

"Macie did a guest spot on *Utopia*." Sam had started out in Hollywood in the ensemble cast of a hit sci-fi drama. She didn't miss the tight and shiny jumpsuits that costuming had made her wear for her role as a half-android, half-human starship officer, but it had been fun to work with a big ensemble cast and some truly remarkable guest actors.

Bex made a tiny squeal. "Tell me what they're like. Is all the dry humor real? Are they hotter in person? I feel like they would be hotter in person."

Sam laughed. She was about to answer when she saw Sloan break away from Chad.

Then she saw Chad start walking toward her car.

No, *to* her car.

"Shit, Bex. I have to go. Text me when you're getting on a plane, any plane."

Sam hit the end button in the middle of Bex's "Okay," just as Chad gestured for her to put down her window.

"Hi there, Chad. What can I do for you?"

"Why are you sitting out here?" His eyes darted around the lot. There was nothing to see. She and Chad and Sloan were the only people on the roof of this parking garage, which no one could access but credentialed actors and studio employees. "Are you waiting for someone?"

"I'm listening to a podcast." The *Craven's Daughter* reunion special had involved Sam and Bex hosting what had become a notorious podcast, so Sam got asked about podcasts a lot by people who assumed she was an expert. She was not. But Chad didn't know that.

The breeze lifted up the waves of his expensive hair, and he furrowed his eyebrows at her. There were tens of thousands of pictures of Chad Bevington making that same furrow between his brows, looking pained, yet artistic, yet hot.

"Did you see me talking to Sloan?" He said this offhandedly, glancing up at a seagull as though its screech had distracted him from his entirely trivial question.

Sam was not fooled. She had spent enough time with Chad in front of a camera to know what he sounded like when he felt a situation had moved too far beyond his control for his comfort. But why control this situation?

"I did spot you with Sloan," she decided to say. "I love to see a man find a style and stick to it. The fedora and sunglasses still work for him."

"Yeah. Whatever. I just mean we were having a private conversation."

He *was* trying to manage this. "And I was listening to a podcast." She raised her eyebrows as if to ask, *Why are you making a giant deal out of it?*

Chad furtively scanned the lot one more time. Sloan stood fifteen feet away, both hands shoved in his pockets, looking like a cardboard cutout of himself.

"Yeah. Okay. I guess you can know. I'm sure I can trust you not to say anything."

Had that been a threat? Chad was still making an effort to sound casual, but he was also staring right at her, his neck tendons prominent. This was how he looked when he brought up his legal team. Sam raised her eyebrows again.

He sighed heavily. "Sloan and I did an episode of *The Howling* together."

It took Sam a few seconds to understand how this statement connected up to Chad's cloak-and-dagger paranoia. *The Howling* was a streamer-original horror series that had become an unexpected phenomenon in its first season due to the wry, winsome appeal of Ramona Watts, also formerly of the Ice Crew. Now filming its second season at StudioHonor with the full resources of Howell Motion Pictures behind it, *The Howling* was generating a lot of speculation regarding whether its star would fall apart under the pressure of her own success.

It was a pattern that had played out more than once for Ramona over the years.

Everyone knew *The Howling* kept a tight lid on its production secrets, but only Chad would treat a pre-airing nondisclosure agreement like a list of nuclear launch codes. "*The Howling*! Oh, wow. With Ramona?"

"Yeah, but shut up about it, right?" He scowled.

Sam mimed zipping her lips.

He looked at the sky again and then smacked the top of her car a couple of times. "Catch you at our prepress."

When he walked away, Sam put up her window.

So strange.

People *were* strange with Sam, in part because she'd been an out lesbian in Hollywood for a long time, in part because she was extremely tall, blond, and famous, and most recently because she was associated with solving a crime. While trying for a second chance on the *Craven's Daughter* reunion special, she and Bex had also used their TV detective skills to close the cold case of what had happened to their friend Jen, the show's makeup artist. On live television before a breathless audience of millions, they'd coaxed a confession from the man who killed Jen, setting off a firestorm of publicity.

The sleuthing adventure was a one-off, brought to their door by circumstances and old secrets. But Sam couldn't say she had entirely put down a certain kind of *awareness* of undercurrents, obfuscation, and mysteries ever since. For instance, it was fun to see how people in her professional life checked themselves in her presence. Being a TV detective turned actual detective made people assume Sam's bullshit meter was finely tuned. It warded off a lot of bullshit.

Sam flipped through the stealth pictures she'd taken of Chad and Sloan. She would be lying if she claimed she hadn't fantasized of heading into a mystery again. She'd enjoyed working through the clues with Bex and her sisters, talking to people she might normally have never met, and baiting a trap to catch Jen's killer. It was fascinating to track the aftermath as the case wound its way through various pretrial motions on a slow path toward justice. All of it exercised Sam's mind and put her invisible youngest-of-five-siblings-and-only-girl powers to use.

A-a-and . . . she was distracting herself from the cocktail of feelings that had hit her system while talking to Bex, with Bex's arrival on the literal horizon. There were so many of these feelings. Sam was never sure which one was going to hit her at any given time.

If there was such a thing as love at first sight, then how Sam had felt about Bex the first time she met her was an argument in its favor. But they were kidding themselves to count on six full weeks together. Six months apart was much more the norm for a Hollywood couple. Something always came up in this business—callbacks, reshoots, "amazing opportunities" that had to be seized before they evaporated. Even now, Sam had half a dozen emails from Bradley's people sitting on her phone, flagging up details to review before she was supposed to be on a plane in seven days, on her way to his rustic mountain retreat to talk about his agenda.

It was how the game was played. He would monopolize her time and make her come to him because he *could*. How else could Sam appreciate how big his dick was?

Not to mention that Sam's brother Fergus was hogging her guest room, which meant she and Bex had no guarantee of privacy at Sam's. Bex had her sister Vic living at home, with Frankie road-tripping her way west from her New York internship and arriving in a handful of days.

With a sigh, she pulled out of her spot to head home and execute Bex's plan. She trusted Bex's plans. They'd gotten the two of them this far, and Sam had no reason not to believe that if she stayed the course, everything would get good, and easy, and they could just be Bex and Sam, always.

All they had to do was make it to the part where they were in the same room at the same time. After that, there would be nothing to worry about.

She was almost sure of it.

You Can't Come Back from a Comeback

"What is this?" Victoria Simon pointed a honey habanero wing flat from Sam to Bex. "Like, what *is* this?"

She sat across the table from them with a smear of hot sauce on her broad cheekbone and a mountain of decimated wings on her plate. The younger of Bex's two sisters, Vic was a sophomore transfer student at UCLA, majoring in biology in preparation for a career in veterinary medicine—a future plan that had not wavered since Sam first met her at age seven.

Vic had been making Sam laugh for just as long with her sneak-attack wit and enthusiastic embrace of the off-screen drama of Hollywood. But it would be a mistake to underestimate her, even if she took FaceTime calls at full volume in public and her biggest recent dilemma was whether she should get heart-shaped rainbow freckles tattooed on her face.

Bex looked up from her plate of tacos. "What is what?"

Her hair had gotten long, frizzing in red coils to her elbows. She wore opaque pink dancer's tights and an oversized vintage sweatshirt that celebrated the Cleveland Browns 1964 championship win. It was very Bex travel attire, familiar in every way. Sam had known this woman for more than ten years, seen this outfit more than once, but the tips of her ears set fire every time Bex glanced at her.

She felt thirteen years old. Her bones were humming, possibly audibly. Ridiculous to think she had fantasized about pulling Bex into her arms and kissing her hair straight the moment she saw her. Right now, Sam felt like she would faint if she so much as touched this glorious creature.

Which was maybe why she hadn't touched her yet?

Sam had done what Bex said. After she spent too long deciding on what to wear all over again and dodging Fergus's questions out of fear he would try to finagle an invitation, she'd arrived at the same time she got a text from Bex that she was thirty minutes away.

Thirty minutes.

Thirty minutes and six months.

Ordinarily, Sam prided herself on her ability to run in a low gear. But her voice had cracked when she'd ordered food—so much food—and she'd snapped at Vic and had to keep checking her appearance to make sure that the way her entire body buzzed with electric anticipation wasn't making her hair stand on end.

Of course, the moment she had made herself sit down, take deep breaths, and sip slowly from a water glass was the same moment Bex burst into the foyer. Sam's surprise caused her to inhale a mouthful of her soothing water, and so she was bent at the waist, red-faced and choking, when Bex first laid eyes on her. Not the impression she'd wanted to make. Bex and Vic pounded on her back until Sam could breathe again. She stood up to accept Bex's hug. But after thirty minutes and six months and a choking fit, Sam freaked out and air-hugged Bexley Simon like she was a fan in a selfie line.

"What is this vibe between you guys?" Vic clarified. "I could have fit a Bible between you during your *one* moment of PDA. So far, we've talked about what food Sam ordered, which was boring because I helped her order it, then about Frankie and her road trip—also boring, we're all on the group chat—and we've debated if Kiki's Wings are spicier than usual or less spicy."

For a child with no job, who'd recently asked for an extension on a paper she'd already been given six weeks to write, Vic looked smug. Bex put her taco down.

"What?" Vic asked, with a glare around a mouthful of wings. "If we do this your way, we'll have to wait another ten years for anything to happen between the two of you, and I'm tired of the paparazzi asking me if you're really, for-real *together* when they should be asking if I was whispering in Catriona Kennedy's ear at the Lakers game or licking it. I do have fans."

"Maybe, Victoria," Bex said, "and please listen carefully, because what I'm about to say includes words and phrases you haven't learned the meaning of, but *maybe* it's none of your business."

"It's definitely none of my business," Vic agreed easily. "But what kind of life am I going to have if I only mind my own business? Why would you want that for me?"

Sam folded the foil that had wrapped her burrito into a neat square. She had nothing to say in response to Vic's fair but brutal assessment of the situation.

Was it true that Sam had come over to Bex's wearing silk briefs as pants and extremely high heels in order to claim something a bit sweeter than a fail-hug? Yes. For Sam, fashion was expression, attention, power, and armor. She had sartorial strategies for every possible situation.

Was it also true that seeing Bex across her dining room table after all this time was like seeing her camp girlfriend in math class on the first day of school? Again, yes.

But Bex's husky alto still gave her goose bumps, and Bex still got more smart words out of her mouth in a minute than anyone Sam had ever met. Being around her bowled Sam over in the worst, best way, just like always.

Sam took a sip of her Jarritos. "You know, Vic, you do have the option of removing yourself from the equation to give your sister and me some time to ourselves."

Vic snorted. "Yeah, right. Like you guys wouldn't self-combust with nerves if you didn't have a buffer. Thank me later."

Sam grimaced around her straw. Bex had raised this young woman, and Sam knew that a lot of this display was Vic projecting her *own* Bex excitement onto Sam and Bex's relationship. "Hmm. I'm sure you're right."

"Anyway," Vic said tartly. She wound a strand of pin-straight blond hair around her finger, tipping her head as she considered a private thought. "Here's something actually interesting. I took a cold plunge with Piper Redwood today."

Sam sat up straighter. Piper Redwood was a young costar of *The Howling* who was Vic's friend. "Tell me everything," she said.

Immediately, she recognized her mistake. It was never a good idea to betray too much avidity around Simon women. Now Bex was staring at her with her giant eyes that missed nothing, leaning forward to better suck Sam into her tractor beam.

"You can't look at me like that," Sam said. "Like I have to explain my interest in at least one of the random sips of tea Vic serves. Piper Redwood's star is rising fast."

"True." Bex's arched brows furrowed. "But you saw Chad Bevington and Sloan Lennox together today, and you haven't told me what Chad came and talked to you about after you hung up on me. I am plenty sharp enough to guess they might have been together at StudioHonor, where *The Howling* is taped, because they will soon appear on the show."

Damn. Bex had put that together in no time at all. Sometimes she was a little *too* sharp. "I didn't hang up on *you*." Sam offered this rebuttal with her chilliest California surfer girl smile. Sometimes that worked when Bex was getting ahead of her. "I had to hang up the phone because Chad came over to talk to me."

"The thing is, *The Howling* is known for sentimental stunt casting," Bex plowed on.

Sam shrugged but didn't look directly at her. When she did that, Bex could reach into her mind and rummage around.

"Let's see. Chad talked to you." Bex was now thinking aloud. Never good. "Maybe Sloan did, too. Or both of them together. You had to go so quickly that you *literally* and *actually* hung up on me, and you never do that. For someone who was born and raised in Oakland, you really embrace the Midwestern goodbye. But now, after running into one third of the Ice Crew in the StudioHonor parking lot, you're super-duper interested in Piper Redwood, who stars alongside *another* famous Ice Crew personage on *The Howling*—namely, Ramona Watts." Bex frowned at Sam. "You're not telling me everything. You're *supposed* to tell me everything. It's a rule."

"Whose rule?"

"Obviously my rule. Not knowing things gives me hives that won't fade until I know the thing."

"Maybe Sam heard what Piper told *me*." Vic pulled out another wing dripping chiles and chopped cilantro. "About Ramona Watts being a no-call no-show for *The Howling*'s taping this morning."

Sam and Bex turned to her as one.

"Is *that* what you were going to tell us?" Sam asked.

"Wait." Bex held a palm up to her sister. "I was wanting to hear what Chad talked to Sam about. Is Vic's gossip about Ramona what one or both of these men told you? Because if it is, they could only know that if they had been guest-cast on the show in order to bring Chad, Sloan, and Ramona back together on screen for the first time in a generation!"

Vic opened her mouth. Sam held up her own palm to forestall any additional commentary. She had forgotten how quickly the conversation could get out of hand when there was more than one Simon in the same room. "I didn't know about Ramona. Chad came up to my car and asked if I would keep it under my hat that I saw him and Sloan together because he and Sloan recently did a spot together on *The Howling*. I guess he doesn't want to violate whatever NDA he signed to keep it a secret. He said he trusted me not to tell, but he didn't say it like he actually trusted me. More as a threat." Sam dropped her hand and watched keen interest spread over Bex's face.

"I *knew* it!" Bex said, pointing at Sam. "See? I figured it out, because I know this town. Ramona is breaking streaming records with her comeback on *The Howling,* reminding her old fans and a whole new generation that she can act her actual pants off anytime she wants to. Naturally, Hollywood is going to ask, 'What cheap trick could we do to get even more viewers? Wait, no, this is perfect! Let's make her act in front of the whole world with the two men she was with on the night their friend died.' " She smiled at Sam in triumph, and then her face fell. "That came out wrong. I didn't mean to make light of a tragedy. I only mean that is what I would *expect*. From Hollywood."

"You two don't know everything." Vic sounded put out at the theft of her thunder.

"Then tell us what we don't know," Sam countered.

Vic exhaled, as long and beleaguered as a person could without passing out. "I'm not sure I want to anymore. I'm feeling very silenced."

"Vic!" Sam and Bex barked this at the same time.

"Now I am feeling empowered again." Vic leaned back. "I wonder, is what I might know interesting to you? Is it interesting to hear that Piper didn't like working with Chad and Sloan—she said they were ick—and Ramona liked working with them even less? Piper told me that by the end of the week, Ramona was pulling out diva behavior. It got messy. But the episode's in the can now, as of Friday. Everyone takes the weekend to grab a breath. Only *then*, Ramona's MIA on set this morning, and we all know what that means. The studio's freaking out."

Vic smiled like a little gremlin and nibbled her wing.

"'We all know what that means,' meaning what?" Bex reached across the table and took Vic's wing from her fingers. "Don't forget I could cut you off."

Vic rolled her eyes with the confidence of a well-loved child. "Meaning they're assuming Ramona's going to turn up in an arroyo in forty-eight hours bombed out of her mind, wearing nothing but a silk scarf. You know, I heard she stole a director's Bentley, parked it at the edge of a canyon, and then put a rock on the gas, sending it into oblivion, all because he hired a body double for her who had bigger boobs." She tapped her chin. "I don't know where I heard that, but that's what I heard."

Bex wrinkled her nose. "I've heard things, too. Like Ramona taking off for months or years to live in the desert after a hospital stay for exhaustion. I feel like there was a luscious profile once with pictures of her living in an adobe hut wearing flowing linen layers. She always comes back, of course, usually with a new religion or exercise practice that purportedly saved her life." She sighed. "The woman is talented with a capital iconic, but doesn't she need this comeback? Surely she only has so many comebacks in her at this point in her career. You can't come back from a comeback."

Sam was rooting for Ramona to stay the course, if only because her IMDb profile looked a lot like the one Sam had thought she herself would have, once upon a time: a mix of independent films and big-studio projects. Roles that made her stretch and learn things. No-money work she took because she believed in the message. That was what Sam had assumed she'd be doing when she moved to Los Angeles, twenty-two years old and fresh out of Yale School of Drama. Instead, she was cast on *Utopia* nearly instantly. After a few years, she made the lateral move to *Craven's Daughter.*

She imagined telling her current team that she admired Ramona's career. Their collective horror was not difficult to picture. Ramona Watts was unreliable and ungovernable. If she were a man, her unpredictable behavior would only enhance her industry-wide reputation. But while a difficult man was a genius, a difficult woman was a liability. This went double or triple for queer people like Sam. Black women. The list went on.

In the arts, it was always better to be unknown, with no history or projects to speak of. Then you could break out like a thoroughbred in the home stretch—far preferable to being a consistently talented actor with a reputation for even a single whisper of struggle. It meant that career longevity for non-men almost *required* a series of comebacks where you could fake to the world that you were shiny, brand-new, and unsullied by experience.

Sam wondered when she would be forced to reinvent herself. She supposed that would be determined by *Theomina*'s box-office returns. Or what Bradley Wilhite decided about her fate.

The thought was so preoccupying that Sam missed the next thing Vic said. She had to mentally rewind to catch up.

"It's worse than that," Vic had just told her sister. "Piper says Ramona's been on thin ice, anyway, because of her past behavior. With the way she acted last week, the director is fed up. She said in front of the whole cast and crew this morning that they can get by shooting without Ramona for a few days, but if she's not in the studio ready to go on Friday morning, she's going to be written off the show."

Bex held up a finger and then bounced over to a credenza in the dining room. She opened a drawer and pulled out a notebook, then returned to the table, where she reclaimed her seat. When she clicked open her pen, Sam's heart skipped a beat.

Bex didn't whip out her famous notebooks to doodle in. One of those notebooks had kept their investigation into the murder they'd solved six months ago from going off the rails.

"So what do we think happened?" Bex asked. "What do we know?"

"Wait." Vic peered at her sister. "You got out the notebook."

"I need to keep my thoughts in order."

"Why?"

"Because we just established that Ramona didn't show up for work today despite a clear ultimatum from the studio that she be on her best behavior. What the director said in front of everyone probably wasn't *just* her blowing off steam. It's likely a condition of Ramona's employment, inked in her contract. StudioHonor is the streaming arm of Howell Motion Pictures, and they aren't known to mess around. That's concerning. Did your friend Piper or anyone else on set or with the studio call the police? File a report?"

Vic blinked. Her blue eyes were huge and, for a few long seconds, blank. Then her mind seemed to come back online all at once, and she bounced in her chair with barely suppressed excitement. "I don't know! But I will definitely find out."

If Bex loved to be right, Vic loved drama of any kind. Particularly the kind she had initiated and was taken seriously by her older sister.

Sam had a sinking feeling about this development. If she and Bex were only going to have a week together, she didn't want to lose it to diving headfirst into the shallow end of somebody else's business.

"If I'm remembering right," Bex said, "Ramona won an

Emmy, a SAG award, and a Golden Globe for her work on *The Howling* in its first season." She jotted notes down rapidly, tracking her pen back to underline words as she spoke. "I find it hard to believe she did all that while being unstable on set, regardless of what might be going on in her personal life." Bex put down her pen. "I don't like it. I don't want to give in to bystander effect and assume someone else has reported this and is looking for Ramona. What if it isn't the kind of thing where time is on your side?"

Sam knew better than to throw down the tire spikes right this second. Bex and Vic would only protest. Loudly. Sam would give it one more page in the notebook and then steer the ship back to Vic and Bex's *own* lives until Vic got sleepy from the sugar in her tamarind soda and wandered off. Then Sam would have an opportunity to see what kind of effect her outfit was having on Bex.

Bex's phone chimed. She picked it up and swiped to look. "It's the security system."

She tapped her screen, and Vic leaned close, peering at it. "What is it? Is it a bad guy or a bear? Remember how I had to call you in the middle of the night last month because there *was* a bear?"

Bex held up her finger, then put her phone to her ear. "Hello?"

There was the sound of someone talking. Sam looked at Vic, who whispered, "I couldn't tell who it was. They're wearing a hoodie."

Bex stood and started walking toward the foyer. "Hold on," she said. "I'm coming." She motioned to Sam to follow her. Something about her energy made the hairs on the back of Sam's neck stand up.

"Are you okay?" Vic asked her sister.

"It's fine," Bex said. "I'm just surprised. There's a visitor for Sam."

In the foyer, Bex turned on the lights and opened one of the huge doors. Standing on the wide, curved steps, wearing a black knitted hoodie and raw denim jeans, was none other than Macie Finn.

Of the Ice Crew.

Of Chad, Sloan, Ramona, and the late Juliette Draper.

What was *happening*?

Actresses, Detectives—It Doesn't Matter

"Sorry!" Macie said. "*So* sorry. Look, can I step in?" They glanced behind them. "I parked on the street, and there's a sedan I don't recognize. I think it might have followed me over here. I'm worried some asshole with a camera is going to pop out of it any second."

Macie Finn was the type of actor whose looks destined them for character or comedic roles. The broad, square jawline, the huge green eyes, the pixie cut—all of it combined with an impertinent, borderline tactless screen presence to mean that Macie had been called "singular" long before coming out as nonbinary. When Sam was young, Macie had been an inspiration by virtue of this very singularity. In every role, they were always indescribably *Macie*.

And now the '90s star was at Bex's door, and Bex was stepping aside to let them in, saying, "Of course." Surreal.

Bex shut the door and killed everything but the security lights outside.

When Macie shoved off the hood, Sam saw that dark horn-rimmed glasses failed to conceal their exhaustion. Despite the star's typically ageless quality, the lines around Macie's eyes were deep.

"Sam," Macie said in the familiar husky baritone, reaching out their hands. "I went to your place first, and your security guy told me you were here. I know he shouldn't have, but I convinced him it was an emergency, so go easy on him."

"Don't worry about it." She squeezed Macie's hands, her heart racing. Vic had come into the foyer and was staring in obvious shock—and Vic was a Hollywood baby who was difficult to shock.

"The thing is, I do have an emergency," Macie said. "If I were anyone else, and if my emergency were about anything else, I'd go straight to the police, but that's a last resort."

"Ramona Watts," Bex said.

Macie's mouth tightened. "Shit. I know the gossip rags work fast, but I can't believe it's already out there."

"No. It's not." Vic stepped forward. "I found out from Piper Redwood, but she only told me that Ramona no-call-no-showed at *The Howling* today. The three of us were just talking about it."

Macie's eyes closed. "Thank God. Okay. Yeah, it's because of Ramona that I'm here. I've been running around asking anyone I can about her all day, trying to track her down without everything going sideways. I'm fucking sick with worry. It's sensitive enough that I didn't want to call. I went by your house, Sam, and like I said, your security sent me over here."

Sam didn't have security. She did, however, have a brother visiting who would not hesitate to give Macie Finn directions to Bex's place.

Macie suddenly stuck out their hand to Bex. "Apologies. Macie Finn. I'm intruding. You're Bexley Simon, obviously. Saw you at the Prince Edward in Soho and cried my eyes out. Never going to be the same." They gave Bex's hand a firm shake, then offered the same to Vic. "Victoria, isn't it?"

"Vic," she confirmed. "It's a pleasure to meet you."

"What's going on?" Bex started leading them into the main living room, turning on lights as she went. The stiff way she moved and the color creeping into the tops of her ears told Sam that Bex was privately freaking out. Macie's effusive greeting had overwhelmed the still-obsessed teen inside of her. The group settled in a rough circle on the comfortable sectional, with Vic on an ottoman.

Macie rocked her body toward Sam's. "I wanted to talk to you. When you did the *Craven's Daughter* reunion, I followed everything about Jen Arnot and how you nailed that little shitbrick, the set designer, for her death. I was breathless listening to the podcast, let me tell you. Ramona and I both were. And so I thought of you, hoping . . . hoping, I guess, that you guys are still doing it."

"Doing what?" Sam asked.

"Sensitive work. Detective work. For people like us. Hollywood people who don't want to get the authorities involved too soon."

Sam laughed, incredulous. How could she and Bex have been doing detective work when they hadn't had a minute together in months?

Macie tipped their head. "Fuck. I'm wrong. Jesus. I'm sorry. It's only that I'm a complete wreck, and I couldn't think where else to turn."

Sam was about to say something sympathetically dismissive when Bex folded her hands together in a move that Sam recognized as something she used to do when playing private investigator Cora Banks. "No. You're right," she said with all of Cora's gentle empathy. "It's not something we talk about, but we might be able to help."

Sam wished she had come over here wearing real pants so she didn't feel like she was going to collapse in front of Macie Finn and Bexley Simon wearing nothing but heels, glorified underwear, and a suit vest. *It's not something we talk about?* No kidding it wasn't something they talked about. They had made it very clear to the public that while it was true they had played investigators on TV—and, yes, had stumbled on the resolution to the mystery of Jen's death—they were not, in fact, detectives.

Evidently in Los Angeles that was a distinction without a difference.

"It's true Ramona didn't show for call this morning," Macie said. "But what no one knows is that she's been gone longer than that. We haven't heard from her since she went to work Friday morning."

It was Monday now. No one had heard from Ramona Watts in more than three days?

Macie wrung their hands. "Most people would probably think it's too soon to say this, but what I know in my heart is that Ramona has disappeared."

Sam turned to gauge Bex's reaction to this news. She found Bex already looking at her. Sam raised an eyebrow and watched both of Bex's dimples sink in, framing her serious mouth.

Sam wanted to kiss that serious mouth. She wanted to kick Macie and Vic out, and then, when they were gone, she wanted to tell Bex to lift up her arms up so that Sam could draw that soft sweatshirt over her head and find out how much softer her skin was underneath. After that, she wanted to do whatever Bex told her to do, one thing after another, until she was exhausted and breathless and full of stupid gratitude.

Unfortunately, Sam also believed Macie. Ramona Watts was missing. And if Macie had come to Sam and Bex believing they could help, they could at least listen to what Macie had to say.

Sam turned back to her visitor. "Tell us what you're worried about."

In an obvious bid to soothe Macie, Bex moved their conversation to a seating area by the pool.

The hot day had eased into cool, dry night with a soft breeze, and whatever night-blooming plants Bex's gardener had tucked into the landscaping released a fragrance that made the whole area smell like an expensive spa. Unprompted, Vic had disappeared in the direction of the kitchen and emerged with a pitcher of hibiscus agua fresca, proving that Bex had influenced her sisters where it counted.

Macie did appear to be fractionally more comfortable in the dim outdoor lights, and sitting outdoors meant they could vape. "You'd think after thirty years shackled to nicotine I'd know better," they said before taking a long, rueful pull. "I wish they'd never made these things. I'd just about gotten off the patch when my agent passed one to me, telling me it was 'healthier,' and that was ten years ago." They blew out a cloud of vapor.

Sam was trying to think of the right question to ask when Macie zipped up their hoodie and put away their vape. "You know, that's the first thing to know about Ramona. She'd never fucking smoke. She doesn't drink at all. Never has. One time she tried weed and found out she's allergic to it. The only substances Ramona's into are mushroom coffee and fancy vitamins. She was drinking green smoothies back when only the cult members were doing it."

Macie glanced at Bex, who had begun taking notes with the slim gold pen she liked best. The soft sounds of the pen moving over the paper blended with the lapping water of the pool. It seemed to settle Macie down to be listened to with such officious attention.

"But that's how she grew up," Macie said. "Her parents were both teachers. She's a Great Lakes kid who had an idyllic childhood, camping and doing children's theater and reading in this magical treehouse her dad built for her. She's never moved out of the first fairly modest place she bought in West Hollywood when she was getting started. Ramona's always been very grounded."

"That's not the version of Ramona that the media peddles." Sam sat beside Bex on a love seat plenty big enough for there to be space between them. Instead, Bex's pink dance tights pressed against Sam's bare thigh from her knee nearly to her hip. Every time she shifted, the sensation of dense nylon stretched over warm skin made Sam want to close her eyes and sink into it.

Macie nodded. "Ramona's strict policy is to refuse to engage, but sometimes I just want to project forty-foot letters on the roof of SoFi stadium saying that Ramona Watts is an introverted coastal granny who keeps herself to herself, not some banana-pants cluster of neuroses who can't stop falling off the wagon. In my opinion, the rumors are because Ramona's private and ambivalent about publicity. It's punishment."

Sam had certainly seen this dynamic play out. A precarious truce existed between the media and celebrity. It was maintained by giving the media just enough access to feed the world's parasocial relationship, but not so much that you were criticized for overexposure. Paradoxically, sometimes ignoring the media led right back to overexposure—usually of a fictitious version of your life that begged you to come out of hiding and correct it.

"It's the break in her routines that has you worried, is that right?" Bex asked. "Tell us more about that."

"Who's missing her, what they expected, what might be out of the ordinary," Sam clarified. Now it was her turn to sound like her *Craven's Daughter* character, hard-boiled FBI agent Henri Shannon. It was an odd sensation with Bex's thigh pressed against hers.

"Yeah." Macie nodded, their eyes on Bex's gold pen. "Sorry. I mean, I should be able to tell you more than I can, considering how long I've known her. I got a call from a producer at *The Howling* around ten this morning. They wondered if I'd heard from Ramona. I tell them no, but it's not out of the ordinary for a couple days to go by that we don't talk. I'm pushing fifty, and I hate texting. Everyone's always misinterpreting what a person means or taking offense because you ended a goddamned sentence with a period. The studio tells me she's not returning their calls, and the same is true for her agent and manager. I offer to drive over to her place. It's locked up, all the lights out. I look around, but nothing's out of the ordinary. I call Ramona, text her, but I don't hear anything back. *That's* out of the ordinary. She always calls me back."

"Even if she were on set or tied up at work?" Sam asked.

"Unless she's in front of a camera, yeah. She's my closest friend. We've known each other since we were kids. Came to this town at the same time from the Midwest with our mamas, naive as fuck, the kind of young this business likes to run through like potato chips, but we're still here."

"Was it when she didn't call back that you started to worry?" Sam asked.

Macie seemed to deflate. "I guess I've *been* worried. Listen, I'm going to tell you something in confidence. It can't leave this group."

"Of course," Bex said.

Macie checked each of their faces before continuing. "I think there's something going on with her. She was under a lot of stress, it seemed like. Some of it was *The Howling*."

"The attention from its success?" Sam asked.

"A little, but more because of the work. A horror show is rough on its leads. Physical. She did three days up to her neck in freezing-cold water for the first-season finale."

"I just wrapped *Theomina*," Sam said. "My bruises have bruises. Filming is so technical, and the expectations are brutal. The schedules."

Bex glanced at her, making Sam's belly hollow. Right now, Bex's warm body was against hers, but in a week, Sam would be in Colorado with an indefinite endpoint on talks for the Theomina series. After that, there would be the next project, the next location, or a grueling set in L.A. that demanded fourteen-hour days. It was hard enough to sustain a career in this industry. How were she and Bex supposed to sustain this relationship?

"You understand," Macie said. "But with Ramona there are other factors, too. This time of year, late May, is always hard on her because it's when everything happened with Juliette."

When Juliette Draper died, she meant.

Sam took stock of what she knew about that accident. It wasn't a lot. There had been a small Ice Crew party on a docked boat in Marina Del Rey. Chad Bevington, Sloan Lennox, Ramona Watts, and Juliette Draper. Juliette was impaired and had gotten into an argument with the others. In the year prior, she'd been engaged to Chad, then to Sloan, but had broken it off with both. There was bad blood. For reasons Sam couldn't recall, Juliette impulsively took a dinghy out into the bay on her own. Her body was found days later, her death by drowning declared accidental because she'd been intoxicated.

"I'm sorry you lost your friend," Sam said.

"I just watched a TikTok about it," Vic said. "It's an incredibly sad story."

"Thanks." Macie patted the pocket they'd put their vape pen in, then seemed to think better of it and adjusted their glasses. "I don't think there was ever going to be a way we could have saved Juliette. But Ramona isn't so sure."

In the violet light from the pool, Sam caught Macie's sudden grieved expression and realized the implication. "You're saying that Ramona *really* struggles with the anniversary. Emotionally."

Macie took off the glasses and squeezed the bridge of their nose. "Ramona feels responsible for Juliette's death. Sometimes, I'm afraid she'll do something drastic. Hurt herself. Or worse."

Bex put down her notebook. "My God, what a burden. But Ramona wasn't held responsible. Did you have any reason to doubt the conclusions of that investigation, or—?"

"No." Macie shook their head. "But Ramona's a private person. To me, she's seemed preoccupied the last few times I've seen her. Moody. I was at her house not long ago when she got a voicemail that made her jumpy, but she wouldn't talk about it. It could have been nothing, the kind of bullshit everybody deals with. Or it could have been something huge and scary. I don't know if there was something unusual going on in her life, but I wouldn't, necessarily. What bothers me is not knowing if *anybody* would know." Macie sighed. "If I take my worry to the police, even if they believe me, there will be a leak. Ramona's reputation will take yet another hit. I don't want this to end with her pissed off at me for feeding the sharks. But what if I don't do anything and she really is in trouble?"

"She's not an anxious person?" Bex asked. "There are a lot of people who would describe me as jumpy after a relatively minor issue that came up on a call."

Macie shook their head. "It's one of the reasons why we've been close all these years. I'm inhibited and a worrywart, but Ramona feels her feelings, even the ones most of us avoid. It means she's almost always very centered, or she's taking care of herself while she works through something. With Ramona, I feel less vulnerable talking about my own shit, and her calm regulates me. She got off that phone call white as a sheet, jumping at shadows, irritable, and, yes, anxious. If it were anyone else, I'd probably write it off. But this is Ramona, so it shook me up. I pressed harder than I usually do to get her to talk. She wouldn't."

"Okay, but why did Ramona think it was her fault Juliette died?" Vic scooted closer to the edge of her ottoman. "From what I understand, the facts are far from mysterious. Chad and Sloan and Ramona and Juliette were all in plain view of the busy marina on the main deck of the yacht. There were pictures of the party taken at the marina from afar. People heard Juliette yelling. When she was found in the water, her toxicology screen told the rest of the story. What could Ramona have done differently?"

"She was in between projects the night Chad and Sloan wanted to party on Chad's yacht. When she heard Juliette was planning to go, she invited herself along to protect Juliette, who was taking pills like Tic Tacs at that point. I don't know a lot about what happened that night, but I know that in a general sense, Ramona thinks she gave up on getting Juliette away from Chad too soon, and that she didn't do enough to keep her from rebounding with Sloan. She didn't get tough enough with her about the drugs and alcohol and media attention that were dulling Juliette's judgment. And Jesus, the media was so loud. It was like the entire plot of *The Lights of Marfa* was playing out in real life."

In the cult movie that instituted the Ice Crew as a cultural phenomenon, the character played by Juliette had to choose between two men played by Sloan and Chad. The film presented the choice between blond, wealthy, traditionally masculine Chad and slim, brunette, bespectacled, fedora-wearing Sloan as a choice between polar opposites, though neither man treated Juliette's character with respect or kindness. In the end, Juliette's character picked Sloan's—a decision portrayed as a tragic, given what the film had shown the audience about the destructive force of his obsession with her.

Sam shivered, thinking about how many young people had seen that movie and thought it was about love.

She understood why Macie was reluctant to involve law enforcement. Celebrity-obsessed media distorted the most minor blips into full-fledged scandals. Add to that reality Ramona's reputation, and if Macie felt it wasn't the time to make their alarm public, Sam had to respect that. But she did need a way to gauge how alarmed Macie was—and how alarmed Macie thought *they* should be. "Just to be clear," she said, "do you believe that Ramona may be in danger, struggling with these feelings?"

Macie pulled out the vape then and took several pulls, enveloping their body in smoke that looked blue in the light. "She has taken time to be by herself before, whenever she needs it. She likes to connect to the outdoors when feelings are hard. But not once, not ever, has Ramona failed to tell me she'd be off the grid for a while. I feel like my heart's hovering right outside my chest, poised to fall on the ground and smash to pieces. If I've learned anything from Ramona, it's not to ignore emotions that are tearing you up inside."

Bex had tears in her eyes. Years ago, she had told Sam that the night her parents died in a car accident in Ohio, she sat straight up in bed, certain there was something very wrong. Within hours, she found out what it was.

"I'm not sure we can do much," Sam said. "Believe me when I say that everything that happened around the *Craven's Daughter* reunion was organic. We were deeply connected to Jen. What's more, we knew the players. I know the world's making the most of the idea of two TV detectives as actual sleuths, but we're actresses."

Macie adjusted their horn-rims in a way that signaled impatience with Sam's line of argument. "What you're saying just proves you can help. The world does think you know how to do this, which means you'll be taken seriously. People will talk to you. And more than that, because you're actors, you understand what Ramona's show means to her. You won't put it at risk. Actresses, detectives—it doesn't matter to me, as long as someone finds her."

Sam leaned forward. "But if we find out she *is* at risk—"

"Then I'll go straight to the police," Macie said. "Right away, if I have a reason to believe she's truly in danger."

Sam was reassured. She was perfectly willing to go to the police herself, if it came to that.

"We'll do it," Vic said. "We'll help you."

"*Vic,*" Bex hissed.

"What? You can't seriously be thinking of saying no? Macie

came to us in the night! A woman is missing! You're both in the same place at the same time! It's *destiny* that you find Ramona. If you don't help Macie, I will. My squad will back me up."

Sam winced. The idea of Vic's action-seeking young Hollywood friends chasing down Ramona Watts made her more nervous than the thought of having to deal with Chad again.

"Sam?"

Bex's thigh pressed hard against hers. In the low light, the freckles Bex often hid under makeup looked nearly three-dimensional against her shadowed skin. "Maybe it couldn't hurt to ask a few questions?" she asked.

Sam glanced at Bex's notebook, which was filled with her tidy handwriting, little boxes and stars, and many underlines. "You don't really mean a few questions."

Bex closed her notebook with a smile. "Maybe however many we need to ask."

Whatever the circumstances, Sam wouldn't say no to Bexley Simon. Even if she could, Sam wasn't the kind of person to turn away a genuine request for help.

She'd go with the flow, same as always, and steal the time and space to connect with Bex wherever they could grab it. Sam knew how to do that. She'd made herself an expert at it.

But she couldn't seem to feel as excited as Vic was or as emotionally invested as Bex already seemed to be at the prospect of digging up Ramona Watts's secrets. And she couldn't tell if that was because her time with Bex was precious or if her intuition was picking up on something darker.

"I'll give you whatever phone numbers and introductions you need," Macie said. "I'll be the muscle where it's necessary, if someone won't take your call. Please."

"Okay. Yes," Sam said.

Bex reached out and touched Macie's arm. "We'll do what we can. Everything we can."

Sam stood up, reaching her hand down for Bex, who took it

and stood up, too. Instead of letting go, Bex twined their fingers together. The tight knot deep in Sam's chest relaxed.

"Stay out here as long as you need to," Bex said to Macie.

Sam pulled on Bex's hand to draw her back inside the house and—if Vic managed to take the hint—offer Macie some privacy.

And to give Sam, finally, at least one minute alone with Bex.

Power Won't Mend a Broken Heart

Sam stood in the marble hallway outside her manager's office on the seventh floor of Elite Talent Associates, smacking a thick envelope against her hand.

It was one of the pale blue letter-size mailers that Sam's agency used to provide itineraries, and it contained Sam's travel arrangements for Colorado. She'd just heard an earful about the Double Diamond Ranch, outside of Telluride, where Bradley Wilhite apparently raised some kind of rare beef for elite markets. The eight a.m. convocation with her manager, agent, and a raft of personal assistants was the kind of thing Sam avoided when she could, not being a fan of meetings of the "could have been an email" variety.

This morning, however, Sam had been the one to call the team together, for two reasons.

Number one, she'd had a revelation. It bore down on her last night after about thirty minutes of tossing and turning in bed, feeling annoyed about Bradley Wilhite and guilty for not telling Bex. The revelation was this: Sam had arrived at a crossroads in her career. It made sense to take a look around.

Sitting at a conference table between her agent and her manager with six assistants of various types arrayed around them and a glass of something called "cold-extracted apple juice" in front of her, Sam had done just that. She'd gotten an eyeful of some of the many people she would let down if she didn't meet her immediate obligations. She'd heard more about those obligations, which included listening to whatever Bradley Wilhite thought of the rough cut of *Theomina* while she sat at his twelve-foot-long aspen wood table beneath a deer antler chandelier.

This far along in her life as an actor, she truly hadn't expected to arrive at a point where her own voice felt muffled by her success. But she had. It did. Sam needed to figure out what to do about that. The truth was, most of the time, she didn't feel as though she had any kind of a good argument why she shouldn't just continue to take the calls, meetings, and projects her team told her to take. That was what she'd been doing ever since she quit *Craven's Daughter*, and it had worked—at least in the sense that it kept her too busy to think about her broken heart. By any conventional metric, she was successful.

Except she was starting to wonder if there was a different metric to measure success by. One that would make her happier.

That was as far as she'd gotten with her first objective.

The second reason Sam had called this morning's meeting was so that she'd have an excuse to be at Elite Talent Associates. This reason had come to her after she got sick of lying awake under the covers, climbed out of bed, did sixty seconds of Internet research, and learned that Ramona Watts's agent had an office in the building.

Macie wasn't wrong—Sam and Bex *did* have access to people and inner circles it would be difficult for the police to penetrate without a warrant. Sam had never been one to leverage her status for more than a runway preview, but the chance to speak to Ramona's agent was one she couldn't pass up.

Her appointment was scheduled for nine o'clock.

If Ramona was simply taking a breather, her agent might know where she was and when she would come back. Talking to April Feinstein was therefore a critical first step in reassuring Macie. If April would talk to Sam. She had a reputation for being formidable. Scary, actually.

Sam tugged the hem of her top, which was styled to look like a giant's shirt collar that a normal-size person could wear as a shirt. A very small shirt.

As her heels clicked down the hall, she considered what Henri Shannon, formerly of the FBI, would ask Ramona's agent. First, Henri would need to find a way to introduce the topic of conversation. Maybe she would have a ruse. Would April Feinstein buy that Sam was Ramona's cousin? That they shared a love of antiques? A rare breed of dog? And Sam needed to know where Ramona was in order to give her a hot tip about an upcoming litter?

No. She was *Sam Farmer*. After all the work she'd done, if she believed her name couldn't open an agent's door in Hollywood without a ruse, then she wasn't giving herself or her team the credit they deserved.

She would simply walk in there and be Sam Farmer.

When she grasped the handle, the doors opened on whisper-quiet pneumatic hinges, and a tall, curvy, gorgeous plus-sized woman with deep red hair that was, if possible, more unruly than Bex's grabbed her by the wrist and pulled her inside.

"Thank Christ you're here," she said in a rush. "Does anyone else know?"

Sam blinked at the woman, who was filling out a pair of short shorts with high-top Converse sneakers and a wrap top. "I mean, just the person I set up the appointment with? Assuming you're April and I've got the right office."

The woman hadn't let go of her wrist. She gazed at Sam's face with her brow furrowed in contemplation. "No one else, though, right?"

"No?"

"Except, of course"—she winked—"Bex. *She* would know."

Bex actually *didn't* know, not yet, but Sam's head was spinning, so she only nodded.

"Right. Follow me. Sorry it's so"—she waved her hands around the office, which contained a long glossy desk with a single chair and nothing else—"Zillow-ready. I'm not in the agent game anymore, ever since I founded my production company with Katie, you know. But I kept one client, because, well"—she leaned against the desk and gestured to the chair for Sam to sit—"one doesn't fire Ramona Watts."

Sam took a slow breath through her nose while she tried to catch up. This had to be April Feinstein. The "Katie" she'd just name-dropped would be Katie Price, one of the most A-list of the A-list, who had recently started directing. Sam had seen a few industry write-ups about the partnership between the two.

April jackknifed her body forward, breaching Sam's personal space with a waft of something expensively citrus-scented. "I was so glad, *so* glad, when I heard you wanted to pop in. You've added years to my fucking life. I'd already tracked down your cell number to call you myself because I didn't see any other option."

"Any other option?"

April widened her eyes. "To find Ramona! I've been out of my mind, and I am never out of my mind. My mind is a steel trap. A titanium trap. As far as I'm concerned, I lost the woman myself. That's how responsible I feel for my people. But what am I going to do, call the cops?" April rolled her eyes. "Categorically not. Then I realized. You and Bex are my only hope."

"Me and Bex?"

"The detectives." April twirled a finger in the air. "For sensitive *predicaments* in this town."

Sam swallowed. "I see."

"I'm sure. So. You'll want a timeline. What I know. I've got something ready for you, too." She paused, having finally observed the confusion on Sam's face. "Do you have something to write with?"

"Yes." Sam pulled her tiny bag covered in twelve-inch-long rainbow fringe into her lap and poked through it until she found a black Sharpie that she'd signed autographs with the last time she wore this purse. She turned over the travel arrangements envelope to write on. "Go ahead."

April raised an eyebrow but continued. "You talked to Macie, so you know what I know. Ramona wrapped an episode Friday. She was due to set yesterday morning bright and early, but she didn't show. I didn't hear from her over the weekend, but I wasn't expecting to. The first I heard of her being out of contact was from the studio. They called Monday to ask if I knew where she was. I didn't. Would I reach out and find out why she wasn't on set? Sure thing. I called, texted, emailed, called again and left messages. Didn't hear back. That's when I start sweating through my clothes. Ramona always calls back."

Macie had said the same thing. "When was the last time you spoke to her?"

"Last week, Thursday. *The Howling* was going to be taping on location Friday, and Ramona had some questions about her insurance riders."

"Was there something hazardous about the filming conditions?" Insurance riders were added to standard studio contracts to improve an actor's coverage for the specific risks or needs of a project.

"She didn't say. Ramona's been burned a lot, so she trusts no one. Plus, the folks running *The Howling* are serious about leaks. The scripts and production details are locked down as tight as Fort Knox. If you don't need to know, you won't fucking know, you know?"

Maybe it was more than just paranoia that had caused Chad's covert behavior in the parking lot. "But wherever they were filming Friday, it wasn't at the studio," Sam said.

"Yeah, though it wasn't so far away that they couldn't get there, shoot, and get back to the studio the same day. I didn't hear about any problems."

"Gotcha." Sam filed the information away. It *was* helpful to know that Ramona had left the Howell Motion Pictures campus on Friday. A location shoot was definitely a lead. "What else can you tell me?"

Mainly, what Sam learned was that Ramona's agent loved her. She described her as gifted, dependable, and delightful to plan projects with. She shared Macie's perspective that Ramona's preference for privacy had a tendency to backfire, sparking rumors about her lifestyle that were not true.

"You said you had something for me to take with me?" Sam capped her Sharpie when the conversation seemed to have reached its natural conclusion.

"Yes." April leaned over and picked up a single sheet of paper from the desk. "This is a list of people who I trust to talk to you about Ramona." She showed it to Sam. There were only a handful of names on it, with contact details beneath. "It's not a lot of folks, and that's because I'm fucking suspicious by nature, and I have a responsibility to protect my people." April reluctantly passed the paper to Sam.

"I promise this goes nowhere except to help Bex and me help Macie."

April gave her a military salute, and Sam scanned down the short list of names. Her gaze arrested on one name, chills washing over her body.

"This is perfect," Sam said, sliding the paper inside her travel itinerary envelope. "Thank you."

"Just find her. Or you'll never work in this town again."

Sam had been so preoccupied with folding and shoving the bulky envelope back into her tiny purse, she almost didn't hear what April had said. Then she did. She whipped her head up in shock. "What?"

"Figure of speech." April laughed, a menacing sound. "Sort of. I could do that. I don't want to do that." Then she sighed, and her eyes went shiny. "I'm sorry. I truly have no intention of tossing around threats, especially when you're helping. It's only that I'm incredibly worried, and even though I am a single woman with cats, at my core I am the same incredibly fierce Jewish mother who raised me, and what they don't tell you is that you can accumulate every speck of power in this town and it still won't mend a broken heart."

"I promise we will do everything we can."

Sam left the downtown building with a busy mind and a heavy heart. When she and Bex had begun trying to figure out what happened to Jen, the stakes were easy to understand. Jen had been their dear friend. She'd died on their watch, at their workplace. But if Sam and Bex started taking on other people's potential heartbreak, it would mean they carried the feelings of everyone who loved Ramona with them everywhere they went. Along with their hope.

Sam was an actor. She knew how to empathize deeply with other perspectives. She had to do that in order to deliver performances that made her audience *feel.* What Macie had asked them to do, what April expected—it was a different kind of engagement. More personal, with the potential to introduce profound change.

It was a lot to consider.

This morning, what Sam had learned in her meeting with her people was that they had plans lined up for the next five years of her life.

Now, maybe for the first time, it occurred to her that she wouldn't mind if she had the kind of career that invited more unexpected turns.

Bex had been an unexpected turn, after all.

"We can't count on being alone," Sam said firmly through the microphone in her Audi's stereo system. "We have to throw that fantasy away. There will always be an audience, Bex, and if they don't want to watch, they can remove themselves."

Their hoped-for private moment last night had been interrupted by a call from Sam's brother, who'd taken a dip in the pool and locked himself out of her house. That was when Sam had arrived at the conviction she was now sharing with Bex, who laughed.

"If they don't want to watch *what*, Samantha Farmer?"

"You're a big talker over a wireless connection," Sam shot back, "but I haven't seen any of those moves live." She changed lanes and had to honk at a guy in a too-furious, souped-up Nissan who tried to cut her off at the last second.

"Where are you? I thought you'd be here by now. I called to make sure I remembered what time zone I was in and it wasn't me who was late."

"Ten minutes away," Sam said. "I set up a meeting this morning because, when I looked up Ramona Watts last night, I realized we're at the same agency."

"Oh!" Bex said. "Good thinking. Did you get in with Ramona's agent?"

"Yeah." Sam turned off the freeway and had to brake as a group of kids in school uniforms crossed illegally at the top of the exit in a laughing scrum. Then she gasped when the guy behind her nearly rear-ended her. "What the fuck is the deal with traffic today?"

"Careful. You sound tired. What did Ramona's agent have to tell you?"

Sam filled Bex in on her meeting, but she held back the contents of the list April had given her. She wanted to save it for a surprise.

"You did good," Bex said cheerfully. "And I'm not shocked Ramona has an agent who knows how to keep her mouth shut, given what Macie told us. On a professional note, I'm jealous as hell April Feinstein reps her."

Sam pulled onto the narrow access road that would take her to Bex's place. "That's what I've been thinking about. The people in Ramona's life and Ramona herself."

"What about them? Because I'm"—there was a blank moment on the line before Bex's voice came back—"layers of privacy."

"Do you have another call?" Sam asked. "I can go."

"No, it's fine. It's not anything I need to take right now."

Sam frowned, unsure how to interpret that. With the singular exception of the five years Bex had avoided Sam and Sam had avoided Bex and they'd both talked about the other through Vic and Frankie, Bex was not someone who put things off to deal with later. "You sure?"

"Completely sure. I want to talk to you."

"Well, the good news is that I'm nearly to your house. I missed some of what you were saying, though. Something about layers of privacy?"

"Just that Ramona's been in this business for a long time, and she entered it on an enormous crest of sudden fame. It would make sense that she's"—the line cut out again, due to what Sam was now certain had to be another phone call—"and to be cautious."

This time, Sam didn't mention the interruption. "There's private and cautious, and then there's secretive." She put in the gate code at the bottom of Bex's driveway. When Sam reached the house and got out of her car, she spotted Bex waiting for her on the sheltered portico outside the front door.

"You're right, there's a difference between cautious and secretive." Bex shoved her phone in her pocket. "But there are miles to go before we get to Ramona's secrets. For now, I'd be happy if she very nonsecretively called Macie and told them, 'My bad, I couldn't resist taking a sudden opening at that Arizona spa I had my eye on.'"

Bex was in another oversized sweatshirt this morning, this one paired with appallingly short shorts that meant her muscled dancer's legs had a sudden chokehold on Sam's attention. She grabbed Sam's hand and pulled her close, not shy at all, and then the only thing Sam could think about was Bex's shower-damp rosemary-scented hair, and her own gratitude that she'd picked out such a small shirt to wear this morning because it meant Bex's other hand snaked around her bare waist.

"Good morning." Sam stepped out of her heels to put herself in a better position for what she hoped might be about to happen.

"No time for idle chitchat or chaste hugs, Farmer." Bex spoke against Sam's neck, making her shiver. "Vic's in there, she woke me up, and she's in a state of excitement that makes me worry about her heart."

"Shh," Sam said. Finally, *finally*, she got close enough to feel the shift when Bexley Simon went completely still, silent in a way she never was except in the hushed pause before their mouths met. Her fingers stroked a restless arch over the skin at Sam's waist. Her lips parted. Sam memorized the curve of her cheek for the thousandth time, the sweep of her eyelashes, and just because she wanted to kiss her more than anything, she held her breath and let anticipation hammer through her, as loud and insistent as her heartbeat.

Six months.

Bex squeezed her waist and rose to her toes, pressing herself against Sam's breasts. She wrapped her free hand around the back of Sam's neck and pulled Sam's head down until their lips aligned. "Don't you dare make me wait." She could feel Bex's breath against her mouth. "Not for one more second."

Sam was smiling when she kissed her, and then she wasn't. The kiss charged through them both, driven by half a year's longing and a decade of thrilling familiarity, of laughing glances that caught and held too long until Sam's desire for the woman in her arms threatened to immolate her just like this, from the crux of her thighs to the nape of her neck. She would die happy if the exchange meant she got to hear Bexley moan, licking her tongue across the seam of Sam's lips, yanking at her hair to bring her closer.

Bex threaded her thigh between Sam's, which ruined Sam to such an extent that she backed her into one of the porch columns and lifted her up, erasing the difference in their height, giving her access to the smooth sweep of a palm from Bex's knee to her hip, with nothing in the way and all the time in the world.

"God." Bex arched her back, and Sam bit her to warn her not to kill her with erotic promises.

"Emergency!" Vic's voice blasted through the security speaker by the door. "You guys need to get in here right away!"

Never Sleep on the Assistant

Sam pressed her forehead against Bex's. Both of them were panting. "How likely is this to be an actual emergency?" she rasped.

In response, Bex turned her head and yelled, "Go away!" loudly enough for Vic to hear her through the thick walnut of the entry door.

"I would if I could!" Vic yelled back over the intercom. "I would go far, far away! But you guys have to come inside, because a woman is in peril!"

"In a few hours, we could be in Mexico," Sam rasped. "There's a resort I've been to. The beds are enormous."

Bex slid down the column out of Sam's grip, then put her fingers lightly against Sam's cheeks. She looked into Sam's eyes for a long moment before she let her hands fall away. "Come on," she said, releasing Sam. She grabbed the front door handle before turning back. "Hey, I've been meaning to ask you. Macie said they talked to your security guy last night? But you don't have security. Unless—"

"It's Fergus." Sam sighed. "He decided to move his paragliding and outfitter's business from the Oregon coast to Malibu, and he's crashing with me while he looks for a storefront to rent."

Sam hadn't thought twice about giving Fergus a key to her house. Because their shared father had a talent for brief relationships that ended in unplanned pregnancy (until he had a vasectomy shortly after Sam joined the world), all four of her brothers had always been in and out of the family home—going back and forth to their moms—and so were the other women her dad dated and their kids. Sam had never known anything but the people she loved moving into and out of her life on an unpredictable schedule. As a teenager, she would've cried tears of joy to see into a future where her brothers willingly spent time with her, or at least spent time at her place. But as much as she loved all of them, she couldn't help but feel like the beloved proprietor of a favored bed-and-breakfast. Fergus had been in the guest room for a week now, and she'd spent two hours in his undistracted company.

"Ah." Bex stepped into the foyer. "I see."

"Indeed." They walked through the open-concept living room of Bex's California ranch, a homey Mission with Spanish tile and skylights studded between the heavy beams gridding the ceiling. Sam loved Bex's house. It never changed. Every one of its spacious five thousand square feet felt like home and had since Bex first invited her over in their *Craven's Daughter* days.

"Is this one of Fergus's businesses you've 'invested' in?" Bex asked.

"What can I say?" Sam smiled as they pushed through the French doors at the back and settled themselves around the poolside table, where Vic was vibrating with the need to talk to them. "I'm a sucker for older brothers with medium-sized ideas they have no money to see through."

"What took you so long?" Vic's hair was in rollers. She wore a bikini top and pajama bottoms. "We have to get out Bex's notebook and make a plan!"

"Sam, could I grab you something to drink? Did you eat yet?" Bex had her back turned to Vic and Vic's energy. "I have those orange-glazed muffins from Deliah's, and there's still agua fresca."

"No drinks!" Vic barked. "No food!"

Bex's annoyed dimple made an appearance.

"As it happens," Sam said, wrapping her arms around Bex's waist and pulling her down onto her lap on the sofa, "I had breakfast at the agency. Where April Feinstein, Ramona's agent, gave me a list of people we can contact. One of them is someone we know."

Bex perched her hands on Sam's shoulders, beaming with delight. "Who?"

"Haris Ahmadi."

"Oh, *shit.*" Vic collapsed to the ground with her hand over her eyes. "This is bad. Bad, bad."

A wrinkle appeared between Bex's eyebrows that Sam associated with this particular dramatic mode of Vic's. "I know that name, but I can't quite place it," Bex said.

"Allow me to set the scene," Sam replied. "It's the *Craven's Daughter* reunion special. A young production assistant comes to retrieve us from our picnic on the steps. It's clear that he knows your sister Frankie, who is also a PA for Cineline. After the live part of the episode wraps and we expose a murderer, Haris fills a small but essential role in our escape by leading us out the side door at Frankie's behest."

"Oh, *that* Haris Ahmadi."

"I am embroiled in a genuine moral dilemma!" Vic shouted from the ground.

With a sigh, Bex slid back off Sam's lap, though she left her legs draped over Sam's thighs. "What is *wrong* with you?" she asked her sister.

"It's real! Like, Sam has just identified Ramona's former assistant. Ramona's agent trusts this person. This person presumably likes Ramona. They know how to keep their mouth shut. No doubt they have insider knowledge of her private life. This person might have kept her day diary and had her passwords.

Although it was a while ago. Probably nothing this person knows is useful anymore. Or maybe we can get it from another source on the list." Vic stuck out her bottom lip. "That's what I will have to do."

"Why does she keep saying 'this person'?" Sam asked Bex. "We're still talking about Haris, right?"

"I think so, but it's hard to think when I've literally never been more annoyed in my life." Bex sat up and crossed her legs in a way that conveyed this annoyance while also managing to expose another few inches of dancer thigh. Sam thought of the suite in Mexico. A bed with a sheer canopy blowing in the ocean breeze.

"Fine! I'll clarify, but only if you promise to protect me from Frankie. I don't want to die." Vic pulled out her phone and started furiously texting.

"What does your sister have to do with anything?" Bex asked. "Who are you calling?"

"*Frankie.*" Vic glanced at Bex from beneath lowered lashes. "I told her to tell you, but she didn't want to yet." Vic scanned an incoming text and thumbed in a reply.

"Want to *what*?!" Bex asked this at a volume that could probably be heard by people in the bars on Sunset.

"Her road trip isn't exactly the lone voyage that she implied." Vic winced when her phone hummed with an incoming text.

"Who is she with, Victoria?" Bex leaned forward. "Tell me right now."

"Haris," Vic blurted. "He's her secret boyfriend. He met up with her in Philly, because he has friends there from college who he was visiting. He's traveling the rest of the way to L.A. with her. And he visited her a bunch of times when she was doing her internship in New York."

Sam considered this new information. The one time she'd met Haris, his interest in Frankie had been so blindingly obvious that it might as well have been painted in neon letters on a billboard. Frankie had behaved as though she barely tolerated his existence.

Now that Sam thought about it, she should have guessed that Frankie's behavior meant Haris's feelings were not one-sided.

"I can't believe Haris's relationship with Frankie is bigger news than the fact that we know someone who used to be Ramona's assistant," Sam mused. "Though I shouldn't be surprised by the assistant thing. I forget that even though L.A. is a big city, Hollywood's a small town."

"You *know* how Frankie is about romance," Vic said pleadingly. "The lengths I went to to figure out who she was dating in high school should earn me a spot with the CIA. *I* only know he's with her because he always texts me when he's with Frankie so that her family knows. He's very protective, but he also respects Frankie's privacy."

Bex wound a long lock of curly hair around her finger and gave it a tug—something she did when she was trying to get a handle on her feelings. "But Frankie invited me to drive home with her!"

"She knew you'd say no. You hate road trips. You don't like having to eat and go to the bathroom on other people's schedules." Vic looked at her phone, then back at her sister. "Okay. Haris is caught up with the situation. Be cool."

The sound of a FaceTime connecting intensified the wince on Vic's face. "Don't be mad," she said to the screen of her phone.

"Why would I be mad?" The voice coming from Vic's phone was cheerful, but Sam had been acquainted with Franklynn Simon for too long to be deceived.

"Because now everyone knows about you and Haris," Vic said.

"We know nothing!" Bex yelled. "Clearly!"

Sam couldn't fail to hear the hurt behind Bex's defensive humor. Frankie and Bex were a lot alike, and they'd spent more than a few of the difficult years after they lost their parents at odds with each other. Bex had a tendency to take Frankie's silences as an indictment of her parenting.

Bex's first priority was her sisters, above everything else. Above what she wanted for herself. It was why she hadn't been ready to respond to Sam's declaration of her feelings when it was clear *Craven's Daughter* would likely be ending soon. Bex was about to lose the security the show provided, with its (relatively) family-friendly schedule and steady paycheck. She hadn't known what would come next. Frankie had taken off to college at a rough time in their relationship, and Vic was only just starting high school and was a precocious, fearless honey badger of a human. Sam hadn't given Bex time to answer yet another demand on her heart before she walked away, hurt that Bex hadn't fallen into her arms instantly.

It meant they'd wasted nearly five years they could've been together. Sam was determined not to mess up like that again.

"Here's Haris," Frankie said, still using the same deadly helpful tone. "I'm sure he'll be happy to answer your questions."

"Um." Haris cleared his throat. "Just the ones about Ms. Watts, actually."

Vic turned her phone around and lifted it up so all three of them would be visible, giving Sam her first glimpse of Haris. He sat on the end of what was obviously a hotel bed, with bland art on the wall behind him framing his handsome face, beautiful deep brown skin, and dark curls. He slid his heavy glasses up his nose. "Hello. Everyone. Ms. Farmer. Ms. Simon. Victoria." He gave a small wave and looked to the side, where Frankie was probably glaring at him from off screen.

"If you'd rather talk some other time," Sam said, "we completely understand."

"No, it's okay," he said. "I want to help. Ms. Watts is really great, and I hadn't heard no one knows where she is. But it's tricky because of privacy. And I worked for her almost two years ago. We're not, like, friends. Now. I would say we were friendly, then. She's friends with my uncle, actually not my uncle, one of my dad's friends who's a producer who I always called my uncle. Nepotism. That's how I got the job."

"We don't know that she's actually missing," Sam said. "Just that she didn't go to work. But if she were missing or in trouble, we'd like the right people to be aware of that. Really, anything you can tell us would be helpful."

Haris pushed his glasses up again. "She talked to Macie Finn all the time, but you know that. Vic said. That's how you know about Ms. Watts being gone. And from Vic's friend Piper. That's not helpful. I'm sorry."

"No worries." Haris's rapid-fire self-doubting declarations were making Sam's pulse race. She made a point of projecting detachment. "It's all good."

Haris did not seem convinced. "Or I could see if she still had her location turned on."

"What?" The question had shot so fast from her throat, it made Sam cough.

"She's given you location tracking?" Bex asked. "Why the hell haven't you checked it already?"

He ran one of his hands through his hair. "It's just that—"

"Turn it on, man!" Vic shouted. "Better yet, share it with me!"

"I wouldn't ever—"

"It's an emergency." Bex was attempting her gentle voice, but the undisguised urgency in it gave off enough decibels that Haris reared back from the phone. "I'm sure Ramona would never challenge someone who used information to help her, even as a private person."

"It's okay," Frankie said from out of view of the camera. "I'll back you up."

Haris's face relaxed, and he looked to where Frankie was with gratitude. It made Sam's chest ache. She had loved Frankie since she was a girl. Frankie deserved someone who looked at her that way.

And kissing Bex had made Sam sappy.

"Hang on." Haris reached around to his back pocket and pulled out his own phone. He stared at it for a moment, then let out a sharp breath, stretched his neck, and squared his shoulders.

"You're not getting ready to slalom down a mountain, Haris," Vic bit out. "Open the freaking app."

He shot a look at Vic that she fully deserved, then swiped and tapped at his screen.

"Well?" Sam hadn't meant to sound so impatient, but if Haris could track Ramona, it would be such a tidy conclusion to the mystery Macie had dropped on them. She wanted to find out that Ramona was camped out at a friend's or holed up in a hotel in Nevada. *Somewhere.*

"It's going to take me a minute," Haris said. "My whole family shares locations. There's so many iPads and phones on here."

Vic closed her eyes. "Haris has a huge family. This could take all damn day."

"Found it!" Haris looked up at the camera. "I'm still connected to Ms. Watts's phone! She never took me off."

Sam crossed her legs and summoned the patience she'd cultivated growing up with five men. "And?"

Haris held up a finger, then went back to tapping. "She's . . . nowhere."

"What?!" Now Bex shouted in earnest, making Sam's ears ring.

"I mean that it says she's offline, and 'no location found.' That could mean a lot of things. Her phone could be turned off. Or she doesn't have an Internet connection."

"Or she stopped sharing with you?" Sam asked.

"No, if she stops sharing, she's gone from my list. She *is* sharing, but she's not online. I have a toggle for if I want to be notified when she connects again."

"Do that, oh my God," Vic said.

"And do you know if she shares her location with anyone else?" Bex was sitting on her hands to keep control of herself. "Macie didn't mention it, and I can't imagine Macie would forget they had that access if they did, but maybe a different friend?"

Haris shook his head, then had to catch his glasses to keep them from flying off. "Not that I know of. She was making an exception for me. She didn't like the idea of being tracked, but when I worked for her, she was doing a movie that shot all over L.A., sometimes multiple locations in a day. She wanted to make sure she kept on schedule and made every call. I shared my location with her, too, so we could accomplish this."

Ramona disliked the idea of being tracked. Was that paranoia or practicality? Or just being part of a generation that wasn't used to leaving digital footprints everywhere they went? Sam thought again about how fine the line could be between privacy and secrecy. "Who took the assistant job after you?" she asked. "If we could talk to that person, they might know more than you do."

Haris shook his head. "She had to fire them. There was some turmoil with a friend in her personal life, and she was concerned this assistant would leak to the tabloids. She didn't hire another assistant after that. Ramona actually contacted me to see if I wanted the job again. That's how I even know about it."

Sam mentally crossed the potential lead off her list. Macie had made it clear that she and Bex shouldn't reach out to anyone who couldn't be trusted to keep Ramona's situation under wraps. She tapped her upper lip. "What about this friend she was having problems with? Do you know anything about that?"

"I don't. Her circle of friends is small. I can say that if she fired an assistant because she was simply worried they would leak whatever was going on, then whatever was going on was probably about this friend acting messy and threatening her private life, not about anything Ms. Watts was doing."

Haris was the third person to tell them Ramona wasn't messy. Sam filed this away.

Frankie stepped into the frame and took Haris's phone from his hand. She tapped the screen. "The notification thing is turned on now. But, you know, it won't work if her phone's dead. Or if she got a new one. People switch phones." When she gazed into the camera, her mouth in a firm line, Sam saw the same disappointed worry in her expression that all of them felt.

People went missing in Los Angeles every day. It wasn't unusual for celebrities and others with industry connections to drop off the map. A starlet walked out of a party and never made it home. A director took a trip to the desert and didn't return. In a town where youth and beauty were a currency, where #metoo had turned over dozens of rocks and exposed the scandals and shame hiding beneath, it was hard not to worry that Ramona was gone in a way that meant she'd never turn her phone back on.

"Maybe you guys could ask her roommate if he knows anything," Haris said from somewhere off-screen.

"Her *roommate*?" Vic asked.

Sam collapsed back into her chair and caught Bex's eyes. "Macie did not, I am positive, mention a roommate."

"I put that wrong. He's not exactly a 'roommate.' " Back in front of the camera, Haris made air quotes around the word. "Colin Worth rents her guesthouse."

"*Colin Worth!?*" Bex was projecting with her full voice again. "*Broadway*'s Colin Worth. The man who I wrote a letter to when I was twelve years old, who graciously sent me an autographed headshot that is *right now hanging in my hallway*?"

"His name is also on the list April gave me," Sam said. "I was saving it, but we got caught up with Haris."

"Well, that's a hell of a secret," Bex said. "I'll tell you right now, if April put Sir Colin Worth on the list, we are giving him a call. But how private do you have to be to keep a seven-time Tony winner stashed in your fucking guesthouse?"

Privacy. Secrets. When it came to Ramona Watts, which one was it?

A Circumspect Woman

"Are you sure he's not the kind of roommate you had when you were starting out in New York, Bex?" Vic lurched forward to stick her head between the two front seats. "Roommates with benefits?"

Colin Worth had invited them to Ramona's Hollywood Hills property to talk. He'd already been given the heads up by April.

Sam watched Bex's face go pink. When she had first hit Broadway as a young woman, Bexley Simon had been notorious for her love life. In fact, the first time Sam had noticed Bex was when she'd seen her on the cover of *American Theater* magazine. She'd been posed without a lot of clothes, lying across the laps of other Broadway babies, holding her Tony in a provocative manner. If Sam hadn't fallen in love the very moment she saw that magazine cover, she'd certainly fallen in *something*.

"Colin Worth is gay," Bex said. "The last I heard, he was with Christian Stanstedt. Which is quite the pull for a ninety-four-year-old." Bex tipped her head. "Though not if you're Colin Worth."

"Christian Stanstedt is gay?" Sam had to lean away from Vic's volume. "He's been Ramona's plus-one for so many premieres! Star Spy said that his look was a perfect foil for Ramona's 'everlasting gamine beauty.' I don't know what 'gamine' means, but it sounds like something I would date."

Bex maneuvered aggressively through the stop-and-go traffic, and Sam, as usual when Bex was driving, held onto the handle above the door. "It describes, usually, someone femme-identified," Sam said. "Unusually pretty and fairylike, but also a bit boyish or enigmatic. It's generally a word for young people, but Ramona is ageless, so she still gets called that. It's one of the reasons why *The Howling* is so successful. Gamine plays well on a monster-hunting show."

"I was right," Vic said. "Would date."

Sam mulled over Bex's mention of Christian Stanstedt while Bex flipped off a delivery truck driver, thankfully from behind dark-tinted windows. Sam had always thought of Christian as the sixth member of the Ice Crew. Partly, that was because he'd been the last to join, but it was also because his skater-boy good looks positioned him as an outsider to Chad's polished blond handsomeness and Sloan's reputation as an edgy, self-destructive artist. Christian injected as much variety as another white man could into the group.

Of course, the Ice Crew hadn't called *themselves* the "Ice Crew." It had been a name the media came up with to explain this group of young actors who were ice-cold cool and getting famous starring in the biggest movies of the day, often together. Was it strange that the entire set of surviving Ice Crew actors—Chad, Sloan, Christian, Macie, and Ramona—all seemed to be connected in one way or another to Ramona's disappearance? Or was it simply the case, so many years later, that Ramona was the one who connected these people?

Sam swallowed a warning to Bex to slow down before she rammed a braking car in front of them. She hadn't missed Bex's driving. Thankfully, the traffic was letting up as they turned off the Boulevard and toward the general area of Chateau Marmont.

"Wouldn't you think Ramona's roommate would call someone and file a report?" Vic asked.

"Maybe he did," Sam said. "It sounds like Macie wouldn't have known, either way."

Macie had told them when they called to update her that Ramona had a carriage house she'd let people stay in as friends or tenants on and off over the years. Macie was aware that Colin was the current tenant but didn't know him well. Ramona kept her friendship with Colin separate from her friendship with Macie.

"Ramona has layers," Bex said. She glanced at her phone, mounted on the dash to help her navigate the confusing streets of West Hollywood.

At the very least, Sam thought, Ramona had a complex decision tree for who was to know what in her life. Her compartments had compartments.

They missed a turn onto Ramona's property twice. It was disguised by camellia and a trimmed row of rose bushes. Finally, Bex rolled slowly up the long, exquisitely maintained pea gravel drive, revealing a fairy-tale olive-green bungalow straight out of the Weetzie Bat books that Sam had devoured in middle school.

Bex turned off the car. "Here we are."

"I guess we walk around the back and find this carriage house?" Sam unbuckled her seat belt.

"I should have changed my clothes." Bex was looking with horror at her sweatshirt and shorts. "This is a momentous occasion. I should have worn something fashionlike."

"It's not an audition." Vic opened her door and hopped out of the car. "Which is good news, given what's happened to your hair."

"Gah." Standing in the driveway, Bex pressed her hands against the huge, curly mass. "I didn't have time to do my whole routine!" She leaned back into the car to look in the rearview. "My *God*."

Sam pulled her toward the side of the house, where there was a series of steppingstones. A row of lemon trees and more neatly trimmed rose bushes threw the path into deep shade. In the warm late-morning sun, it smelled delicious. Birdsong filled the air.

"Maybe I should get a place around here," Vic mused. "Or Laurel Canyon."

"Are you putting in an order?" Bex asked. "Because I'm not a vending machine for actual whole entire houses in the most expensive neighborhoods of L.A."

"Hmpf," Vic grunted.

They walked through a stone archway and found themselves on a large circle of lawn surrounded by English-style plantings. There was a small, tiled lap pool in the middle of the space, and another stepping-stone path to a second archway that framed a pink Dutch door that Sam guessed must be the entrance to the carriage house.

"This is beautiful," Bex said. "It doesn't feel like a property that was closed up before the homeowner took time away. The pool's open. The flowers on that patio table aren't even wilted."

"Hello?"

They turned toward the voice and watched an elderly man who was unmistakably Colin Worth unlatch the bottom of the Dutch door and emerge in tennis whites.

"Mr. Worth?" Bex called out. "Hello!"

Colin, as tall as Sam and not the least bit stooped, stopped in front of them. Other than his snowy hair, looked thirty years younger than ninety-four. "Fuck me, it's Bexley Simon in the flesh."

Both of Bex's hands went to her mouth. "You *know* me?"

"Shouldn't I? You don't leave Broadway, Broadway leaves you, and that's only if you get too old and sad. I saw your debut, the one you got the Tony for, and wondered all the way to my pied-à-terre in Hell's Kitchen if there was anyone I cared to collaborate with on a musical for you to be the lead. And who wasn't a *Craven's Daughter* fan?"

He winked at Sam. "Thank heavens you're both here. I called the community policing line when I couldn't get ahold of Ramona and she didn't come home. I didn't name names, partly because I was afraid she'd walk in the door and lecture me, but I asked some questions. They told me the only adult missing persons cases that tend to get seriously investigated are those where there's reason to worry about the person's mental state or vulnerability, or there's evidence of foul play. I don't have any of that. I was thrilled to find out Macie pulled you in."

Bex didn't seem to be able to speak after receiving Colin's verbal mash note, so Sam took the lead. "Macie asked us to discreetly see if we can find out where Ramona is, and if we can't, they'll involve the authorities."

Vic stepped between Bex and Sam and stuck out her hand. "Victoria Simon, associate."

Colin grinned as he shook it. "Now, I've seen *you* on the gossip sites."

"Thank you," Vic said warmly. "I appreciate my fans."

He laughed. "Well, come on. I would take you into the carriage house where I stay, but there isn't room for more than two to sit. I do have a key to Ramona's to feed her cat when she's away. Maybe it will help your project to look around *respectfully*. If Ramona found out I'd let strangers go through her things, she'd not let me hear the end of it."

Colin led them to the back porch, talking to a pink-cheeked Bex all the way, as Sam took in how utterly *fine* everything appeared to be. She couldn't imagine that the authorities would visit this meticulously kept property, talk to a famous and gregarious roommate, consider the size of the paychecks Ramona earned, and believe that any trouble had come to her. At least, nothing worse than a sudden whim to shop in Paris or meet a lover.

Maybe that was what had happened.

Except Macie was terrified. When Sam and Bex had been in and out of each other's pockets in the *Craven's Daughter* years, if Bex hadn't shown up on set, Sam would damn well have known if it was a one-off or if something had gone seriously wrong.

Seeing everything in its place, as neat as a full-color spread in a design magazine, filled Sam's stomach with heavy dread.

"Here we are." Colin led them into a four-seasons room lined with bookshelves. The furniture was vintage, with curvy lines showcasing velvet and leather aged to perfection. There was art in an eclectic mix of frames everywhere there weren't books, and at least three abandoned cardigans and shawls. A cherry-red Fender leaning against a small amp in a wooden case looked recently and frequently played. A funky pair of reading glasses and a small stack of mail sat on an occasional table with a smooth amethyst stone top.

Sam was reminded of the Oakland Victorian she'd grown up in. When she'd bought her own house, a sleek California contemporary, she'd been focused primarily on its convenient access to Bex's place, just a ten-minute walk on a canyon path separating them. But Ramona's home looked like somewhere a creative person could retreat to find inspiration.

"Does she have housekeeping?" Sam asked. "Or any other kind of service?" They sat down in the comfortable furniture. At Bex's elbow was another small table, this one topped in what looked like lapis lazuli. The finished end of a stick of incense stuck out of a ceramic holder. A bit of ash had fallen on the table.

"Oh, no. Nothing like that. Ramona takes care of everything herself. The house is small, and the garden plantings are well-established. She put them in when she was young. Not to say she isn't very fit now at . . . forty-eight? Fifty? But even a busy actress can look after this place. That's why she's kept it."

Colin leaned forward to greet a petite calico who had trotted into the room, tail high with the excitement of guests. "Hello, my dear Miette. Look at all the laps you have to choose from!"

As if she understood perfectly, the cat surveyed the guests and then meowed elegantly and leapt into Vic's lap. She made biscuits with her front paws as she settled in, purring astonishingly loud.

"Animals adore me," Vic said, petting the cat. "I'm going to be a veterinarian."

"Outstanding." Colin smiled. "Very smart to avoid this town's business. Now. What questions can I answer?"

Bex opened the flap of her purse and extracted her notebook. She flipped it open to a fresh page. "It would be helpful if we could start to get an idea of Ramona's movements. We know she didn't show up on set Monday morning, and we know she filmed on Friday. Macie's understanding is that she hadn't been seen since. We'd like to narrow in, if we could. When did you last see her?"

"When our schedules align, we eat breakfast together. We did on Friday. She was heading out for work."

"When should you have seen her next?" Bex asked. "That is, when would you normally expect to?"

"Weeknights, we often watch something together on her big television, but on a Friday, I have no expectations. I may not see her on a weekend, or I may spot her in the garden and spend time talking. I didn't begin to worry until the young man from the studio stopped by looking for her. This was late yesterday morning."

"Do you happen to recall his name?"

Colin looked out the window for a moment, then shook his head. "Sorry, I don't."

"Where does she go when she's not here for the weekend?" Vic asked.

"She sometimes travels for press events, or she'll have a premiere and get a hotel so she can use the spa the next day. Of course, she'll plan getaways with friends and the like."

"Does she tell you where she's going?" Bex asked.

"Only if she wants me to feed Miette or she's canceling plans we made."

"So she was on set on Friday, and you never make plans with her on a Friday evening, but as far as you know, she didn't come home?" Bex was clearly checking this information against what she'd written in her notebook.

"After the man came by, I looked at the feed from the security camera over her garage. I checked Friday afternoon and evening, you understand. There was nothing on it, so I took a look at Saturday and Sunday. No Ramona. And then I got confused."

"Because she should've come home?"

"Because I backed the footage up to Friday morning, and her car never left. The security system covers the whole property. I never saw her or her little car come and go, so I opened the garage. It's still in there, as well as the truck she drives when she goes to one of the garden centers. I don't know how she got to work on Friday."

"I sometimes use a car service," Sam said, "if I know the day on set is going to be exhausting and I don't trust myself to drive home late."

"It could be. I discovered the cameras don't cover the area out front where one would naturally pull in to pick someone up who was waiting."

"They had a location shoot that day," Sam said. "Her agent told me. She might not have driven herself if she wasn't going to the studio."

"And there had been recent diva moments," Vic added. "Maybe she wanted to swan onto the studio lot with a driver to make her look fancy."

Colin gave Vic a quizzical look.

"*The Howling* brought on Chad Bevington and Sloan Lennox as guest stars for the episode they shot last week," Vic explained. "According to my friend who's on the show, Ramona went into full diva mode with them, and it was an entire cold war that made everything nearly impossible."

Colin huffed out a breath. "Good lord. Ramona didn't breathe a word of that. Maybe she was a bit more tired than usual last week, but if she was difficult on set, she didn't bring it to me. I have to believe that your friend who called her a diva was most likely witnessing a woman of an age to be in her full powers refusing to suffer assholes one moment longer than she had to."

"Probably," Vic said. "Piper is weirdly suspicious of people over thirty, so that tracks."

"Could someone have used the dead spot in the camera to drop Ramona off Friday night?" Bex asked, steering the conversation back to the timeline she was making.

Colin put an index finger to his temple. Only his hands belied his age. He had gotten paler as they talked, and Sam noticed a mild tremor in his hand. "Perhaps, but the security system doesn't log anyone coming into the house Friday evening or at any point since. No one disarmed it until I did. Again, I checked after the man came for Ramona."

"Can we see camera footage of the man?" Bex asked.

Colin reached into a snapped-closed pocket on his tennis shorts and pulled out his phone. He swiped it awake, tapped the screen, and handed it to Bex. "You can download any of that footage you want. Email it to yourself."

Vic snatched the phone from Bex's hand, and then they were bickering quietly, huddled over the phone as they tried to figure out how to pull photos and stills to Bex's account.

Sam noticed that one of the framed pieces on the wall behind Colin was a movie poster featuring a group shot of the Ice Crew. "That's interesting," she said, pointing. "I thought I'd seen all the Ice Crew movies. At one point in film school my friends and I made a project of tracking down the entire catalog for a weekend film festival. I guess we missed that one."

Colin turned to look at the poster Sam indicated. "It's a little bit of a joke, that one. It's the poster for a documentary that was never distributed. *Ice.*"

"By Archie Blasingame," Sam read from the bottom. "I sat at the next table over when he won an Oscar a few years ago." She rose and stepped closer to read the fine print of the copyright statement, then let out a low whistle. "It was going to release the same year Juliette died. I'm guessing the timing had something to do with why it never made it to theaters."

"Perhaps. It's funny you noticed that poster, because it was on Ramona's mind recently. She's been looking at some of the old footage from the documentary and taking notes."

"Why? Is the project being revived?" If someone had taken an old documentary out of mothballs, that could explain why it seemed as though all of the old Ice Crew were emerging just as Sam and Bex tried to find Ramona—because they had already positioned themselves to be noticed ahead of the release.

"Couldn't tell you." Colin gave a dry laugh. "Oh, Ramona. A circumspect woman. Keeps her friends close, never speaks of her enemies, and holds everyone in her life as far away from each other as possible. If she was part of a project with"—he gestured at the poster—"no one would know until it officially hit industry announcements. Her inclination is to trust people and to love them, but I imagine she was betrayed so many times early on that she had to develop some kind of workaround to keep the friends she had left."

Sam thought of the stories she'd seen over the years about Ramona. Dozens of blind items and breathless tabloid accounts of her instability. Someone, or some *ones*, had given those stories to the news media. Former friends or significant others?

Celebrity could be vicious.

"My friendship with her is a bit of an example," Colin said.

"What do you mean?" The tone of Colin's voice had arrested everyone's attention. Even Vic had stopped tapping on the screen of Colin's phone to listen. Sam didn't like the ominous hush in the room.

"I mean that by taking my side in a matter of the heart, Ramona necessarily made a bitter enemy."

"Who?"

"Christian Stanstedt," Colin said. "My ex. He and I adored each other when it was good, but the end was very bad indeed. Ramona confronted Christian over his treatment of me, and after an ugly bit of business, she cut him off and opened the carriage house to me. She's meant a great deal to me in what's been a dark time. Christian has not forgiven her."

Sam thought of what Haris had told them. Ramona had fired

an assistant not too long ago, simply because she was afraid the assistant *might* leak about a messy issue going on between Ramona and a friend.

Christian could be the friend. If so, it meant Ramona had a lot of feelings about stepping in on Colin's behalf and her estrangement from Christian as a result.

Colin looked down, then at the three of them. There were tears in his eyes. "Christian can be a toxic person. And I'm afraid he hates Ramona more than anyone else in this town."

Hollywood Official

Sam took a sip of her honey latte and watched the espresso ruin the peacock design in the foam. They'd stopped at the Melrose Urth Caffé after leaving Ramona's, having mutually decided they needed sustenance and an opportunity to regroup.

Bex slid into her seat and set her phone down on the table. She folded her arms tightly across her chest—a response, Sam guessed, to the attention on them and their grim faces after talking to Colin.

Typically, Sam avoided places where celebrities went to see and be seen, but she had a nostalgic attachment to the Melrose Urth, because she and Bex used to come here for brunch with Vic and Frankie in the first few seasons of *Craven's Daughter*.

The number of people watching them, whispering, and trying to be subtle as they filmed them was reminding Sam why they'd stopped coming. There had to be at least a few invisible paps with telephoto lenses pointed at them through the café windows right now, taking pictures that would briefly bomb the Internet with clickbait headlines like FIGHTING ALREADY? SAD SAM WITH BOSSY BEX OVER PASTRY.

"Did you take your phone with you to the bathroom?" Vic asked her sister.

"Yes. I didn't want to be overheard."

Vic snorted. "Like that's ever stopped you before. Remember that time you took a call from your agent in the middle of my school concert, and your phone whisper drowned out the soloist?"

"The viral videos were unkind," Bex said. "I was *trying* to be quiet. It wasn't my fault that child didn't know how to sing from her diaphragm."

Sam laughed at the memory, but she agreed with Vic. It was unusual for Bex to be private about a phone call, even if the circumstances justified it. Combined with the calls Bex had ignored earlier when they were on the phone together, it made Sam wonder if something was going on that Bex didn't want her to know about.

And if what was going on with Bex was anything like the multiple calls and emails from her team that Sam was currently dodging.

"Anyway," Bex said, "I was thinking about Christian. I know someone who's connected to one of his projects."

"You hate Christian Stanstedt's movies," Vic said, biting into an enormous chocolate croissant. "You said you've seen better writing on a jar of face cream."

"I know that! I'm not *actually* interested in whatever this project is. It's a pretense to talk to Christian."

"I don't think he has anything to do with Ramona's disappearance." Vic licked her finger and picked up croissant crumbs that had rained down onto her plate. "No one that hot with that many connections should have only managed barely half a page on IMDb after so long in the business. He's lazy."

Sam forced herself to refocus on the conversation instead of fretting about the things she needed to tell Bex and if there was anything Bex hadn't told her. "What makes you say that? There's hundreds of reasons someone doesn't break out in this town."

"You think handsome white guys are impeded by 'hundreds' of reasons?" Vic let her air quotes hang. "Even when they're *monsters* to work with—even when they end up in jail, or their demands are expensive and compromising—all of their bridges are fireproof. Christian's not even *out* out. *I* didn't know he was queer, so that's not holding him back, either. He's coasting on a dragon's hoard of family money."

Bex put down her fork. "I did not know that."

"Nepotism is one of my areas of interest. He inherited from Brinley Downs."

"No kidding," Sam said. Brinley Downs was Old Hollywood. Her heyday had been the 1940s, when she played a femme fatale in some of the original blockbusters. After retiring, she'd become a silent partner in more than one big production company. "I thought Brinley Downs was famously single and child-free."

"Yep. Christian is her favorite niece's kid, and she left him everything." Vic reached across her bright orange boba tea to snag a bite of Bex's breakfast burrito. "He's worth hundreds of millions, but he's done fuck-all with it. He lives in the Swan mansion in Beverly Hills and swims in a lap pool of gold coins in the basement, I guess?"

"My knowledge of Christian Stanstedt hasn't been updated since I was eleven," Sam said. Middle-school Fergus had been deeply into Christian's indie debut, a troubling skater movie called *Halfcab*, whose dark moment involved a head injury at a skate park in Helsinki. As a preteen queer possessed of zero interest in cis men with poetic hair, Sam was not into it.

"I went to a party at the Swan." Vic raised her eyebrows at Bex's shocked gasp. "What? You've been on location, and you won't let me throw a party at our house! School is stressful. I have to unwind somehow. But my point is that he hasn't made any kind of notable career for himself despite every opportunity, he was obviously a shit boyfriend, and even if he had actual real feelings about Ramona Watts's role in the end of his relationship with Colin, I can't see him luring her to the Swan and pulling a Black Dahlia. It's eleven thirty. I doubt he's even up yet."

"Why didn't you tell us this before?" Bex asked this as a

group of young women sat down at a table near them. They were plainly excited to spot Sam and Bex. And, hell, probably Vic.

"You were too busy postgaming our Colin encounter with Sam, and you won't let me sit in the front seat."

Bex closed her eyes. "No, I *won't* let you sit in the front seat, because Sam is my"—she glanced at Sam, clearly panicked at having to supply a term—"my *Sam*."

Sam smiled at her. "Your Sam?"

"Don't tease me. You can't." The strain of trying to hold down her volume was making Bex go hoarse. "There is almost too much going on to keep track of"—she held up her notebook and shook it—"which I hate. Also, I'm not used to hanging out with Vic this much, and I don't have a nanny anymore."

"Hey!" Vic shot Bex with laser eyes.

Sam stayed out of the bickering argument that followed, musing instead about when she would have a chance to call this woman "my Bex."

If only they could get a minute alone.

First, though, there was their favor for Macie. It made a certain amount of sense to talk to Christian. They had to find time to review the security footage and track down the man who had come to the house looking for Ramona. Call Macie with an update. Reach out to the few people remaining on the list from Ramona's agent. If Ramona was truly in trouble, there was a clock ticking to find her, and that pressure was alongside the clock counting down six precious days before Sam would have to go to Telluride.

But she was determined to find at least *one* moment to whisper "my Bex" into her fellow detective's ear.

"You know what?" she asked, breaking into Bex and Vic's argument. "I don't think we need a pretext to talk to Christian." She tucked her tiny pleated skirt under one thigh as she crossed her legs, and the toe of her heel brushed the bag of one of the young women seated near them. "Sorry," she mouthed, giving them a grin that one of them snapped a picture of. As she turned back to Bex, her eyes caught the stare of a woman her age with dark bobbed hair at the table on the other side of the fans. The woman looked back to her phone quickly.

Bex glanced at the women Sam had grinned at, and her mouth compressed just a little. Jealousy? That was . . . Well, Sam wasn't one to *condone* jealousy, but falling for Bex did mean it hit different.

"Our characters on *Craven's Daughter* always needed a pretext, but that's because they were regular people," Sam said. "We're famous *TV* detectives. What's the point of being TV detectives if we can't just walk up to someone's door with full confidence he'll let us in?"

"Is that what you want to do?" Bex asked. "Just walk up to Christian Stanstedt's door?"

"Yeah, why not? Because it's looking like Ramona may very well be in some kind of trouble. Her agent *and* her best friend *and* her guesthouse buddy *and* her former PA say this isn't typical Ramona behavior. We've learned a potentially dangerous man has strong feelings about her—"

"Who used to be her friend, if we believe all the premiere photos," Vic interjected.

"—and he just happens to be wealthy and important, not to mention that the entire rest of the Ice Crew may be involved in one way or another. Then there's Howell Motion Pictures and the threat that Ramona could be terminated in three days. If she were, then everyone who trusted us to track her down safely and privately would find themselves in the middle of a shitstorm of rumors and bad press."

"You're talking about our reputation," Bex pointed out. "Because apparently, we're detectives now."

"You're Hollywood official," Vic said. "Or at least you've soft-launched being officially official detectives."

"Unless you want to go to the police?" Sam dropped her voice even lower. The woman with the dark bob would not look away from them.

"Colin said we'd have to be able to show them Ramona was vulnerable or in mental distress," Bex said. "We haven't got any evidence of that."

"I think we're still in the zone where Ramona's reputation will get in the way of law enforcement's taking us seriously," Sam agreed. "And then, for sure, it would leak. Beverly Hills isn't far. Why do we have all this fame if we can't drop in on a guy at his mansion?"

"You're saying that we, right now, should drive to Beverly Hills and pull up unannounced to the Swan mansion, a historical and stately edifice with twelve-foot-tall gates, in the hope that Christian Stanstedt will order up a tea service and talk to us?" Bex dipped a bite of burrito into salsa.

"I have the gate code," Vic said. "Unless he's changed it. But probably he hasn't, given the things I've seen at the Swan."

Sam and Bex stared at her in mute disbelief.

"He gives it out to people who come and party! And I went to a party! I wish you had a better car, though, Bex, if we're going to gate-crash."

"It's a Mercedes!"

"Eh." Vic shrugged.

Bex paused with a forkful of burrito halfway to her mouth. "But we can't. Colin told us Christian hates Ramona. He called him toxic. We don't know anything about who's at that mansion, who Christian keeps around, what kind of security he might be hiring, or even"—Bex attempted to lower her voice even more, which made it raspier but no less loud—"if he might be the one who's done something to Ramona. We know the statistics. If she has been hurt, it would most likely be by someone she knows well. She ended her friendship with Christian, probably presenting him with a picture of himself he didn't want to see. It's not safe."

Vic looked like she might argue, but then her shoulders dropped. "That's solid. We should probably wait for your fake work-meeting-thing to come through and figure out who else to talk to in the meantime."

Bex shook her head. "No, I have a better idea. Let's get Fergus to come with us."

Sam laughed. "Be serious."

"I am. He's six foot three and madly fit."

This was true. He also had no job and nothing to do, and this morning, she'd opened her refrigerator to discover that he'd eaten all of the meals she had delivered.

When was the last time she'd asked her brother to do something for her? Anything?

Sam came up blank.

"I guess he might get a kick out of meeting Christian Stanstedt." She yanked her fringed purse from the back of the chair and poked through it for her phone. The blue itinerary envelope unfolded itself and dropped clumsily to the floor. Bex retrieved it for her, and Sam shoved it back down into her bag, her heart racing. Another one of those things to discuss when she and Bex had time alone. Not now. But soon. For sure.

She shoved the envelope down further, then grabbed her phone and tapped her brother's contact.

Bex and Vic watched her with identical expressions of Simon curiosity.

"Sammy!" It sounded like Fergus was outside. The wind whistled through the phone.

"Hey, Ferg. Listen, I have to do something, and it occurred to me that maybe you could help out."

"Yes."

"Sorry?"

"Yes. Yeah. I'm there. Whatcha need?"

"You don't even know what it is. I thought you were scoping locations in Malibu."

"Malibu will be there tomorrow. You're my sister. Are you headed back my way?"

Sam pulled the phone away from her ear and looked at it to make sure she'd dialed the right number.

"Is he coming?" Vic whispered. "He's my favorite one of your brothers!"

"Um, no. Actually, I'm at Urth Melrose right now. I was hoping you could meet us somewhere we can park Bex's car, and then you could take us to—"

"Say no more. Gotta get a shirt on, but then I could meet up with you at—Where'd you say you were going?"

"I didn't. Beverly Hills."

"Sweet. And you're at Urth Melrose. Let's get together at the Beverly-Canon garage. Grab a spot, and I'll call you when I'm pulling in."

"That's a good idea." Sam felt like she was having an out-of-body experience. Was this the same brother who'd made her pay him a dollar per minute if she wanted to be in charge of the remote control as a child?

"I'll roll out of here in five."

"Thanks."

"Absolutely. See you."

Sam put her phone down on the table. "He'll meet us at the Beverly-Canon garage, and we'll try Christian's place in his Rivian."

"*That's* a cool vehicle," Vic said.

"And he can—you know—make sure we're safe."

Bex studied Sam's face, her brown eyes searching for something. Then she slid her hand across the table. Sam grabbed it, lacing her fingers with Bex's. "Look at that. Your brother's going to help us." Bex smiled. "How does that feel?"

Sam cleared her throat as she studied their interlaced fingers, which no doubt would show up on social media momentarily.

She bit the inside of her cheek and looked back at Bex's beautiful smiling face. "It feels good. I think it feels good."

"I bet it does."

Then, unbearably, Sam was grateful for how many years Bex had been her best friend when she wanted more, because all that time they'd spent getting to know each other meant Bex understood. She knew what it meant that Sam had asked one of her brothers for help with something and that Fergus had said yes without hesitation—a development that might have been lost in translation if they had less of a history or had gotten together too soon.

"My girlfriend," Sam said.

"What?"

"That's what you should call me."

Bex's eyes widened. A blush raced from her collarbones to her hairline. "Then that's what I'll call you. And what you'll call me."

"That's enough." Vic put her boba tea down. "I just ate."

Bex's jaw clenched. She slid her hand from Sam's. "Jesus, Vic."

"Sorry." She glanced toward the women at the table beside them. "I shouldn't have said that. I'm just going to retreat to my thoughts until my ears stop feeling like they're on fire."

They finished up in awkward silence punctuated by even more awkward attempts at conversation. By the time they left, the handful of paparazzi who always hung around Urth Caffé had swollen to a crowd. Pictures of Bex and Sam as a couple were worth money to the celebrity sites and online news, and they hadn't been seen together since the immediate aftermath of the reunion special. Vic cut a pathway through the paps, her powerful Viking thighs parting the sea of shouting men and flashing lights.

Bex held Sam's hand. In this town, it meant they were official. Hollywood official.

They made it to Bex's SUV and then to the garage in decent time. Fergus was already there, smiling and waving from the open door of his truck. He wore board shorts with sandals and a T-shirt that said "Crazy for Swayze" over a line drawing of the *Dirty Dancing* star in profile. Vic was hugging him before Sam had finished extracting herself from the car.

"Ironic?" Vic asked, pointing at Fergus's shirt.

"You'd think so, but no, not remotely." He gave Vic a crooked smile. "*Point Break* was, like, formative for me."

Bex slid a protective arm around Sam's waist. "Hey, Fergus."

He pointed at her. "Bexley Simon. I love you, but please don't hurt my sister."

"Never," Bex said, completely serious. "Never again."

There were a few beats where nothing filled the void but the echoing roll of tires in the garage and noise from the street, and then Fergus gave Bex another one of his crooked smiles that had convinced thousands of people to jump off a cliff holding onto a few hundred yards of nylon and have fun doing it. "All right, then." He rubbed his hands together. "Tell me why you're pulling me in on this. I have to say, I'm pretty worked up. If I have too much fun, I might change careers."

Sam shot him a look, and he laughed.

Bex filled Fergus in on Macie's visit and their amateur investigation of Ramona Watts's disappearance. Fergus became more solemn as he listened, asking questions about everything they had learned so far. "I don't love how dicey this could get," he said finally.

"If you're not comfortable, we have our plan B," Sam assured him.

"No, I'm good. If I'm going to deliver protection, though, I don't want to roll up like this." He swept his hand over his daily uniform. "Hand on. I've got a duffel in the frunk."

Sam yielded the front seat of the Rivian to Vic and sat in the back with Bex while Fergus changed by the tailgate. When he came around the driver's side, he wore dark jeans and a white button-down that wasn't too wrinkled. Since he'd unbuttoned one more button than was standard, rolled up the sleeves, and added Ray-Bans, he looked every inch the muscle Macie had mistaken him for.

As he pulled into traffic in his silent electric truck, explaining various features of the flatscreen on the dash to a happily chattering Vic, Sam let herself relax and take a minute to just be in the moment—on her way to Swan mansion with Bex and Vic beside her, her brother behind the wheel, the sun baking the hot pavement, the world bright and real and alive.

It was because she was looking out the window and seeing West Hollywood through the Technicolor lens of her gratitude that she noticed the woman. About her age, with dark bobbed hair. It was the same woman Sam had seen at a nearby table at the café. The one who'd been watching them.

And now she was pulling out of a parking spot just outside the Beverly-Canon garage, sliding into the stream of traffic a few cars back.

The Beast of Swan Mansion

Christian Stanstedt sat with one arm draped along the back of a mint suede sofa, jiggling a cracked flip-flop off and on his foot by flexing and relaxing his toes. Sam thought Vic must be correct—this man hadn't been awake long. He'd answered the door in an open cotton robe patterned with parrots, beneath which he was bare-chested, with only an extremely small pair of terry running shorts providing a breath of modesty.

Sam was struggling with the shorts. They revealed so much she didn't want to know, with an ongoing threat they might show her more every time he shifted position or crossed his legs.

He squinted at Bex while scratching idly at his chest hair. "Nobody stops by," he said flatly.

The Swan mansion perched so high above Los Angeles that the air felt different up here. They'd wound their way uphill in Fergus's truck until they reached a pinnacle of Hollywood that Sam had, despite her very privileged position, never attained.

The mansion was exquisite, with panoramic views of the city framed out in Spanish-inspired scrollwork, littered with Turkish carpets and trimmed in old-growth hardwoods that Sam felt guilty for admiring. But Christian wasn't the one who'd built it, or even who'd selected the enormous age-spotted vintage mirror that reflected the view and brought all of L.A. into the library he'd invited them to sit in. He'd done nothing to earn this magnificence.

"*We* stopped by." Bex's face was as empty and guileless as a kitten's as she gave Christian the most famous version of her guileless smile. Sam took it as a cue to lean back, let her cropped silk shirt ride up, and cross her legs, every one of her seventy inches a study in entitled boredom.

Christian raked his hand through his hair. It stood up fully six inches from his forehead before swooping lavishly to one side. At least half of Christian's fame had to be due to his hair's sculptural magnificence. He touched it often, tossing it to and fro, and it obediently fell into a flattering salt-and-pepper romantic disarray that perfectly set off his three-day stubble.

"Whatever." He stood up and shuffled to a breakfront built into the library shelves, where he slid open a leaded glass door to reveal a bar. "Anyone want a drink?"

"Scotch and soda," Sam said. She never drank Scotch and soda. She hardly drank, period, because anything alcoholic predictably gave her a cluster of pimples right along her hairline that took forever to heal. But she decided, given how Christian smelled, that the kind of functional alcoholic he was likely to be would not be keen to drink alone.

"Nothing for me," Bex said. "I'm cleansing."

Sam suppressed a laugh. Bexley Simon had never done a cleanse in her life.

"I'm twenty," Vic told him. "Not enough of my cerebral cortex has developed to drink. But I'll take a Coke with lemon."

Sam couldn't help but feel a secondhand maternal pride in Vic and her ability to make good decisions despite what some might believe about a twenty-year-old nepo baby with free rein of the Greater Los Angeles area.

"How about you, General?" Christian shouted this to Fergus across the room. "Want to wet your whistle?"

Fergus pushed away from the column and took a few casual steps closer, pushing his hands into his pockets. "Same as she's having, if it's not any trouble." He indicated Vic with the flick of one finger. "Since I'm on the job."

"No problem. If I'd have known I was throwing a kid's birthday party, I would've hung up a few balloons, but to each their own." He handed Sam's heavy pour to her with a wink.

Lord.

"So." Bex sat up straighter. "This is the Swan mansion!"

"Mmpf." He took out half his highball in one swallow and uncapped the Scotch to ready a second pour.

Sam took a closer, longer look at Christian. There was tension around his shoulders and in his jaw. He'd winced when he'd knocked back the Scotch. Sam would have expected a man in a robe drinking before happy hour to be accustomed to the burn.

He'd let them in with little comment. He'd recognized them, sure, but he hadn't asked any questions.

She studied the lines around his eyes with the experience of reading an acting partner.

Christian was *sad*.

There could be a lot of reasons for that, but this was an unfathomably rich man with a lot of power. Sam thought of her conversation with April Feinstein. Power and money couldn't preserve the relationships that meant something to you.

"You wanna swim?" Christian topped off his drink. This time, he didn't bother to put the cap back on his Lagavulin. "You don't need suits."

"No," Sam said at the same time Vic said, "Yes." She shot her a quelling look. "Actually, we're here because we had a few questions about your old friends. The Ice Crew. It seems like there's more than just your friend Ramona working the comeback. I had a wild hunch to check if you had any projects coming up with anybody from the crew."

Christian's face turned gray the same moment his neck and chest went bright red, as if his heart couldn't pump properly at the very mention of—what? Ramona? The Ice Crew?

It made Sam feel like she might be onto something.

"If you're interested in the crew, talk to Chad or Sloan," he said. "If you like *The Howling*, talk to Ramona." Christian waved his drink in a circle. "If you're into torture, that is."

Sam pretended to take a sip of her drink. It seared her nostrils when she got it close. "Not your besties?"

Christian laughed. "Fuck, no. Chad's a hack trying to skate by on what's left of his jawline, and Sloan's as irrelevant as that hat he wears. If it wasn't for *Lights of Marfa*, nobody ever would've heard of either one of them. You know *Halfcab* was in the can before their movie?" He clucked his tongue. "Got stuck in post because we needed to reshoot the ending, but my costar was pregnant and wouldn't do it until she'd had the baby and lost the weight. By the time it released, all anybody wanted to talk about was fucking *Marfa*."

Sam desperately wanted to exchange a look with Bex to transmit her surprise that it was so easy to rile up Christian about the old days. It meant he still had ego in the game. Vic had told them in Fergus's truck on the way over that the rumor was that something had gone down between Christian, Chad, and Sloan back then, leading to Christian's being literally iced out of the crew. Maybe being recently friendship-dumped all over again, this time by Ramona, had been a serious blow to Christian's ego.

Serious enough that he would have retaliated against Ramona?

But why bother? It could be that Christian's waters ran a lot deeper than it appeared, but he didn't seem like a planner to Sam. She had no idea if Vic was right and his money had made him complacent, but at the very least he was numbing *something* with substances, parties, and attitude.

"That's a bad break." Fergus spoke from behind Sam's chair. "*Halfcab* was majestic. I hate guys like Chad—entitled tools who need validation so they can hitch themselves up high enough to punch down. You're smart to walk away from that shit."

"Thank you." Christian raised his drink to Fergus and then

put the empty highball glass on the bar. "If the Ice Crew is all you wanted to talk about, you can see yourselves out. Or go ahead and use the pool, what do I care? It's got a hell of a view of the city."

Vic looked worriedly from Bex to Sam. "Don't we have a lot more we want to ask about Ramona?"

It took a great deal of self-mastery for Sam to prevent herself from spilling Scotch on her shirt. To their credit, both Bex and Fergus remained self-possessed in the face of Vic's blunt question.

"Sorry?" Christian turned around where he was walking through a cased opening that led out of the library. His cheeks were maroon.

"There's a rumor going around town that the whole crew is getting reunited again," she lied. "Maybe you've talked to Ramona recently. Like, since Friday."

"*Vic*," Bex warned.

Vic turned to Bex. "But isn't that really why you wanted to stop by? To confirm the rumor, because you're so into Ice Crew and are hoping for a reunion? Everyone knows you're obsessed with reunions after the *Craven's Daughter* reunion and everything." Vic opened her eyes wide at her sister, willing her to take the bait. It wasn't a graceful move, but Sam could admit it was a direct way to learn if there was anything else Christian would give them about Ramona.

"So obsessed." Bex smiled at Christian, but it was a pained attempt. "Is it true? Can we expect to see the entire Ice Crew on the big screen again?"

Christian's cheeks were mottled purple. Sam could hear the bubbles popping in her glass.

"What is this?" His question bristled with hostility.

Sam slowly uncrossed her legs, on edge due to the palpable mood shift. She did not like this man. She could not imagine him ever having been worthy of Ramona's friendship or Colin's love. If he had been, he'd left that version of himself behind.

"Ramona didn't show up on set Monday," she said. "She

hasn't been home. Her friends are worried about her. Including Colin."

Christian tipped to the side, stumbled, and caught himself against the wide wooden trim of the curved library opening. "Well, I haven't seen her! I don't see her anymore!" He wiped his hand over his mouth. "Jesus, she's serious with this?"

Surprisingly, he directed this question to Fergus. Sam assumed someone like Christian Stanstedt was more comfortable investing authority in another man.

"Dead serious," Fergus replied. "When did you last see Ms. Watts?"

"A while ago. Did Colin tell them I would know something?"

"What do you think Colin Worth would tell us about you and Ramona?" Sam asked.

Christian's eyes went black, but Sam watched him try to affect unconcern. "You said she didn't show up to work on Monday? It's, what, Thursday?"

"It's Tuesday, Captain," Fergus said. "Almost three in the afternoon on a Tuesday in May."

Christian rattled the ice in his glass. "Okay, so, Monday to Tuesday, that's nothing. She's taken off. You'll find out from the gossip pages that she got married to a supplement millionaire she met in Vegas, or she moved to Bali to study kundalini yoga." He pushed away from the doorway. "Ramona's the comeback queen. She fucks up, fucks off, and disappears. You don't hear from her for years so she can turn right on time to remind you how much you loved her. It's a game, and Ramona knows how to play it better than anyone. *The Howling* is at the top of the ratings? Time for her to go."

Sam had to admit there was veracity to what Christian was saying, anger or no. Lasting a long time in Hollywood, surviving at all, *did* often mean finding a game you could play. It wouldn't be a bad strategy to build the public's interest in your work by disappearing. Sam had heard the word "overexposed" more than once in connection to *The Howling*.

Maybe Ramona wasn't in danger after all. Maybe she was only trying to make it to the next round.

When Sam looked at Bex, she gave her an almost imperceptible nod. Sam transferred the message to Fergus through sister telepathy.

"Sorry to waste your time," Fergus said, easy as warm honey. He walked over and held out his hand, and, thank God, Christian took it. "We appreciate it."

"Shit happens. Next time be straight about it. You can find your way out?"

"You bet." Fergus clapped Christian on the shoulder. "Thanks, truly." He gave Christian a look like, *I have to humor these women, but we both know their drama is part of the job.*

It was remarkable. Her brother was a good actor.

Finally, he turned his attention to Sam, Bex, and Vic. "We rollin'?"

They followed his broad shoulders out through the labyrinth of the Swan. They were subdued as they passed between the fifteen-foot doors and onto the marble portico to a gorgeous day, everything gleaming, with Los Angeles laid at their feet.

In Fergus's truck, the cool silence made Sam feel entombed.

"Well," Vic finally said. "That was terrible. First of all, we haven't done anything to help Macie or find Ramona. Second, that guy is trying to kill pain that I have no way of understanding, but I *will* say it is a big hit to the aura to be around it. And finally—and keep in mind I really think it has to be acknowledged—what Christian said about Ramona doesn't sound wrong. It sounds bad, and it doesn't sound like how Macie talks about her, but it doesn't sound *wrong*."

Sam sighed. "I want to disagree, but we do know that Ramona's self-reliant and smart. And *The Howling* was in large part so interesting to audiences because it was Ramona's big comeback. But—"

"—that part of the sparkle is starting to fade," Bex said. "If the episode with Chad and Sloan airs after Ramona's disappeared, that's a huge, mysterious platform to launch herself off of a few years from now. And what kind of role was she going to get after *The Howling* came to an end? At her age, there might not be one. There *should* be, but there might not. Unless she emerges from the mist one more time."

Sam was staring out the window of her brother's truck, trying to process Ramona's disappearance through the lens of these freshly depressing perspectives, when Vic's phone made a soft noise and she gasped.

"What's wrong?" Bex asked.

"Ramona Watts. She's emerged from the mist."

The Truth According to Star Spy

Vic twisted around in her seat and held her phone up so Sam and Bex could see the screen. "According to Star Spy, the 'evergreen trendsetting and retro-cool star of a popular horror series' was spotted enjoying the weather and signing autographs at the Exposition Park Rose Garden this morning, her signature perfectly messy brunette locks showcasing the crystal hairpin collection from Chloé accessories line."

Bex had been tapping on her own phone, but now she dropped it in her lap and pushed her hands over her eyes. "I can't get Macie to pick up. They should know about this, but they're not answering."

"We'll tell them," Sam said. "If we have to, we'll go to them." She felt as though a heavy blanket had been laid down on top of her own feelings. Sam hated Vic's news. That was the truth. She didn't hate that Ramona was alive, but she *did* hate that they'd just found out Ramona was perfectly fine, enjoying the spring weather, chatting up her fans at the rose garden.

Why would she do that?

Bex gave her a pained smile. "So much for her private and enigmatic reputation, huh?"

Sam nodded. But then she really heard what Bex had said. "She *is* private and enigmatic. But now she's signing autographs right out in the middle of the busiest part of L.A. on a pretty spring day?"

Something felt off. The Star Spy item was *too much* of a letdown, too much confirmation that it was ridiculous for two former TV detectives to drive all over Los Angeles gathering "evidence" to find a missing actress.

She and Bex were not ridiculous people. Neither were Macie or April Feinstein or Colin Worth. Call it what you wanted, headline it however it got the clicks, but *Sam and Bex: TV Detectives Who Can't Resist a Real Case* were also real people who had made other people feel like they could get to the bottom of a real problem.

"You know what we need right now?" Vic turned fully around in her seat. "Perspective."

"Yeah?" Fergus started his truck and began rolling down the endless driveway. "I know just the place."

After a quiet drive and small hike over the sand toward the roar of the ocean, they were gathered in a small circle on a cluster of rocks. Sam watched Vic fight the wind as she set up her phone so everyone could hear Frankie.

"Our perspective is at a Missouri truck stop," Vic said. "She doesn't have enough signal to video chat. You should know I told her about the blind item, and she's pissed at us if we say we believe it."

Here on the beach, they were a stone's throw from Marina Del Rey, where Ramona had gone to a party on a yacht the night of Juliette Draper's death. But Sam knew that wasn't the reason Fergus had chosen to bring them to Santa Monica. The beach was where Fergus could always think best, where he went to heal. He'd structured his entire life around the Pacific Ocean.

"Who am I talking to?" Frankie's voice was clear in the lee of the big rocks. She did sound pissed, but Sam wasn't bothered. Frankie had been in middle school when Sam met her, with a caustic wit and a tendency to lock down her feelings until they exploded in bursts of furious recrimination.

"Me and Bex and Sam and Fergus," Vic said.

"All right. Vic has indeed filled me in." Frankie sounded ready to give them one of her ranting lectures. "Have you guys actually forgotten there is nothing the world loves more than putting a woman in the public eye on a pedestal and then ripping her apart when they're bored? Women and marginalized famous people are always fighting the minimal tolerance the public has for them in the first place. Bex—for example. Star Spy once placed you at Nobu throwing up in a Birkin bag when you were actually with me at the orthodontist getting my braces tightened. They ran that right after your Emmy win and *Vogue* cover."

"Well, that's true." Bex pulled her wild hair on top of her head and wound an elastic around it. "And it's probably the least of what they've gotten wrong. Until this Star Spy thing, there hasn't been anything from any source about Ramona. By some miracle, unless I've missed something from all the alerts I've set up on my phone, it still hasn't even leaked that Chad and Sloan are going to be on her show. Most of what's out there right now is gossip speculating with varying degrees of accuracy about the relationship between me and Sam and listing the places we've been spotted."

Sam nodded, thinking aloud. "No one who was with Ramona on Friday has leaked that Ramona didn't show up Monday. *The Howling* is good at confidentiality. I can't decide if that's good or bad under the circumstances."

Frankie sighed loudly. "It's good. You don't want to follow leads generated from gossip and the Internet. That's my fucking *point.* You should know that Haris checked his location tracker, and it *still* shows Ramona as unfindable. And look, if she was signing autographs in L.A., would her phone be turned off?"

"This whole town gossips," Bex said, taking in Frankie's argument. "Information leaks and gets distorted."

Sam rubbed her temples. She could still hear the shouts of the paps as she and Bex walked out of Urth Melrose holding hands. Her publicist had already left her a voicemail saying to give her a call when Sam had a "quick second" for a "rundown" of the agency's "strategies" for dealing with the surge of press. Sam guessed if she looked on the Internet right now, every headline about them would be at least partly wrong.

Ramona knew herself. That was what they'd learned about her so far from visiting her home and talking to the people who were close to her. In her career and in her life, all of Ramona's decisions grew from her understanding of herself. It was why the news from Star Spy had churned up Sam's feelings so quickly—because the behavior it described didn't make sense for the person they were getting to know, even though they hadn't met her yet.

Sam wanted to listen to Ramona, not the noise. Not only because it was the right thing to do, but because the woman they were looking for had come to mean something to Sam.

It was true that she didn't know what was coming next in her life. She could feel the hours ticking closer to the moment she was either on that plane to Telluride or not. But that clock wasn't ticking as loud as the one counting off the hours Ramona had been gone.

Sam had to believe there was a reason Macie had brought this problem to her door.

And as far as spending time with Bex? Making up for lost time? Bex was right here. Sitting next to her, a hand on her knee. Right now, they were together.

Sam stood up. "We don't know yet if Ramona's still in trouble," she said. "Not until what Star Spy says is definitively confirmed. Does everybody agree with that?"

"Yes," Bex said. Frankie, Vic, and Fergus chimed in with their own affirmatives.

"That means we need to check in with Macie and Colin, and if Ramona's still not calling them back, it's time we start looking at what was happening on the set of *The Howling.* Maybe Ramona shared her plans with someone. The only thing we know so far is Ramona had to shoot with Chad and Sloan last week, hated it, and then didn't return to set. It's fair to wonder if something went down."

Vic nodded vigorously. "Yes. And we haven't found out anything about that guy who came looking for Ramona at her house on Monday morning. Colin said he came from the studio. If that's true, we should be able to verify it."

"I can get us on the studio lot with my credentials from the *Theomina* reshoot," Sam said, "but I doubt we can use them to access the *Howling* set."

"I'm going to call Piper," Vic said. "She's where this started, in a way. Maybe she can get us in after they wrap today. It's what, four o'clock?"

"Four thirty. What a day." Sam held out her hands and pulled Bex to her feet. The freckles across Bex's nose and cheeks washed a wave of tenderness through her that made her knees weak.

Bex laid her head on Sam's shoulder. The ocean breeze had pulled half of her hair down from its impromptu bun, and as Sam gathered her close, the loose locks blew against the exposed skin of Sam's throat. She inhaled the familiar smell of Bex's shampoo and kissed the top of her head.

Bex's phone started ringing from somewhere in the depths of her bag.

"I want updates." Frankie's voice interrupted the muffled ringtone. "I'll try to think of anything else we can do to help."

After they packed up and began moving back toward the parking lot, Bex hustled ahead and dug her phone out. She was poking at the screen when Vic caught up to her and asked her something, but Sam couldn't hear what it was. The ocean drowned them out.

She walked next to her brother, whose Oxford shirt had come untucked. The tails were blowing in the wind. "You look like a men's fragrance ad," she told him. "Half squinty, half empty-eyed bonehead."

"It's called cool. You wouldn't know." He smiled, not quite in her direction. "Are they all like that?"

"Who's they?"

Solemn lines bracketed her brother's mouth. "Christian Stanstedt. I must've seen that skater movie a thousand times. Thought he was so fucking aspirational." He shook his head. "What a wankhammer."

"I'm sorry I dragged you over there."

"Nah. I've always gotten a kick out of the behind-the-scenes drama of your career. I'd prefer a total lack of danger, but I appreciate the chance to pick up the pretty, shiny rocks and see what's squiggling in the dirt underneath them."

Sam tried to get a bead on her brother, whose interest in her work had always seemed to be limited to watching her shows and movies when they released. In her TV days, her older brothers had sometimes visited her on set or tagged along for a premiere, but not Fergus, even though he'd been her closest brother growing up. When Sam said *my brother,* she still always meant Fergus. "I'm glad you were there, but you can bail now if you want. We can go by the Beverly-Canon and Bex can get her car. You don't have to pick up any more rocks. I promise that Bex and Vic and I will stay safe."

Fergus stopped walking. "You're kidding, right?" There was a palpable thread of tension behind the question that matched his hands, fisted now in his deep pockets.

"No." Sam was surprised to have prompted such a strong reaction. She wasn't sure what he was reacting *to*, but his tone made her stomach tighten. "I know you have meetings and wanted to scout some properties in Malibu. This is a working trip for you, right?"

Fergus laughed. "If you don't hang out with me, it is. Look. I'm here. I'm doing this. I get why you might think I'd rather be doing something else, but that's old pain that you and I should talk about sometime. Hopefully in more relaxed circumstances when we both know we can escape the conversation the minute it gets too much into the feelings."

Sam's stomach relaxed. It was a relief for the tension between them to be acknowledged. Maybe they finally *would* talk.

That was when she noticed the sedan.

She touched her brother's arm. "I didn't tell you this yet, but I'm pretty sure I saw that car when we left the garage in Beverly. And the woman in it was the same person I saw watching me and Bex and Vic at Urth Caffé."

Fergus pulled his phone out of his pocket, swiped the screen, and started filming.

"I'm probably wrong," Sam said. "Why would someone follow us? I mean, people follow me, especially me and Bex together, but women don't, usually. And this woman was *inside* the café, which is also not normal for the people who tend to follow celebrities around. And they don't drive from West Hollywood to Beverly Hills to Santa Monica."

As Bex and Vic got closer to the Rivian, Sam watched the woman's head swivel to watch them.

"Can you zoom, Ferg?" She picked up her pace, and his strides lengthened.

"On it."

Then the woman was looking right at Sam. Her heart skipped, but she kept her gaze steady. She heard the woman's car start up. "Can you get her face?"

"The sun's so bright, it's washing out the details, but she's around my age, maybe a bit older. Dark hair cut into a bob. I got her plates."

"For sure the same person." Sam watched the car slowly pull away as Bex and Vic made it to the tailgate of Fergus's truck. "A stalker is not something I need right now."

Fergus lowered his phone. "That was unsettling. Not to get all protective big brother, but it will make me feel better to live closer by you. At least then you can call me if you need me."

Sam was trying to think of how to respond when her brain snapped with a new Ramona thought. "If that woman caught up with us at Urth, then she knows we went to the Swan mansion. But she could have been following us before that, when we were at Ramona's house. Everyone I've talked to so far has assumed Bex and I were looking into Ramona's disappearance in an official way. That means there's an impression out there in the world that we weren't done once we figured out who killed Jen on the *Craven's Daughter* set."

"You're saying you think that woman knows you're looking into Ramona?"

Sam tapped her mouth, thinking. "If she does, it would mean she *knows* Ramona. Well enough to know she's missing, I mean. So why hasn't she talked to us? Unless—"

"—she's a bad guy," Fergus finished. "And I hate that. I can't even tell you how much I hate it. What should I do with this video? With the plates?"

"I could send them to the person who does my security when I need a detail. He has the connections to figure out who she is. But if I call him right now, it will initiate an entire series of events that are about me, not Ramona, and God knows what would leak. I think we should hold onto what you have until after we talk to Piper on the *Howling* set."

"You're the boss." They caught up to Vic and Bex, who were waiting for them. He unlocked the truck for everyone. "Let's head to the studio. See where the magic happens."

Stalking Monsters and Monsters Stalking

"VIP at Coachella this year was embarrassing." Piper Redwood lounged on a futon sofa near an empty craft table, nibbling a baby carrot she'd taken from a plastic bag in her lap. Her nose wrinkled in disgust. They were the only wrinkles touching the elfin, wide-eyed features that had made her famous and her role as the daughter of Ramona's character believable.

Yesterday morning, Sam had been in a different building for the *Theomina* reshoots, which fell under Howell Motion Pictures but not its StudioHonor streaming arm. She'd never been on this part of the campus. The double soundstage that belonged to *The Howling* was dominated by a massive set piece of a family home from the nineties, complete with wood paneling, printed vinyl floors, and sculpted carpeting. Certain areas were hung with sound and lights, and there was a slight smell of prop cigarettes made from nontoxic herbs, probably due to the overflowing ashtrays on the set's end tables.

On the way in, they'd passed a space near the outside wall of the soundstage where a number of the show's animatronic prop monsters had been stored on shelves and in cubbies. Sam had stared at the pink eyes of a flayed face, most of its skin peeled away, and told herself they would find Ramona, and she had nothing to be afraid of.

There were so many monsters stalking Ramona. Sam really hoped one of them hadn't pounced.

"You didn't miss anything good," Piper was telling Vic. "I just forgot to fill you in. I was supposed to see the headliners with Sera and Matty, but of course they couldn't even go near the main stage VIP because Linus was there, and *you* know."

"I *do*," Vic moaned. "But I still can't believe I couldn't make it. I was going to have that woman who body painted Liv do me, and it would have been one legend moment after another, but instead there was a lab for Developmental Biology? No. The worst."

"Amazing that you do the school thing, though. As soon as I'm twenty-five, I'm going to have to start playing moms."

"So, hey." Bex interrupted what promised to be an interminable catch-up conversation with a wave and her big voice. "Nice to see you, Piper. This is Sam Farmer and her brother, Fergus."

Piper stood up and pulled her long, dark braid over her shoulder. Her wide-eyed gaze focused in on Fergus, who she stepped toward and offered her hand to. "I saw you at Sushi Park, right? With Ryan Gosling."

Fergus laughed as he shook her hand. "No, you didn't, but it's lovely to meet you."

"Hmm." Piper didn't let go of him. "That's right, you have a little feud with Ryan, I think." She grinned. "Doesn't matter to me. You can call me, though, the next time you go."

Fergus tried to take his hand back. "I don't have your number?" Sam's clueless brother looked hilariously confused.

"*You* do." Piper looked back at Vic, just a quick glance, raising her eyebrows.

"My brother's not in the industry." Sam held out her hand,

forcing Piper to let go of Fergus. "It's really great to meet you. Love your work on the show."

Piper gave Sam a closemouthed smile and took her hand away. "Thank you. I'm sure your project with Chad Bevington will be interesting, too. I was surprised you were cast as Theomina. I imagined her much younger when I read the book."

"She's a three-thousand-year-old mage," Sam said, unbothered. "I think the casting director thought there was a bit of range in the part. We're actually here to talk about Ramona and why she's missing shooting this week."

"Ramona Watts?" Piper tipped her head as though she might know dozens of Ramonas.

"Yes. The star of this show. Your colleague. Ramona Watts."

"I mean, okay, I *guess* I'll help with damage control, even though I kind of despise her right now. But should we do a quick tour of the studio first?" She gripped Fergus's arm. He held it out from his body at a strange angle, as though he had to remain motionless to prevent a viper strike.

"We're kinda in a tight schedule sitch." Vic gave Piper a sympathetic look of annoyance.

Piper huffed. "I can't *believe* she emerged from her seclusion just to sun herself and sign autographs. Did you know we've been shooting around her not being here for two days? I've got to do all these scenes from different episodes completely out of order. Like, I can't. I learn my parts in linear progression, emotionally, and now I have to deliver these completely random feelings with no concern about how that affects my process. I'm so *effing* peeved, I'm starting to think it's better if she doesn't come back and they have to make it so one of the monsters ate her."

Sam moved to stand closer to Bex. She could smell sun and sea in Bex's wild hair. "Star Spy's blind items aren't the most reliable," she said. "We're looking for confirmation from people who know Ramona that they've seen her. Have you, or have you heard anything from the other cast and crew?" she asked. "Rumors?"

Piper flopped back onto the futon. “I’m very method, so I don’t commingle.” Vic sat next to her, and the rest of them grabbed stage stools. “But I can say she still hasn’t checked in.”

“How do you know that?”

“My agent and I took a meeting with Honor last night to discuss future projects.” She widened her eyes at Sam as if to ask if she knew who Honor was.

“Honor Howell,” Sam said obligingly. “The studio head.”

“Yeah, and I overheard her on the phone talking to someone about Ramona’s being AWOL. She was demanding an explanation, which means she doesn’t have one, right? And if Honor doesn’t know why Ramona’s not here, I can promise you nobody else does.”

“Thank you,” Sam said, distracted, because now she was much more worried. They’d just ruled out any plausible professional explanation for Ramona’s absence. “It’s helpful to know that no one involved in Ramona’s job has been in contact with her.”

“However.” Piper gave Sam a sly smile and reached into her back pocket for her phone. She waggled it at them. “If I had seen *this* last night, I could’ve helped Honor out. I’m officially on to you guys. I’m not totally sure how much I want to help you shape the narrative or whatever, since it looks like Ramona doesn’t care anyway.”

Sam glanced at the dark screen of Piper’s phone, then at Piper again, completely lost. “What are you talking about?”

“You don’t have to go around pretending to look for Ramona anymore. She updated her Instagram a couple of hours ago.”

Vic’s jaw dropped. “Um, can I take a look?”

Piper shrugged and handed her phone to Vic. “Sorry she made you go to all this trouble. I’ve heard she’s like this, even with her friends.”

Sam’s palms itched to see whatever was making Vic’s pale eyebrows meet her hairline. She swiped several times, then looked up at Sam, Bex, and Fergus. "These are pictures on a lurker account," Vic said. "There's no way we could've found it. The account is private. But it really seems to be Ramona's."

"It is," Piper said. "She added me so I could follow her ages ago. Usually, it's just her cat and recipes, and she rarely updates. You can see for yourself it's nothing worth talking about."

"I wish you'd told me about *this* post," Vic said. "The new one. It's a bunch of scenery shots from the Maldives. No selfies or pictures of Ramona. It's someplace fancy, like a resort hotel." She squinted at the screen. "No, the art's too good. Resort hotels don't have marble sculptures propping up the balcony. Maybe it's a high-dollar rental. Could she have gotten to the Maldives as of a couple hours ago?" Vic tapped at the phone screen, presumably doing a search to find out how long it took to get from L.A. to the Maldives. "Barely. Is *this* really how she was going to let her friends know she was okay? An Insta post without even a caption? That's . . . not okay."

Piper shrugged. "Whatever."

Sam's radar must've been tuned up high, because she didn't miss the hurt in Piper's voice. She studied the young woman, thinking about her self-protective body language. The way she'd talked since they arrived. The flirtatious behavior. The aggressive nonchalance.

Piper *liked* Ramona.

All of Piper's attitude since they started asking about her costar was because Piper was having some big feelings that she didn't know how to handle. She hadn't believed Ramona would do something like this. Walk off the set. Leave her hanging.

Sam couldn't really make herself believe it, either.

"You said none of the pictures actually have Ramona *in* them?" Sam asked Vic.

"Not in this new set." Vic passed the phone to Bex, who started scrolling through, biting her lip. "But it's definitely Ramona in some of the cat pictures from before."

"The caption just says 'the Maldives,'" Bex pointed out. "Vic's right, though, the art looks expensive."

"Wait." Piper leaned forward and took her phone back to study the photo set again. "What are you saying?"

"Piper, do you genuinely think that Ramona fucked off to the Maldives and is on the beach now ignoring phone calls from her studio head?" Sam asked. "Does that fit what you know about her? Does it feel correct?"

Piper shoved her phone back into her pocket. She suddenly looked young. "She always takes the time to help me with my craft," she said softly. "She actually worked with Meisner when she was my age. Like, Sanford Meisner himself, not at one of his studios." Piper looked from Sam to Bex. "And I saw Star Spy. She couldn't be in L.A. and the Maldives at the same time."

"No. She couldn't. I think someone wants anyone who's paying attention to think Ramona's living up to a bad reputation that she didn't earn. I think they might be doing that to distract people who care from noticing that she's in trouble."

Piper's eyes filled with tears. "What do you want to know?"

Bex rose from her stool and settled on the futon beside the young actor. "We're trying to figure out all of Ramona's movements from the end of the workday on Friday to Monday morning when she didn't come in." Her voice was the same gentle one she'd used to soothe Vic's scrapes and bruises. "Did anything unusual happen at Friday's shoot? What time did you wrap on Friday? How does everyone usually leave the studio? Does Ramona go straight home in her own car, or does she have a driver? What are her habits? Those are the kinds of things we need to know. Anything you can think of."

The tip of Piper's nose had turned pink. "I guess as far as habits, she doesn't talk to anyone much. She texts a lot on her phone and makes a lot of script notes. This season, especially lately, she sometimes hangs with her boyfriend."

Sam didn't check, but she was sure the shocked expressions on Bex, Vic, and Fergus's faces were the same as her own. "Ramona has a boyfriend?"

"Yes? Or maybe not. She's pretty guarded about her personal life. Respect." Piper dove her hand into her pocket and pulled out her phone again. "Here." She swiped on the screen, then handed it to Vic. "That's him. I was taking a picture of someone else, but you can see him standing next to her."

Vic took the phone. Sam watched as the edge of her pale blond hairline went red. The sides of her face flushed, splotchy and hot. She handed the phone to Sam.

When Sam saw the man in the background standing next to Ramona's chair, her goose bumps reactivated. "Jesus."

"Who is it?" Bex leaned against Sam and looked at the picture. "Vic, isn't that the man who was in Colin's security cam footage?"

"It is."

Sam's hand started trembling. "Archie Blasingame. Ramona's boyfriend—that's the same Archie Blasingame who made a documentary about the Ice Crew that never got released. Colin told me Ramona's been watching footage from it and taking notes. It was Archie who went to her house looking for her the day she was supposed to be on set."

"Oh my God," Bex breathed.

Piper was staring at her phone now that Vic had handed it back. Her thumb tracked slowly up the screen. "Ramona normally changes out of her costume and goes home. There's a parking garage. She has an assigned spot. I've seen her get into her car. She doesn't use a driver."

"On Friday?"

"We weren't here. We shot on the mountain—which, I wasn't the one to tell you that." Piper covered her mouth with both hands for emphasis. "Seriously. It can't leak. If it does leak, it can't be me who leaked it. *No one* knows where the shoot was. *No one* knows who the guest stars are. The NDA was scary. The studio wants the episode to shock the audience."

"What mountain?" Fergus asked.

"Baldy."

Mount San Antonio, known locally as Mount Baldy, was a ten-thousand-foot peak on the border of San Bernardino County. It would take at least ninety minutes to get there from the studios.

"They sent us up in vans," Piper explained. "Trucks had gone the night before with filming equipment, and some of the crew had been there all day Thursday. We do a lot of wilderness exteriors."

"Were you up at the peak or more in the foothills? Do you know if it was west, the flat, the bowl, the notch?" Fergus leaned his elbows on his knees, his tone casual. He was trying to make sure Piper stayed comfortable so that she didn't freak. Sam had seen him use the same supercool affect while teaching anxious people how to hurl themselves off a cliff wearing a nylon glider.

She did the same thing. When emotions rose around her, Sam shifted into a lower gear. It was why she had a reputation for being unflappable. She'd never thought about it as something she and Fergus had both learned growing up in the high-energy, high-emotion Farmer household.

"Not at the top," Piper said. "It's like in the wilderness, with the giant rocks. Where the river is?" She pulled her braid back over her shoulder, then picked her phone off the futon. "I have some more pictures." She swiped them open and handed her phone to Fergus.

He studied the photos. "It's hard to tell, since most of these are closeups of your costars, but looking at the foliage and the terrain, yeah, I think it must be somewhere in the watershed. There's a big wilderness preserve."

"Yes! That was it. It was the worst shoot. We only had the

day, because the studio was paying out the nose for the permits to have such a big crew up there, and it all had to be cleared with the government."

"To make sure the filming wouldn't have a negative impact on the environment." He bobbed his head agreeably, looking right into Piper's eyes.

"Yeah, although I don't see how we could. It's just a huge wasteland of nothing up there. We had rehearsed on the lot—at least, some of us did. The principals were going to work more improvisationally. You know, with the natural environment."

"By 'the principals,' you mean Ramona, Chad, and Sloan," Sam clarified.

Piper slapped her hands to her cheeks. "Who told you about Chad and Sloan?"

"Chad did. I had a reshoot for *Theomina* with him on Monday morning over in Building D, and he let it slip."

Piper immediately relaxed. "As long as it's not me. The three of them had their own crew and cameras. The rest of us were in a different area."

Fergus crossed his legs, clasping his knee. "On Friday, the sunset would have been around seven forty-five, so—"

"How do you know that?" Piper interrupted.

"I have an outfitting and paragliding business, so it's pretty much my job to know when the big light turns off. Did they use lighting rigs on the mountain, or were you leaving before sunset?"

"They had lights, but they were all gelled with different colors, and there were some digital light effects. We had to wait in the vans for almost an hour while they wrapped with Ramona and—you know who. I seriously can't say it." Fergus's guide persona had relaxed Piper into speaking more fluently, her memories flowing now. "They went long, and then the trucks had to finish loading. Finally, all the vans with cast and crew drove down together. Everybody was packed in, and it took forever. We had to go slow since the trucks were in front of us."

"The vans dropped you somewhere here?"

"At the parking structure, where the valet office is. The night valet retrieved our cars while we waited next to the office."

"Did you notice anything about Ramona that seemed unusual?"

"She wasn't in my van, so I didn't really get a chance to notice her at all. Sloan gave her a ride home. Chad was on his motorcycle." Piper shook her head. "That's what I can remember."

Had Sloan been the one who picked Ramona up on Friday morning, then taken her home that same night? Or taken her somewhere else?

Sam added the question to her list of things to find out.

"So just to recap the timeline, you wrapped at sunset," Fergus said. "Ramona, Chad, and Sloan finished shortly after, and everyone waited in the vans for the trucks to get done breaking and packing the set. Then you drove back here to the parking garage, stood around waiting for your cars, and Ramona left the studio with Sloan around . . . ?"

"It was almost midnight by then. Almost Saturday," Piper told him.

"Got it." That was helpful. Bex had retrieved her notebook from her bag a while ago, no doubt marking out with bullets whoever they would have to follow up with, but Sam committed the basics to memory.

Ramona had left her house by some unknown means early Friday morning for the studio. She'd been transported to location in a van, worked all day on Mount Baldy, returned to the studio parking garage with the full cast and crew, and then left the parking garage with Sloan close to midnight Friday night. Colin and Macie hadn't seen her over the weekend, and no one Macie talked to had heard from her. Her location tracking was unavailable. She didn't go to work on Monday morning—the same morning that Sam had been at the studio reshooting for *Theomina* with Chad and later saw him in the parking lot with Sloan. The same morning Archie Blasingame went to Ramona's house looking for her.

Star Spy had heavily implied that Ramona was in L.A. this afternoon—which must mean the studio was scrambling to figure out what the hell was going on—while Ramona's private Instagram account put her in the Maldives.

It was Tuesday night.

Sam was officially terrified.

"You'll find her, right? That's what you guys do. Help people like us." Piper's arms were wrapped around her body.

"Yes." Sam put every bit of her famous calm reassurance into the affirmative. "We will."

She sounded like Theomina. Fighting monsters and trying not to cry.

After saying their goodbyes, they left Piper to her work and exited the studio together. Vic was doing something on her phone. "Wait," she said. "I just looked it up quick. Archie Blasingame is married."

"But not to Ramona." Sam wondered how many gotchas this day was going to have.

"No."

Was he an affair partner? A friend? An enemy?

Bex stopped on the path to the parking garage. "Let's try Macie again. There's just too much. As it is, I'll be writing in my notebook all night."

Sam had tried calling Macie from the Rivian on the drive from Santa Monica, but they hadn't answered. Now Bex retrieved her phone from her bag. Sam spotted missed-call notifications on her screen. It appeared that at least one of the people Bex had been dodging was her manager.

Bex put her phone on speaker. After a few rings, Sam heard Macie's worried voice. "Hello? My God. I'm so sorry I missed you earlier."

Bex's voice was sure and steady as she caught Macie up with the latest developments in the investigation.

"Listen," Macie said after Bex had filled them in. "That Star Spy item is bullshit. Ramona doesn't sign autographs. She hasn't for ages."

"Thanks for that," Sam said. "It didn't sound right, but it's good to know you think so, too."

"Yeah, and the other thing. Ramona's not having an affair with Archie. They're just friends. We both met him when he was working on the Ice Crew documentary that never happened. Later, she helped him get work on some of her other projects. They've always had each other's backs. My guess is that if Piper was seeing him with Ramona on *The Howling* set regularly enough to think he's her boyfriend, it means Ramona needed a bit of support there."

Sam let out a long breath. "That helps, too. It means we need to talk to Archie. I'd like to hear what he has to say before we try to question Chad or Sloan."

"The other thing is that I did call and talk to Ramona's parents," Macie said. "I don't want to mess up your investigation or anything, but—"

"No," Bex interrupted. "That's a good call. What do they want to do?"

"They're talking to a few different people close to law enforcement, trying to figure out how they can file a missing person report without causing a media circus. They want you to keep asking questions. In the meantime, they're going to fly out here."

They ended the call with Macie sounding somber. The light was fading. As they made their way to the parking garage, Sam tried not to think about what could have happened between the last minutes of Friday night, when Ramona got a ride home from Sloan Lennox, and Monday morning.

They reached the lot. The Rivian looked humongous in its narrow space. She was temporarily confused when a set of bright

LED headlights beamed at their group like a giant laser, but then Fergus started running toward the lights, waving both arms and yelling, "Hey!"

As the headlights swung away, Sam recognized the car. It was the woman who had been stalking them all day. Fergus had caught up to it and was jogging alongside the sedan. He smacked the top of the sedan, then sprinted to stand in front of it, blocking it from leaving.

"Fergus!" Sam yelled.

The sedan stopped. Its headlights went dark. Fergus approached the driver's side and knocked on the window, and it eased down.

Sure enough, it was the same woman with the dark bob who Sam had seen at Urth Caffé, then again outside the parking garage and at the beach. She'd followed them to Culver City.

"Who the fuck are you?" Fergus asked, with surprising calm. "Because this lot is covered in cameras, and you've been following us. You can't do that. We'll call the police."

"What's going on?" Bex grabbed onto Sam's forearm.

"That's the woman who's been tailing us," Sam said. "Who I told you Fergus filmed."

Bex made a noise that prompted Sam to put an arm around her. "Oh, she's getting out of her car. I don't feel great about this." Bex leaned over and grabbed Vic's hand and made her stand behind them, ever the big sister.

"Please, don't get excited!" The woman slowly eased from the driver's seat, keeping her hands palms out. "My name's Ashleigh. Ashleigh Chambers."

"We don't know an Ashleigh Chambers," Fergus said. "But you seem to know us, so we're going to need more than that before I reconsider calling nine-one-one."

The woman pushed her car door shut with her bottom. She was curvy, older than Sam and Bex, though she probably regularly passed for younger. Her French bob was inky black, and so was her sharp winged liner and lash extensions.

"Do you know her?" Bex asked in a low voice.

"No." Sam watched as the woman pulled a wallet out of her cropped blazer, the pocket too tiny for a weapon.

"My ID is in here." She handed the shiny red bifold wallet to Fergus, who opened it. He looked back and forth between the wallet and the woman.

Then he turned around and held up the wallet, showing Sam, Bex, and Vic that it contained an ID.

"Looks like Ms. Chambers is a private investigator."

The Other Hollywood Detective

Sam stood with her her hackles up in a private detective's office housed in a Van Nuys strip mall. The not-white-not-yellow walls were covered with wood planks bearing inspirational phrases like *don't let yesterday take up too much of today*. Everything else was a stack. Stack of folders. Stack of papers. Stack of binders. Stack of filing cabinets.

"You have a lot of art." Vic picked a chair and sat down. Bex was already seated, her hands folded in her lap with prim reserve. Ashleigh had gotten them here by telling them she could help "the other Hollywood detectives" with their case. They didn't want to be in this office, but they hadn't been able to dismiss the possibility that the PI knew something potentially useful to their search.

Ashleigh grinned as she dropped into the chair behind her enormous L-shaped desk. "Thank you!" she told Vic. "I do those myself at this place I am *addicted* to called Board and Brighten on Ventura. When I sit and paint, everything just floats away."

Sam watched Bex subtly master her expression. It was impressive, considering how long the day had been. Fergus had volunteered to grab everyone tacos at a nearby taqueria. He'd also exaggeratedly turned up his volume to the loudest setting possible and suggested, out loud, that Bex and Sam predial emergency services on their own phones. All while looking Ashleigh in the eyes.

Sam wasn't worried about their physical safety. The strip mall was busy, with plenty of people visible through the office's plate-glass front windows. Ashleigh had shown them her credentials. More to the point, they'd learned on the drive over here that Vic knew Ashleigh, or at least knew *of* her as "that PI in Van Nuys everybody hires when they need to prove they're getting cheated on." By "everybody," Vic meant celebrities, Hollywood VIPs, network executives and their young wives and angry daughters, and nepo babies.

This information was enough to convince Sam that Ashleigh was legit. It did not reassure her about Ashleigh's *character*, however. "Since it's so late," she said, "could we get right to it and talk about why you've been tailing us?"

Ashleigh's expression went from welcoming to professionally blank in the blink of an eye. "The short answer is no. We can't."

"We're going to have to." Sam marshaled the remaining crumbs of her self-control. "Unless you're interested in talking to the police. What you've been doing all day is a crime."

Ashleigh held up a finger, her shiny, gold-on-burgundy acrylics catching the light. "You are welcome to initiate a cease-and-desist with me and my legal associates, which I will share with my client."

"And who is that?" Sam dropped into the last available chair. It looked like it had seen some things. She crossed her arms, trying to affect the full power of her celebrity. It was difficult. She felt rumpled, gritty with sand, slightly windburned, and so hungry that her eyes were crossing.

This time, Ashleigh's smile was a sharky one. "No."

It was a complete sentence.

Sam regrouped. If what Vic had said about Ashleigh's reputation was true—mainly that Ashleigh always delivered for her clients because she knew everyone and everything—then Sam could reasonably assume the PI was aware of their interest in Ramona.

Moreover, since Ashleigh had said she had a client, they could assume Ashleigh's client *also* knew they had a connection to Ramona and her disappearance.

Sam did not like that.

She liked even less that Ashleigh, an investigator in the know about Ramona, seemed willing to make decisions that didn't prioritize Ramona's well-being. As far as Sam was concerned, it meant that this PI worked for the *other side*.

Bex straightened and scooted forward in her seat. The shift in position allowed her to plant her feet on the floor. "I'm stuck on figuring out a puzzle. Why would a PI who has a reputation for being the best of the best at surveillance make herself so obviously known to us?" She pointed her chin at Ashleigh. "Sam has spotted you repeatedly since this morning. I have to ask myself, *Did Ashleigh Chambers, perhaps, want to be seen?*"

Bex somewhat lost control of her volume with this final question, such that Vic had to use her index fingers to protect her ears. Sam leaned back and crossed her legs, letting Bex's angry shout ring into the corners of the tatty office while she worked through the implications of Bex's astute observation.

Ashleigh had not been subtle. Not at all.

"You wanted us to know you were there," Sam guessed. "You *wanted* to get us alone here, after you'd gathered as much information as you could by dogging our heels all day. But that's over now." She sounded satisfyingly like FBI Agent Henri Shannon. Agent Shannon remained Sam's most useful character to summon in everyday life.

Ashleigh's expression remained bemused. "Is it? I would say we're at a stalemate."

Maybe they were. She and Bex needed to figure out who had hired Ashleigh to follow them. Who else knew Ramona was missing and would hire Ashleigh?

Sam was hit with the visceral memory of Chad leaning into

her driver's side window. His false nonchalance. All the time between takes on *Theomina* that he'd spent chasing down who said what to whom about whatever he was worked up about that day. His much-too-frequent threats to call his "team."

His part on *The Howling* had wrapped on Friday, before Ramona disappeared. Sam couldn't be sure if Chad found out that Ramona was MIA on Monday morning, when he was filming reshoots for *Theomina* with Sam. But if Chad had hired Ashleigh to follow Sam, he certainly knew *now* what Sam and Bex were up to.

"I don't have any illusions that playing a detective means I am one," Sam said. "But I'm pretty sure I've worked out who your client is."

Ashleigh tipped her head but said nothing.

"It's Chad Bevington." Sam narrowed her eyes at Ashleigh. "You're well-known, which means you're busy, which means the only way you're working this case today is if someone important gave it to you yesterday. It would have to be a person with connections, and likely somebody who's worked with you before. Chad's suspicious, anxious, and controlling as a baseline, plus litigious as fuck. I've got no problem believing he's deranged enough to have you in his back pocket. I think he asked you to follow me."

"Why would he do that?" The softness in Ashleigh's question made Sam hear the anger in her own tone.

"You tell me."

Ashleigh folded her hands on her desk and gazed at the three of them for a long moment. "You're looking for Ramona Watts."

Bex opened her mouth to say something—to deny Ashleigh's statement, confirm it, or change the subject, Sam wasn't sure—but Sam beat her to it. "Tell us what Chad wants."

Ashleigh responded with another mild smile, this one aimed in Bex's direction. "You shouldn't be surprised. You've done nothing to conceal your purpose. I figured out Macie had gone to you and Sam for help when I saw them show up at Sam's house. After drawing a little map of your Hollywood tour today, I also figured out they must have come to you for help to find Ramona."

"Shit," Vic said. "The sedan Macie worried was following them last night? That was *Ashleigh*."

Bex sat up straight so fast, her hair tumbled from its haphazard bun. "You were at my house last night?"

Sam had gone cold. Ashleigh wasn't confirming or denying Chad's involvement. If Sam's hunch proved correct, Chad must have hired Ashleigh within the hour after talking to Sam at the studio lot.

Why? Was he only trying to make sure Sam didn't spill about his guest spot on *The Howling*, like he'd said? Or was there something else he was trying to control—possibly something involving Ramona?

"I was asked to surveil Sam, so I did," Ashleigh said. "I surveilled her to Bex's doorstep, where I noted Macie Finn's arrival. Macie's connection to Ramona Watts is well-known to me. Macie has no known connection to you, Sam, or to you, Bex, and so it was reasonable to suppose that they went to the two of you for help with something. I, like everyone else, followed the *Craven's Daughter* reunion and your debut as sleuths. I got all the confirmation I needed when you drove to Ramona's home address and spoke with Colin Worth. And yes, Bexley, I did, in fact, make certain Sam clocked me at Urth. I often do that when the person I'm tailing may need to be put on a leash."

"Oh, fuck you," Sam said. This woman made her want to grind her teeth. "We get it. You've found out a lot today about what we're doing for Macie, and you've made a big effort to tell us about it instead of simply telling Chad. Your client. In fact, you *revealed* yourself to your client's target. What are you loyal to? Chad's money or our mission?"

Ashleigh fluffed her hair. "I'm always loyal to my client first. No one in this town forgets that—it's why they hire me. But sometimes, in the course of an investigation, I'm willing to market my services to someone I think may have a much more interesting case, especially if I know something they don't. Something they might pay for."

The woman was a double agent for sale to the highest bidder. Even if they paid her for what she knew, she would sell anything she learned from them to someone else. They might get ahead temporarily, but sooner or later this kind of shady business would drag them down. It made Sam feel dirty just thinking about it.

"We're done here." She stood up and held her hand out to Bex. "Ready?"

Bex reached for her bag. Vic's shoulders were slumped. Sam didn't look at Ashleigh. She was too angry. They still had no idea where Ramona was. Bex took Sam's hand, and they walked out the door to stand on the sidewalk beneath a flickering safety light.

"I'm sorry if I didn't handle that right," Sam said with a sigh. "I do want confirmation that Chad hired her. I want to know if she's learned anything we haven't and what Chad will do with this information about Ramona. But I've met enough people like Ashleigh Chambers in this town to know she won't tell us anything except what's sufficient to get what *she* wants. It's not worth it."

"I know." Bex squeezed Sam's hand. "You did just fine." Her phone rang inside of her bag. She reflexively reached for it, looked at the screen, and silenced it.

An impulse rose up in Sam that she knew she ought to ignore.

She would have if she had eaten more. Slept more. If she weren't hyperaware of her sweat-damp underarms and the greasy residue on her skin of a day spent in and out of the sun. But she had no resources left to tamp down her bad impulses. "Whose calls have you been ignoring?" she asked. "You never ignore calls. Ever. You once closed a deal on a supersecret project with Pixar while you were in a checkout line paying for a literal case of organic tampons."

Bex held her phone to her chest. "People are always trying to get ahold of me. I'm not ignoring anything."

"She's lying." Vic's voice was sullen. "Look how her lower lip got tight when she said that."

"Vic!" Bex barked.

"Sorry. I forgot how annoying it is for you to spend this much time with me." Her neck was getting red.

"I can't do this," Bex said. "Not here. Not now."

Vic threw her hands up in the air. "Whatever."

"Whatever?" Bex asked. "Neither of you knows what you're talking about! I'm simply doing exactly what I want, what needs to be done, for *Ramona*, and I don't want to be bothered by show business! What's given either of you the impression that I am anywhere I don't want to be?"

"Maybe your phone," Sam shot back, viciously suppressing an intrusive thought about Telluride and the zero amount Bex knew about it.

Bex waved her phone in the air. "You want to know what's going on with my phone? I'll tell you. *Nothing*, because I'm being offered Sally in *Follies* at the Evermore in New York, and I don't want it, because I want to be with you!" Bex dropped her phone. It landed on the sidewalk like a digital brick.

For a moment, Sam couldn't take it in. She was simply elated for Bex. Sally in *Follies* was the role of a lifetime. It was a part Bex would slay in, one she'd dreamed of playing one far-off someday at the pinnacle of her career.

But then the rest of what Bex had said began to sink in, and Sam's delight drained away. She'd said she didn't want the role. Because of Sam.

Because of what she thought Sam wanted.

The trouble with being at this particular crossroads in her life, Sam suddenly understood, was that she wasn't here *alone*. She'd been behaving as if the decisions in front of her involved only her and the people who worked for her, but that wasn't true. Not anymore. If she played her cards right, it would never be true again.

"So yeah, what*ever*." Bex's voice was rough with tears, though she wasn't crying. "I'm not going to go live in New York for three months, maybe longer. Although I'm not sure why I'm hesitating, since you're going to take off anytime now. Maybe I should've picked up the call."

Sam's stomach sank. "What do you mean?"

"I mean that fat blue envelope from your agency that you've got stuffed in your purse. I know what those are. I've watched you open them. It's an itinerary, the kind they give you right before you get on a plane and go far, far away. I guess we're even."

"Bex. Don't," Vic whispered.

Sam swallowed over an enormous lump of regret to say, bitterly, "I don't even know if I'm going."

"Oh, okay. Sorry I presumed, based on all the information I don't have."

It was right on the edge of her teeth to fire back. She knew how. She had four brothers.

But then Sam remembered what had happened the last time she'd reacted to what Bex said when she was surprised and upset. At the end of *Craven's Daughter*, Bex hadn't responded to Sam's declaration of love with instant commitment. Sam's response was to walk away from Bex for more than five years and to miss her every single day.

This might be a good time for Sam to learn the fucking lesson.

"That's not true," she said. "I do know. I feel like I know."

She took in a breath, but when she tried to find words for the next thing she wanted to say, everything was blank inside of her mind.

Bex's jaw clenched. "Where are you going, Samantha?"

"Colorado. To read with Bradley Wilhite and join talks for a Theomina series. To work out how to fit it in around the Marvel shoot schedule and the time-slip sci-fi thing in Australia. But I didn't know about *Follies*, Bex. Why didn't you tell me? Why—"

"Ladies." Ashleigh had just flung open the office door behind them. "Please come back in. Give me the opportunity to plead my case. I'm not quite the bottom-feeder you think I am."

Sam and Bex just looked at each other. Sam knew that Bex's expression of despair-filled fatigue likely mirrored her own. She wished she'd held it together. "The elevator version," she grumbled. "And we're not coming back inside."

Ashleigh leaned her shoulder against the doorframe. "Ramona Watts is gone. You're limited as far as what kind of effective move you can make next, but I'm not. I have sources in places you can't imagine. Hire me."

"*Hire* you?" Sam felt like she was floating somewhere above her body. "Why would I hire someone who's in Chad's pocket?"

"Allegedly." Ashleigh held up her finger. "I could be convinced to help your cause and drop my other client. Including a clause that anything I learn related to Ramona Watts stays with the two of you alone."

"You could be *convinced*? With what argument?" Bex's tone was beyond incredulity.

"Money," Vic said. "She means money again."

Ashleigh laughed. "Yes. But it might surprise you that I want something *more* than money. I'm proposing we work together. Nothing formal—none of us want a paper trail—but I think if you two are going to keep taking cases, you need someone with experience in the seedier side of this business. We can write a little bit of history together. The kind that's whispered about until we're ancient and telling our stories to a famous biographer. I like *The Hollywood Detectives* for a title, but I'm open."

"I literally have no words." Bex closed her eyes.

Then, she shuffled sideways and leaned her head against Sam's shoulder.

When Bex opened her eyes, she was looking up at Sam. Only at Sam. "I am good at making plans," she said. "And I am equally good at making plans with someone else, if that someone decided—if they *knew*—it was important to . . . collaborate."

Sam had to clear her throat before she could speak. "You do always make the best plans." Her voice was barely audible.

"You know," Ashleigh interrupted again, "if Ramona *is* in danger, it's been four days. Rescue is beginning to look unlikely. You're heading into much darker territory. I could help. Whatever you think of me, surely that puts us on the same side."

Sam slid her arm around Bex, looking into her serious brown eyes. If there were sides, she was on Bex's. Exclusively. She wanted to make sure Bex knew that as soon as possible.

But first they needed to wrap up this conversation with the *other* Hollywood detective. If Ashleigh wanted to work with them, as preposterous as the idea sounded, it meant they had a little bit of leverage. And that meant Sam might be able to get something out of Ashleigh after all.

Sam's distaste for Hollywood games hadn't prevented her from learning to play them.

"How do we know you can actually help?" she asked Ashleigh. "The fact that you're notorious doesn't mean you're good at what you do."

The PI's eyes brightened, and a wordless acknowledgment passed between them. Ashleigh understood that Sam wanted proof she could be useful. A boon in the form of information.

"The Star Spy piece on Ramona was planted," Ashleigh said. "I don't know by whom, but a source told me that it was called in. That's not necessarily interesting. What's interesting to me is that Ramona Watts signing autographs for fans on a pretty day in May is *not* interesting. It's the kind of celebrity sighting Star Spy would rightfully ignore as boring. No one's canoodling. No one's fighting. No one's making a brand-new relationship Hollywood official." Ashleigh waggled her eyebrows.

"Okay?" Bex huffed out a sigh. "So what's interesting to you about Star Spy running a piece that's not interesting?"

"The man who called it in paid not a small amount of money to make sure that blind item ran."

Sam's stomach yo-yoed in shock. They had guessed the Star Spy item was fake, but if someone from outside the newsroom had paid for it to be released, then that person needed people to believe Ramona was where Star Spy said she was.

Sam was thinking about her next move when they were caught in a flood of headlights. Fergus climbed out of his truck carrying two huge bags. "That took forever, but good news! I come bearing tacos and soda." He surveyed the women on the sidewalk. "For now, I will chalk this very complex vibe up to hunger."

Sam wished Ashleigh had led with the tip she just gave them. Hearing it so late in the game just made Sam leerier of the PI. And what Ashleigh had said about the "darker territory" they were heading into, with Ramona gone four days, was high on Sam's list of worries.

She didn't want to be too late.

"For now, you've told us enough," Sam said to Ashleigh. "If we have questions that we think you can answer, we'll call you. If you're willing to *directly* tell us information that helps us find a woman safe, call us. In the meantime, you might consider thinking about what kind of mark you actually want to make in Hollywood."

Ashleigh nodded, her expression serious for once, and she disappeared into her office, leaving them on the sidewalk in the flickering light.

Whether the PI's information proved useful or not, this was real. Ramona was gone. Chad was involved somehow, if only to serve himself. Someone was using fake blind items and maybe even strange social media posts to try to keep anyone from looking closer.

And time was running out to find Ramona alive.

Night Swimming

Under different circumstances, being in Bexley Simon's pool under a dome of black night sky would have been everything perfect.

It had been a long and quiet drive to the parking garage in Beverly Hills, followed by an even quieter drive in the passenger seat of Bex's SUV, where Sam had ended up when Bex asked her to come back to her house so they could talk.

When they got there, Bex had wanted to check in with Vic first, and she'd left Sam alone. Sam had gone out to the patio. Then, before she could think it through, she'd stripped to her bra and panties and slid into the still water. After the day they'd had, the relief of the water was so good that Sam lost track of time, her mind synching with the hum of the pool skimmers and slowly, blissfully, emptying.

That was why it surprised her when she heard the water break near her, and she opened her eyes to watch Bex slide into the pool in a soft-looking bandeau bra and her tiny shorts. She tipped her head back into the water. The huge, fluffy mass of her hair dissolved like candy floss in a cocktail. When she straightened, it streamed down her back in dark, shiny ribbons.

"Your hair," Sam said, thinking of the trouble Bex usually took to protect it. "Didn't you just wash it?"

"I did." Bex sighed. "But I'm going to have to start over. No amount of product could rescue what happened to it today."

This was Sam's opening to talk about the day they'd had. It was hard to remember that sometime at the beginning of it, she'd kissed Bex. Especially because, here at its end, they'd had their first real fight as a couple at a strip mall in Van Nuys. No surprise that it was about the circumstances that had been so difficult over the last six months. And the likelihood those circumstances would continue.

Sam swirled her hand over the surface of the water. "Isn't it interesting how everyone keeps assuming we're detectives now? Even when we were in the middle of finding out how Jen died, I didn't think of myself as a detective. Just someone who wanted to know what happened to a friend."

"I was trying to figure out how to keep me and my sisters from falling apart." Bex sounded thoughtful. "You were back in my life. It was messy. Isn't a detective supposed to be someone who is in control? Obsessed only with the case? Or someone more mercenary, like Ashleigh?"

"Maybe you're the kind of detective who solves people's messy problems from a position of empathy with messy problems."

"Maybe *we* are." Bex smiled.

Sam wasn't quite ready to talk about *we*. She needed to ease in, like she'd eased into the water. "You had a hard time finding your feet with Vic and Frankie once they finished high school."

"Yeah, but everyone who parents does, I think. Family's hard. Adult family's hard, too, just in a different way. The actual problem was that I made the problem about *me*." Bex circled her face with her finger. "One of two things you absolutely cannot do when you are a parent. The other thing you can't do is believe you're uniquely cursed. Thinking that means you try to hide your problems and only show the world the things about your family that are the same as everyone else's. It's stifling."

Sam couldn't remember a time when she hadn't been acutely aware that her family *wasn't* the same as everyone else's. She'd learned to make a show of it, as if she were the star of a sitcom about a little girl from Oakland. Instead of having a mom, she had a dad and *four* older brothers! Men everywhere! No wonder she turned out queer! Pause for the laugh track.

But Sam had felt stifled, too. Hidden.

Until the first season shooting *Craven's Daughter*, when Bex had brought her sisters to the set. That was when Sam had learned family didn't have to feel that way.

"What did you and Vic talk about before you came out to the pool?" she asked.

"She's hurt. I don't blame her. I told her I was sorry I had taken out my feelings on her, making her feel like she was annoying and messing up what I wanted to do with my time. She may or may not have forgiven me, but we did hug. It was a good hug."

Sam centered her lower back over a jet, hoping it would work out the hard knot of muscle there. It was easier to talk in the murky shadows and lavender light from the pool. The water muted their voices, and the air was just cool enough to be a perfect contrast to the heated water.

"What feelings were you taking out on her?" She was jumping in feet-first now. No more easing.

Bex pulled the wet hank of her hair over her shoulder. "I felt like my plans had been upended."

"You hate that."

"I very, very much do, especially since my plans involved you dressed as you are right now, except with even less clothes." Bex's smile was a little bit sad. "I didn't plan on Macie showing up on my doorstep. Or feeling out of touch with Frankie because I didn't know about Haris. Or hurting Vic's feelings. Or having a constant low-level panic attack about this offer to go to New York."

"I didn't have 'detective' on my bingo card for this week either. I don't have 'detective' on any card, actually."

Bex tipped her head back, looking at the sky. "What do you have in your cards, Sam? Seems like you've been holding them pretty close to the chest."

Sam liked the sharp shape of Bexley's chin pointing at the stars. "I have. I'm sorry I kept my plans to myself. I genuinely *don't* want to put on cowboy boots and tromp around a meadow admiring Bradley Wilhite's beef cattle."

"That's real?"

"But then I think about how my agent had a baby last year and wants to buy a house, and all the other people in my circle who are looking out to make sure my bottom line stays healthy so their cut is enough to live on. It feels complicated."

Bex lowered her gaze. She reached out her hand and let it settle over Sam's hipbone, where the cool press of her fingers sent a sweet throb through Sam's middle. "You're empathetic. I love that about you. But you and I both know *you're* the one who has to live with the decisions you make, not your team or your staff."

"I do know that." She stroked her fingertips over Bex's wrist. "The thing I liked about Theomina is that she's all values and violence. If they're going to throw her away on Wilhite, I guess I'd just as soon not be a part of it."

"And you despise him."

"There's that." Sam cupped Bex's elbow in her palm. "*Follies*, though. I thought we had enough history together that you would come straight to me and tell me about this amazing thing happening to you, and we would open a bottle of champagne. Not fight in front of a morally gray private investigator's office."

"I had a weak moment," Bex said. "There's too many divorce ghosts in that office." The ropes of her hair were plastered across her shoulders. She closed the rest of the space between them, laying her wet cheek against Sam's neck, and pressed a kiss there.

"I'm sure of you, Sam. Not knowing how we'll do this next part in our relationship doesn't keep me from trusting you or from wanting to see what you're going to do next. I've already preordered all the Theomina action figures from the movie. I can't wait for the premiere. I told Vic she can dress me. She promised corsetry." Bex rose to her tiptoes and kissed the corner of Sam's mouth.

Sam reached out to lift a long, dripping lock of Bex's hair, running her finger down it and then resting it against Bex's bare collarbone. She moved closer. Hearing Bex pull in a breath made Sam warm in new places. She dipped her head down to taste the pool water off Bex's collarbones, then kissed her cool skin, taking a moment completely separate from the twist in her middle that reminded her nothing was settled about what came next for either one of them.

Nothing except that there would be a both of them.

For now, it felt like enough.

"Bex!" Vic yelled, her voice coming through the French doors that led into Bex's room. "I'm having another emergency! I got into your shower, but I forgot to bring a towel. I require rescue!"

Bex shook her head. "How did she survive when I was away?"

"She did fine," Sam said. "She's just getting all the love she wants now that you're here."

Bex swam to the edge of the pool. She put her hands behind her on the deck and levered herself out of the water with a single effortless push that reminded Sam she was a dancer, with a dancer's control of her movements. Sam swallowed at the sight of the small, wet clothes clinging to her body.

"I will give her the towel," Bex said wearily. "I need to call Frankie. I need to wash my hair again. And sleep. You're—"

"I'm going to head out." Sam took note of the angry dimple sinking into Bex's cheek. "Don't look like that. I'll call in the morning. We'll figure it out."

Her voice was the one she often used in tough situations. Laid-back, go-with-the-flow Sam.

It made her chest ache to hear how it sounded.

She walked to the edge of the pool, close enough to see the furrow in Bex's forehead. Bex looked like she might be about to say something else, but then Vic shouted her name again. She stood up with a sigh and started walking toward the French doors.

Sam couldn't leave it like that. "I do want to stay the night," she blurted. "If that's what you were going to ask. But I know you still have things to do and think about here. You weren't just away from me all this time. You were away from your sisters. Your life. But here's the thing, Bex. No matter what, I'll be here. I'm not going anywhere. Whatever else gets upended in your life or mind, I'm your constant."

Bex walked back over and bent down, and Sam lifted up from the water to meet her kiss. "I'm your constant," she said again. "You can plan on it."

"I will."

Sam watched her disappearing into the house, already talking to Vic.

It was time for her to go home.

When Sam got there, she was surprised to find it so quiet. Fergus usually kept late hours. She guessed they'd worn him out today.

She husked off her clothes at the threshold of her bathroom and took a shower in the dark. Her limbs were leaden. As she soaped, she found new hurt places on her body. Her skin throbbed along her bra line where the costume she'd worn for the reshoot pressed uncomfortably. The tender crease at the back of her knees felt pebbled against her fingertips. Contact dermatitis. Sam wasn't sure what she'd touched, worn, or rubbed against that her skin hadn't liked. It stung at the slightest touch of her fingers.

She padded on damp feet, navigating from her bathroom to

her bedroom in the pitch-dark. Her body knew how many steps it was from the sink to the closet hook where she kept the T-shirt she liked to sleep in. She shrugged into it and collapsed into bed.

She'd put a downpayment on this sleek house, with its sharp corners, glass, and views, after Bex had used her first real money from *Craven's Daughter* to buy her home ten minutes away via a hiking trail. Sam could admit she bought her house as a gateway to Bex's. When she wasn't on set, she'd passed most of her time with the Simons, eating, playing with the girls, and mostly, spending every minute she could with Bex.

The years they were estranged after *Craven's Daughter* had led, in large part, to Sam's large career. She hadn't wanted to be here if she couldn't pull on her tennis shoes and ball cap and walk through the chaparral, sage scrub, and oaks to spend a few hours flopped on Bex's giant sectional, reading scripts or listening to Bex sing in her practice room. She'd signed on to every project that took her away or required long days on tough sets. Her rising fame made a different kind of cocoon for her to rest inside of.

She thought about Ramona's bungalow in West Hollywood. It was a home only for herself and the people she loved. It reflected the life she'd made.

Had Sam made a cold, expensive life that she didn't want to live in?

A lot of people looked at her every day, just as she'd hoped they would when she was a little girl, from a chaotic family, who only wanted to be seen. But it didn't feel the way she'd imagined it would. Sam didn't know any of the people looking at her. What they saw was a mirage made of flashbulbs and sequins.

She arranged her pillows under her head, afraid that her thoughts and the events of the day, her worry for Ramona, would keep her awake. But she fell into a black sleep almost instantly.

When she woke, the room was gray, the rain a gentle sound between rumbles of thunder.

Sam was standing in front of her glass-front refrigerator, still in her pajama T-shirt and some vintage cotton bloomers she'd found on the floor of her bedroom, when Fergus came in. He appeared fresh as a daisy in what looked like the black-tie version of zip-off hiking pants and a blue T-shirt that still had the fold lines in it.

He reached around her to open the fridge and began pulling out a stack of items. "Sit down. I'll make you Caesar's eggs."

"For real?"

"I stopped for groceries last night. I don't know if you noticed, but I ate all your food. I still remember how to make them."

Every Saturday morning, their dad had made what he called "Caesar's eggs" in a huge skillet that was always on the stove and fed them to whichever of his children were at home. It was the only all-hands family tradition they really had. Sam watched Fergus break eggs into a pan, adding green olives and lots of shaved Parmesan. After he put the plates down on the table and sat down, he rubbed his hands together.

"What's on deck for today?"

Sam shoveled in a bite of almost-too-salty, delicious eggs. They hit her homesick button hard. "Your deck doesn't involve meeting with suits in Malibu?"

He looked right at her. "Sam, this is the most real, meaningful time I've spent with you for years. Yesterday, and *just* yesterday, is the L.A. trip I've wanted for a long time, but my little sister's hard to pin down."

Her pulse picked up. "Oh."

"Oh." He pushed her shoulder, gentle but firm. "I'm not so boneheaded that I don't already have a location in mind to rent. I have a guy in Malibu doing the legal heavy lifting. But you really think I came out here to eat your food, wander around Malibu Beach, and then ask you for money."

"I wouldn't put it like that."

He took a bite of his eggs, the tight movements of his body

signaling the change she'd caused in his emotional weather. Fergus hadn't been an angry kid, but he was intense, and it had always seemed like he needed big views, big water, big sky to take up his feelings.

If someone had asked her, Sam would've said Fergus wasn't intense like that anymore. She'd been watching him yesterday, though, and the attention he had paid to the situation—to their feelings and what he needed to do—was just as tightly focused.

The last time he'd visited her was nearly a year ago, before the *Craven's Daughter* reunion. That visit was when her brother had come out to her as ace. Understanding this identity had given him tremendous peace and a lot of room to contemplate what relationships he wanted to give his heart to, which was a couple of lifelong close friends and his family. Her.

Her cheeks heated as she admitted to herself that she hadn't taken him seriously. She'd believed he said it on a whim, and he'd forget all about her once he left L.A. They hadn't spoken about it again. She'd more or less forgotten.

And now Fergus was making her Caesar's eggs and driving her and her girlfriend and her girlfriend's kid sister around in an expensive electric truck that Sam had not purchased for him. She couldn't remember the last time he'd said more to her about his business than that it was doing "well." He was understating.

Because Sam had a habit of underestimating him.

"You're really moving here to be near me," she said.

"I told you I wanted to."

"I know. I'm sorry."

He grimaced. "Right. Well, don't be too hard on yourself," he said. "Caesar's an okayish dad, but I don't think it ever occurred to him to maybe give his five kids with five different moms a little goddamn guidance on how to be a functional family. Every one of us just spun off in a different direction."

"You think?"

"I know. Take Primus, now on marriage number three. I

wish him well, even though he's an asshole. Then we've got Magnus, and he and Katie seem solid, so I guess monogamy is working for him? But if he gets any farther off the grid, I'm going to have to start sending him letters by Pony Express, and that worries me. Rasmus and Amber already have seven kids, and now they're talking about foster-to-adopt like one of those families that ends up on a reality show."

Sam covered her mouth with her hand, shaking her head. "It's possible that some of my fears around getting what I want in a relationship are about avoiding even the slimmest possibility of getting what I *don't* want, given Dad's example."

"Oh, so walking down the aisle so many times you wear a hole in the carpet's not good enough for you?" Fergus reached over and pulled her hair. "You know what Dad says. 'Life's an adventure.' "

"He's a periodontist in Oakland."

"But you couldn't ever claim he was a man who doubted." Fergus lifted his eyebrows.

"Might have been good if he'd been plagued with a *few* doubts. Like if his youngest, motherless child might need to hear a little more than 'Way to go, Tiger' at periodic intervals."

"Yeah. And he didn't even come up with an amazing name for you. He could've called you 'Deltron' like Magnus wanted, but no, you were a girl, so it had to be 'Samantha.' Probably wasn't easy being queer on top of all that."

Sam shrugged, and Fergus laid his hand on her shoulder, serious again. "You deserve to have people who are for you, Sammy," he said. "You deserve the life you want. That's why I want to be down here and be a part of it."

"Fuck." Sam pressed her fingers to her eyes. "Don't make me cry."

"You want a noogie instead?" He wrapped his arm around her neck and pulled down.

"Jesus! No. Let me have a few minutes to pretend you're my emotionally intelligent sibling."

They separated, smiling at each other. It was good. Sam felt good. She took a drink of water. Fergus picked up the pan and shoveled the last of the eggs onto his plate.

"It's been surprisingly nice having you here," she said. "You were a big help yesterday."

"Yeah, about that," he said. "I gave Vic my number, and she's already sent me about twenty texts this morning." His eyes were warm when they met hers. "Would it be all right if I tagged along again today?"

"I would love that."

"Good, because Vic's inviting us to meet up at Bex's in twenty minutes. She said to feed you so you wouldn't get low-blood-sugar crabby again—her words—and to bring the truck in case we need to 'crowd together or haul something big.'"

"Just let me get changed quick."

Sam fortified herself with a very small black dress with thigh-high leather boots she'd been saving to be particularly shocking. In deference to the weather, she threw on an oversized wool cardigan in the colors of the lesbian pride flag. Eggs in her belly and double-take fashion meant that when she and Fergus arrived at Bex's house, Sam felt fully human again.

"Hi." Bex sat at her dining room table with perfect, obedient red ringlets. There was a notebook and an array of highlighter pens, colored tabs, and glitter Post-its surrounding her spot at the table. She had also fortified herself.

"Hi." Sam hovered in the doorway, soaking in the sight of her. "Are you ready for today?"

"I have a plan," Bex said with a brisk nod. "It came to me while I was diffusing my hair, and I refined it while my face steamed. I want you to know that I have already noticed your boots. I know what they mean. I will cash that check after we find Ramona."

Sam lifted one eyebrow. Flirting with Bex was something she'd practiced for years. She liked to strike an erotic match across a situation just to see it flame, and Bex was unfailingly receptive to her moves. "I'll hold you to it. What have you got?"

Bex pinched a tab that stuck out of her notebook and flipped to the page she'd bookmarked. Sam moved to sit across from her at the table. Before she could pull out a chair, the door to the patio banged open.

"I hate it when L.A. gets weather in May. No one knows what to do. It's just rain, people! We circled at LAX for a thousand years. I felt like I was the dice in a Yahtzee cup from all the turbulence." Frankie Simon dropped her bag on the floor and raked her hand through her short dark curls, spraying raindrops onto the tile floor.

"Frankie?!" Bex's voice was loud. She moved to stand up, then sat down again. "But you're in the Ozarks!"

"Haris is in the Ozarks." Frankie pulled off her black hoodie, revealing a black tank that matched her black cargo pants and combat boots. Sam hadn't seen Frankie wear anything but tech black since she was a freshman in high school. She was backstage to her core. "I guess he wanted to sleep at night instead of lying awake listening to me talk about Ramona Watts after a full day of driving that I spent talking about Ramona Watts. He put me on a plane in Tulsa and said he'll drive the rest of the way on his own."

Sam couldn't help but note the unaccustomed thread of swoon in Frankie's tone. She glanced over at Bex, who clearly had also noticed.

"Shut up," Frankie said cheerfully. "You'll get nothing else on that topic from me. One hundred percent of me is for finding Ramona."

"*Frankie!*" Vic burst into the room and ran to Frankie, throwing her arms around her, hilariously a foot taller than her big sister. "Never leave me again."

"Franks!" Fergus stepped into the room behind Vic. "Back from the Big Apple!"

Frankie cast her eyes at the ceiling, trying to extricate herself from Vic's tight grasp. When she failed, she dragged her sister, still clinging to her body, over to where Fergus was and gave him a hug with one arm. Vic grabbed tightly to both of them.

"This is everything I wanted," she said.

Sam swallowed over a batch of inconvenient tears.

It was everything she wanted, too.

Cracking the Ice Crew

"Okay, everybody!" Bex said this in her dance rehearsal voice, a five-foot-tall woman who could project as much volume as an air-raid siren. "Come sit at the table and listen to me!"

They'd already packed several hours' worth of catching up into thirty minutes, all of them crowded around in Bex's kitchen with Vic opening and closing the refrigerator door to fortify them with drinks and the fancy fruit Bex liked to buy and forget to eat. Vic had been in on Frankie's plan to fly home early. It was why she'd gone to so much trouble to get Sam and Fergus over to the house in time for her sister's arrival.

Now, they arranged themselves around the table, Sam seizing the chair next to Bex and shoving it sideways until their knees touched. Bex flipped through several notebook pages densely filled with the spikes and whorls of her distinctive handwriting. She stopped on one that said SUSPECT LIST at the top.

She'd underlined the words three times.

It made Sam uneasy. "Suspects" inarguably suggested that someone had harmed Ramona, not just that she was missing.

"I've got too many people on this list," Bex said. "Today is going to have to be about crossing out and narrowing down." She raised a finger. "First, Sloan. We don't know how Ramona got to work on Friday, but we know she was on location and then rode back to the studio parking garage with everyone else. Then she got a ride home from Sloan. If we discount the Star Spy item and the pictures from the Maldives, that makes Sloan's car her last known location. I'd like to talk to him. We should figure that out soon, because if he was the last person to see Ramona, the police will go to him first after Ramona's parents file their missing person report. After that, we'll never get at him."

Sam agreed. "We'll have to ask Macie if they have a number for him."

Frankie leaned across the table to peer closely at Bex's list. "You should keep Ramona on the suspects list. I don't think we can discount the Maldives or Star Spy yet."

"Why?" Bex held her notebook out of Frankie's reach so she wouldn't grab it and add her own notes.

"Because Ramona *could* have posted the Maldives pictures. I know your PI nemesis said that a man planted the Star Spy piece, but she could have had someone do that *for* her. As cover. Haris doesn't think she would. He's never known her to do anything like that, and I know everyone you talk to keeps vouching for her integrity. Plus, he's been watching her location tracking like a hawk, and it hasn't so much as flickered on for even a minute."

"But you don't agree with Haris?" Sam asked.

"Haris is cute, but he's as naive as a dog in a stroller when it comes to the human condition. It's actually shocking when you consider how long he's worked in Hollywood. *I* think Ramona could've used another phone or disabled cellular data. She might not be herself. We should plan for the worst while we hope for the best."

Bex reluctantly made a note on her list.

Outside, thunder rumbled. A streak of lightning lit the sky behind the hills. Sam sent her hundredth hope into the universe that Ramona was okay.

Bex placed the tip of her pen on the page of her notebook. "Second, Archie Blasingame. We haven't dug up any information about Ramona having a partner, lover, or special someone. But we did find out last night that Ramona's been seen several times with Archie on the set of *The Howling*. Macie says Ramona and Archie are old friends. Colin says Ramona was doing something with the documentary recently. So we need to talk to Archie today."

"Another contact that Macie may have," Vic said.

"Yes." Bex moved her pen down. "Third, Chad, with an asterisk that connects him to Juliette. We've been told by Macie that Ramona felt responsible for what happened to Juliette. Sam, did Chad ever mention Juliette to you?"

"Chad only talked about himself. And even if he *had* been interested in talking to me, I was hiding in my trailer as much as I could to avoid him."

Sam had meant for this comment to be lighthearted and diverting, but now her brother was frowning, and Bex's eyes had gotten sad.

When *Theomina* wrapped in Vancouver, Sam had thought she was exhilarated. But she hadn't acted like an *exhilarated* woman. She'd slept ten or more hours a night for days afterward. What she'd really been was exhausted. For weeks on end, she'd had to protect herself and the actors around her, slipping into the kind of codependency that a little sister who wanted everyone to get along was good at. When she received the call for the reshoot, her internal reaction was so panicked that it had felt like getting bad news in the middle of the night.

"About that." Vic dipped an enormous piece of dragon fruit into yogurt she had spooned into a mug. "We have to understand the dynamics better."

"Of what?"

"The Ice Crew." She took a bite of her fruit.

Frankie sighed. When Sam wasn't looking, she'd yoinked Bex's notebook and was scanning rapidly through the pages. "I'm not sure we have the time for one of your little meta-analyses of other people and their friends that you and your crew like to do."

"Ugh! Maybe we should analyze the dynamics of us, huh?" Vic made a circling motion between herself, Frankie, and Bex. "Should we get into why neither of you takes me seriously? Which one of you got an A on your Comparative and Evolutionary Physiology final? Or knows how to do calculus? Or walked Celine's runway for their spring preview? You know, my friends and I aren't *just* about getting smoothies at Erewhon wearing bikinis as tops. We see things. We protect each other and play the game against the system. It's not easy, and it's a delicate balance because of how difficult this town and fame are."

Sam felt guilty. Vic had mostly grown up in Hollywood as the sister of a popular TV actor, and she'd always been good at building alliances to other young people in her social circle—some of them working artists, others behind the scenes, many related to established Hollywood talent. From the outside, they could look a little aimless or irresponsible, but Sam had spoken to enough of Vic's friends to know they were passionate, bright people who'd witnessed what Hollywood did to their parents and grandparents, and wanted to call their own shots.

"Sorry," Frankie said.

"You looked so pretty on the runway." Bex patted Vic's hand.

"How could knowing the dynamics of the Ice Crew help us find Ramona?" Sam asked.

"Not *this* group. Not now. But the dynamics back then, and why—*exactly* why—it all fell apart. On the outside, it looks like they fell apart because of Juliette's death, but that's the kind of thing that could make a group of people tighter, too. My guess is there was something else going on. Something in addition to Juliette's death, or something that ricocheted through the group after her death that was always going to come back to haunt them."

"Yikes," Fergus said.

Vic pointed at him. "Exactly. When I say you need to understand the dynamics better, I mean that understanding the dynamics *could* show you that none of those people should be on your list, or that someone you don't know about yet *should.* Sam, you don't like Chad."

"I do not."

"You can't even stand to be near his aura, but he has the most successful career out of all six of the Ice Crew. Why? We know it's not the outcome of his talent."

Frankie was nodding. "Or there's Sloan. The general impression people have is that he left the crush of Hollywood behind for a more artistic lifestyle," she said. "How come? He was considered a talented actor back then. Did he even want to do *The Howling* episode?"

"What about Christian?" Sam asked.

"He should have been bigger than Chad," Vic said. "He's better looking and had more range. But he didn't successfully navigate his queerness, and Hollywood, and inheriting money when he was in his twenties, and now he's fried and hates them all."

"Except Ramona," Bex piped up.

"Except Ramona," Vic agreed, "who he was close to until she friend-dumped him for his treatment of Colin. And Macie comes across like Switzerland. They've done projects with Chad. I was able to find pictures of them at a few arty events with Sloan as recently as a few years ago. They're besties with Ramona. I've seen pictures of Ramona, Macie, and Christian together. I wonder if Macie has something on all of them, or are they just that easy to get along with, or does everyone have something on Macie?"

"*This* is what you and your friends like to do?" Bex shook her head. "This is unsettling."

Vic dipped her fruit again. "There is nothing in this town more fascinating than interpersonal dynamics. You've been to the awards-show after-parties. How many times has someone whispered something in your ear as another person approaches to give you a five-second rundown of why you shouldn't mention that person's husband?"

"So many times."

"Dynamics." Vic crossed her arms. "Your lists aren't complete until you have them."

"If that's true," Sam said, "then our next action is to go back to Macie. They're the only person we have access to who can fill in what we don't know about dynamics."

"And who can maybe connect us to Archie and Sloan." Bex grabbed her notebook back from Frankie and flipped it closed as she rose to her feet. "Sam, you drive, and I'll call Macie on the way. Vic and Frankie, why don't you and Fergus—"

"I read your notes," Frankie interrupted. "I just completed an internship on Broadway. I was a PA on a highly rated hour-long family drama that included golden retrievers and copious use of wind machines. I can handle home base."

Bex's smile was relieved. "Fantastic. See ya." She started toward the door.

Fergus reached into his pocket for something and held it out to Sam across the table. It was the key fob for his truck. "Drive safe," he said. "Might be better if you're in a car no one associates with you."

Sam gave her brother a quick hug, grabbed her bag, and went to the entryway. She opened the closet near Bex's front door and started rummaging around.

"What are you doing?" Bex asked.

Sam found it. She held up a big golf umbrella she'd once received as swag when she took her dad to the Masters Tournament in Augusta. "Looking for this. To protect your hair."

The marquee above the red door of the Velvet Chair read NEU RAL ILK HOTE 2-25. A few of the black letters were missing from the name of the band, which had broken up in the late nineties.

For decades, celebrities and music lovers rubbed shoulders in the dark interior of this famous club. The Velvet Chair was one of those places that an artist who ordinarily played stadiums would show up at on a Thursday for a surprise set. Its owners were known to look the other way at the debauched antics that played out in its shadows. But Sam had never been here, and not because she didn't love music or the chance to check out a place with so much intense Hollywood history.

She had never been here because the legendary club on West Sunset had closed more than twenty-five years ago.

The windows alongside the double doors were backed in brown paper to keep the curious from looking inside. As she and Bex approached, Sam noticed the graffiti. The entire alcove around the door had been tattooed with decades of statements inked in Sharpie, overlapping and so dense that they read at a glance like a painted design. Close up, she could pick out messages from fans and tourists beside autographs from Kurt Cobain and Kathleen Hanna. It gave Sam goose bumps on top of the goose bumps she had from the unseasonably cold and rainy weather.

"It's something else, huh?" The low rasp of Bex's voice seemed correct in this alcove, in front of this door. Sam had a sacred feeling about it. "I've texted Macie."

Because Macie Finn, they'd learned, was the secret owner of the Velvet Chair. When Bex had called to ask for a meeting, it was Macie's suggestion to meet here. "If you're going to try to understand," Macie had said, "we might as well sit with the ghosts."

The club had shuttered after a tragedy involving an overdose in the mosh pit. Macie quietly bought it and sealed it up like a time capsule. Or a tomb. It was true that the Velvet Chair had been the place where the Ice Crew held forth, and so it would hold significant memories for Macie. But the purchase seemed to Sam to indicate feelings a lot more complex than nostalgia. Macie had never done anything with the property.

Vic was right. There were dynamics at play that needed airing if Sam and Bex were going to find Ramona.

After a few moments, the brown paper behind the glass flanking the door rustled, and the door opened.

Macie wore layers of jersey over leggings and an enormous wool scarf that climbed nearly to their ears. The circles under their eyes were puffy and purple-black. The excess of emotion in their face made Sam worry.

"Come inside." Macie tried to smile and failed. "Sorry I didn't clean up for you."

They walked into the foyer. The black-and-white checkerboard floor was worn in the path to the ticket booth. It was the glassed-in kind, with a small mousehole opening to exchange tickets and money. The multicolored flyers and posters on the walls overlapped in layers upon layers of paper, staples, and tape. There was a cigarette machine in the corner by the beaded curtain that led to the main floor. The machine had a hand-lettered sign above it: DON'T FORCE THE LEVERS YOU CRETINS.

If Sam closed her eyes, she could almost smell sweat mixed with cheap beer, perfume, and clove cigarettes. She hadn't been part of Macie's generation, but her oldest two brothers were on the cusp. Sam could remember being curled up in the back of Caesar's Mercedes wagon in her pajamas one of the times he'd had to go pick up Primus and Magnus from a club like this. She had been fascinated by the people milling around the entrance in their striped tights and baby doll dresses.

"It's incredible," Bex said.

Macie rubbed their hands together. "It's just the same as it was the day they handed me the keys. I gave the last owner all of my savings. Paid him in cash. Anything I talk about in here will probably be pretty raw, but I'm guessing that's how you'd rather hear it."

They stepped between the wooden beads of the curtain. The interior of the Velvet Chair was a huge black-painted space. The stage sat piled with speakers, mic stands, monitors, and stools at one end. There was even an electric guitar on the stage floor, the strings broken and curled around it like something dead.

The round wooden tables and their wood-backed chairs had been shoved around the edges of the main floor. The long bar was covered in stickers, and its row of top shelf was gone. Or it had never had one. There were sleeves of red plastic cups beside beer taps heaped with dust and grime.

"My God." Bex spun around, taking everything in. "It's not a time capsule, it's time *travel*."

"Let me get some chairs." Macie went to the wall and dragged over three chairs that they set up in the middle of the mosh pit, then went back for a fourth chair and a black plastic ashtray. They pulled a pack of Camels and a lighter from their sweater pocket as they sat down. "I stopped at a gas station for these. I'm not going to vape in the Velvet Chair. If you're allergic or object, tell me now."

"Go ahead," Sam said after looking at Bex, who compressed her mouth to indicate permission as she began digging through her purse. She came out with her tin of lubricating lozenges and a device that she turned on after filling it with water from a bottle, also in her purse. Vapors curled out of it. Bex took a breath through the mouthpiece. "Are you sure?" Sam asked.

"I am protecting my voice." Bex looked at Macie. "But one time sitting by you smoking in a huge room won't take it out. My voice has some legs."

Macie lit the cigarette, drawing in smoke that they held in their lungs before letting it out in a long exhalation.

"I'm scared," they said. "I'm beyond scared, really." They lifted a trembling hand to their cheek. "Ramona's parents got here a few hours ago. They're talking to an LAPD detective who's known to be discreet. I'm keeping them up to speed with what the two of you are doing. I don't know if Ramona's being gone is connected to any of the shit from when we were young and stupid, but I'm starting to feel like this is more than any of us have dealt with before."

And they'd dealt with a lot, Sam thought. Including the death of a good friend. "What does being here make you think about?"

Sam watched Macie take another long drag, blow it away, cough, and then set the cigarette down in the ashtray. "We filmed a lot of the documentary here."

"Really?"

"It was such a nineties project. Handheld camera, interviews on sidewalks outside this place and other bars, dark cut-ins of grainy footage of the crew piled on sofas on the set of *The Lights of Marfa* arguing, talking. The boys, me, and Juliette were often drunk or high. There were some talking heads." She pointed. "Shot them against the wall back there in the corner."

"And this documentary was something all of you wanted to do?"

Macie shrugged. "How were any of us deciding what we wanted to do? Everyone around us wanted to make money. We were what was for sale. My agent told me the only career I could ever have was playing the weird sidekick, and I didn't have the 'privilege' to turn down anything."

Oof. Autonomy was hard to come by in the industry, but it would have been much worse for actors so young, who had so easily captured the imagination of America.

"Tell us about Juliette." Bex popped a lozenge and leaned forward, her curls gleaming in the low light of the club.

"She was funny. Hilarious. Nobody ever talks about that. But she had a hard time. She grew up in a fundamentalist church that was essentially a cult, and when she left for Hollywood, her whole family and everyone she'd ever known shunned her, basically. She's seventeen, with the kind of beauty that makes casting agents see God, and she's got this need to be loved that's screaming inside her, insisting she's nobody if she doesn't belong to someone."

"Seventeen," Sam said. "Jesus."

"When we met. This was on the first movie Tom Kessler wrote and directed with us, *Karma Revisited*, before *Lights of Marfa.* Chad had already done a few projects. He was twenty-two. Ramona and I were eighteen. Christian wasn't around yet. Kessler brought him in later. Chad was the big draw."

Macie tilted their head and flipped long, imaginary bangs off their forehead in a rakish manner that was exactly Chad.

"He does have a quality, and the camera loves him. At first, if he wants to, he can make you feel like you're the only person in the world and the best thing that ever happened. But the minute you're ready to take a step out of the love bubble and focus on anything but him, he's done. Chad spits out people like sunflower seed shells."

Macie stopped to pick up the Camel. The rain drummed on the building's roof. "I want to say, it took me years to understand any of this. If it was easy to see, no one would be destroyed by Chad. They'd just walk away. But it's not. He piles up his concern on you. His worry. You get so you're willing to do anything to make him feel better, and *that's* when he starts telling you what to do. By then, you're relieved. He's given you an instruction book. You think if you follow it, everything will work again."

"But it never works again," Sam said.

Macie danced the tip of the cigarette through the air. "The problem is that it works sometimes. Just often enough you keep trying. You keep hanging on until your whole life is anticipating the mercurial needs of Chad Bevington, and you don't know who *you* are anymore."

"And then he's done," Bex broke in.

Chin lifted, Macie mimed spitting out a sunflower seed shell.

"This is what he did to Juliette?" Bex asked.

"It's what he did to everyone. I was first. I wasn't a romantic interest—I don't date men—but I guess I was auditioning to play the part in Chad's life that ended up going to Sloan. It took me a long, long time to rebuild my own brand of cool after Chad was done with me. By then he'd joined forces with Sloan, after *Marfa* wrapped, and he was zeroed in on Juliette. She'd become famous enough for him to pay her the attention she'd been wanting from day one."

"Not to be an armchair psychologist, but Chad's starting to sound like a narcissist," Bex said.

"Could be," Macie said. "I'd never heard of a narcissist back then, and I wasn't focused on what might be wrong with him. I was focused on what he'd told me was wrong with *me*. When I'd put myself back together enough to want to avoid him, I went with 'I don't need this fuckin' drama,' and then I peaced out and snuck into the lesbian bars."

"How did Sloan respond?" Sam asked.

Macie took another drag on their cigarette. The white smoke hung heavy in the air around the cluster of chairs.

"The two of them were about who owed what to who. No matter what, though, Chad made sure that whatever Sloan gave him, it wasn't good enough. Chad sometimes gave Sloan love and attention, and things that he wanted, but other times he wouldn't even look at him, or he'd be cruel. It meant Sloan was constantly trying to figure out what worked. Like a slot machine. Keep feeding it money, keep pulling the lever. You can't stop because there was that one time you hit the jackpot, but the house always wins, right? You know what was the biggest prize Chad held over Sloan's head?"

"Juliette," Sam guessed.

Macie tapped ash into the plastic ashtray. "Chad would joke that when he was done with her, Sloan could have her. Or later, he'd say, 'You've only got her because I gave her to you.' But with the press, he'd play like his breakup with Juliette had been amicable. He and Sloan and Juliette were all cool."

"None of that is okay." Bex's cheeks were pink, her anger at Chad's bad behavior as palpable as heat shimmer coming off the highway.

Macie's smile made their red-rimmed eyes look ghoulish. "I hate to say this, but Juliette . . . I guess the way I'd put it is that she wasn't a completely real person to anyone but Ramona. She hadn't had a chance to figure out who she was. In the cult, they told her what to do. Then everyone here was making decisions for her. Juliette wasn't stupid. She knew Chad didn't make her feel good, and Sloan made her feel like a prize he'd won at the county fair. When she was high, I think she felt free, and she convinced herself *that* feeling was *her*. What did any of us know? We were all acting, or reacting, on instinct, making money for everyone around us, counting love by the number of magazine articles about us or how many dollars we had in our bank accounts. As a queer person closeted by my agent, I assumed I was here for a good time, not a long time. The best I can say about those years is that I survived. Juliette didn't."

"What about Ramona? How did she survive?"

Macie didn't answer right away, and Sam could tell the older actor wouldn't be able to keep talking about this for much longer. They seemed to keep getting smaller as they spoke. They weren't looking at Sam and Bex anymore, but into the club.

Sam wondered what Macie saw, staring into the empty space. Was it the crush of bodies and ear-ringing volume pouring from the speakers, drinks spilling over fingers in cheap plastic cups, the singed hole from a cigarette they found on the sleeve of their blouse when they stood in line for the bathroom? Had it been exciting? When did the drugs come out? Or were there drugs before they even went to the club, another kind of ticket to the show? They were famous, in a dark club with flashing lights, L.A. crushing in around them, maybe crushing them.

How would they have known when it went too far, or how to pull back when it did?

Sitting in this empty relic of a club, Sam thought that Ramona's tidy garden, books, and privacy made sense. Ramona just wanted to live, not crash through one sensation after another.

"She's the best of us," Macie said. "The best actor. The best person. You know she only had one scene in *Marfa*? No one remembers that. She stole the movie. Around then was when Tom started calling her his muse. Not Juliette, the lead. Ramona. He lined her up for three more films."

"The muse thing is creepy," Bex said. "Ramona was, what, twenty years old? Tom Kessler was already a successful writer and director in his thirties." She tapped her lip. "But I guess I get it. I rented every DVD I could get my hands on with Ramona in it when I was a kid, trying to figure out how to emulate what she had. It's a quality that's not just about what she looks like. She's effortlessly talented."

"Not effortless." Macie's green eyes looked almost black in the dim club. "She worked hard. Kessler worked her harder than he should have. Juliette was going through her breakup with Chad, then her thing with Sloan. Ramona was preoccupied with the projects Kessler had her doing. She believes she should've paid better attention. Tried harder. Maybe she could have found a way to convince the police of what really happened."

"What did really happen?" Sam asked, conscious that they'd put this question to Macie once already.

"I don't know, I'm just repeating her words. Ramona implied there was more to it than an impulsive, fucked-up kid who didn't know how to swim getting into a boat in the dark."

Sam inhaled the caramel reek of Macie's secondhand smoke. There was a headache forming right between her eyes. From the dust, from the smell, from this story. She pictured Ramona's pretty four-seasons room. It smelled like the eucalyptus she had in big bunches in an enormous Chinese vase.

Then she remembered the movie poster. The canceled documentary. "You've stayed friends with Ramona. I know she and

Christian had a falling out recently. Was Ramona close to anyone else?"

"She and Sloan saw each other on and off. I wouldn't say they were *close* close, but close enough that he was one of her guesthouse tenants several years back. Occasionally, he joins a dinner party at my place or Ramona's. I did reach out to him on Monday when I started trying to find her. I left him a message. Just, like, 'Get back to me when you have a chance, I have a question about Ramona.' He hasn't called, but he's bad about keeping in touch."

"And Ramona doesn't see Chad."

"Never. Not since Juliette."

"What about Kessler, the director?" Sam could tell, from Macie's posture, they were feeling pushed, but the questions she wanted answers to were coming fast.

"As far as I know, they parted ways after the last project they did. *Apartment 313*."

"Archie has been friends with Ramona ever since he was making the documentary?"

"That's right. They clicked."

"And he would hang out with her on sets?"

"Sometimes. Like I said, *The Howling* has been rough. Ramona loves the project, loves the story, but once the guest stars started coming on and the shoots got more physical for this second season, she's been at the edge of her capabilities. Ramona takes exquisite care of her body with weightlifting, hiking, green juice, all that—but you know, fifty is fifty. If Archie's hanging out with her on set, she needs him."

"We'd like to talk to him."

"I can reach out and see if he might meet with you. I'm not sure he will. Archie's circle is more of a line between him and maybe two people, other than his wife, who he can stand."

"If you could give him your best pitch, that would be great."

"Hold on, let me make the call." Macie stood up and walked a few paces away with their phone.

Bex pushed her chair back, bringing her vapor device with her so it blew into her face. "What are you thinking behind those piercing baby blues, Samantha?"

Sam leaned back in the chair, making it creak. "In the time before Ramona disappeared, it sounds like she had positive relationships with everyone but Chad."

"Chad and Christian."

"Right. She falls out with Christian, who at this point hates everyone for no clear reason. She starts having problems on set. She brings her emotional support buddy to work. Juliette's death anniversary is getting close. And then Chad shows up at her work with Sloan, and Piper says Ramona hates it. Then she's gone."

"Before we even think about approaching Chad or Sloan, we've *got* to talk to Archie and find out why Ramona needed his support. Especially if you're right that Chad hired Ashleigh to tail you. We need to tread carefully there. *Was* Ramona coming apart? Was someone coming after her? Oh! Remember that Macie said they saw Ramona get a phone message that made her upset?"

"Yeah. And as far as Sloan, I get that he's Mr. Unavailable, but if he does care about these people, why hasn't he answered Macie's call? He gave Ramona a ride on Friday! Is it as simple as he knows where Ramona is? But then Sloan should be willing to reassure Macie that Ramona's okay, so that's fucking suspicious." Sam took in a short breath. "You know what? He drove her home, right? He's been to her house. They all have. They all know where she lives because she's lived there for years. She hasn't lived anywhere else. They knew that house. They *know* that house."

"Colin didn't see anybody on the cameras, but Chad was on his motorcycle that night. Easier to dodge the cameras? Lay in wait somewhere he knows in the house? But why? For what?"

"I don't know." Sam rubbed her temples and forehead with

the flat of her hand. "I just know this is ugly, and it keeps getting uglier."

"I'll never doubt Vic again. Figuring out the dynamics was the right way to go. She's saved us precious time by helping us focus on talking to Archie."

"And Sloan."

"Right." Bex stood up and held out her hand for Sam. "Let's make sure Macie tells us how to find those two. Then let's get the hell out of here. This club makes me feel like I'm walking on a grave."

Sam looked around, and this time she didn't imagine loud music or young people dancing.

She didn't imagine anything.

This place should have been let go of a long time ago.

When We See Ramona Watts

"Are you warm enough?" Sam reached for the climate controls in her brother's truck. She and Bex were in Laurel Canyon, on their way to Encino to meet with Archie Blasingame. He had reluctantly agreed to give them ten minutes, if they could make it to the Gymboree before the end of the child's birthday party he was attending with his daughter.

Bex adjusted her seatbelt. "Yes."

Sam turned the wipers up, not because it had started to rain harder, but because if she didn't do something with her hands, her heart was going to explode.

She felt restless thinking about the Macie she'd seen in that dark club, hands cupped around a lit cigarette. She felt like she'd witnessed something she wasn't supposed to. Sam hated it when Hollywood did that.

Some things were meant to remain behind the scenes.

"Maybe some music?"

Sam had never been so glad Bex could pick up on her moods. It precluded her having to actually talk about her feelings. "Yes." She grabbed her phone and handed it to Bex. "Here. Play whatever you want."

"Don't you need the navigation?" They'd decided to avoid the 101, knowing it would be a mess in the rain.

"The car can do it. On the screen." Sam gestured at the backlit control screen in the center of the dashboard.

"What do I push?" Bex had swiped Fergus's console menu open, creating a swirl of rainbow colors. Sam's phone, in Bex's hand, pointed out that they had just missed a turn.

"Goddamnit." Sam slowed and tried to figure out what had happened. "What is it telling me to do?"

"It wants you to take a U-turn at the next intersection."

"U-turns are illegal. I can see the sign from here."

The phone's navigation told them Sam had missed the turn after the U-turn. *Return to the route.* She bit the inside of her cheek. "Why is the map yelling at me?"

"It wants you to take the 101 to go to Encino."

Sam checked her mirrors, then changed lanes. "If I wanted to play bumper cars, I would have made Fergus take us to Pacific Park when we were in Santa Monica yesterday. Turn that off. I'll take Mullholland through the canyon. I need to look at something pretty and play with this truck."

"I'm looking at something pretty." Bex ran her index finger along Sam's kneecap, softly up her thigh, between the top of her boot and the hem of her dress.

Sam felt the psychic grime from the Velvet Chair fall away. "Why, Bexley Simon."

Bex laughed. "Can you believe that a couple of days ago I was calling you from an airport lounge in Denver?"

"Easier to believe than you right here, right now." Sam gave Bex a quick smile and moved her leg closer to where Bex had settled her hand over her thigh. "Can *you* believe we haven't seen each other, shared a car, a meal, a glance, in six months? That's much harder for my body to believe. It feels like it will be even harder for my body to give up."

Bex didn't reply. Understandable. Sam focused on navigating the turns of Mulholland. She caught glimpses of stucco and wooden gates grown over with bougainvillea on one side, the gray mist heavy over the canyon on the other.

"I think I have to do *Follies.*" Bex had put on Tom Waits. It was "Long Way Home," one of her favorite songs when she wanted to feel mellow.

"You do have to do *Follies.*"

"The Evermore is in New York."

"Last I checked."

"The limited run is eight weeks. There's a month of rehearsal before that. And press."

"Yep. You've done a limited run or two."

"They're putting me up in an apartment in Stella Tower. In Hell's Kitchen."

Sam whistled, low. "Nice. You'll be able to share an elevator with Edie Falco."

"You can't walk to the Stella from your front door in ten minutes, Sam. Or from wherever they want to shoot the Theomina thing."

"Exteriors in Vancouver. Everything else at Howell here in L.A. But I haven't committed to the Theomina thing yet. It all depends."

"On?"

"Whatever I decide." Sam raised her eyebrows at Bex. "My career. My life. Us."

Bex held her tongue, though Sam could appreciate the energy coming off her in waves as she restrained herself from pulling them both into a big conversation they weren't quite ready to have.

"I love you," Bex blurted.

Sam laughed. She couldn't help it. "Good *night*, Bexley."

"I know! It's not the time. The valley doesn't even look pretty. . . . But I do love you. I just wanted to get it out of the way, because you said what you said by my pool last night, and this is not some will-they-or-won't-they bullshit here. This is *it* for me." Bex squeezed Sam's thigh a little painfully. "We've avoided it so far, but if I genuinely do have to figure out how to do dirty things on FaceTime without dropping the phone on my face, I will. I'll buy a tripod. I'll hire a crew."

"Whoa, there." Sam's heart was doing something cataclysmic. A supernova of exultation that crowded out her ability to think.

"My point is that I am committed. And *you* shouldn't think that any decisions you make about your career or that I make about mine can mess us up. In twenty years, we're going to be a Hollywood couple they write those mawkish articles about, like 'Hollywood Romances with Staying Power.'"

"Ten years. Ten years equals twenty years in this town."

"Well, I'm here for fifty Ohio years at least."

Sam swallowed over a few tears. Ridiculous. She was *happy* with this woman. She was okay with not exactly knowing what came next. And anyway, she was starting to have an idea. "I love you, too."

"Thank God," Bex said. "I've only wanted to tell you for months, but I didn't want to in a text. I considered and rejected sending you a voice memo. I had designs on at least two hours without a collection of our relatives around us and a throat-grabbing mystery."

"So did I."

The song finished, then started again, and Waits began to sing his gloomy descending notes. Sam wound around a broad curve, hoping that the LAPD detective talking to Ramona's parents was smart and would know what to do. Hoping she and Bex made it to the Gymboree in time to talk to Archie.

Hoping.

"Hey, Sam?" Bex turned the volume down on the music. "Do you see that car in your rearview?"

Sam glanced at the mirror. "No." Then there were headlights

coming around a curve, far behind them. "The one way back there?"

"I swear it's been following us."

"Mulholland doesn't give you a lot of options to turn off. Why do you think it's not just a car that happens to be behind us?"

"I first noticed it when it took the same turn you did to drive up into the canyon. It was a little weird, because you turned on a surface street by that church and then navigated through a residential area. Not a common way."

Sam scouted what was ahead of her. "In a quarter mile, there's an overlook. I'll turn in there and let it pass."

"What if it stops?"

"The turnout I'm thinking of faces the driveway of a house that used to belong to one of my stylists. Right near the entrance, there's a very-hard-to-see shed on the left-hand side. There's plenty of room around the gate. We run and duck in there."

Bex's head dropped back. "Jesus Pete, Sam. I admire your quick thinking, but you know how short my legs are. You would dust me. This is a bananas thing to be talking about."

"Get nine-one-one ready on my phone like Fergus had us do."

Bex picked up Sam's phone from the console. "This is why I don't get booked for the action-hero stuff. I'm made for period pieces that style my hair over my corseted boobs."

Sam let up on the gas. Through the curtain of rain, she couldn't make out any details of the vehicle behind them. "I'm going to slow down enough that if they *are* just another car, they'll think I'm turning and go around me. No one is coming from the other direction."

"That's right, you did your own car chase stunts when you played the hot bank robber."

Sam choked on a surprised laugh. "This is not stunt driving. Or a car chase."

She slowed, then slowed some more. The car didn't go around. It slowed with her.

"Fuck. Okay, I'm taking the turnout."

Bex blew out a nervous breath. "Ready."

Sam pulled into the turnout, watching her mirror.

And then the car was close enough to see. It was a sedan driven by a woman with a dark bob.

"Son of a bitch!" Bex shouted. She opened both of the glove boxes in front of her seat, one after the next. They were empty. Then she flipped open the lid of the compartment between their seats.

"What are you doing?"

"Looking for a weapon." Bex pulled out a carabiner and tested it in her hand.

"You are not going to brain Ashleigh Chambers with my brother's carabiner. Come on."

Sam hopped out of the truck as Ashleigh got out of her sedan and opened a bright red umbrella. She looked as glamorous as she had yesterday, now in navy cigarette pants with a soft pink blouse bow spilling out over the neckline of a matching cashmere sweater. Her red lips were on point, her stilettos so high that even Sam's arches throbbed in sympathy.

"Ladies!" Ashleigh shouted over the rain. "Nice day for a drive, isn't it?"

Sam handed Bex the golf umbrella. She nearly took Sam's eye out when she opened it. They were both soaking wet already. "Why the hell are you here?" Bex shouted.

"I'm following you. As I was hired to do. I've offered to let you buy my loyalty to you and you alone, but you didn't call, so here we are. Where are you two headed? I would have loved to get a peek inside the Velvet Chair again. I could tell you some stories. Is Macie holding up?"

"Tell me why I shouldn't call the cops right now, Ashleigh." Bex brandished the screen of Sam's phone with 9-1-1 dialed in.

"Because I have information you need that you can't get from anybody else. *And* because if you report me to the police, it will cause a detonation on every media platform within an hour. That would mean you had to step aside while other people try to find Ramona. People who don't know any of the things you know. People who *might* fail to take Ramona's absence seriously enough to get to her in time."

Bex pointed emphatically at the PI, jostling the umbrella and sending an ice-cold rivulet of rainwater down the back of Sam's neck. "I do *not* like you."

"You don't have to like me to find out what I know. But at this moment I am bound by my existing contract."

Cold water had begun soaking through the leather soles of Sam's boots. "Even if we buy out your contract, we have no guarantee you wouldn't share everything about us with your client," she said. "Or that you even *have* this other client and aren't just in this for yourself. *Or* that you would tell us anything useful!"

"True. You don't know. You can't." Ashleigh inspected her manicure, a bright red that matched both her lips and her umbrella.

"How much?" Bex asked.

Sam turned to her in surprise. "For real?"

"Believe me, I *know*," Bex said. "I don't like this any more than you do. But we're on a critical timeline, and I only care about Ramona at the moment. Ashleigh gave us useful information about Star Spy before. Maybe she'll tell us something that helps. Even if she doesn't and it turns out we're paying her to go away, as long as we get a receipt, we have a case for a restraining order if she pops up again."

Sam sighed. She turned back to Ashleigh. "How much."

Ashleigh cheerfully named her number.

"Fuck me!" Sam shouted. "There is no way anyone is paying you that much to follow people around."

"A reductive description of what I do."

Bex already had her phone out. "Venmo? CashApp? Some kind of creepy gray web app that only traitors use?"

"Bank transfer. I'll text you the invoice and my paperwork that makes it clear what I can and cannot do, should you need it for the judge."

Sam held the umbrella while Ashleigh and Bex manipulated their phones. Finally, Ashleigh got a notification that Bex's payment had gone through. The PI made a phone call. "Good morning!" she said cheerfully. "I regret to inform you that we're done. My final invoice and contract cancellation are already in your inbox."

She hung up, interrupting indistinct male shouting coming from the other end.

"Now, then," she said. "You're welcome to record what I'm about to tell you. I'll follow up with a written report."

She waited for Bex to open a voice note and begin recording. "Okay, go ahead," Bex said. Sam held the umbrella, feeling useless.

"Sloan Lennox left his loft in Koreatown at seven fifteen this morning. He made his way straight to Leading Edge Artists Agency, didn't pass go, not even for a coffee, didn't seem to be on his phone, smoked out his window the whole time."

"Is he represented by Leading Edge?" Sam asked.

"He is," Ashleigh confirmed. "One of the staffers in the pool that assists Sloan's agent happens to be one of my paid informants."

"For real?" Bex asked. "You have a mole."

Sam had to admit that was impressive. She admitted it to herself. Not to Ashleigh.

"I do, and so I can share with you what I learned from this person," Ashleigh said. "For a while now, Sloan has been positioning himself for a career reboot. He's got new representation. His agent took a risk and reached out to Chad's people with the idea that Sloan would gain maximum visibility by cashing in on old associations."

Not a surprising plan and also not a bad one. The association between Chad and Sloan had been enough to arrest Sam's attention in the studio parking garage, had captivated Bex when Sam told her about it, and had then become the subject of their reunion dinner conversation with Vic. Audiences would be similarly engrossed.

"Chad was interested, but he had conditions," Ashleigh said. "He's in a good position right now. *Theomina*'s got an unproblematic dream cast, including you, Sam. Huge budget. Being in a dragon-riding fantasy is good for his brand. It's going to introduce his face to a new audience. With that in his pocket, does Chad want to be reconnected to Sloan and the Ice Crew again? After Juliette died, it was a bad deal for Chad to be associated. On the other hand, now it's retro. He gets points for knowing the beautiful dead girl."

"That is revolting," Bex said.

It was. But to Sam's mind, it tracked. Chad liked to talk about how easy it was to lose a good reputation. He'd made Sam's agent do a sit-down with his agent before *Theomina* so that he could be reassured that the press around Bex and Sam's solving Jen Arnot's murder was positive and wouldn't "curdle" on him.

"Chad wants to build on *Theomina* to fully produce and star in a project from his new company. It's a sci-fi picture. Eight novels, and he has an exclusive license to the IP. The story centers around two rival space pirates who are forced to buddy up to fight some greater evil. Chad's costar isn't cast yet. If Sloan landed such a big studio project, it would be a coup for him."

A gust of wind blew up from the canyon. Sam shivered. "You're telling us *The Howling* guest spot was a soft launch of Chad and Sloan working together. To see how it landed."

"Yes. If it lands well, Sloan's casting in Chad's movie will be greenlit."

"That makes Sloan dependent on Chad's career decisions," Bex said. "Not a good position to be in."

Ashleigh leaned closer. "Right now is a moment made of the thinnest glass for Sloan, and of outsized power for Chad. Sloan can't do anything that would remove him from Chad's good graces. But if Sloan pulls it off, we could be watching the two of them pilot a space pirate ship alongside a revolving cast of female costars for years to come."

Sam reached back and gathered her wet hair, squeezing it out in her fists as she tried to prevent her thoughts from flying off in a million different directions. "Sloan is a *lot* more interested in a comeback than we've been led to believe."

"Honey, in this town, everybody's either at the top of their game or trying to come back. If Sloan didn't still want to be famous, he wouldn't be in L.A. He wants a blockbuster. He wants the excited whispers to break out when he enters a room, the cameras following him wherever he goes, the endless media takes. All eyes on him. Why do you think he wore a fedora and sunglasses? He wants Sloan Lennox to be a brand that no one can say no to. The problem is, he's never been blockbuster material. According to my former client—"

"Chad," Sam interrupted.

Ashleigh finally acknowledged the relationship with an incline of her head and a conspiratorial smile. "According to *Chad*, Sloan feels that age is on his side. He's no longer an idiosyncratic-looking youth best suited for playing the wry outcast the girl doesn't pick. The camera transforms all the crow's feet and snowy temples into a sly silver fox."

"Imagine age being on your side." Bex snorted. "I was recently told I was too old to play a thirty-eight-year-old. I *am* a thirty-eight-year-old."

"And Sloan's an egomaniac whose only shot at fame rests in Chad's hands," Sam said. "Fine. But how does all of this help us find Ramona?"

"Oh, sweet summer children, you will learn this trade in time. Chad hired me after you clocked him and Sloan in the studio lot. He needed to know how much *you* knew and what you would do with it."

"What does that mean?"

Ashleigh slowed down her words as if she were speaking to a small child. "You saw them together. No one had seen them together in the wild for many years."

"We were on the top deck of a secure studio parking lot."

"In Chad's head, this was a momentous breach in security. What would you do with this information? How would it ruin everything for him? This is how Chad thinks. By that time, Macie had likely called him to ask if he'd seen Ramona—or if she hadn't, Sloan had. Did *you* know anything about that? Chad was aware you'd worked with Macie before. Would you leak something or, God forbid, 'go all fucking Harriet the Spy' on him—direct quote. These were the thoughts in his head when he hired me to follow you. Macie went to *your house*, and from there to Bexley's. Chad blew at least three gaskets. He felt the situation was getting out of his control."

That made sense to Sam. She'd witnessed Chad overreacting to any number of situations he believed were getting out of his control.

"Men with overwrought reactions make me curious," Ashleigh continued. "So I let you see me while giving him reports on your movements that suggest, yes, the two of you *are* going all Harriet the Spy. From this moment on, he knows nothing more, but he certainly is aware that you're on a road that leads to, among many other places, Encino."

"Does he *care*?" Sam asked. "Does he want us to find Ramona?"

"Hmm. Can't speak to that. If I were mentoring you in the art of private investigation, I would certainly suggest having your ducks in a row before you spoke to someone as openly hostile as

Chad has revealed himself to be. And I would also point out that the two of you looking for Ramona directs public sympathy and interest to her that Chad would prefer be pointed at him. When this episode of *The Howling* airs, he wants the moment to be about Sloan and Chad, not poor missing Ramona Watts and the adorable sapphic duo who couldn't find her. Or who did find her." She waved her hand dismissively. "Either way."

"I hate it here," Bex said. "Doesn't anybody get that Ramona isn't a pawn for her or anyone else's comeback? That she's a real live person who people are worried about?"

"Oh, no." Ashleigh smiled. "They do not. But take a note that *I* wanted to help you. Not Chad."

Sam was cold. The rain and wind made her feel like an irrelevant speck in the middle of the big ocean. She had to admit that Ashleigh's insight into Sloan and Chad's motivations was useful, but it wasn't a full picture. Chad was controlling, not stupid. He didn't act without *reasons*. The reasons Ashleigh was giving them didn't add up to a motive that made Sam suspect Chad in Ramona's disappearance.

"You've got your money," she said.

Ashleigh didn't protest. She moved to her car door and opened it, snapping down her umbrella and shaking it out as she put one leg into her car. "You'll call me again," she said. "You need what I can do, however distasteful you think it is."

Then she got in her dark sedan and drove away.

"I have no idea if I like her or not," Bex said as Ashleigh's taillights faded into the mist.

"Maybe the world would be a better place if it wasn't important if a woman was likeable," Sam said. "I'm not sure we *won't* call her again."

Once they were back on the road, with the truck's heat blowing them dry, Sam found herself thinking of Juliette, alone on a boat in the frigid Pacific.

It was hard to think about Juliette.

Hard, too, to think about Ramona, screaming out at the dark water while her friend drifted beyond her reach.

"I've always looked up to her. Ramona." Sam's voice sounded peculiar against the drumming of the rain. "I don't know if I've said that. I'd like to get a chance to meet her."

She glanced at Bex in the passenger seat. Her auburn hair was sparkling with raindrops, her skin damp, her eyes full of all the feelings Sam wasn't handling as well as she wanted to.

"Then you will," Bex said firmly. "We'll find her, and you'll get to meet her. Frankie will act like it's no big deal. Vic will say something outrageous. You'll wear an outfit that makes me feel feelings I don't know how to categorize."

"Don't you?"

"And I will bustle and talk too loud and possibly cry. That's what's going to happen when we meet Ramona Watts. And it's all I'm going to say on the subject."

Sam felt a little warmer from Bex's reassurance. "Consult your notebook, then, and tell me what's next."

"I hate to tell you this, but what's next is the 101."

"That's him," Bex said as they turned into the parking lot of the Encino Gymboree.

She pointed at a tall, huskily built man, with brush-cut hair and deep brown skin, standing outside the building beneath an awning. He had a cup of coffee clasped between his palms. His tweedy jacket gave him the air of a college professor.

Sam pulled into a spot ten feet away. Archie stared into their car, positively glowering.

"Yikes," Bex said. "We're on time. More or less."

"Remember, he hates everyone, so it's not personal," Sam said. "Probably."

They jumped down from the truck and dashed under the Gymboree awning. Even through the glass double doors, Sam could hear the happy screaming of children and the beat of primary-colored music.

"Hello," she said with an understated wave. "I'm Sam, and this is Bexley. Macie told you why we wanted to talk to you, I think."

"My daughter is done in five minutes." Archie's accent sounded London-born.

"We understand," Sam told him. "Thanks for meeting with us. Long story short, in Macie's search and our helping, we heard you'd been spending time with Ramona on the *Howling* set, and Ramona's home security cameras captured you looking for her on Monday morning after she didn't show for work. Colin Worth let us know that you may have been collaborating with Ramona on a project related to your Ice Crew documentary. We thought it was important to talk to you about where you think she might be, given all of those"—Sam searched for a word that was not *clues*—"connections."

Archie took a long, pointed drink from his coffee cup, watching the two of them with discerning eyes. Then he leaned out from beneath the awning to throw the cup away. He seemed not to notice the rain running off his inky hair and beading on the shoulders of his jacket. "You're the TV detectives. Who's Ramona to you?" He directed the question to Bex.

"We're helping at Macie's request."

"That's not what I asked."

"Ramona's parents are filing a missing person report," Bex said. "But even though Ramona's famous, law enforcement is less likely to spend resources on a missing adult unless the adult is vulnerable or known to be in distress. No one wants to miss anything. Or waste time. She could be in grave danger." There was more than a thread of warning in Bex's tone.

"She could be in Cabo," Archie countered briskly. "It's none of your business."

"Her friends are worried," Sam tried. "You must be worried, too. You drove to her house."

Archie's face somehow went both blank and furious at the same time. "If Ramona wanted the world to know what she was doing, she'd issue a press release. If she wanted you lot to know, she'd ask her manager for your phone number. She hasn't done that, has she? That tells me what she would want *me* to tell *you* is 'Back the fuck off and leave her be.' "

Well. That was definitive. Sam clenched her hands in the pockets of her sweater.

Bex took a step closer to Archie. Then another. When she leaned up toward him, the difference in their height meant he had to rear back and crane his neck to make sure she wasn't about to attack.

"I appreciate your concern for Ramona's privacy," she said. "But she has other friends than you, and she isn't answering their texts. She isn't returning their phone calls. Macie says it's out of character. We know that Ramona's phone has either gone off the grid or been disabled. It's been like that for days, so it doesn't *look* like she's on vacation. It looks like she's gone. *Furthermore*, it looks like there are people who might have had a reason to harm her. You're right to say we're not anything to Ramona Watts. We are, however, people willing to do whatever we can to make sure she's okay, and that's a good thing. Objectively."

Archie's eyebrows knit together. "Are you done?" he growled.

"I am. Sam?"

"You covered it."

The music inside turned off, and there was a change in the noise of the children. "That will be my daughter," he said. "I don't have anything else to say to you."

He went to the door. Just as he put his fingers to its handle, he paused.

Sam held her breath.

"If you want someone who will tell you what you want to know and a lot you don't besides, talk to Kessler. He's the type who will be delighted instead of horrified that two actresses have started messing about in other people's lives, deputizing themselves with their own make-believe." Archie pushed open the door. "Leave off with your stunts. And leave me the fuck alone."

The Biggest Story in Hollywood

Bex Simon had the patience of a saint.

Sam leaned against the blue-velvet-curtain-covered wall of Tom Kessler's home theater, eating from a paper bag of freshly popped popcorn and watching Bex give the legendary director her full wide-eyed attention as he cued up yet another clip of the Ice Crew back in the day. Sam had lost count somewhere around the fourteenth or fifteenth "You have to see this," but Bex's interest showed no signs of flagging.

Despite his being arguably one of the top five most important men in this town, it hadn't taken long for Bex and Sam to get themselves invited to visit Kessler at his Malibu mansion. All Sam had to do was ask Ramona's agent, April Feinstein, to give him a call.

"Fuck, yes, and thank you, absolutely I will do that," April had said. "He owes me more favors than I can count. But pin the shitgibbon down or he'll bore you to death with stories of the bad old days."

At least the man provided snacks to go along with his running commentary for candid video of young actors flipping off the person behind the camera while chain smoking.

"You can really get a sense of the on-set culture at that time." He rubbed his hand over his close-trimmed silver beard, looking like a man accustomed to sharing sage thoughts. "The process was more collaborative than it is now. I was letting the cameras roll after scenes ended, because I'd often catch live, intimate moments that gave the films texture. Oh, you know what's an excellent example? Take a look at this one."

He cued up another clip as Bex widened her eyes at Sam and mouthed *Help me.*

Sam had to cover up her laugh with a cough. The huge theater screen filled with a scowling Sloan Lennox wearing a leather jacket with a pair of polarized Oakleys. Sam recognized the costume and the scenery behind him, an interior from *Karma Revisited.* Macie and Chad had been the leads in that project, but this candid clip featured Juliette with Sloan. It was the first clip Kessler had shown them with Juliette in it.

"Get off!" She was laughing, but there was pressure in her demand, which she made in response to Sloan tickling her. She gave him a hard shove. He stepped away, grinning.

"This isn't the one I wanted," Kessler said. "Hang on."

But Sam wasn't listening. Juliette had captured her attention.

"Sloan thinks tickling is funny." Juliette spoke to someone outside the frame. She wore an oversized blue T-shirt with a red-and-black flannel tied around her waist. Her hair was loose, big and frizzy in a way that pre-dated salon blowouts. Her eyes were direct. Cutting. "I worry he didn't get as much attention as he needed as a child."

Whoever held the camera snorted, and Sloan, still laughing, said, "Hey!"

The screen went dark. Sam stared at it, the image of Juliette still burning inside her.

She'd thought of her as delicate. A fragile, lost person. But the young woman in that clip wasn't anything like the Juliette Draper in the movies.

Why did Hollywood have to take someone perfect and young and whole, just to turn them into something they weren't? Juliette manifestly had a lot to offer to cinema—much more than was captured when she was acting from a script this man wrote.

Maybe she would still be alive if she could have been seen for who she was.

Sam moved off the wall. She'd run out of patience. Kessler's career was built on the backs of six talented young people, and one of them was dead. Another had gone missing, possibly for reasons connected to the work she'd done for him. If he didn't understand that he owed Ramona a great deal more than this tedious tour of his greatest hits, Sam would explain it to him.

"Macie asked us to talk to you about Ramona," she said. "Colin Worth is worried sick about her. We've been to see Christian Stanstedt, who seems like someone no one wants to talk to. Piper Redwood's scared. You know Ramona hasn't reported to work, isn't home, isn't anywhere. We think she's missing involuntarily."

The director grimaced at Sam's blunt approach. She thought of what Ramona's agent had told her. *Pin the shitgibbon down.* She pressed on. "Chad and Sloan have recently resurfaced in Ramona's orbit. Chad made a preemptive hostile move against me, hiring a PI to follow me after I found out that he and Sloan did a guest appearance on *The Howling.*"

Kessler crossed his arms protectively over his chest.

"Yep. Your body language"—Sam waved at Tom's posture—"is where we've been living the past few days. It's not a comfortable situation that Bex and I have gotten ourselves into. Chad's surveillance means he *knows* we're looking for Ramona, which makes him more volatile. His appearance on Ramona's show is vital to a comeback project he's cooked up with Sloan. They're on our list to talk to once we have more of the information that too many folks are reluctant to give us."

Bex leaned back to catch Tom's eye. "Any idea, for example, why agreeing to help Macie figure out where Ramona is has put us in the position of getting followed by dark sedans, kicked out of actors' homes, and yelled at by prestige documentarians? I don't expect a red carpet wherever I go, but I do anticipate help when I'm looking for a *missing woman.*"

"*Thank* you," Sam said. "Look, we know Ramona has been grieving and processing Juliette's death for years. We tried to talk to Archie about his relationship with her, and he sent us to you. Actually, every person we've talked to has sent us to someone else. Surely, *Tom*, the buck stops *somewhere*. We've been in your viewing room for an hour. You start a new clip every time me or Bex try to say something other than 'That's so interesting!' "

Kessler wiped his hand over his mouth.

"You should know that Ramona's parents are talking to the LAPD," Sam added. "Whatever you can tell us that could help find her that you *don't* want law enforcement to know, leak, and potentially take to court, now's your chance."

Kessler smoothed his hands over the sides of his silver-white hair. He wore it long, swooping over his forehead, as if in tribute to the young men he'd made famous thirty years ago. "That's direct."

"I hate that in Hollywood the truth is *always* considered too direct." Bex folded her arms on the back of her theater seat, fully turned around to face them now. "I want all the time back I've spent couching everything I've ever said in euphemisms. It's not as if we don't know that everyone in this business has an opinion." She held out her empty popcorn bag to Kessler. "Or a secret."

He took the bag and stood up to toss it in a discreet mahogany wastebasket. There was a white ring around his mouth. He was probably angry.

Sam didn't care. There were a lot of naked emperors in Hollywood, and someone had to point their finger.

"Cineline mothballed the documentary," he said.

"We know that," Bex said. "Everyone knows that who still remembers there was supposed to be a documentary. They killed it after Juliette's death."

Now Kessler leaned back against the wall. "Do you know why?"

"Out of respect for Juliette?" Bex's confusion was evident on her forehead. "But, as I say that out loud, I'm surprised I believed it."

"They put it away after they'd spent more on fighting Chad's lawsuits to stop the release than they'd spent on the documentary or could ever hope to make from it."

"For fuck's sake." Sam shoved her hands into her hair.

"A few months ago, Archie told me he wanted to buy the rights back from Cineline, but they wouldn't sell to him. I offered to produce it. And by 'offered,' you understand that I'm saying I cashed in a chip with the studio head, Niels Shaughnessy."

Emotional debt really was the most important currency in show business. "We're following," Sam said.

"My involvement gave Archie the opportunity to step back into the project and assume creative control. Chad's career is big enough now that Chad has to be a lot more careful about his litigious behavior. He cowered behind the cover of respect for Juliette's death the first time, but another lawsuit would make him look like he's trying to hide something. You know how it is."

Sam didn't. She was not inclined to sic lawyers on people to cover up anything she'd done. "*Is* Chad trying to hide something? Is there something in the documentary he's trying to suppress?"

Kessler scanned around the theater like he was looking for someone more interesting to talk to at a party. "Why don't we go outside? Change of scenery."

"We will go outside with you and give you five more minutes, as a courtesy, so that you may master your feelings and tell the truth," Sam said. "But if it takes you longer than five minutes, I will be *so* direct."

This was the beginning and end of any threat Sam could make, but Tom did go a little pale. He motioned for them to follow him from the room.

Bex and Sam walked behind him down the whitewashed, wood-paneled halls of his home. The ceilings soared above them.

Every surface seemed designed to softly reflect light. It was effective even on this gray day. Money could buy the weather.

On Kessler's deck, Malibu's collage of jagged rocks and smooth beaches were filmed in a fog so heavy, it almost seemed like another round of rain had begun, though Sam didn't feel even a sprinkle. Multiple outdoor heaters ringed a covered seating area. The deck, made from blond woods and glass, had an uninterrupted panoramic view of the Pacific. It was surreal, and so warm that Sam slipped off her cardigan while the unseasonal storm swirled around them.

Tom leaned against the deck's glass railing. His hair curled in the fog. The smell of the marijuana he lit and drew through a small pipe drifted in and out of awareness in the wind.

"I'd like to tell you what I know," he said. "This mess of pain and lies should've been dealt with years ago. Ramona confided in me what happened the night Juliette died. She needed help."

Sam felt weak. She braced her elbows on the arms of her chair. "We understand she felt like she'd failed to keep Juliette from partying too much."

"That's not what she felt responsible for."

"Oh." Bex's voice was so hushed, so unlike even her whispers, that Sam wished she'd kept her sweater on to ward of the chill of dread. She wasn't sure she wanted to hear this story after all.

She didn't tell him to stop.

"Juliette was invited to what she believed would be a party on the boat. Ramona went with her because she didn't think it was a good idea for Juliette to go alone to *any* party Chad and Sloan were throwing. They'd both given interviews where they talked about their romantic relationships with her. Chad had implied in more than one interview that he'd taken her virginity. It was crass."

Bex made a noise in her throat she usually reserved for things she found in the pool skimmer.

"Even though she was no longer involved with either of them, the media speculation hadn't died down. Ramona told me Juliette wanted to talk to them together, to try to get them to stop jockeying over her. It was affecting her career and her mental health. She wanted a chance to start over. She'd recently gotten a spot at a good treatment center. But when they got to the boat, it wasn't a party. It was just Chad and Sloan. They'd been expecting Juliette to come alone."

"What did they plan to do?" Bex asked.

"Ramona wasn't sure. She knew Sloan wanted to get back together with Juliette. She thought maybe Sloan and Chad had a plan to try to convince Juliette she'd made a mistake. Chad being a wingman for Sloan, that kind of thing. But whatever they had in mind, they were unhappy to see Ramona."

"She got in the way of their being able to manipulate Juliette," Sam said.

"Yes. Ramona told me that at first things went well. There were drinks, but not many. Ramona made sure she and Juliette stuck to soda. She poured them herself. But after a time, Sloan made a pass at Juliette, and Juliette seized the moment to make her request. She wanted an end to any appearance of a love triangle. No more statements about each other's private lives in the press. She was going to rehab. There was a role Juliette wanted, not one of my projects, and the casting agent had told her it would be hers if she made it through her upcoming program. Chad and Sloan didn't take Juliette's new request to publicly part ways well."

"In what sense?" Sam reached for her sweater.

"They made it sound like Juliette was blowing their behavior out of proportion. Being hysterical when they'd just been shooting the shit in their interviews. Locker-room talk, that sort of thing. As if Juliette were the one who was creating the problem, not them, and her request for them to stop was just more evidence of her instability."

"Gaslighting," Sam said.

"She became upset. Juliette was shouting, 'Fuck you, you're such an asshole,' things like that, which witnesses on the nearby boats overheard. She was agitated, and Sloan was angry, getting in her face. Chad was furious."

Kessler took a long toke from his pipe. Sam thought of Christian's drinking and Macie's vaping and cigarettes. Bex started picking at the skin alongside her thumb, a nervous habit she'd defeated ten years ago. "What happened, Tom?"

"Ramona stepped into the middle of the argument and reminded Chad and Sloan there were people at the marina. They would attract attention. It calmed them down. She tried to get Juliette to leave with her, but Juliette wanted to go on good terms. She was like that. The guys went belowdecks for food and more drinks. Juliette was still sticking to soda. Ramona relaxed. This kind of thing happened often—a big blow up, and then, once the feelings had been discharged, everyone was okay. They were just kids, you know?"

Sam did know. The clips Kessler had shown them were of children playing, roughhousing, pulling faces, having emotions that were awkward in their rawness. He didn't seem to understand they'd needed an adult to protect them.

The people who could have accepted that role had elected to sit behind a camera instead, collecting checks.

"Ramona noticed Juliette slurring her speech like she was really drunk. She had stopped watching Chad and Sloan as closely. She got upset, thinking they must have put something in Juliette's food or a drink, and she'd missed it. Juliette realized it, too. Ramona said she started yelling again, but she wasn't making sense. Ramona tried to get Juliette to stand up so she could help her walk out, but something happened. Ramona sustained a blow to the head that knocked her unconscious. Chad would say later that she slipped on the deck while she was trying to get Juliette to make the step onto the dock. He claimed she fell down and hit her head. Ramona wasn't sure if that was true. She didn't have a memory of how she got the injury. When she woke up, Juliette was gone."

"In the dinghy," Bex said. "Juliette got into it while she was under the influence?"

Kessler gave a tight nod. "They found the drugs in her system. Chad and Sloan said that when Juliette stepped into the dinghy, she was angry and high. She started the motor instead of letting them help her back onto the boat. She took off. She didn't remember the dinghy was tied to the boat, and it ripped off a cleat. That was confirmed. There was a line with a cleat dragging behind the dinghy when they found her. The engine had run out of gas."

Sam studied Kessler closely. His emotions were difficult for her to read.

She focused on the story he was telling them. "But *you're* saying Chad and Sloan were the only people who would know if Juliette got into that dinghy under her own power, started the motor, and pulled free from the yacht. Ramona was unconscious. Juliette didn't make it. What about the witnesses at the marina?"

"The dinghy was on the opposite side of the boat from them. They could hear Juliette, but they couldn't see anything that happened with the dinghy. Ramona came to after Juliette and the dinghy were gone. But she overheard Chad and Sloan talking."

Kessler looked out at the ocean. Sam's heart was beating madly in her throat. She and Bex were about to hear something few people knew.

"Ramona heard Chad tell Sloan, 'Don't say *shit*.' She heard Sloan say, 'But she can't swim.' Chad said, 'I don't care. She said she wanted to leave, and now she's fucking left, hasn't she? If you tell anyone, I'll kill you.' Ramona was clear about all this. I've never forgotten the exact words as she spoke them to me. She'd been having nightmares."

Sam felt her blood drain away, replaced with ice that slowed her heart to a drum that started beating in her ears.

Chad and Sloan had known Juliette couldn't swim. They'd known she was impaired, because they were the people who'd put her in that state. They'd understood that their actions endangered Juliette's life, and Chad's response was to threaten to kill Sloan if he told anyone.

That was conspiracy. Manslaughter. Possibly murder.

It meant that Chad *wasn't* paranoid. He and Sloan bore responsibility for Juliette's death. They'd known it then. They knew it now.

A man responsible for a woman's death had put surveillance on Sam and Bex. He knew their movements across L.A. He knew who they had been talking to, at least until the moment they'd pulled into a turnout on Mulholland Drive. Chad was a man who imagined worst-case scenarios, who jumped to conclusions and accused everyone around him of subterfuge and sabotage. He'd been keeping this secret for a long time. He'd never had more on the line.

Would he stop at lawyers, lawsuits, and stalking to guarantee Sam and Bex's silence?

"Why didn't Ramona tell the police?" Bex asked.

"She did."

"Then how come Chad and Sloan were never arrested?" Bex's big strong voice was reduced by half. Sam felt sick to hear a tremble in it.

"By the time Ramona gave her statement, the police had already interviewed people on nearby boats. The witnesses said Juliette was agitated. They'd heard her yelling. Chad and Sloan had failed sobriety tests, and they said they were *all* drinking and drugging. The police on the scene recorded that Ramona smelled like alcohol, too, and had hit her head. The cleat was torn out.

Juliette's absence got the searchers on the water, but where they eventually found the dinghy in the morning made it clear it had taken off fast enough to catch a seasonal current that took it way out. There were too many converging details to make it look like anything other than a bad accident. And the police consume media, don't forget. No doubt they were biased by reports of this troubled love triangle."

Bex made a noise of protest.

"But what Ramona heard means that Chad and Sloan *put* Juliette on the dinghy," Sam said, working out her thoughts as she spoke. "Incapacitated, it sounds like. Because right before Ramona was hit—right before someone *hit* her, surely—Juliette needed help to walk. How was she supposed to have gotten herself into a dinghy when she couldn't *walk*? And Chad made a sick joke at her expense. 'She said she wanted to leave, and now she's fucking left, hasn't she?' He knew she *couldn't* leave. *They* were the ones who made sure she left."

"They loaded her unconscious body onto that boat, started the motor, and sent her out onto the ocean in the dark!" Bex's distress was absolute. "They knew she was impaired! They knew she couldn't swim! They knew they'd knocked out the only person who would care enough to help her! But they didn't do anything to rescue her from certain death until *Ramona* came to and got the police, and by then it was too late? My *God*."

Kessler didn't say anything to refute Bex's conclusions. He'd reached the same conclusions years ago and said nothing.

Sam was glad for the bigness of the Pacific, half obscured by rain. The ocean was big enough, she'd always thought, to wash anything clean.

But it was also a graveyard full of ghosts.

"You called her your muse," Sam said. "She trusted you, but you didn't help her. Why the hell not?"

Kessler looked mournful. "At the end of the day, I didn't feel that I had any more to bring to the situation than Ramona had already given to the police. I did check to make sure the police had the report. Her story was in the hands of the only people who could do something about it. That was my feeling at the time. Especially after I talked to Chad and Sloan to get their story of what happened."

"Why did you need to get *their* story?" Bex asked irritably. "What did you think, that they would provide independent confirmation of a *murder*? Of course they blamed everything on Juliette."

"What they said seemed to match what the witnesses on other boats heard. They'd failed sobriety tests. It was hard to believe they were in a state to conspire to murder."

"Did Ramona fail her sobriety test?"

"No."

Sam pulled her sweater tighter around herself, needing to feel the protection. "That means Ramona could have fallen in a spill. She could have been doused deliberately, for that matter."

"Chad sent a hoard of lawyers after her. After Archie, too, because of the documentary. I'm sure that's why Archie wasn't helpful to you, beyond his loyalty to Ramona. He had to hire an attorney back then."

Bex growled. "Oh my God, spare me the tedious legal abuse of this man!"

Sam wondered if Juliette's death had been the origin point of Chad's threats to bring in his legal team. It was a pattern he still fell back on. It had worked so well for him. He'd kept Ramona from telling her story. He'd kept the documentary from being released. "He stopped it," she said. "But *why* did he stop it? Is there evidence in it? How could there be, if Juliette's still alive in it?" She looked at Kessler, who hadn't answered this question when they asked it earlier. "Was there any footage for the documentary filmed after Juliette died?"

"No, it was already wrapped and edited. Cineline had been running a marketing campaign in advance of the release."

"Right. They'd already done the movie poster. All six members of the Ice Crew posed together, maybe for the last time. But then they pulled it because Chad and his lawyers made it too expensive to bother distributing." That made sense. What didn't make sense was why Chad had gone to such lengths to suppress the documentary. What was he afraid of?

She thought of the Velvet Chair. The cigarette machine with its sign, DON'T FORCE THE LEVERS YOU CRETINS. Macie smoking in the abandoned club, telling them about the documentary. *Handheld camera, interviews on sidewalks, dark cut-ins of grainy footage of the crew piled on sofas. The boys, me, and Juliette were often drunk or high.*

Then Sam's mind jumped to Kessler's home theater.

The Ice Crew had made this man famous. He'd been living steeped in that nostalgic glory for so long that he'd become an archivist of it. He'd been waiting a long time for someone to come along and tell him the jig was up.

"*You* know," Sam said. "You *know* what was in the documentary that Chad is afraid of. Show us."

Kessler took a long pull from his pipe. The sharp smoke shuddered out from his lungs. Then he reached into a pocket, pulling out his phone. He swiped at the screen for long enough that Sam wanted to smack it out of his hand. Finally, he handed it to her. Bex drew close to watch over her shoulder as Sam pushed the white "play" triangle hovering over Chad Bevington's twenty-something face.

"Oh, you're going to take a girl home tonight, Lennox?" Chad was laughing, sitting on a huge beanbag chair with Sloan, who leaned forward to tap his ash into a tall glass vase on the floor.

"Shut up. I'm a gentleman." Sloan flicked his butt in the direction of the camera, which caught it sailing off screen. "If the Smashing Pumpkins move the souls of the fair sex tonight, let's just say I'm soulful."

Chad snort-laughed, and the way he couldn't stop giggling at

Sloan's performance of painful coolness suggested there was something helping his laughter along. His red eyes were more evidence. "I know how you move a girl's soul," he said.

Sloan bent to light another cigarette, and Chad knocked his fedora off. "Shut the fuck up, Bevington."

Chad kept snickering as he picked up a can of beer that had been between his knees and then mimed pouring something into it from a vessel between his fingertips. "Here you are, milady. Just close your eyes and enjoy your soul moving."

Sloan hit him with his hat.

Sam paused the video and set the phone down on the table. Her neck was hot. Nausea landed in her stomach with a sick punch.

"Stupid joke," Kessler said. "That's what I thought at the time, but it was just the kind of jokes guys made."

"No," Sam said. "Rape has never been a joke."

Kessler swallowed. "But after everything with Juliette, and what Ramona told me, her version of events, I thought about it. I thought about it more when Chad suppressed the movie."

"You think he was afraid that the circumstances of Juliette's death were suspicious enough for people to see that scene in the documentary and believe she'd been roofied," Bex said. "Even if Juliette's death wasn't reinvestigated, he and Sloan would have been convicted in the court of public opinion."

"And that threat never went away," Sam said. "It's as true today as it was back then." She speared Kessler with a pointed look. "Who knows about this favor you cashed in for Archie with the head of Cineline? Is it possible Chad found out about the documentary coming out of the vault?"

The director shook his head. "Niels has kept it locked down. The subjects' contracts were such that the footage belonged solely to the studio. I've been scrupulous about keeping my involvement quiet. I'm not looking for a headache from Chad or anyone else."

Sam took a deep breath, considering Kessler.

Something was off.

"How does it benefit *you* to cash in so many chips with Cineline and resurrect this documentary?" she asked.

He didn't respond. He didn't look at her.

"Ramona," Bex said. "You feel *guilty*. All these years later, you want to do something, and calling in this favor with a studio executive is the only way you can think of to make amends. Not going to the police and giving them a statement. Not apologizing to Ramona and asking her what *she* would like to do. All you can think of to do is release this film into the snake pit of public speculation and, of course—of *course*—earn box office at the same time. For fuck's sake." Bex looked disgusted as she turned her face away from Kessler's suddenly flaming cheeks.

"Is there anything else you want to unburden yourself of?" Sam asked. "Any confessions you might otherwise end up taking to the grave?"

Kessler knocked out the contents of his pipe into an enormous blown-glass ashtray on the table, then rubbed his thumbnail with his index finger. "Just . . . if Ramona's missing. I've never known her to—well, to be anything but someone a person can count on."

"*I* know that." Sam stood up. "But you could have told the rest of the world. If you'd wanted to support Ramona, you could have sacrificed and stuck your neck out for your *muse*." She said the word with heavy sarcasm. "When we find her, I'll be sure to tell her just what a help you've been, Tom."

Sam's phone buzzed from her bag. Bex put her hand on her own, then opened the top and slid out her phone for a fast peek. "It's Frankie."

"We're finished here," Sam said.

"Well, you know where to find me." With this, Kessler got up and led them through the fog and down the halls of his beautiful shiplike home to the drive.

Sam didn't feel sorry for him.

In Fergus's truck, Bex slipped out of her shoes and crossed her legs on the passenger seat. She retrieved her notebook and began furiously writing. Sam started the engine and backed slowly out of Kessler's driveway, pointing them in the direction of downtown.

They drove for a little while. Sam listened to the soft scratching sounds of Bex's gold pen and let her mind empty of everything but the foggy road in front of them.

"Do you really believe there isn't *any* way word of the documentary rerelease hasn't leaked?" Bex asked after a few miles.

"Ramona knows," Sam said. "It's hard to believe she's the only one."

"Right." Bex made a quick note. "If what Ashleigh told us holds up, Chad was hot and bothered about Ramona being missing because it could mess up *his* plans. If he knew this documentary footage could get out there, or Sloan did, there's no telling what they'd do."

"It's possible," Sam said. "The clip Kessler showed us implicates Sloan, not so much Chad. It might be a hit to Chad's reputation, but that's what publicists are for. Leading men have done worse and kept working. Is there really anything like motive here?"

"I don't know. I guess if word of the documentary got back to Chad or Sloan, what I'd expect to see is lawsuits, not an elaborate scheme to kidnap Ramona or something. We know Sloan drove her home from the studio parking lot, but are we supposed to think he locked her in a dark room after that? To what end?"

Sam tapped on the steering wheel, thinking. "We know more now about why Ramona feels responsible for what happened to Juliette. What if the first thing Macie told us is the most important to focus on? They came to us worried about Ramona feeling distressed about Juliette's death. Archie had been around, reminding her of the old days. Colin saw Ramona watching tape, taking notes. What happened to Juliette was a gut punch, and Ramona's been preoccupied with it lately, right after she lost her friendship with Christian to an ugly argument. Then Chad and Sloan are in her studio. Maybe it all got to be too much."

Bex pressed her hand to her forehead. "I was thinking when Kessler told us what happened that it might be the biggest story in Hollywood. I'd hate it if the story ended with Ramona taking her own life."

Sam's phone started to ring. Frankie again. She tapped the truck's display screen to put the audio through the sound system.

"Finally." Frankie's voice was more than the ordinary amount of sharp. It made Sam's scalp tingle.

"What is it?"

"Vic and I have been cleaning up loose ends. There were a couple more people on the list from Ramona's agent. We called them, but nothing useful came from that. Then I was reviewing everything with Vic about Ramona's timeline. You guys have the last time anyone saw or spoke to Ramona at around midnight on Friday. She got into a car with Sloan in the StudioHonor parking garage, where they'd just been dropped off by the location vans that drove them down from Mount Baldy."

"That's right," Bex said. "And?"

"Vic and I agreed that everything alleged on the timeline should be confirmed by at least one source, if possible. My thought was that we had Piper *alleging* Ramona left the parking garage with Sloan, but I wanted to figure out another person to talk to in order to confirm that as a fact. I had Vic call Piper to ask her for a name. But that call didn't go how we expected."

"Because?"

"Piper *didn't* see Ramona get into Sloan's car with him."

"She told us she did!" Sam said.

"Vic says Piper told you guys it *happened*, not that she saw it. Splitting hairs, I know, but Piper was just trying to tell you everything she could think of that would help. It didn't occur to her that she needed to physically witness Ramona climbing into Sloan's car with her eyeballs."

"How did she know it happened?" Sam asked.

"She overheard Chad say something like, 'Ro, you can ride with Sloan.' "

"But *someone* must have seen Ramona leave," Sam insisted. Her armpits had gone slick with sweat. She forced herself to take a deep breath and loosen her grip on the steering wheel.

"Put a pin in that," Frankie said. "Since Vic and I don't have Ramona confirmed in the parking garage by anyone, much less by two sources, I called a woman I know at the studio who's a tech PA for *The Howling* and asked her if she could get me access to the van manifests."

"What's that?" Bex asked.

"You know what it is. When you shoot on location, there's someone like me checking you into and out of transportation. They've got a clipboard or a tablet with the van manifest."

"Oh, right."

"Here's the problem. The van manifest should have shown Ramona boarding a van on the mountain and getting checked out of it back in the parking garage. But my friend at Studio-Honor who went to pull the manifest for me couldn't find it. It wasn't where it was supposed to be. And the PA who recorded that manifest, who was responsible for it, *resigned* three days ago."

Bex had stopped writing in her notebook. "What about cameras? In the garage or the van?"

"Maybe, but you'd need a warrant or a subpoena, I think. Vic and I are chasing down what we can. It's not easy, because *The Howling* keeps itself buttoned up, but any second now we should be getting a contact sheet for the full crew, including van drivers. We'll work the phones, don't worry."

"Ramona's parents," Sam managed to get out over her tight throat. "They should know."

"I already talked to them. I made Macie put me on a conference call so I could *confirm for myself* that I was talking to them and getting the information to them to share."

"We hear you," Bex said. "All these stupid notes in this stupid notebook, and it doesn't occur to me to double-check basic facts around the last time anyone saw Ramona?"

Sam shook her head. "No. Listen. With the exception of Archie, everyone who knows we're doing this has been confident in our talents, and that's nice, but we are *TV* detectives. We are capable of learning, but if we think we have to be perfect to help people, then I guess we're—I guess we're *Kessler*."

"Okay. Okay. Frankie, do you think we could get in touch with—"

"Logan. The PA. His name is Logan Widi. He lives in Koreatown. Rents a place on South Kingsley. I'm texting you the address. I think you need to talk to him in person. He's not returning my calls."

Sam's neck was so tight that she could feel it pull in her shoulders when she put her foot on the gas. "We're in Malibu. It's more than an hour to Koreatown. Could be two hours in this rain."

Bex sat up straight. "Don't worry about it. Sam, turn around up here."

"I guess I could go over there myself," Frankie said. "Though I'm not sure he'd open the door to me, versus for two famous actors."

"I've got this," Bex said. "I can get us there fast." She started scrolling through her phone. "I've just got to call in a favor."

"Some favor." Sam smoothed her hand over her hair, tangled from the downwash of the rotors of the helicopter that had just flown them from Malibu to the construction site of a medical office suite a few blocks from Logan Widi's place in Koreatown.

"It's too much to go into right now." Bex was unwinding the

silk scarf she'd wrapped around her head. The rain had stopped, but the sky was foreboding. Sam assumed it would start up again shortly. "But when a board member of SoFi really, really loves his wife and wants her serenaded on her birthday with a medley of her favorites by her favorite singer, it's almost always better to do it in exchange for a future favor instead of for cash. Board members of finance companies have helicopters."

A few moments later, the map on Sam's phone delivered them to a pale yellow stucco house with the same collection of succulents and yucca plants that every house on the block had, all fenced in behind vinyl-coated chain-link. Sam spotted a small dog in the big front window. It was staring at them and trembling.

"Ready?" Bex lifted the latch for the gate.

"It looks like he already knows we're here." Sam gestured toward the doorbell camera as the inner door opened, leaving only a security door with ornate metalwork. They closed the gate behind them and stepped up onto the small concrete porch.

"It's really Sam Farmer and Bex Simon." A man Sam assumed must be Logan Widi held the dog under one arm. Its eyes were glazed with cataracts, but its little tail whipped back and forth nonetheless, and its nose wiggled in the air to confirm the presence of visitors. "The TV detectives in the flesh."

Logan was having a hard time meeting their eyes. Sam couldn't figure out if he was shy or nervous. She was used to people who didn't know how to act around celebrities, but Logan was a PA. He ought to have been accustomed to working with talent, even very famous talent.

Of course, he wasn't meeting them at a studio or shoot, where everyone had a role to play. A woman was missing, and he'd been one of the last people to see her. He'd left his job, and the timing did not look good. Logan Widi had excellent reasons to be nervous.

They followed him inside to an open-concept combined living and dining area. There was an opening to the back, probably to the kitchen and a postage-stamp backyard. "Have a seat. I'd offer you something to drink, but my wife is taking a nap, and our new baby is in her bouncer on the kitchen floor. She likes to stare at the light fixture in there. Sometimes it helps her fall asleep. If I go in and get a drink, she'll wake up, and then my wife will wake up, and everything will be so much worse later." The dark circles under Logan's eyes matched his black T-shirt and hiking pants.

"How old is your baby?" Bex sat down in a leather recliner, while Sam took the end of the burgundy sofa opposite. The room was pretty. Someone had styled the big wall at one end with a collection of round, carved Mayan calendars in materials ranging from colored stone to painted wood. There were hand-woven round, shallow baskets interspersed between the calendars, echoing the shape with texture.

Logan reached up to adjust the ball cap he'd already taken off. His dark hair was smashed into a position it had probably settled into overnight. It was easy to imagine this young man drifting off in a recliner with a baby, stealing an hour of sleep before he had to go to work. "Two months. It feels like we might be over the rough stuff. Her name's Olivia."

The little dog jumped up beside Sam and leaned against her hip, asking for pets.

"That's Bombón. He's nineteen years old but pretty spry." Logan perched on the edge of the white brick fireplace hearth. "You're here about Ramona."

He put on and readjusted the cap on his head again, then took it off. His knee was bouncing double-time. Sam tried a technique she'd learned way back in Yale Drama. She took deep breaths, emptying her mind of everything she *assumed* Logan was feeling, and asked her body to react to what Logan's body was telling her.

While she breathed, Bombón climbed on rickety legs into

Sam's lap and started trembling harder. The dog was naturally doing what Sam was asking her body to do—reacting to Logan's fear.

Everything in her body, in the dog's trembles, told Sam that this young man was afraid. Not nervous. Petrified.

Of what? Of whom?

"We are here about Ramona," Bex said. "And we're short on time, so I'm just going to dive right in, if that's okay with you?"

Logan nodded.

"Are you aware that she didn't show up at the studio on Monday?"

"Yeah. I wasn't there, but I did hear that from another one of the PAs."

"As far as we can tell, no one has seen Ramona since Friday night." Bex paused, watching Logan for a reaction. He nodded again, then rubbed his palms on his knees. Bombón was shaking like a leaf. "Did you know that already, too?"

"I didn't, because I left. The job. Nobody told me. But today one of the other *Howling* PAs gave me the heads-up she talked with your sister, so I knew Frankie was trying to confirm Ramona's transpo on Friday. Frankie left me a message. She tried to pull the manifest from Friday, and it wasn't there. I didn't guess Frankie's message would be followed by a visit from you two, but here you are." He gave Bex a self-effacing smile. The small dog trembled on Sam's thighs, craning its nose as high as it could to smell her chin and the area around her mouth.

There was nothing overtly sinister about this young man, with his cheerful home and his well-loved dog, but Sam felt more than uneasy. She felt certain something wasn't *right*.

"Here we are," Bex agreed cheerfully. "You want to tell us what the hell is going on?"

Logan blinked. The dog put both paws on Sam's shoulder and stared into her eyes. "Ye-e-eah." The crack in Logan's voice made Bombón whine. "I fucked up. I didn't want to get fired for fucking up, because then I'd never get another PA job. But I couldn't figure out how to fix it, so I took the manifests from Friday." He shook his head. "It's bad, I know. It's so bad. Monday morning when I was supposed to be at work, I called in to resign. I said it was too hard with the baby. They were nice about it. Made me feel worse. It was almost a relief when Frankie called me. It's a chance to come clean about what I did with the studio."

He scrubbed his palms over his knees again. There was a hole in the armpit of his T-shirt. He shot a quick glance at Bex, who raised her eyebrows. "Go ahead," she said. "Come clean. It will be good practice."

The air gusted out of him. "Okay. Yeah. Well, I was taking roll call on the vans. The shoot went late. I'd been up all night Thursday with Olivia, and I was barely keeping it together through the set strike. I get to Ramona's name on the list. She'd come up the mountain in the morning in the same van as Chad and Sloan, so I go to that van. They tell me she's going to be riding down in a different van, the one Piper's in. Without even checking, I mark Ramona's roll call in Piper's van. But then I get myself together and go to Piper's van to officially mark Ramona on roll call, and the AD in Piper's van tells me no, Ramona isn't there. She has not been there. I go back to Chad and Sloan's van, and they tell me she *is* in their van now, sorry about the confusion, but she'd just stepped away by the trees to knock mud off her shoe. So I mark her present in Chad and Sloan's van, but I forget to remove Ramona from the roll call in Piper's van. Now Ramona's on the manifests twice. I fucked up." Logan's shoulders were tight. "I can't believe I'm saying this to Bex and Sam. I used to watch your show after I came home from school. *Craven's Daughter*. Badass. Didn't imagine I'd end up in the hot seat." He gave an unconvincing laugh that lifted the hackles on Bombón's neck.

"Logan." Bex's voice was firm. "When is the last time *you* saw Ramona? With your own eyes."

He cleared his throat. "Lunchtime Friday. I helped catering

pass out the box lunches. Ramona had ordered a vegetarian box. Those were the ones I was passing out. I directly handed a boxed lunch to her. She said thank you. She asked how Olivia was doing. After that, she was shooting through the afternoon."

"What about after the shoot?" Sam asked. "You never saw Ramona after the shoot?"

The room dimmed. Low thunderclouds had rolled in, and Sam heard a rumble of thunder. Logan lifted and put back on his hat, pulling down the bill, throwing his eyes into shadow. "No. I didn't. I saw her at lunch. Then I didn't see her again."

Sam gently stroked Bombón's back until he settled and laid down on her lap. A portentous calm had settled over her. Behind it, in the back of her mind, the thoughts she'd been trying not to think since Frankie called had begun howling. "You didn't see her get out of a van in the studio's parking garage?"

"No." Logan looked out the front window at the rain. The miserable shape of his mouth made his chin pucker. "Chad told me she'd already got in Sloan's car. He was taking her home from the studio's parking garage. I didn't see Sloan either. I fucked up. I know. I know it. We learn not to let the talent keep us from doing our jobs. They teach us to do what we need to do, even if they don't like it. But it isn't easy. Not when it's someone like those guys."

Sam heard the patter of rain on concrete. Her headache throbbed back to life as the facts lined themselves up for examination.

Logan had not seen Ramona in Piper's van.

He had not seen her in Chad and Sloan's van.

He had not seen her in the studio's parking garage.

He had not seen her in Sloan's car.

Piper had not seen Ramona in the parking garage.

Both Piper and Logan had been told, *by Chad*, that Ramona was in the van, and she'd gotten a ride home. But Colin had never seen her come home on the cameras. No one had entered the house.

Not a single person Bex and Sam had spoken to had seen Ramona Watts since Friday afternoon.

The thunder rumbled again, much louder. In the kitchen, the baby started to cry as lightning strobed the front window and the sky opened up.

"For fuck's sake," Sam said over the hammering rain. "Is Ramona still on that mountain?"

We Won't Stop Until They Find Her

Sam never drank coffee after noon, but she was grateful for the huge ceramic mug full of steaming French press that Fergus pressed into her hands.

She'd cracked open the door to Bex's back patio so that she could watch the rain churn up the surface of the pool. "Is it ever going to quit coming down? I don't remember it raining this much in May."

"Any given day this month, there's about a sixteen percent chance of rain." Her brother's smile was sad. "But I hear what you're saying."

They'd made Logan give them a ride back here. It was the PA's decision to stick around. He wanted to help, and he had useful contacts. Logan and Bex's sisters had been working their way through a list of *Howling* cast and crew who'd been on Mount Baldy Friday, asking everyone when the last time was that they'd seen Ramona. They weren't finished. They were being thorough. But a clear pattern had already emerged.

No one had seen Ramona in the parking garage.

No one had ridden down with her in a van.

These were the facts that had finally enabled Ramona's parents and the detective they'd been working with to activate the full resources of the LAPD.

"I still don't understand why LAPD can't bring Sloan and Chad in for questioning," Sam complained. She and Bex had spoken to the detective to provide a quick summary of what they knew. They were supposed to go to the station in the morning to be interviewed. The detective had assured them the LAPD was doing everything in its power, and rescue teams were launching a search of the location shoot site.

With this, Bex and Sam had been dismissed.

"They don't have evidence yet that anything's happened to her," Fergus said. "Without it, they can't compel someone to talk who's lawyered up. They have to know what they're dealing with first. For now, it means the focus has to stay on finding Ramona."

The late afternoon light was starting to fade. The rain reduced visibility to near zero. Search and rescue would be limited in what they could do tonight, but they were still up there, looking.

"What are the chances, Ferg?" Sam let out a shaky breath. "It's been five days."

He leaned his shoulder against the wall beside her and looked out at the hills. "I've known search and rescue folks. They're experienced outdoors people who can operate in nearly any conditions. They know where to start looking, which helps narrow the parameters."

"Sure, but if the crew just left Ramona behind close to where the vans were parked, she'd have called a car or hitched a ride back by now. Something bad happened. What are the odds, if Ramona didn't die from whatever was done to her, that she's still alive now?"

"It's hard to say. Overnight temperatures up there are survivable. It's rocky and steep, with a lot of abrupt changes in the terrain that can make it disorienting. Looking at the map Frankie got her hands on, they were shooting in an area near the river where there's a little more ground cover. If Ramona's mobile and conscious—if she's not in shock from a serious injury—she likely could have found or made a shelter and be in better shape. But on Baldy, the rain will change the terrain quite a bit. It might reveal waterways that weren't there when it's dry. It will make some areas impassable." He swallowed. "The rain means she can potentially collect fresh water that's safer to drink, but no doubt she's cold and hungry."

"She's a petite woman in her fifties in extremely poor weather conditions, without food or clean water, wearing no more than a shirt and pants and a light jacket. If she had an injury to her head or is bleeding a lot—"

"—her survival would be a miracle delivered by freak favorable conditions. Like if she was able to make an effective tourniquet and had water or an energy bar. Head injury scares me, always, when it comes to outdoor activities. Our brains swell fast. We can't recover from losing oxygen or from the kinds of traumatic brain injuries that are possible out there."

"But Macie says Ramona is fit and self-reliant. She's a gardener. Maybe she would know what she could safely eat." Sam felt herself grasping at straws. She rested her head against the doorjamb.

"Sammy. Look at me." Fergus pushed against her arm, his tone firm enough that she lifted her head. When she turned to face him, he clasped both of her shoulders in his hands. His fingers were firm through her fuzzy sweater. "Help is on that mountain because of you and Bex. The information you found out is what sent help to Ramona. You haven't slept. Barely ate. Search and rescue will be just as tenacious."

"I know, but—"

"You *don't* know. I'm telling you. You've done everything you can."

When she looked into her brother's hazel eyes, Sam could see how deep his certainty went. It helped. She didn't believe him, but it helped anyway. She managed a weak smile. "How much do you want to get in your truck and drive up there, though? Dad took us on so many camping trips. I feel like we trained our whole childhood for this moment."

"I wouldn't be much use. The experts aren't going to let civilians on the mountain in the dark if they can help it. All they need is to lose someone else. And you left my truck in Malibu. But yeah, of course I want to beat through the bushes yelling, 'Ramona Watts!' until my voice gives out."

Once, when Sam was around thirteen, her dad had taken them on a camping trip in southern Oregon, where they'd gone whitewater rafting on the Deschutes River. In the middle of a rapid, Sam had been flipped out of the raft and into the water. She got caught in a current, what the rafting guide later called a "hole," that pulled her under and wouldn't let her go.

Fergus was the one who'd jumped into the water to save her.

She'd forgotten about that.

"Look, I know it feels like the next step is physically finding this woman," he said. "But the reason I've stayed relevant in outdoor recreation is because I am anxious and methodical. I'm obsessed with the newest safety equipment. I hire people who are just like me. If you want to paraglide off a cliff without so much as breaking a fingernail, I'm your guy. But when every minute counts, you want the person who knows what to do in the worst-case scenario and when even the worst-case scenario goes tits up."

Sam knew he was right.

She also knew she would have nowhere to put the screaming energy roaring through her body until Ramona was found.

She looked over at Logan on the phone. His face was so pale, he looked gray. She'd always thought that was a figure of speech. Guilt was riding him hard.

But it wasn't really his fault, was it? As much as Sam wanted to find Ramona, there were two people who had never wanted her to be found. At *least* two people. Chad and Sloan had lied about Ramona's being in the van. What had they done to her? What else had they lied about?

And were they the ones who'd planted the Star Spy item and posted fake pictures on Ramona's Instagram? Had they stolen her phone to do it?

But wouldn't that mean Haris would have seen Ramona's location tracking turn on, even briefly, around when those photos were posted?

What had happened to her phone?

Had Bex and Sam really done everything possible? The LAPD detective strongly implied they should hunker down and let the professionals take over, but until Ramona was found there was no *crime*. Without a crime, the LAPD wouldn't begin an investigation.

If there was no investigation, there was technically nothing for Sam and Bex to obstruct by asking the questions Sam still wanted answers to.

Most likely, the search team wouldn't find Ramona until the morning. They *would* find her in the morning.

That left the rest of the night. Hours and hours until dawn.

"Bexley!" Sam turned and shouted into the dining room.

Bex had been pacing back and forth, flipping through the pages of her notebook. "Yeah?" Her cheeks were red-hot. The tension around her eyes and mouth was awful to see.

"If we can't help find Ramona on that mountain, maybe you and I should figure out what happened to her *before* she was left behind. I want to know who planted the Star Spy piece and how those pictures from the Maldives got on her account. I want to paint an entire picture in oils of Ramona's life that led to her getting left behind so we can hand the LAPD a fat report in the morning. And tell StudioHonor who to fire on Friday, because it's sure as hell not going to be Ramona."

"Fuck, yes. I've got an idea." Bex jogged over to Vic, who had just hung up a phone call and was wrapped up in one of her plush hoodies. She had been taking the turn of events incredibly hard. Sam was worried about her.

"I know you want to help," Bex said to her sister. "I have something only you can do. I need you to raise an army."

Sam sat in a chair in Piper Redwood's pool cabana—or, more accurately, her parents' pool cabana. There were young people everywhere. Every one of them wore something that sparkled or showed skin or boasted a label. Everyone's hair was stylist-casual in a glossy way and their makeup breathtaking. But the expressions on their faces were grimly determined.

Bex had told Vic they needed an army. What she'd meant was this entourage: a crew to carry out counterintelligence and analysis more powerful than the machinations of men still pushing the same buttons of power they'd been pushing for thirty years. Bex and Sam had enlisted these digitally savvy young minds to ferret out who was responsible for the Star Spy item and the Maldives fakes. They required their communication skills and their ability to triumph even while being underestimated.

Vic's thumbs on her phone had never moved faster, and within the hour Sam and Bex were in Beverly Hills, in Piper's parents' cabana, with their army, dressed in their sparkles, deploying the resources of their combined furor, which was considerable. They also had a security guy, a driver, and Colin Worth, who'd called Sam up and asked what he could do. Colin was here to bear witness and represent his friend while Macie stayed with Ramona's parents. Vic, Frankie, and Logan were still at Bex's house, reaching out to the remaining cast and crew of *The Howling* for any crumbs of information that might help the search team.

A young man with shiny gold extensions braided into his long hair walked up to where Sam sat as still as possible so that the current star of a wildly popular BBC Regency romance show could finish covering her face with setting spray and testing the lace edge of her brunette wig.

Bex and Sam would be in disguise tonight.

It had been almost too easy. Vic's crew, and their crews, leaned on Christian to host a party. Piper had a friend who'd once had Sloan slide into her DMs, and this person was willing to follow up and invite Sloan to the Swan mansion. Sam had scarcely been able to follow the rapid-fire developments, but she knew the details didn't matter. What mattered was that all of Vic's friends wanted to do the right thing for Ramona.

The right thing at this moment involved a party at the Swan attended by Christian, Sloan, and hopefully, Chad.

"It's go time," the young man said. "Bex is ready. Sloan is already there, holding court with our forward line. We need to go before he gets handsy."

Sam nodded and stood, glad for the coverage of her designer tracksuit on such a cool night. The sneakers from someone's elite footwear collection were keeping her weary feet warm and dry.

The goal of the Swan Mansion Party Mission was to gather as much information, digital or otherwise, as possible. Maybe Christian was in league with Chad and Sloan and digital receipts could be procured from either Christian or Sloan's devices. Maybe there were other players in the circle Sam and Bex still didn't know about. Maybe Christian and Sloan would talk openly at the party, or even argue in front of their spies. Maybe they would slip away and someone could listen in. Maybe, maybe, maybe.

If there was anything to find, Piper and her crew would find it and report back.

Meanwhile, Sam and Bex would lay low, disguised as Piper's friends, and gather any information that the others might not think to collect.

If Chad didn't show, Plan B was to track him down and throw everything they had at him. But they trusted Ashleigh enough to heed her advice about Chad. They would avoid him until they saw no other way forward in their investigation.

Colin approached and held out a pair of oversized sunglasses to Sam. "These are from Ramona's collection. A gift from Jackie O. Ramona always said they were lucky. They'll go with your party look."

Sam smiled. "Thank you. They'll also disguise the fine lines around my eyes that I refuse to get Botoxed."

Colin tried to smile back but had to firm his chin against trembling. "Christian never uses Face ID on his devices. He doesn't trust it. All his passwords are 6969."

"Why are old people so weird?" Golden Braids wrinkled his nose. "Not, like, *you* guys. Not, like, *genuinely* old people, I don't think. But, like, old people who think they're still not."

Colin put his hand on Golden Braids's shoulder. "A conversation for another day."

"Come on my channel," he replied. "We can talk about real Hollywood."

This is real Hollywood, Sam thought. *It has always been like this.*

Bex came over. Sam had seen how hair and makeup could transform Bex before, on stage and on screen, but she wasn't sure she would know this woman if they had a conversation in line at Whole Foods. Her wig was short, blond, waved in finger curls with edges. Bex's eyebrows were gone, slicked under makeup in favor of dark, stylized wings with lots of glitter. Her lush mouth was disguised with an exaggerated cupid's bow, and she was dressed for action in tuxedo pants and shirt. She looked like a Manic Panic pixie dream butch and fit right in with the glittering New Hollywood crew.

It wasn't unaffecting.

"Ready?" Bex's voice was getting hoarse from all the commands she'd been dispatching. She made a formidable general. She was going to have to go on total voice rest for a week, wearing one of her warm neck wraps and drinking the foul-smelling tea that her voice coach made.

"I am. We'll stay back at the perimeter of the party. The first objective is to get access to Christian's phone or devices for intel. If there's nothing about Ramona on there, we can rule him out as a suspect. Sloan is trickier, but everyone has instructions to make sure the party goes all night. That gives us time to keep the players in our Venus flytrap while we find out whatever we can. Tonight, L.A. belongs to us. The media is on to us, Bex and Sam back together again. We've been seen all over town. But in disguise—"

"—we find out what happened, once and for all." Bex grinned.

The other partygoers piled in with the driver to meet up with those already at the mansion. Sam and Bex got into the car Colin had loaned them for the night, a nondescript electric hatchback that Sam felt was particularly freeing.

When they walked up from the end of the drive to the grand entrance, the house was spilling light all over the grounds. Despite the rain, a few of Sam and Bex's undercover partygoers were outside standing under the portico. Vaping, but actually waiting for them in order to whisk them inside.

Once they were in, they were led down a dark hallway to what looked like a study by a young pop star who had recently won three Grammys. "Wait here," she said. "Someone already has info for you."

She melted back into the crowd and returned moments later with the daughter of the Dodgers' right fielder.

"Guys." The new arrival stepped close to Sam and Bex, still holding the pop star's hand. "Sloan has scratches on his neck. *Fingernail scratches.*"

Bex frowned. "That's concerning. But I suppose there's no way to tell if they're from a scuffle on Baldy, from filming a tough scene, or if he got them in a bar fight last night."

"Wait." Sam pulled off her sunglasses and dove her hand into her silky tracksuit pocket for her phone. "There might be a way."

Sam went to her photo album. Bex looped her arm through Sam's and inched closer. She smelled like hairspray and waxy-floral cosmetics. Like show business. Like *hers*. "The pictures you sent me from the parking lot!" Bex said. "Of course."

Sam found them. She tapped, pinched, and zoomed. "There they are! Bright red scratches. Fresh. And look!" She turned the phone around. "Chad has them, too, on his forearms. If *only* Chad or *only* Sloan had fresh scratches, the injuries could be chalked up to something like the bar fight you mentioned," Sam said. "But the odds are slim that they would both randomly be scratched up at the same time for an innocent reason."

"I'll tell Piper to connect with wardrobe and makeup, or even an assistant or dresser who was on the mountain. Someone would have taken their costumes. Someone would know about the scratches. Have seen them. Maybe Chad or Sloan gave an explanation for where they came from."

"Good. And text Vic to reach out to wardrobe at *Theomina*. Whoever put Chad into his chroma-key suit might have seen his scratches, too. We want to confirm and document as much as we can."

"We're going back out there." The singer pulled the baseball player's daughter back into the party.

Sam looked at Bex as the importance of what they'd just learned started to sink in through the jittery buzz of her adrenaline-and-fatigue-soaked brain. "She might have fought them. Ramona."

Bex bit her lip, nodding. "I hope she's still fighting."

Sam shoved her sunglasses back on. "You up for some spycraft?"

"You bet."

They leapfrogged from group to group, and the crowd seamlessly moved around them to keep them from being noticed. The party was getting bigger as rumors flew through town of something interesting going down at the Swan. Sam used the advantage of Ramona's Jackie O sunglasses to peer around for Sloan, but she didn't spot him. She hadn't seen Christian, either. She really needed to know if Christian was involved, and if he was, how deeply and why. Could the men of the Ice Crew have decided *together* to hurt Ramona? Why? What was at the bottom of all this?

"Sam," Bex whispered. Her voice didn't register at first. Sam was looking past the bar, certain she'd spotted a fedora. "Sam!" Bex squeezed her hand.

She turned to look, and Bex pointed to a gallery wall over a white grand piano. "Third row. Right in the middle."

Sam's belly flipped when she saw what Bex had spotted. "You're kidding me. It's nearly the same picture!"

The photograph showed a beautiful ocean view from a white balcony above the water. Marble sculptures held up the balcony railing. Here at the Swan, framed on the wall, was a view identical to the one that had been posted on Ramona's Instagram. Sam pulled out her phone and took several bursts of pictures.

"It must be Brinley Downs's place in the Maldives," Bex said. "That whole arrangement of photos on the wall looks like it's been up there for ages, and they're all pictures of properties and parties at those properties. No way are those *Christian's* candids of a lawn party in Palm Springs with a young Frank Sinatra."

"We really need to look at his phone," Sam murmured. "Or a laptop, tablet, anything."

"At least six people are working on it," Bex said. "If the tech Christian uses is anywhere in this mansion, someone will find it, but clearly he's involved *somehow*. He didn't want anyone to look for Ramona. He must have posted those Instagram shots from the Maldives on Ramona's account literally *as we were leaving his house* after we came here to ask him questions. I think we should have people look for *any* phone. What if he has Ramona's?"

"Unlikely, but who knows? We need to be more careful if we're pretty sure he's in league with Chad and Sloan. He wouldn't notice us at a glance in these disguises, but if he talks to us or gets close, he will."

Sam thought she caught another glimpse of Sloan's fedora and started to lead them in the opposite direction. "Come with me. Hurry."

She was focused on Bex, whose cooperation was never easy to obtain without an explanation, when she smacked face-first into hot, stinky silk.

"Watch it, kid."

Sam glanced up. *Fuck.*

It was Christian, wearing a silk robe over board shorts. He had a piece of yarn around his neck strung with what looked like gummy peach rings but were probably edibles. He held a bottle of Scotch by the neck.

"Pardon." Sam used her best British accent, holding tight to Bex's hand, already pulling away from him.

"No worries. Hey. Wait." The tone of Christian's voice was suddenly sober.

Sam dared to glance at him. He was focused on her face. Her eyes. "Those are Ro's sunglasses."

Then, as Sam watched in horror, his expression contorted with animosity.

"What the actual raw *fuck* are you two doing here? And why the fuck are you wearing Ro's sunglasses?"

Christian hauled them both down the same hallway where they had discovered the scratches and then pointed the way into the study. The noise of the party got briefly quieter as Sam and Bex's people realized what was happening, but Sam caught Piper's eyes and shook her head.

Don't blow your cover.

Piper signaled something to the security detail who'd come

with her, a former Navy Seal who worked full-time for Piper and her family. It made Sam feel a lot better to know that he and an entire mansion of partygoers had their backs.

Christian slammed his Scotch bottle on the green-leather-covered desk and glowered at them. "What the hell is this? I don't remember sending either one of you an invitation."

"We're here for the same reason we came the last time." Sam gave him FBI Agent Henri Shannon's best grim stare. She didn't know if it was as effective while wearing a tracksuit and a long brunette wig with barrel curls.

"Then you'll have to leave with the same thing I told you last time. I don't know what you're so worked up about. Ramona does this. She's in the wind."

Bex stepped to him. "Like the wind in the Maldives? Or the wind on Mount Baldy? Ramona often heads off to the properties of her estranged friends? Was that before or after she signed autographs in the middle of L.A.?"

"Mount Baldy?" Christian looked down at Bex like he was trying to get her into better focus. Sam would chalk his peculiar expression up as a response to their disguises if it weren't for the sudden uncertainty creeping into the back of her mind.

How was he involved? Why hadn't Bex's aggressive questions swung this volatile man instantly to the defensive?

Christian sounded authentically confused.

Bex's phone made a noise. She pulled it out of the pocket of her trousers without taking her eyes off Christian. When she glanced at the screen, a storm cloud moved over her expression, and Sam's limbs filled with molten lead. "What is it?" she asked.

"The search team found blood near the filming site." Bex brought her glare back to Christian. "And a smashed phone."

Sam could hardly pull enough to move over her rage-frozen vocal cords to speak. "She was your *friend*," she choked out at Christian. "What did she do to deserve getting hurt while she was working on that mountain? Was it just because she held you accountable for your behavior with Colin, so you decided to sic your old buddies on her? Did you dangle some prize in front of them? Money? You might as well start talking. Everyone at this party is here because of Ramona."

Christian's head shook slowly from side to side, trying to get his thoughts to surface like the die in a magic eight ball. "Where's Ramona?" His voice was hoarse with worry.

Sam's creeping uncertainty came back.

Then she remembered that once upon a time, Christian Stanstedt had been a decent actor. "It's disgusting to pretend you don't know what I'm talking about."

His jaw clenched. "*Where* is Ramona, Sam? Where is she? There's blood? What the fuck is going on?"

Bex scoffed. "Don't pretend that—"

"I posted the Maldives pictures," he spit out. "You got me. Fine. But I didn't hurt her. I wouldn't. I posted them to help her."

"How is posting pictures that keep people from looking for Ramona going to help her when she's missing?" Bex asked.

"I didn't think she was actually *missing*! Why would I think that? I wanted her to be able to live her life! I was trying to get ahead of some fucked-up blind item saying she was wandering around a mesa doing drugs with cult members!"

"What?" Bex's question rang through the room. Sam's stomach felt too tight, her breathing wrong, but her sense that something was off the rails had become a solid belief.

Christian wasn't acting.

He held up a finger. "Give us a minute. Give me a fucking *minute*." He started pacing. "Start further back. Tell me from the beginning. Please."

Sam crossed her heavy arms to keep from leaning against something. "Ramona had a shoot on Friday. It was on Baldy, on location. With your buddies, Chad and Sloan, as guest stars. She didn't show up for work on Monday morning. Everyone has been looking for her ever since. Right now, West Valley Search and

Rescue is on Baldy in the dark, in the rain, trying to find her after van manifests and questioning a ton of people proved she never came off the mountain. We didn't know that until tonight, because, again, *your* buddies lied to the production assistant. They left her up there. And the scratches on Chad and Sloan's arms and necks, combined with this news"—Sam coughed and, to her horror, realized she was choking on tears—"about the blood, and her smashed-up phone, means that not only did they leave her there, they hurt her. And *you've* been making sure no one looks for her with the blind item and the Maldives photos."

"Why didn't you tell me?" Christian's body collapsed against the desk. He'd gone pale, with red spots on his cheekbones. "When you came here the first time, why didn't you tell me what was going on?"

"We did!" Sam protested.

"No, you fucking didn't! *You* said she didn't show up on Monday for work!"

"And time-date stamps prove that you understood well enough," Bex put in, "since you posted the Maldives pictures right after we left."

"I understood that she didn't go to work, not that she was *missing*! Ro sometimes *does* need a break. I believed it when I told you I thought she'd just taken off for a while. Why wouldn't I? I had no idea Chad and Sloan were shooting an episode with her the week before! If I had known that . . ."

"Then what?" Bex asked. "If you had known that, then what?"

"I'd have fucking strangled Sloan and Chad is what I would've done! But you two were too busy playing detective to be straight with someone who could have helped."

"We were supposed to look for help from the guy who Ramona had to cut off because of how bad he treated Colin?" Bex angrily swiped a tear off her face. "Unlikely."

Christian closed his eyes. He looked his age. Maybe older. He'd lived fast and rough the last several years. "I care about Ramona. I always have. She was a real friend to me when I was a newcomer to the Ice Crew. It wasn't easy, and just as I got comfortable—just as I thought I might have real friends in this town who were interested in more than my family connections—I was stupid and decided to come out to everyone. Chad and Sloan started making my life hell. Luckily, I didn't have to deal with them much after what happened with Juliette, but Ro and I were tight for a long time. Look, I don't make good decisions—although that's none of your goddamned business. But I would never hurt her."

Sam couldn't read Bex's expression. Her own body told her Christian was telling the truth, but so many things didn't make sense. She hadn't even had a chance to process what search and rescue found, much less worry about what else they might find before morning.

What did she *know*? Chad and Sloan had deliberately left Ramona on the mountain. They'd lied and pretended she was in the van, then lied and pretended Sloan drove her home.

Just like they'd left Juliette in a dinghy and then lied about how it happened.

Don't say shit.

But she can't swim.

Sam shook her head. "But *why* did you think that your Instagram post would get ahead of rumors? How could pictures from the Maldives possibly help Ramona?"

Christian grabbed the bottle and started to bring it to his mouth, then set it back on the desk. "Chad and Sloan came back around here a few months ago. There were a lot of mea culpas. Talk about how we were young and stupid. I kept it casual. Hardly talked to them much at all. Then Ro and I imploded, and—listen, I've been angry, but not at her. Just angry. I'd have kicked me to the curb for what I did, too. But then Chad and Sloan are back here, talking shit about her. I knew Chad hated her, but Sloan surprised me. He had been friends with her, too.

But I didn't care. It felt good to moan about all the ways she sucks with those guys. I'd fallen off the wagon, messed up the best thing I ever had, and got eighty-sixed by the one person who'd put up with me longer than anybody else. I was ready to numb with whatever was available, including pure meanness. But then . . ." Christian took a drink from the bottle.

"Then *what,* Christian?" Bex's voice was a sledgehammer.

"They started confiding in me. As if I'd think what they had to tell me was funny. Turns out, they were the ones responsible for Ramona's reputation."

"How?" Sam's middle had dropped away, leaving her sick.

"The rumors. The 'insider' leaks. It was them all these years. They didn't tell me outright like that. More in inference. Bits and pieces. Paying low-rent paparazzi sleaze, paying hackers. Doctoring pictures. Mirroring her phone. A tracker on her car."

"That's stalking," Sam said.

"It's fucking vile. I called her up to warn her. She'd told me not to call anymore, so I wasn't surprised she didn't answer. She didn't call back, but I told her in my message to stay away from them. They weren't her friends."

Sam remembered Macie telling them about Ramona getting a message that had upset her. Ramona hadn't wanted to talk about it. Was this the message she'd meant?

Christian wiped the corners of his mouth. "Then I find out that Chad and Sloan were working on a big movie. Franchise shit. And I figured out why they'd sought me out again after ignoring me for so long."

"Not your personality," Sam said.

"No, it's always fucking money, isn't it? 'Chris, you've got the connections. Chris, maybe your production company could invest.' I'm hearing this . . . a week ago? Little longer. They weren't around last week, I guess because they were filming this episode on Ramona's show that no one told me about. But I'd already decided I was done with those fucking leeches. Then you guys show up. I didn't think Ramona was in real danger, but I was definitely worried Chad and Sloan were getting up to more of their shit. That's why I did the Maldives thing on her Instagram. They'd given me her login when they showed me how they fucked with her. I figured if I made it look like Ramona was on a tropical vacation, it would mean *they* couldn't make shit up about her this time. Whatever they planned to say she was doing when she was a no-show at work, they wouldn't be able to say it. *That's* what I meant when I said I was trying to help her."

"What about Star Spy?" Sam asked.

"What about it?"

"The same day you posted the Maldives pictures, there was also a blind item that Ramona was in L.A. signing autographs."

"That I did not do."

Sam's vision narrowed to a point at the same time that Bex grabbed her elbow, and then all she could feel was the pressure of Bex's fingers and the freefall of what it meant that Christian hadn't planted the Star Spy story.

It must have been Chad or Sloan. They'd done it before, and other things like it, misrepresenting Ramona's movements and actions to give the public a false impression that she was unreliable. To give the industry that impression. Even Sam had believed it.

But this time they hadn't fed out a story that put Ramona out of town, bombed out of her mind and stargazing nude. They'd gone out of their way to make the world believe she was *here*, in downtown Los Angeles.

Because she wasn't. Because she'd never come down from Mount Baldy. Their bodies told the story of a violent incident. The blood at the filming site. Her smashed phone.

They'd left her there, the same way they left Juliette on that dinghy surrounded by the fathomless Pacific Ocean. Left her there to die.

They'd had the means. They'd had the opportunity.

"Motive," Sam said aloud. "We need motive. We need to understand why they hurt Ramona. No one expected it. Ramona didn't."

"If she had, she might have tried to get out of working with them," Bex said, quickly catching on to Sam's train of thought. "Her agent has the clout to step to StudioHonor if that was what Ramona wanted. But she didn't, because Ramona didn't ask her to."

"No. She checked in on the insurance riders. That tells us she was uneasy about the location shoot, maybe, but not in fear for her life. Something changed at the last minute. We need to find out what it was, and the person who might know is Archie. He's the one who was coming to the set, keeping close enough by Ramona that Piper thought he was her boyfriend. He's the one who was digging up the past with the Ice Crew documentary."

"He wouldn't talk to us before," Bex said.

"No, but things have changed. Archie didn't know Ramona was left behind. He won't know about the search yet. I have to think he'll want to help once he understands how dire the situation is. We need to go back to Encino and tell him."

"It's after midnight." Bex glanced at Christian. "We're still trying to get Chad here. There's Sloan to talk to first. We have a whole plan."

Sam shook her head. "If we don't pin down motive—if we don't have some solid evidence of what really happened and who did what to who—then we're not going to be able to drag anything out of those two but another bullshit story. Chad will call down his lawyers to put up a wall we can't push past. We need something solid enough to pry them apart and make them turn on each other."

Christian lifted his hand, drawing their attention. He was still leaning against the desk, listening to them, but his posture was no longer insouciant. His eyes were alert. "I have bad news, ladies."

"What is it?" she asked.

"You're gonna have to trust me."

Bex wrinkled her nose. "Come again?"

Christian wrapped his robe around himself, and for one heartbeat, Sam could see how much distress he was in. "It's like you just said. What good are you two going to be here? *You're* not going to get anything off Sloan. He'll recognize you quicker than I did and clam right the fuck up. So go do your Nancy Drew shit. Find out everything you can from Archie. I'll keep the party going, make sure the booze and drugs go light except for Sloan. And I'll get Chad over here."

"Why, so you and Chad and Sloan can all take off together?" Bex put her hands on her hips. "You could flee the country and hole up somewhere we don't have an extradition treaty with, and Ramona will never have justice."

"I get why you don't believe me, but you're going to have to." Christian reached into the pocket of his robe and extracted his phone, which he held out to Sam. "Look through it if you want, but don't judge. There's nothing on there that puts me anywhere in the solar system of hurting Ramona. When Sloan showed up here tonight, I almost sent him home. I've been avoiding him. But one of these kids said he was supposed to be here for someone, so I let it slide."

Sam took the phone. It was a solid weight in her hand.

She checked in one more time with her intuition.

Her intuition informed her it was leaning hard in Christian's direction, as bizarre an ally as he made.

"I trust him," she told Bex. "It's on me if he fucks this one up, but I don't think he will."

Christian held up his fist for her to bump. She obliged him, touching her knuckles to his. "Solid, Farmer. Why *are* there so many under twenty-fives in my house tonight, by the way? I rolled with the reach-outs for a gathering, but I didn't realize I'd have to plan on a snack time and lifeguards. Is everyone out there really here for her? For Ramona?"

"Yeah," Sam said. "They are."

Christian nodded, slow. He seemed completely sober. Sam understood that he'd dropped a mask.

His mask made it easy to assume the worst of him. Now she was likely looking at who he really was—the Christian Stanstedt who Ramona had maintained a friendship with.

"Okay, then," he said. "Consider me their prisoner of war. I've just got to ride this out and lure Chad into the trap." He pushed his hand through his poetic hair. "You two go talk to Archie. Find out what happened so you can nail these guys. And when you see Ro." He coughed, then swallowed, and Sam noticed his eyes had filled. "*When* you see that girl alive and well, maybe you tell her I helped."

"Maybe," Bex said. "Or maybe you figure yourself out so she can trust you when *you* say it."

"Better. Yes. I'm going to get back out there. Take my phone. Give it to one of your spies. If you need to get a message to me, use the same number. I'm wearing my watch." He pulled up his robe sleeve to show them his smartwatch.

Sam looked at Bex. "Okay?"

"Yes," Bex said. "I'm the one who makes the plans. You're the one who reads people. If you vouch for him, I trust you."

"Sweet." Christian lurched his body off the desk. "After you." He gestured toward the door.

They followed him into the party, and Sam felt dozens of eyes on them. Piper made her way over.

"You found our host!" Piper shot a look at Bex and Sam that meant *Is everything okay?*

"And his phone!" Bex dangled it in front of her. "He's decided to help. Too much to explain, but keep the party going. Keep Sloan here. Get our people to look at his phone and find out whatever you can. Christian thinks he can get Chad to come, and we hope that by then we can spring this trap. Of course, if Christian doesn't help . . ."

Piper snatched the phone from Bex with a small, terrifying smile. "That's where my special friend comes in." She gestured with her head at her security detail.

"No worries, Piper. You're in charge. You know I know your mom?" Christian held eye contact with Piper. "When she was still acting, we did this experimental piece together at the Guthrie. She was sick as a dog the whole time. Turns out, it was because she was pregnant with you. Never seen someone so happy she was going to be a mother."

Piper's eyes went wide. "You're serious?"

"As a heart attack. I bet the two of you geek out together over all kinds of deep art shit. I can see you're a lot like her."

She shook her head. "Old people are incredibly confusing."

Christian laughed. "I confuse myself, Piper. Let's go sit somewhere that's not assaulting my eardrums, and you can tell me the ten ideas you probably already have to get Chad over here."

"Okay, then." Piper looked at Sam. "If we pull it off, I'll make sure my security guy keeps both Sloan and Chad here. I have total indemnity from his methods. My dad wrote the contract." Piper took Christian by the elbow. "Ready, old man?"

Sam watched as he pulled on the mask of a rich Hollywood washout. It really didn't look right on him anymore. She took Bex's hand, and they made their way to Colin's little car at the end of the drive, the music and light from the mansion dimming behind them. The rain had let up a little, but there was still enough drizzle that Sam could feel the products in her wig softening when she touched it.

As soon as she was seated behind the wheel, Sam's mind began unhelpfully flashing images of a rain-soaked Ramona limping through dense foliage. Curled up in fetal position in a pool of blood.

No. They would find her.

"Hey." Bex smiled at her and stroked her cheekbone with her thumb.

Before Sam could fully accept the comfort Bex was offering, a sudden burst of light made her rear back and squint. A vehicle pulled to a stop in front of them, much too close to the bumper of Colin's car.

"What the hell?" Bex said.

The headlights snapped off, and Sam watched Frankie jump out of Fergus's truck.

She opened her car door. Frankie ran around the front of the truck to crouch down in the rain next to her.

"They found Ramona. She's been shot."

Only a Hollywood Detective Could

Frankie clambered into the backseat of Colin's car to get out of the rain. "I don't know much." Her lips were bloodless, her breath coming short. "Macie got the call from Ramona's parents. Someone from search and rescue asked them to come in. The police only said where Ramona was being taken, so Macie and Ramona's parents are meeting them at the hospital. She's in critical condition."

"She's alive." Sam could feel her pulse in every part of her body. "Holy shit, she's alive."

Bex made a noise. She was crying, her makeup going everywhere. Maybe Sam was crying, too. She couldn't tell. There were so many emotions coursing through her.

"I know," Frankie said. "We came here as fast as we could. It didn't seem right to call. We didn't know if you knew anything new. We didn't want to talk to police if you were close to getting something important."

"She was *shot*?"

Hearing Bex say it again did nothing to blunt Sam's surprise.

"I heard that from one of the crew who helped the search team get to the right location. She didn't know anything more, just what she witnessed as they got Ramona out."

Sam made herself breathe. *Shot.* Shot on a *set*. That was never supposed to happen.

She and Bex had starred in a TV series that had guns in nearly every episode. Sam had heard stories of the tragic accidents and negligent horrors that had been perpetrated by prop guns, which were often real guns, unloaded or loaded with blanks. If there was one thing never permitted on a television set, it was an unauthorized gun.

But also, Bex and Sam had been part of a show where a coworker and friend died—not from a gunshot wound, but by being pushed through a gap in an on-location balcony to her death in the alley below. They were hauntingly familiar with this kind of tragedy, and they knew what it would be like in the confusing aftermath.

On-set deaths could linger in investigative limbo for years as studio execs pushed for them to be classified as "accidents." But what happened to Ramona on that mountain couldn't have been an accident. If she'd been shot as part of a scene gone wrong, she would have been airlifted out immediately in full view of the cast and crew. Instead, the only people who knew she'd been shot were the ones who shot her, *away* from the cast and crew. Intentionally. And they'd said nothing.

"I don't know how to tell you this, but it gets worse." Frankie ran her hand through her damp hair, making her curls stick up all over. "Actually, stay here. I'm going to grab Logan."

"Logan Widi? The production assistant?" Bex asked.

"You know another Logan?"

Sam experienced a spectral memory of Logan's dog trembling in her lap.

Yes. Logan Widi. Because the story he'd told them at his house hadn't completely explained what he was afraid of.

A gun, though. A gun might explain it.

Frankie dashed out of the car. When she opened the back door of Fergus's truck, the interior light came on, illuminating Sam's brother in the driver's seat with Vic beside him. Sam had never been so glad to see Fergus.

That was the unlikely moment when she felt, for the first time, her new family take shape.

Logan followed Frankie, and then they were both in the backseat of Colin's electric car.

"I'm going to the police," he said. "I want to tell you that first."

"You better tell us everything else right the fuck next," Bex snapped. "Why was there a gun on the set of *The Howling*? It's got monsters, but they don't fight them with guns. *Was* it a prop gun? Or an actual, unmodified, real gun, on a set? A set that crews and production assistants are responsible for. A gun makes noise!"

Logan held up both palms facing out. He let out a shaky breath. "I know, okay? I know. We drove up the mountain in the morning after the actors saw costuming. The assistant from costuming came with the on-location crew and had the final pieces for everyone to add once we got there. Talent had already been told to stay by their vans when we arrived, and costuming would come to them." Logan's knee hammered up and down as he spoke. "I was circulating between the vans, noting when each of the talent were fully in costume and could be seen by hair and makeup, who were set up in another area. I'm wearing a headset, with multiple people in my ear. I'm documenting."

Sam had been talent many times, monitored by Logans on location. A shoot could look like chaos from the outside, but most were tightly orchestrated.

"Chad was already with hair and makeup, but I needed to circulate back to Sloan, who was still at the van. When I approached, Sloan was standing just outside of it, with the slider door open. I could see he was ready, but he was messing with something, leaning over the seat. From where I was, I could see his whole body and the inside of the van, so I saw when he pulled a gun from a seat pocket on the back of his seat and shoved it, the gun, in one of those concealed carry holsters on his lower back."

"Motherfucker," Sam said, marveling.

Sloan Lennox really had brought a firearm to filming and concealed it on his person.

Ramona Watts really had been shot and left for dead in the wilderness.

"Why didn't you tell someone?" Bex asked. "Right then, why didn't you shout 'Gun on the set!' like you're supposed to?"

Logan winced. "Sloan caught me. He saw me see him. He came right for me and stood in front of me, close. Like, an inch." His hands closed into tight fists. "Look, I'm an A/V nerd. I grew up in Burlington, Vermont. My parents are hippie professors. I have three sisters. I've never been physically threatened in my life. Never. He grabbed the front of my vest in his fist. His face was right in my face. It was—it was horrible. You see something like that on TV and don't think anything of it, but when someone is nearly pulling you up off the ground by your clothes, and his nose is touching yours, and he's *angry* . . . I couldn't think."

"What happened after that?" Sam kept her voice easy.

"He did something with his knee that knocked my hip, hard. Made me lose my footing. When I almost fell down, he hauled me up again and kicked my foot back into place. He said, 'Fucking stay here and look at me,' like I'd tried to run away or something. Later, when I was home, I realized I had a knee-shaped bruise on my hip."

"Then what?"

Logan blinked a few times, fast. His cheeks were hectic pink. "He let go all at once. He shoved me back, and it was such a relief to get away from his body. He said, 'You didn't see shit, did you?' I don't know if answered him or just shook my head or what, but he said, 'Good.' Then he walked off."

"Keep going," Sam urged, because she could feel the pressure coming off Logan, pushing into her skin. There was more he wanted to say.

"This is where it gets bad."

Sam schooled her face. It was already so, so bad. "It's better if you tell us all the details you remember. Best for Ramona, her family and friends, for the show, for your work."

Logan twisted his hands together in his lap. "Later, after the shoot had wrapped and the trucks had been mostly packed and moved to let the vans through, I started documenting the talent and which van they entered. I finished with the background actors, and as I was going to the other vans Chad stopped me. He slapped me on the back and said, 'Thanks for everything today. Check your Paypal.' Then he went toward the vans. I looked at my Paypal on my phone." Logan's whole body was shaking. "There was fifty thousand dollars in there. The memo on the payment said, 'For your wife and baby. I hope mama gets her papers soon.' Here's the thing." His voice cracked. "No one knows my wife's documentation is up in the air. Not even the hospital where she had our baby. She works from home for a data analysis company in Mexico City, and she's on my insurance. I have no idea how he found that out. I never even talked to him before that. How could he have found out about my wife? Or what my Paypal email is? It was even scarier than Sloan hurting me and threatening me. The idea that someone could so easily discover those things and use them against me. Threaten my family. All I could think about was my wife getting detained. Separated from our baby. No way to reach us. Deported. You know the horror stories."

Sam couldn't hear anything over the sound of her blood whooshing in her ears as she considered the enormity of what Chad was willing to do to get his way. It made her dizzy.

Juliette. Ramona. Decades of lies.

That soul-sucking beast.

Bex was shaking her head in disbelief. "When it comes out about Ramona being shot, everyone's going to circle their wagons, just like Cineline did when Jen died on location for *Craven's Daughter*. *The Howling* and StudioHonor won't want to answer to their insurance carriers, much less to stockholders. It will be impossible to get at the truth."

Ramona would be at the hospital by now. Nurses and doctors and staff would know about her condition and how she got there. Word would be spreading, person to person, that Ramona Watts had been found shot on Mount Baldy. The tower of NDAs that got printed in the morning would be taller than the animatronic monster on *The Howling*'s set. Whatever inside advantage Bex and Sam had gained over the past few days by knowing more than the people around them would be lost when the rest of the world caught up and the police investigation took over.

Their time was running out.

Sam turned back to Logan. "I'm sorry about your wife, I really am. But you need to get out your phone and call your lawyer to help her while my brother drives you to the closest police station to tell your story. If you don't have a lawyer for your wife, tell Fergus to call mine and get him on retainer."

"I can do that," Fergus said. His voice came from right beside her. Sam hadn't realized he'd left the truck. He'd probably come to back her up as soon as Logan got in her car.

Ready to jump in the rapids for her and hers.

"Fergus, I'm sending you the recording I just made of Logan's conversation with Sam," Bex said. "Sometimes you need more than your notebook."

Fergus raised his eyebrows at Logan. "Okay?"

The young man let out a shaky breath. "I'll call on the way. We have an immigration lawyer. I can't lose her."

His face broke, and Fergus nodded. "Come on. We need to go." He leaned close to Sam. "You be careful. I mean it."

"I know. I will."

"Is Vic okay?" Bex looked toward Fergus's truck. "Does she need anything?"

Fergus smiled as Logan appeared beside him. "She's focused on being command central. She has both of you on location tracking. She has a group chat with the army. She's missing nothing. Where are you two headed?"

They had to find the *why* of all this. If they didn't, Chad, Sloan, and the studio would all be pointing fingers at each other. They couldn't count on Ramona being able to tell her story. Even if she was okay, she might not know why they'd shot her. Trauma could obscure her memory of what happened.

"Encino," Sam said. "Let's go talk to Archie."

Sam and Bex stood on the wide porch of Archie Blasingame's mission-style home. The rain had broken, but wind had taken its place, and his leafy street was filled with shadows that projected onto the pale stucco of his house. Just as Bex lifted her hand to push the brass button set into a flower of Spanish tiles, the door opened.

"What are you doing here?" Archie was in sweatpants and a battered Howard University T-shirt. The sleep attire made him no less intimidating than the blazer he'd worn the last time they spoke to him at the Gymboree.

Sam put her shoulders back. "Search and rescue found Ramona. She's alive but in rough shape. She'd been shot and left for dead. We don't know who pulled the trigger, but we have a witness saying Sloan had a gun on him, and Chad knew and helped cover it up."

Archie slumped against the doorframe. "My God." He took off his heavy glasses and ran a hand over his eyes, then opened the door wider. "Come in out of the weather."

They followed him through a formal sitting room to the kitchen, where there was a large booth. A tall woman in a full-coverage robe and a red silk bonnet came through a doorway at the back of the kitchen. "Archie?"

"It's Bexley Simon and Sam Farmer. About Ramona." He gestured toward her for Bex and Sam's benefit. "This is my wife, Jasmine."

"What happened to Ramona?" She turned on another light in the kitchen and leaned against the counter.

"Those assholes shot Ramona and left her for dead." Archie's gruff, precise London accent made it difficult to read his mood. He looked at Bex. "Go through it. Efficiently."

She already had her notebook out, with a freshly bulleted list she'd made on the drive to Encino. "Here's what we know," she said. "Macie told us Ramona feels responsible for Juliette's death. You're strongly associated with that era of Ramona's life. You've been seen with her on set lately and went looking for her at home the first morning anyone noticed she was gone. You sent us to Kessler, and he told us you're working on a release of the *Ice* documentary, which Colin Worth told us Ramona was involved with. Given how much the Ice Crew's past is tangled up with the present, we're wondering if you might know anything about Ramona's state of mind leading up to Friday, and especially about anything she might have said or done to, let's say, *activate* Chad or Sloan. Or both of them."

"*Mercy*," Jasmine breathed. She stood for several seconds with her hand to her chest, thinking. Then her jawline firmed. "I'm going to make some coffee. Warm up some sweet rolls."

"Thank you." Sam realized how little she'd slept, taken the time to eat, anything, since they'd started on this case.

"You're after motive," Arthur said.

"We *are* looking for motive," Bex replied. "For any reason at all that Chad and Sloan would have to hurt Ramona. And we want to find out what that reason is before either one of them has time to get a counternarrative in place, which really only gives us tonight. Very few people know yet that she was on the mountain, but that circle is already getting bigger. She's going to be recognized by anyone who so much as sees her name on an IV bag at the hospital. LAPD will have deployed a lot of people, some of whom talk to paparazzi. I have news alerts set up, and so far, I've only seen stories that say search and rescue was dispatched to Baldy, not for who, and of course about Sam and I being seen around town together, but those are just speculating about our relationship, not what we're up to."

"I'm sure that's going to change fast, too," Sam said. "We found out Chad and Sloan have been leaking damaging information about Ramona to the media for years. Once they hear she's been found, if they haven't already, there's no telling what they'll do or say. We've enlisted Christian Stanstedt's help to keep them occupied tonight. We're hoping they stay in one place and are distracted, but you can see how we only have a few more hours, if that, to gather evidence that helps Ramona and can be used to hold the right person accountable for doing this to her. Or the right people."

Archie stroked his chin. Jasmine was shaking her head. The coffee machine dripped and hissed. Otherwise, the kitchen was silent for long enough that nothing felt quite real, and Sam's thoughts began to soften and drift.

She was *tired.*

Archie cleared his throat. "I got a call. First thing Friday morning."

"Who called you?"

"Some bellend who represents Chad. Says he was giving me a 'courtesy call' to tell me I'd be served cease-and-desist papers shortly. I wasn't to distribute, to anyone in any form, any footage I might have of Ramona Watts describing the night Juliette Draper died. I wasn't to give verbal confirmation of the existence of such footage. I wasn't to share any evidence Ramona may have provided to me that Chad and Sloan had slandered her in the media, contributing to her reputation with the public as an unstable, unreliable, and unwell actress who is difficult to work with. I wrote this down as soon as I got off the phone. I can give you the direct quotes. I was told if I didn't comply with this so-called courtesy, this attorney would proceed with defamation suits and ask for damages that, frankly, exceed what either one of these knob-heads could expect to make in five of their careers."

"This happened first thing *Friday* morning," Sam repeated. "What time?"

"Few minutes after eight. Soon as I finished making notes, I went direct to the studio to see Ramona, but she wasn't there. They'd gone out on a location shoot. I waited here for the courier to turn up with the cease-and-desist papers so I could hand them over to my attorney. Never happened."

"It was an empty threat?" Bex asked. "Chad was trying to scare you off?"

Archie shook his head. "That man damn near bankrupted me to keep *Ice* from being released. There was no good reason for him to do that, mind, since what happened to the film was out of my hands. Cineline had the distribution. But Chad sued me personally, and it took six years and everything in my savings to settle up. If he had his legal people phoning to tell me papers were coming, I believed they would come."

"But they didn't," Sam said. "Something changed in between when you got that call and when the papers were supposed to be sent over." She thought about it. "This was the same day Chad was on Mount Baldy and someone shot Ramona. He either did it or watched it happen. Afterward, he couldn't afford any kind of scrutiny, including from a lawsuit. He had to be cautious. He called off his legal dogs. But something *had* happened that prompted him to come after you, something earlier in the week that resulted in a Friday morning phone call. What do you think it was?"

"That fucking documentary," Archie said. "Cursed from the

start, wasn't it? I thought it was going to make my career. I spent every waking moment with these people. The Ice Crew. Six movie stars everyone wanted a piece of, or to be them, and there I was, looking around, wondering, *Where's the adult?* I was barely five years older than these guys, and following them around for twenty-two months gave me panic attacks, insomnia, problems with my stomach. Then Juliette died. I didn't want anything to do with it, not ever again."

"They broke his heart," Jasmine said. She put a hand on his shoulder. Archie covered it with his own.

"The best thing to come out of it was Ramona," he said. "She's been a friend to us both ever since. But even still, when she came to me asking if I would pick the project back up, I said no. Until she told me why."

"Juliette," Sam breathed. It had to be. Ramona's feelings of guilt and regret about Juliette were what had set this in motion.

"Yeah. Juliette. Ramona wanted me to take my raw footage and edit it again. She asked me to peel back the glamor and show they were barely older than children, drowning in their own celebrity. And she wanted to sit down for an on-camera interview where she finally talked about what happened that night in the harbor."

Bex's eyebrows rose nearly to her hairline. "Where she talked about it in the sense of her feelings, or more in the sense of what *happened*?"

"More in the sense of whose fault it was, ethically, morally, and legally. She wanted to put pressure on the authorities to re-open Juliette's case."

It was an elegant plan. All that valuable old footage resurrected from the archives? Recut, released with the power of Tom Kessler behind it? With Ramona's new interview as the headline-grabbing bombshell? The effect would be powerful. Even if it didn't put Chad and Sloan behind bars, it would have destroyed their reputations and ended their careers.

That was motive.

"We didn't tell a soul," Archie said. "I didn't even tell Jasmine. Only Ramona and I knew what we'd planned. We had the interview set up for this week. My first thought when I got that phone call Friday morning was that if Chad had decided to pay a lawyer a pile of money to sink what Ramona had to say, it was because *Ramona* must have told him she was finally going to say it. I sure as hell hadn't. And goddamn her, I'm not surprised, because she has integrity. It would have been important to her to give those two at least a general idea of what she planned on doing. Her empathy is limitless." He frowned. "But the courier didn't show up, did he? Instead, Sloan took a gun to work. I'd say he and Chad were scared shitless. Is that motive enough for you?"

The coffee maker had stopped. Jasmine went into the kitchen and poured coffee into mugs. She set them down in front of all three of them, and one for her, along with a carton of cream and a sugar bowl.

Sam fixed her coffee light and sweet while Jasmine retrieved a plate of pecan rolls and moved into a seat next to Archie. She put her arm around him and pressed a cheek to his temple. "Will you give us the information for the hospital that's taking care of Ramona?" she asked. "I'm sure we'll want to head over there as soon as we can get someone here for the kids."

"Of course." Sam took a roll. None of them spoke while they ate the early breakfast.

It made Sam think about how her father's main strategy, when Sam felt bad and he didn't know what to do, had been to bring her something sweet. A popsicle, the baklava he loved, a cold soda. Because his whole job was fixing the teeth that sugar ruined, it was a concession of such a high order, Sam had understood what it meant even when she was little. *I recognize your feelings are huge and valid and hard, even if this is all I have to offer. I hope you feel better soon.*

Sam hoped they would all feel better soon.

But this long night was far from over.

Bex and Sam stood on a granite-tiled patio, arranged with teak furniture, toward the back of the Swan's property. They'd texted back and forth with Vic on the drive from Encino. She and Piper had everything under control. Christian had come through for them. Both Chad and Sloan were in the house.

The trap was baited and set.

But now that Sam had good food in her system and coffee lighting up the corners of her brain with something other than adrenaline, she had a serious case of stage fright.

"We've been all over this town in the last couple of days." Bex was looking out at the lights of Los Angeles below them, pulsing and glittering gold. The weather had been clearing by the minute, and the early-hour view was breathtaking, the moonset making racing clouds glow.

"From here, the 101 doesn't look so bad," Sam admitted.

"From Beverly Hills, there isn't anything about Los Angeles that looks bad. Such a vibrant, creative town, and yet a handful of people keep trying to ruin it."

"But that just means even more people keep trying to make it work. I know it's hard to remember sometimes, but it's true." Sam slid her arm around Bex, remembering that standing close to her had always been the best stage-fright remedy.

Her favorite actor. Her favorite person.

There was no one she'd rather solve a crime with.

"You're all right, Samantha Farmer." Bex tipped her face up and smiled. The blond wig suited her, but then again, Sam couldn't imagine anything that wouldn't. It would be lovely to see how gray hair made this woman beautiful someday.

Sam leaned down, meaning only to kiss her forehead, but Bex rose on her toes, offering her mouth, so Sam really kissed her. It made her warm all over. It made her glad. It made her a little horny, also, but mostly it made her realize she could do this.

She had her Bex.

Bex eased away and kissed Sam's nose. "Are you ready to hear the plan?"

"Lay it out, Bexley."

"We're ready to hear it, too." Sam and Bex jumped at the sound of Fergus's voice. When they turned, Sam saw her brother on the patio with Frankie, Vic, and Piper beside him.

Their support team. Their family.

"We got Logan handed off to the LAPD. It's up to him now." Fergus rolled his shoulders. "We came out to make sure we had our orders."

"Christian has a handle on things inside," Piper said. "He's ready when you are."

"What did you get from Archie?" Vic asked.

"Motive," Bex declared. "Archie believes Ramona must have told Chad and Sloan that she planned to film a new part of the documentary. She was going to let the world know what they did to Juliette. She hoped it would reopen the investigation."

"They were worried about going to prison, so they decided to kill Ramona?" Vic rolled her eyes. "I'm not impressed with the logic."

"Not quite," Sam said. "I think it's more that when people do something that works, that's the way they keep doing it until it stops working. It's the reason why, when Chad needs to cry on camera, he always thinks about his dog dying. Because it works."

"Or why Bradley Wilhite makes people come to his ridiculous ranch in Colorado before he starts a project," Bex suggested with a wry smile. "He's successful. He thinks the way he does things is what made him successful. That's why he makes people follow the same script he always follows."

"Right." Sam smiled at Bex as she made a mental note to figure out what to do about *Theomina*, Bradley Wilhite, and Colorado as soon as they got to the bottom of this murder attempt. The to-do list really got long when you were on a case. "Chad and Sloan's script is to isolate and attack. They invited Juliette, and Juliette only, onto that boat. But Ramona came. To carry on with whatever their plan was, they had to get rid of Ramona. They incapacitated her so Juliette would be isolated with them."

"Wait, do you think they *planned* on killing Juliette?" Frankie asked.

"I'm not sure, but they wanted something. Whether that was Juliette alone in a location hard to leave with drugs in her system, or murder to satisfy some other end, we may never know. But my point is, it *worked*, at least in the sense that they never got caught."

"So they stuck to the script," Bex said. "Isolate and attack."

"Yes. We can assume they had a plan to isolate Ramona on location. As for what happened when the three of them were alone, that's what we want to find out next."

"They'll lie," Bex warned. "They did last time. They said Ramona was drunk. They told her she slipped and hit her head, and passed out. We can expect them to blame Ramona the same way they blamed Juliette."

"Yeah, and I don't love that Chad knows Macie talked to us and that we've been asking questions. But they don't know Ramona's been found, probably. All we can do is try to use what we know to discover if either one of them or both had an opportunity to isolate Ramona for long enough to shoot her."

"And there's Christian," Bex said. "They don't know his allegiance, which could be a big help. They still want his money. But it is a gamble. We could be walking into a trap that Christian turned *our* trap into."

"I don't think so," Piper offered. "I've been watching him. Chad and Sloan treat him like a dumb younger brother, but he's got the upper hand. I'm starting to think he might be a good actor."

"Let's not be hasty," Bex said. "His hair does most of the acting."

"Yeah, but his hair is fucking amazing," Fergus said. "It's aging like a diva."

"Oh! That reminds me," Piper said. "I told Vic that Ramona was being a diva when Chad and Sloan were on the set. I take it back. It's true she didn't go out of her way to be nice to them. If one of them made a joke, she would be the only one who didn't laugh. She didn't even come out of her dressing room except for when she had to. But now that I know they *killed* her *friend*, I would say she was being incredibly restrained. When this is over, I'm going to make sure every last one of the cast, crew, puppeteers, catering, *everyone*, makes statements about what they saw and heard. This isn't going down like with the *Craven's Daughter* stuff. That was olden times."

"It was six years ago," Sam said, amused.

"Well, this is now. *Now*, these studios know we stick up for each other. If they don't know, they're about to find out."

Vic gave Piper a giant hug.

Piper squeezed Vic, then looked at Fergus. "I told my security guy what's up. He screened Chad and Sloan when they arrived, all official, so we know nobody has a weapon. He also got the detective's contact information from Macie, and he has other people he's reached out to in order to give them the heads up. He promised me he can get the sirens here when and if we need them."

"Good to know," Sam said.

"Oh! And Christian's phone is clean," Piper added. "Well, not *clean*, but clean in the sense he hasn't been threatening Ramona or anyone else. There are a lot of half-written apology texts to his ex in the Notes app and about a thousand soppy animal videos. The man needs professional help. I'm going to give him the name of my therapist."

"Are we ready for the final battle?" Fergus asked.

Sam grabbed Bex's hand. "We are ready for absolutely anything that comes next."

Plenty of Motive

It made Sam break out in a cold sweat to be in the same room with Sloan Lennox.

He sat in a large white upholstered chair, looking at his phone, and all she could think was this was the man they'd been talking about since they started looking for Ramona. This was a man who might have killed two people.

She moved closer to Bex until she could feel her steady presence along the side of her body.

Fergus, Vic, and Frankie were keeping to the background, eyes on the party. Despite the weak dawn light at the very edge of the horizon, there was still conversation and laughter. Their army had come through, keeping everything going.

Christian was near a bar that served the pool. He broke away and sauntered over, exactly like Christian Stanstedt normally would have when two new people came into his lair. But he winked at them.

Sam hoped this gamble paid off.

"What do these people want?" Sloan had looked up from his phone. He addressed the question to Christian.

Close up, Sam could grudgingly admit that as far as the camera was concerned, the misfit look of Sloan's youth had mellowed into something more marketable. He was fit—Sam could give him that. He had the physique of a bantamweight boxer and held his body just as aggressively.

The scratches on his neck were a scabbed maroon.

Christian leaned over and whispered in Sam's ear. "Chad's through there, in the pool."

She nodded. She could see him in the water from where she stood. She walked over to where Sloan sat and offered her hand. "We haven't met."

Sloan looked at her hand, then looked away, but Sam continued to hold it out until he was uncomfortable enough to clasp it briefly with his own.

Ha.

"I'm Sam Farmer," she said. "That's Bexley Simon."

He tried not to react, but he brought his bottle of beer to his lips a little too quickly to hide his surprise, and it knocked against his teeth.

"Bananas, right?" Christian collapsed into a nearby chair. "I met them the other day. Everyone in town's talking about these two."

"Hadn't heard." Sloan glanced in the direction of the pool.

"Oh my God!" Bex exclaimed in her preternaturally loud Bex-voice. "Is that Chad *Bevington* in the pool? Sam promised we could meet." Bex caught Chad's eye and waved enthusiastically. "It's me, Bex Simon! We heard you were looking for us!"

Chad did a double take and started pulling himself out of the water.

"Chad and I worked together," Sam told Sloan in a confiding voice. "*Theomina.* But also, he paid to have us followed earlier this week."

Sloan glared at Christian. "What the hell's going on?"

Chad appeared in the doorway, a towel around his middle. He looked back and forth from Sam to Bex, his furrowed forehead dashingly familiar.

Sam ran her fingers along the loosened edges of her wig and slid it off. Her skin was sticky with rain-damp hairspray. "We were tired of the media talking about us wherever we went. Decided to try a thing tonight."

"What's this, Christian?" Chad asked. Sam recognized his faux-pleasant tone as one he used when he was trying to recover. She'd seen him go too far with crew more than once, melting down over some small matter he couldn't control, and then just at the moment he realized he'd made a scene, he'd flip a switch.

Sam had grown to prefer his tantrums and sniping over this manic civility that felt like a threat.

"Chad," Sloan said. "They know about your private investigator."

Chad waved a hand, smiling. Sam's gaze went to the ring of fading and scabbed scratches circling both his forearms. "Fuck. You caught me," he said jovially. "Look, hon, no hard feelings. I got spooked after I told you that Sloan and I were guesting on *The Howling*. Until it airs, we aren't supposed to be seen together. I needed to make sure you weren't going to leak."

"You want me to believe you had us tailed by a private detective to keep from violating your NDA with StudioHonor?" Sam lifted an eyebrow. "I know you're neurotic, Chad, but that's taking it a bit far even for you."

The word *neurotic* hit him like a slap. It took him three seconds to recover. Sam counted. "I'd think you would be happy I'm careful. *Theomina*'s a big movie for both of us. We can't afford any bad press when the fast-food chains are about to start bidding on licensing. Right now is the time to tread carefully and keep that bottom line healthy."

A threat. Interesting. Sam was starting to understand she held the full house on this gamble. Chad didn't know what she and Bex had discovered over the past few days. He didn't know they knew about Juliette, the documentary, Ramona's rescue, Logan's confessions, any of it.

The last of her stage fright melted away like a *Theomina*-branded bath bomb, and she took a seat in the last of the empty overstuffed lounge chairs.

"It's nothing personal," Sloan said, with a glance at Chad, who loomed over him, dripping pool water onto the arm of Sloan's chair. "He's just trying to protect some things we have in the hopper. Business."

"Sure. Maybe I would believe that if it weren't for Ramona being missing."

"Jesus H., this again?" Sloan made a strained chuffing sound. "Can't wait to hear where they find her this time."

Chad was the better actor. His smile was *almost* the right mix of sad and bemused. "I feel sorry for Ramona. She really used to have something no one else had. Something special."

"But then the stress got to her, is that right?" Bex asked. "She went back to the drugs. Probably she left town to get her fix in private."

"You'll find her driving a Yugo down the Pan-American Highway," Sloan said. "Something batshit like that."

"Yeah." Bex bobbed her head, tilting it to untangle a lock of red hair from her wig. Once she had the wig in her hand, she pursed her lips at it as if something Sloan said had confused her. "The only thing is, Sloan, *you* were the last person to see Ramona."

Chad crossed his bare arms with a frown. With the pool water glistening on them, it was an affecting reminder of his power.

"Because I gave her a ride home Friday, you mean." Sloan sounded like he was scrabbling for a good handhold on a crumbling ledge.

"Mm." Bex leaned over to drop her wig on the chair next to Sloan's thigh. "More because she wasn't in the van, at all, on the way back down the mountain."

Chad's voice boomed over Sloan's head. "Who told you that? They're lying. She was in our van. It was just the three of us and the driver." He squinted into the middle distance. "But, you know, maybe that was a bit of a cry for help. She said something in the van about being ready to 'tell her story.' She wasn't making a lot of sense. She got aggressive with me, accusing me of killing Juliette again. You know she went to the cops with that? Drunk? There's a reason that tragedy was closed so quickly. I hate it, *hate* it, when she throws that at me. It's disrespectful to Juliette. Sloan helped smooth things over."

"I said I'd take her home," Sloan offered. "Because we're friends. I can handle her. Ask anyone." He was talking a little too fast. "I got her calmed down, real easy, but when the valet brought my car, she wasn't where I told her to meet me. She must have taken an Uber. I know that was her plan earlier. She'd grabbed one to work that morning."

"Sloan, Ramona wasn't in the garage that night." Bex sounded apologetic. "No one saw her there."

He shrugged, his eyes dark and almost filmed over with a lack of expression. "I have nothing to say about that except she was."

Sam was over this. Sloan's story sounded like a monologue he hadn't rehearsed enough, and she felt the way she'd imagined Theomina would at the end of her tiresome adventures. Even bloody-minded from the beatings she'd taken at the hands of her enemies, hollowed out by grief, Sam couldn't convince herself these men could possibly win. They believed in nothing. They had no principles. "Search and rescue found blood at the site where *The Howling* filmed Friday," she announced. "They found Ramona's smashed phone. And we spoke to Logan Widi."

The party went quiet behind her.

"Who?" Sloan's too-smooth forehead seemed to lower in his confusion. Sam watched Chad's eyes. They'd been the only part of him she could see when he wore his chroma-key suit, and she'd grown accustomed to reading the nuances of his emotions.

She watched recognition dawn. His hands twitched when he figured out he didn't know how much Logan had told them. Chad was the one who'd sent the bribe to Logan. He'd probably paid Ashleigh Chambers to find out the private information that he used to threaten Logan and his wife. Blood rushed to the base of his throat, creeping up his neck.

"One of the crew had a nosebleed." He couldn't quite pull

off good humor anymore. "Ramona lost her phone. She'd asked me to help her find it, but we weren't able to locate it in the brush. It's dense up there. The shoot was grueling. They had us in the trees, rocks, and vegetation." He glanced down at the faint lines on his bare arms. "I got scratched up."

"A crew member got a nosebleed, Ramona lost her phone, you got scratched in the bushes, she lost her mind on the way down in your van, and Sloan was a pal and offered her a ride home, but she took off without a word. No one's seen her since, and her friends and family are *so* worried, *so* certain that this isn't like Ramona at all, that they got West Valley Search and Rescue and the LAPD involved." Sam crossed her legs. "That's the tall tale you're going with?"

"I don't know what to tell you," Chad said. "I have a sense you know about Ramona's most recent field trip because you imagine you're one of her friends. Chris can tell you where friendship with Ramona leads."

"Yeah, that's for sure," Christian said. "Leads to a fuckload of emotionally intelligent conversations, for one thing. Self-reflection. Inconvenient personal growth. I experienced a lot of consequences from being held to account for my behavior. And then there's her risotto. Fucking ruined me for any other recipe forever."

It would have been comical to watch Chad and Sloan freeze-frame at the same time if it weren't for the fact they'd put Ramona in the hospital.

Chad's nostrils flared. He covered it with a smirk. "Chris. I thought you were over the sucking up. Are these two your new best friends? After Ramona spread rumors about your toxic thing with the old dude? Sam, I should tell you, because you have an amazing career to protect, you'd better keep far, far away from this guy. No offense, Chris."

"Amazingly, none taken." Christian finger-gunned Chad. "There was a time, I admit. But then I remember that I light my bong with hundred-dollar bills, and the pain floats away."

Sam was still trying to decide about Christian, but she could admit he was coming out ahead.

"You know what I keep asking myself?" She pointed this question at Sloan. "I keep wondering, what does Chad owe you? Isn't that how you two used to do everything, trading back and forth who owed what to who? But it was never even." Macie had given them this ammunition in that painful trip down Memory Lane at the Velvet Chair. "Somehow, you always owed him more than he owed you. Why would that ever change? He was better looking. He got better parts. You were a sidekick, and then you were next door to a nobody. But now you're right at the cusp of your comeback, this time as Chad's equal. I asked myself, how did Sloan pull that off? *I'm* thinking he's giving you that part in the sci-fi franchise in exchange for keeping his secret for another thirty years. What's a second murder between buddies when you've already gotten away with one?"

"Of course, Chad's only ever going to have Chad's back," Bex said. "You know that better than anyone. Logan Widi, the PA, told us about seeing you with a gun. I guess he decided his integrity was worth more than fifty thousand dollars and a cruel threat to a young family. I wonder whose DNA will come back from the blood on the mountain? For that matter, I wonder what DNA might come back from under Ramona's fingernails? You know they do that. Collect evidence from victims of violent crime."

"Those are such good questions," Sam said, smiling at her partner. "You always ask the best questions, Bexley. I'm sure Ramona will clear everything up when she's interviewed, now that search and rescue's pulled her off the mountain and gotten her the medical care she needs." Sam met Sloan's wide eyes. "Chad has his little militia of lawyers on the ready. The only firepower *you* have is who talks first."

Sloan's body went so lifeless, Sam had to clench and unclench her fist to make sure time hadn't frozen.

Then he broke the moment with a wordless shout that ended with a growl, making Sam and Bex both jump. "You think I've wanted this shitass career?" he yelped. "I've had to lay low. Chad has taken everything he can from me and about a pound of flesh more, just so he has enough to cover his own ass. Like with Juliette." He sneered at Chad. "I *loved* her."

"You're high," Chad scoffed, but his lips were as gray as his neck was blood-red. "You're going to sit there and snitch me out for Juliette? You're going to let them hand you the rope to hang yourself with when we have the project of a lifetime on the line? Sober up, Sloan. Walk out with me right fucking now."

Christian leaned forward, robe parting over his spread thighs, and balanced his elbows on his knees. "Thing is, Sloan, either Chad will throw you under the bus or you'll decide to tell the truth. But whether Chad goes down or you do, this thing he's promising you isn't going to happen. Do you get that? This episode you did of Ramona's show, if it ever airs, will be about the crime against Ramona. She's alive to tell whatever tale she's a part of, and I do know her, so I know she *will* tell the truth. You lose no matter what. You've already lost."

One of Sloan's hands gripped his knee, every muscle popping into relief. "Jesus *Christ*. It was my gun, but I wasn't going to use it. We just wanted to scare her a little. Make her leave the past in the past. Juliette's been gone thirty fucking years. What happened on that boat still gives me nightmares, but nothing we do will bring her back. That's what Ramona needed to understand. We'd been talking about it at the studio. Why she needed to leave the past in the past."

Chad stepped closer, looming over Sloan, and Sloan shoved at his hip to make space between them. The sudden violence knocked Chad off balance. He fell to his knees, then surged back to his feet as Sloan shot from his chair, ungainly enough that Bex had to jump backward to keep from colliding with him.

"Shut the fuck up, Sloan!" Chad roared.

"She didn't even *look* at the gun. She wouldn't stop talking. It was fucked up." Sloan was speaking to Christian now, moving in a sliding, sinuous dance to evade Chad's attempts to grab him. "I hated it. Talking and talking, messing with my head like she does, and then she goes for Chad all of a sudden like a fucking demon. I tried to pull her off and get her away from him. My hand was shaking so much. The safety wasn't on. He pushed her toward me. It just got out of control, right? *You* understand." He kept backing away from Chad. The look he gave Christian was pleading. "It got out of control. It wasn't like what they're trying to say. Back then, on the boat, or with Ramona."

Chad caught his arm, and the back of his fist connected with Sloan's nose. He went down, then rose up again with astonishing speed, one arm around Chad's neck, the other connecting a closed, vicious fist with his face.

Sam hooked her arm around Bex's waist and pulled them both back into the deep cushions of her chair. She saw blood splash on the white marble floor.

Piper's security detail appeared. In one movement, he had Chad and Sloan separated, both of them breathing hard, both of them bleeding. "LAPD's on the way," he said.

Chad let out a noise that was probably an attempt at a scoff, but he didn't have the air left in his body to pull it off. He spit on the ground at Sloan's feet. "I'm done. Christian's right. You can forget about working with me, and not because Ramona's finally *really* lost it. So determined to hurt herself! She's a lost cause. I tried to stop her and take your gun from her before she *could* hurt herself. You just stood there! I thought you were different. I thought you got it. I thought the time you spent away was what you said it was. Reflection. Improving your craft. But you're just as grasping as the rest of them."

Chad heaved several more breaths after finishing this disjointed speech. The skin around one of his eyes was an ugly pink, swelling fast. Dripping blood from his mouth, he turned and headed for the door. Sam was sure he believed he'd gathered all the information he needed to go right to the police with a story about Ramona's tragic attempt to take her own life. Probably he would mention his subsequent catatonic shock and the threats he'd received from Sloan, whose gun it was.

But Chad still didn't know everything.

In front of the doorway, a group of young Hollywood's best and brightest blocked his path two-deep. A check of the room's other exits revealed the same barrier. They were surrounded.

"Who the fuck are you people?" Chad asked.

"They're the part of Hollywood that isn't about secrets and who owes what to who," Sam replied.

There would always be bad people attracted to bright lights, but there were more people like her, who only wanted to let them shine on her to figure out who she was, to tell people good stories, and to earn the kind of power that lifted people up and kept them safe.

This was not an army who would let Chad go.

Piper's security detail looked at Christian over his shoulder. "When the heat gets here, can you be ready to show them where to pull security footage from your system?"

"Will do, brother." Christian slapped the other man on his back. "I'm going to order pizzas for everyone. Better not be any underage drinking going on here." He pointed at the partygoers, Vic's army. "I already showed you guys where I keep the sodas."

Sam tugged Bex even closer against her body. "Do you want to stay for pizza?"

Bex kissed the top of Sam's head. "I'm starving."

Chad paced with his hands in fists, his phone to his ear, making demands of whichever member of his coterie of lawyers he'd managed to reach first. Sloan kept to the corner, where he tried to stanch his bleeding nose with his shirttail. Sam held the woman she loved in her arms and listened for the sirens.

They would probably never get the whole story from these

two, but they'd gotten more than enough to hold whatever lies Chad and Sloan told up to the light. Everyone had heard their admission that Sloan had brought a gun with him. Chad had known about it. They'd intended to scare Ramona. There was an argument, a physical altercation, a cliff.

The LAPD already had Logan's statement. They would hear from Archie. Bex and Sam would tell them everything they'd learned, and Ramona's injuries would corroborate that a crime had occurred.

When she was ready, Ramona could tell the whole story at last.

This wasn't a dark night on a marina thirty years ago. No one had been able to save Juliette. No one had backed up Ramona against the force of Chad and Sloan's lies.

This time, it would be different.

Once the first police officer burst through the door of the Swan, everything happened in slow motion, and very fast.

Suddenly, the men were everywhere, dressed in black tactical gear. The partygoers moved to the edges of the huge rooms. The inside of the mansion strobed blue and red. Sam and Bex got up from where they had been sitting and shifted to a corner with Fergus, Vic, and Frankie, and even though Sam knew this was the inevitable beginning of what justice was available to Ramona, the entire scene felt like barely controlled violence.

"Hold up!" Chad yelled. He was sweating, bloody, absurd in his poolside outfit. Two officers flanked him, one talking into a radio. There was another cop speaking to Piper's security detail, both of them murmuring in low voices.

"Fuck!" Sloan's voice was hoarse, the blood on his face nauseatingly red. "What the fuck are you doing?" His arms were held behind his back.

The four officers isolating Chad and Sloan from each other remained expressionless. A female officer next to Chad held Flexicuffs in one hand. Her other hand rested on her holster.

"We received a report of an assault at this address. Security directed us to you and this other gentleman. It's clear an assault took place." The officer indicated Chad's bloody mouth. The blood on the floor.

Chad dropped to the ground, swiping his leg out to kick at the woman.

Everyone in the room gasped and moved closer to whatever safe corner or wall they had retreated to as the police subdued Chad with shouts, a gun pointed at him, and eventually the Flexi-cuffs. They handled him roughly as they dragged him to his feet. Sam missed Sloan's arrest, but she saw him in the middle of a tangle of uniforms, following an incoherently screaming and detained Chad out the main entrance.

Once the noise was muffled behind inch-thick hardwood doors, the overwhelming ugliness moving out of range, Sam noticed her heart beating fast enough that she couldn't take a breath.

"It's okay," Bex said. "Inhale. One short breath in, through your mouth. Then drop your jaw and take in all the air you can through your nose. Blow it out."

Sam listened to Bex's instructions, and her tunnel vision eased. Her face was damp with tears.

There were three officers still in the mansion. They'd begun lining people up, asking them for their identification and telling them to stay. Piper's security detail was rearranging furniture, bringing chairs into groups for people to sit.

The night wasn't over. They would be here a long time yet answering questions. They might have to go to the station even before their appointment in the morning.

But Ramona had been on a mountain, shot, for five days. Maybe Sam wasn't as level-headed and extremely chill as her reputation suggested, but she could get through this. She was ready for whatever came next.

"Thanks, Bex," she whispered.

"Anytime."

"Sit." Frankie offered Sam a chair. Vic opened the doors that led to the pool as wide as they would go to let in air and, Sam hoped, release the horrible energy from the fight and the arrival of the police.

Fergus rested his hand on Sam's shoulder. She looked up at her brother. "I'm so glad you're here," she said. "I really am."

He smiled. "You're not getting rid of me anytime soon."

It was a long night. The police permitted the pizza delivery.

Sam told her story as the sun rose on a clear day in beautiful Los Angeles, California.

She Would Have Hated It

Sam couldn't take her eyes off Bex.

She'd spent more time than she should have getting ready for this morning's appointment. When Fergus had noticed, and commented, Sam asked him how *he* would dress to meet an iconic cult-favorite actor for the first time while trying to cover the rash your leather gauntlets had given you when you were dragged in for secret, contractually nonnegotiable *Theomina* reshoots because your former costar on a fantasy blockbuster was a bail-denied murderer, and *also*, you were going to see the woman you hoped would let you lesbian U-haul yourself into her life for the first time in over a week, not counting a single exhausted hug in the hallway of the police station where you'd both spent endless hours—separately, always separately—answering the same questions again and again.

Fergus had no answer. Well, he *did*, but the answer was that he'd wear his favorite jeans and a pink T-shirt that said *Aloha!*, so it was a useless answer.

They'd driven to West Hollywood separately. Bex's SUV was already parked in Ramona's driveway when Sam got there. With a little wave, she hopped out and walked to the front door alongside Sam.

Bex was wearing *fashion.* It wasn't her way. Bex famously didn't wear fashion even on the red carpet. But what Sam knew, and the media didn't, was that Bex *did* wear fashion when she was trying to feel erotically powerful. When Bex put on this lace poet's blouse and leather short-shorts with hot-pink wedge sandals that were *not* comfortable sneakers, she had been thinking of *Sam.*

"You look amazing," Sam said. "Why haven't I seen you for a week?"

Bex rang the doorbell. "Because I've been giving the same statement to seven different officers from four different agencies?" she asked. "I promise, that is the *only* thing I've been doing in between conversations with my agent, my manager, my publicist, my assistant, and my housekeeper. I think she's going to quit."

"Olive? But she's been with you forever."

"Yeah, and I've never had this many people in and out of my house before. Vic and Frankie are enough by themselves, but now there's Haris, and Piper, too, and yesterday Logan Widi and his wife came over with their baby. It's mayhem." Bex pulled on the hem of her shorts with prim anger. "I'm leaving out the fact I have to wade through photographers and unsolicited press gauntlets because of the leaks about us being involved in the investigation." She crossed her arms, which shifted her silky blouse into the territory of wardrobe malfunction, so she quickly dropped them and, Sam was certain, repressed the urge to swear.

"I love you," she said.

"I love *you,*" Bex returned. "I particularly love that you didn't go to Telluride, because it means that after we do this I get to have you to myself."

The first thing Sam had done when she was finally released from the clutches of the LAPD was loop her agent and manager into a phone call to let them know she wanted to "step aside" from the Theomina series with Bradley Wilhite. As she'd predicted, they did not like this decision.

However, they didn't try as hard to change her mind as she'd expected. *Maybe* that was because Chad's arrest threw a bit of a pall over the future of the Theomina IP, but Sam liked to think it was actually a sign that all the time they'd been telling her what to do, her people had secretly been waiting for her to figure out what she wanted.

People did what they knew how to do until it stopped working. Then they learned a new way to get through the emotional tangle of making a life.

She placed her palm at the middle of Bex's back and slid it slowly down to the swell of her backside.

Macie opened the door.

"Hi." Macie stepped out and closed the door behind them, standing with Sam and Bex on the bungalow's porch. "It's really good to see you both. Especially now that it's—I don't want to say it's all over, but there is something that's shifted, at least in the universe I occupy, and it's easier to stand up straight, you know?"

"We know," Sam said. She and Bex weren't privy to the details of the investigation, but they'd been told Sloan was cooperating and had provided statements to the police about the assault on Ramona. Both men had been charged with a long list of offenses ranging from attempted murder to the unlicensed carrying of a firearm. No doubt the charges would be pled down, but no one expected Chad or Sloan to escape prison. There were rumblings that Juliette's case might be reopened.

"I'm glad we got to here," Bex said. "You're sure Ramona wants visitors? We were flattered she invited us over, but she only got out of the hospital yesterday. She must be exhausted."

Macie had told them Ramona suffered a gunshot wound to her left chest wall, thankfully far enough to the outside of her body that her heart, esophagus, and major nerve centers weren't affected. The bullet had collapsed her lung and caused significant bleeding, however, and a fall down into a rocky ravine had broken an ankle and wrist.

What no one but Ramona had known was that she'd hired a backcountry guide only a couple of years previously to spend a two-week vacation hiking part of the Pacific Crest Trail. During this time, she'd learned good trail first aid and a bit about navigation off-trail and what to do if she was injured and alone. It was while Ramona was on this trip and out of contact, incidentally, that Chad and Sloan had leaked to *People* magazine she was "experimenting with the psychedelic ayahuasca and younger men in Baja."

On Mount Baldy, Ramona had tried to call for help and get attention right away, but the noise of striking the location set, as well as the trucks, had disguised both the gunshot and her calls for help, which Macie said were affected by her collapsed lung.

But she'd sailed through two surgeries already, and her overall good health meant she did well in recovery. She'd been discharged with orders for a daily nurse visit and a lot of physical therapy. Ramona had wanted to talk to Sam and Bex right away, but LAPD had insisted on getting everyone's statements first, and then Sam had been tied up with the meetings about *Theomina* made necessary by Chad's ejection from the project.

"Oh, Ramona definitely wants you here," Macie said. "I'm so fucking happy she asked me to stay with her and help out. She's never asked me for something like that before, but she's been on me every day to get you two out to see her as soon as she was home. She bossed Colin into setting up food and drink in the garden, so we can walk around to the back."

Sam followed Bex, mainly so she could get a look at her ass in the shorts and the way her curls bounced over her bare spine. It was an excellent view.

The garden seemed completely transformed. In the wake of the record-setting rain, they'd had endless sun erasing all memory of the bad weather. In the light, the colors and birdsong were almost overwhelming, and the plantings looked bigger. The previously empty patio set was dressed with a tablecloth and food. There were cushions on the chairs and even rugs laid about. It looked like a bohemian fever dream.

And on the comfiest looking chair sat Ramona Watts, her big dark eyes just exactly like they were in the movies. She had pillows and cushions propped around her to keep her comfortable, but there was something about her that gave off an incredibly lively feeling, as if she'd run over to embrace them.

"Oh, God, hi!" Ramona pointed at one of the rugs. "Be careful there. Miette chose that spot, and she's not moving. Colin, for fuck's sake, pull the chairs out. Do you two want coffee? Or tea? I have Coke, too, not diet, I don't trust it even though everyone says it's fine. I would get up and ask for a hug, but some motherfucker shot me."

"Hi!" Bex stepped carefully around the cat and leaned over to kiss Ramona's cheek. "It's a complete honor to meet you."

Sam reached across Colin's chair and squeezed Ramona's offered hand. "It's *perfect* to meet you. I feel like we've been getting pieces of a portrait of who you are. Every new piece has been fascinating, but this is so much better."

Ramona beamed as they found seats. Colin patted them both on the back while pouring them the drinks they requested. Macie came to whisper in Ramona's ear, then disappeared through the doors that led to the four-seasons room where they had talked to Colin last time they were at the house.

"Macie is going to take a well-deserved break and check in with this realtor they've been talking to. They're selling the Velvet Chair, thank God. It's almost worth getting shot to know someone's going to gut that place. But the sale has Macie freaked, not to mention that I'm a terrible patient. I haven't taken a single one of the opiates they prescribed for me, which means

Macie has to make me up a glass of filtered water with ten different healing tinctures in it four times a day, and they're completely over it."

"They told us they're happy to be here," Bex said.

Ramona adjusted her position, only wincing a little. "That just makes me feel worse I've boxed them out so much over the years." Ramona picked up a tea mug with the hand that wasn't wrapped into a cast. Birdsong took over the silence as she took a sip and set the mug back down.

"We're so glad you're here, dear," Colin ventured. "It will take all of us some time to resettle."

Ramona patted his arm, but she was looking at Sam. "I wanted to meet you. It might be that I discover I have a question or two for you." She lifted her brows, famously shaped nearly like elegant question marks lying on their sides. "Or you have one or two for me."

"If you're up to it," Sam said. "If it were me, I'd take what the doctor gave me and sleep for days."

"I probably should. I promised my mom I would, but I'm pretty attached to consciousness at the moment. I'll crash before long, I just wanted to see you two first. Macie said I wouldn't be here if it weren't for you." She smiled at Bex and gave her a winsome shrug. "You know, I've *never* wanted to meet you. I was too much in love with Cora Banks to give her up for whatever you turned out to be like in reality. Or Henri, for that matter." She gestured at Sam. "Isn't life strange? I would never have thought my favorite TV detectives would be the ones to save me after Sloan shot me and Chad pushed me off a cliff."

Bex inhaled sharply, but Sam liked that Ramona went right at the thing. "We're mutual fans, then," Sam said. "With the difference that I'd always hoped to meet you someday."

Ramona shifted in her chair. "I understand you've talked to a lot of people about me. Archie and Jasmine filled me in. I got a letter from Christian, if you can believe that. Never thought I'd hear from him again. It made me think he's been listening to me a lot more than I thought over the years. He said he would visit soon, after he came back from the rehab center he's checked himself into in Oregon. Even Tom Kessler sent flowers."

"Your friends care about you," Bex said.

Ramona looked away, watching a dove hop up on a higher branch of an avocado tree. When she turned back, her expression was wistful. "My mom and dad had to go home this morning. It's always strange for me to say goodbye to them. When I first came to L.A., my mom lived here with me full-time for a couple of years, and my dad was back and forth from Wisconsin whenever he could make it work. They wanted me to have what I wanted, but they didn't want me to get hurt. No one did that for Juliette. I think even before she came to L.A., no one had ever done that for her. And there wasn't anybody on Tom's sets who was worried about a single thing other than giving Tom what he wanted." She looked at Bex. "You have little sisters, I remember. Teenagers now?"

"Not anymore, but it wasn't so long ago. Vic is friends with Piper Redwood."

Ramona nodded. "Teenagers are so fucking pure. They're just raw creativity, constantly making things, trying to connect and share who they are inside with the rest of the world. The older I am, the more I love working with them. Piper is a revelation. Rachael, in our supporting cast, is seventeen. She goes to school on set, and her mom picks her up early on Fridays so she can go to 4-H. When Juliette was sixteen, she got cast opposite Stephan Chasez in a raunchy summer camp comedy. He was twenty-seven years old. That was her first kiss. They filmed her braless, soaking wet. There were posters of her for sale at the mall. She was legally emancipated from her family, making her own decisions. She told me she'd had no idea Stephan would put his tongue in her mouth, and it was disgusting."

Sam had to remind herself to relax her hands in her lap. "Everyone we spoke to told us what a good friend you were to Juliette."

Ramona's smile was pained. "She just wanted to be loved. Her death was so stupid. She would have hated it. I do. I hate that she's gone, and it's because of these two men with no ideas, no beauty, just a pit of grasping, soulless need. It's why I couldn't be part of propping up the careers of Chad or Sloan with my silence anymore. I used to be afraid of them, but it got to be that I was more afraid they would win."

"You've tried so hard to get people to hear the truth," Sam said.

Ramona took a long sip of tea. "The good thing about the truth is that it doesn't go away, right? Someone in the LAPD showed me my original statement about that night on the boat. They wanted me to *confirm* it. Ha! The truth roots out every single person and entity that ever denied it. I think Juliette will get her comeback. She'll have her day in court, everyone will watch her movies and remember what a gorgeous, glowing light she was, and I will look forward to starting a hard conversation about what it is we protect and don't protect in this town."

"Call us when you want backup," Sam said. "I like a good fight."

"I will." Ramona smiled at Bex. "I think you want to ask me something."

Bex leaned forward in her seat, her knees as far apart as they would go in her leather shorts. "We worked out that you told Chad and Sloan what you were going to do with the documentary. That's what set them off. Is that right?"

"Yes. I told them. Did I tell anyone else I had told them? No, and that was my mistake. The problem with the truth is that it tends to make one feel a little invincible sometimes."

"No one should have to have the forethought to prevent their coworkers from attempting to murder them," Bex said sharply.

"My God. Rehearsal, boundaries, and a breath mint for a kissing scene should be sufficient advance planning for comfort on set."

Ramona started laughing, then pressed her good hand against her side. "Oh, shit, I can't. My ribs are not healed enough to laugh that hard. Phew. And you are so right. I did tell them, though. And, if I could jump ahead, the day on the mountain was actually pretty okay. I felt like they understood why I wanted the documentary. I had no doubt they already had lawyers involved, and I was prepared for the defamation and libel suits, but I was clear, and I thought they were clear. I wasn't afraid of anything. Chad asked me to take a look at a view he'd spotted, so I followed him off the trail. It was lovely. I thought it was, you know, a peace overture, and we would talk for a few minutes. When I looked back, Sloan had a gun on me."

Sam pressed a hand against her stomach.

"As soon as I saw it, I remembered everything I'd learned about survival. I told myself that I knew what I needed to know to live, and if I didn't make it, it wasn't because of something I did or failed to do. I tried to talk them out of it. When I couldn't, I fought. When I understood they wouldn't let me leave, I tried to run away. The bullet hit, and I kept running, but Chad was closer than I thought, and he pushed me off that cliff. After that, my memory is blank until I wake up and realize I can still hear the engines of the trucks. I'm not dead. Survival kicks back in. Survival mode is where I stayed until a very hot woman in a climbing helmet and a bright yellow jumpsuit tenderly eased me onto a gurney and told me she'd take care of me. And she did, but she hasn't called me." Ramona smiled. "Yet."

Sam laughed, and then Ramona started asking questions of her own. The conversation flowed, as easy as Sam could have wished and twice as interesting. But she couldn't help but wonder how much more of the world Ramona might have sparkled for if she hadn't been forced to concentrate so much on survival.

If, instead, she could have only been Ramona.

Sam had to admit, however, that every single bit of Ramona's success, the love she'd found in friends, her wisdom, and her joy were things she had gotten from the light she shined on herself. No one else's.

It gave her a lot of ideas about how to be Sam.

Her Bex

"Whatever we decide to order—and, let me be clear, it will be biryani from the kabob house in Little Bangladesh—I insist you change into clothes as soon as we get inside the house." Sam watched Bex punch in numbers and lay her fingerprint on the secure entry keypad.

"I am wearing clothes," Bex said. "Which I will continue to wear while we eat chicken and waffles from Roscoe's." She yanked at her leather shorts and pushed open the door.

They entered the cool of the tiled foyer. Sam took Bex's hand and pulled her into a dim corner, where she leaned down and whispered into her ear. "You and I both know this outrageous outfit is not clothing. It's a honey trap you set for me."

Bex draped her arms over Sam's shoulders, gazing up at her. "Is that what you think?"

Sam slid her hand down Bex's side, her lower belly going tight when she felt the combination of skin and silk against her palm. "It's what I *know*." She dipped down to kiss Bex's neck, punctuating the kiss with a small bite that made Bex sigh satisfyingly against her shoulder.

"I mean, if you want me to get undressed," Bex loud-whispered, "I'm not sure why I would put clothes back—*goddamnit!*" Bex dropped her arms from around Sam's shoulders and hunched over her shorts. "The fucking zipper broke."

Sam looked. Bex was holding her shorts on with a fist while they peeled away from her hips like a wrinkled and spent cocoon. "Oh, no." She started laughing.

Bex's angry dimple came out, but her eyes were bright with amusement at her predicament. "This is your fault."

Sam lifted one eyebrow, just to provoke her.

"I would have never worn this ridiculous garment that I can't breathe or move my legs in with this blouse"—Bex pinched the silk and yanked it with irritation—"that wants to reveal my side boob to God and country, if you weren't *you*."

"If I weren't . . . ?"

"The one that I want," Bex clarified primly. "I'm going to step out of these torture devices Yves Saint Laurent calls shoes, and you're going to pick them up and follow me to my bedroom, where I will change into some *real* clothes that will fit even after I eat my enormous dinner from Roscoe's. After which I will remove my clothes again and have you for dessert."

Still laughing, Sam kissed Bex one last time, then bent over and picked up Bex's sandals. She followed along as Bex minced into the big living area holding up the shorts, only to stop at the sight of Frankie, Haris, Vic, and Fergus lounging in various poses on the massive sectional.

"Ms. Simon!" Haris jumped up and ran his hand over his hair. "I'm so sorry. Frankie invited me over, but if it's too much trouble for me to be here, I can—"

Bex held up her palm. "At ease, Haris."

"We're doing family," Vic said, unbothered. "There's huge containers of biryani from the kabob house in the kitchen if you want to get a plate and join us."

"No." Bex glowered at Vic. "I'm on my way to get changed, and then we're having Roscoe's." She waddled to the back of the house and disappeared down the hall that led to her bedroom.

"I might have some biryani," Sam said. Following Bex to her bedroom was frustratingly off the table. "Carry on."

"I'll come with." Vic got up, shedding at least three soft blankets and a hoodie she'd had on backward. "I need chocolate milk."

In the kitchen, Sam fixed herself a bowl heaped with lamb and rice and bread while Vic leaned against the counter and drank chocolate milk. It reminded Sam of when she'd impulsively taken Bex and her sisters to an all-inclusive resort in the Caribbean for spring break. She cherished a mental snapshot of Vic on that trip, wearing huge sunnies and a metallic swimsuit, calling Sam's name to get her to look right before she cannonballed into the resort pool.

Family time.

"I can't remember when I last ate a real meal," Sam said before shoveling a bite into her mouth. "This is exactly what I wanted."

"Then why did Bex say you were having Roscoe's?"

"She wants chicken and waffles." Sam tore off a chunk of garlic naan and folded rice into it. "We were debating when we walked in."

"Ah." Vic sighed. "Sam?"

"Vic."

"I'm glad you and Bex is finally happening. You make my sister happy. You always have, but I like knowing that now you always will. I know I play the girl who doesn't want to leave home, and that's partly true I admit, but also? I don't want Bex to be alone. I can't think of her alone when she's done so much for me and Frankie. I know I drive her up the wall, but I also know I wouldn't have the life that I have without her, and it's such a good life. Please give Bex an amazing life."

Sam swallowed her food, tears in her eyes. "That is my whole plan for my life, actually. To give Bex and me an amazing one. And to watch you and Frankie have amazing lives, too."

"Frankie's getting it done. Haris is a peach. She quit the job everyone wanted her to feel lucky to have and did the scary theater internship in New York, and the Geffen here in L.A. has already called her, begging for her genius. She seems almost mellow. It's disconcerting. In a good way."

"Whoa." Fergus stopped at the entrance to the kitchen. "There is a strong emotional vibe. I wasn't here. Carry on."

"We've completed our family talk, Ferg." Vic nodded at Sam. "She's all yours. Sam?"

"Yeah?"

"You have rice on your face." Vic pointed.

Sam laughed, wiping at her cheek. "Thank you, and I love you."

"To the moon and back." Vic smiled. "That's what Bex always told us. She said it's what Dad used to say."

With that, she left, and Fergus came all the way into the kitchen. "Is there still enough food left for me to grab some more?" He was eyeing the biryani. "I underestimated my appetite."

"Help yourself."

He fixed himself a bowl and sat down next to Sam. "I'm going to head out tomorrow morning. I found a buyer for my house. I need to get back to Oregon and start packing up."

"Oh. That was fast." In the week Sam had spent in police interview rooms and corseted on a soundstage, her brother had closed on the commercial space he wanted in Malibu. He'd been looking at apartments with an agent. "Did you find a place to rent?"

"No, but I was thinking. What if I bought your place?"

Sam stopped with her fork halfway to her mouth to stare at her brother. "Where do I live in this scenario?"

"In this scenario, we're roommates until the inevitable."

The inevitable. Sam was quietly thrilled, but she also felt her face turning red, because this was her brother. "Okay."

"*Are* you okay?" Fergus's brow was wrinkled in confusion.

"You can buy my house. Please don't say anything until I have a chance to tell Bex about the inevitable."

"Baller." Fergus put down his fork and held out his knuckles for her to bump. "I already hired a contractor to put in surfboard storage and a workbench for my bikes in your garage."

Sam rolled her eyes. "Make yourself at home."

But that was it, wasn't it? He was making himself a home. Here. A ten-minute walk away from where hoped *she* would be, making Bex happy.

She ate more of her food, laughing at her brother's jokes because he liked that, and then heard Bex roar with laughter in the living room. "Hey, did you walk here?" Sam asked Fergus. "Because if you did, you should take my car back to the house when you leave. Didn't you say you were leaving now?"

He waggled his eyebrows.

"Shut the fuck up," Sam said pleasantly. "My keys are in my bag hanging in the foyer."

Her brother made his way out, and Sam returned to the living room, where Bex had sunk into the only unoccupied portion left on the sectional.

"Bex gave my new boyfriend the third degree." Frankie put her hand on Haris's chest and *mooned* at him. Sam had never seen Frankie do that in her entire life, unless it was at a new piece of lighting equipment. "He did so well."

Haris smiled down at her. Vic was right. It was good to see.

"All of you are young and pretty," Sam said. "Aren't you supposed to be out having experiences? It's a beautiful evening. A brand-new, fresh summer. Get your passports and drive to Tijuana. Go camping at Joshua Tree."

"You don't want us here," Vic said.

"I do not."

"She doesn't mean that." Bex sat up. "Look, Vic, I want you to know that I love spending time with you. I need to work on not lashing out when I'm upset. If you want to be here, you can be here, it's not—"

Vic laughed. "Oh my God. I *know*. Anyway, Haris and Frankie already told me they would go with me to Hannah Hearts Cat Rescue. I'm adopting a cat. Then I have a whole bunch of cat stuff to pick up and a catio guy I want to talk to."

"You're adopting a cat?" Bex crossed her arms. "You didn't talk to me about this. You understand that you have to take care of this cat. I'm not going to deal with a litter box, and neither is Olive. It's a lot of responsi—"

"Let me interrupt you again before you ruin your previous speech about how desperately you love me and want to hang out with me. I don't know if any of you have noticed, but I am pre-vet. Also, Bexley? Frankie and Haris are moving in together, and you and Sam aren't here much. It's lonely. You're lucky I'm only getting *one* cat."

Bex rolled her lips in.

Sam understood. Doing family wasn't easy, but it was worth it. "Good for you, taking care of your needs," she said. "I can't wait to meet this new member of the household. Tomorrow. *And* spend quality time with Haris. Also tomorrow. Frankie? Congratulations. You must have a lot to do."

"What, you have some needs of your own to take care of?" Vic asked with a grin. "Some*one*—sorry, some *stuff* that you need to do?"

"Goodbye," Bex said. "Get out."

They left.

It was heaven.

Bex had changed into leggings and a cut-out-neckline T-shirt with Frankie's junior high school basketball team mascot on it. Sam squeezed in beside her, crossing her legs and leaning back into the soft cushions, feeling better than she had for . . . six and a half months.

If acting was the only kind of work that made sense to how Sam wanted to talk to and about the world, Bexley Simon was the only person who, when Sam was with her, made sense of life itself.

"How can you wear those all day?" Bex asked, toeing Sam's high heel with a foot covered in slipper socks. Her voice was scratchy from the excited talking they'd done at Ramona's, and from a singing performance she'd given at Ramona's insistence. It wouldn't be long before Bex started freaking out about that husky scratch and boiling a huge pot of gross-smelling tea and warming up her facial steamer to breathe, but Sam liked it.

"You've asked me this so many times over the years." Sam turned her body toward Bex.

"'Because they're beautiful' is not an answer. My leather shorts were beautiful when the woman at Loewe brought them to my dressing room and zipped me into them, but I was under no illusion I would like wearing them."

Sam reached over and traced her index finger over Bex's exposed collarbones. "Your body was meant for a seventy-two-year-old veteran costumer of Broadway to dress and no one else," she said. "Someone who has dress forms with people's names signed on them and who knows that Bernadette Peters has two different sizes of feet."

"Bernadette Peters's feet are perfect. I've never heard they are anything but exactly the same size." Bex stretched her arms over her head and then let her hands feather over Sam's hair and tug the neckline of her blouse. "I saw Fergus leave in your car."

"You did? That rascal." Sam slid off her heels and scooted close to Bex, pulling Bex's legs into her lap.

"The house is so quiet." Bex watched Sam's face with a secret laugh in her expression. "I'm not sure what we'll do?"

"Surely you have a plan."

"I might. If I knew it was foolproof."

Sam squeezed the sock-covered feet in her lap.

"But did you order me chicken and waffles?" Bex asked.

"The good news is that I did. The bad news is that they're going to take at least an hour. And there's something I want to tell you." When Sam breathed in, she felt a hitch of fear, but she didn't let it hold her back. She didn't want to compartmentalize her life like Ramona had to in order to be able to trust the people in it.

She didn't want to get so much power and money that she had nothing more to look forward to than a midweek party in a giant house.

And she didn't want to pay the cost of fame for fame itself, keeping track of the lies and secrets fame required until she was broken by acrimony or violence.

"I want to pack the same suitcase," she said.

Bex tipped her head. "What do you mean?"

"I mean that no matter what's next, I don't want to be alone in my bedroom, with stuff from my closet everywhere and my agent on speaker while I pack to go on location, knowing I probably won't see you for months. I want to pack the same suitcase as you, knowing *we're* going on vacation, or *we're* going for work where one or both of us will do something amazing. I want to start to make big decisions together and bring opportunities to you, and you bring yours to me, and we plan a life that makes us happy and keeps our toothbrushes in the same cup. If, you know, that's something you also want to do."

"Samantha Farmer." Bex laughed. "You'll flirt outrageously with me in sky-high boots and an even higher hemline, but whenever you're up against confessing what you really want, you scuff your toe against the ground like a schoolboy."

"Let's see you do better, then." Sam inched closer to Bex's ear. "Talk right to the love of your life and try to choke out what you want like a person who has to ask to get it."

Bex leaned close. She put her fingertips on Sam's shoulders, her thumbs pressing into her collarbones. "You know what I think would be great?"

"What's that?"

"If your toothbrush was in a cup with mine at Stella Tower in New York. Though not really in the same cup, can I say? I'm hoping that's a metaphor. I have a whole oral hygiene routine, and when I'm performing, I can't get sick."

"I would love to keep my toothbrush far away from yours in our bathroom in Stella Tower. Tell me more."

"And while I was there singing and dancing, you were probably doing something fabulous—I can't wait to find out what—but also, at the end of the day, you would give me a foot massage. I would drink my licorice bark tea for my throat while you told me about shooting at a New York sound studio, or meetings at 30 Rock. Then the foot massage would get dirty, and you would have to tell me exactly, explicitly, what to do, because I wasn't allowed to talk. I would have to remain perfectly silent in order to preserve my voice."

The fantasy lit up Sam's inner thighs at the same time it outlined her secret heart in lights. She tugged a lock of Bex's hair, gently at first, and then when Bex let out a sigh, she curled her hand into a fist and pulled her close enough to kiss. She put her thumb over the pulse at Bex's throat and thought, *I love you, I love you,* with every beat of her heart.

Sam reached out for Bex's waist, warm and strong beneath her palms, and eased her onto her lap, where Bex settled happily, winding her arms around Sam's neck. "Logistically, packing together is going to be complicated because of having two wardrobes in different houses," Sam said. "And I'm not a light packer. I like a good costume change. But it will get easier when we're living together."

She held her breath, her lower back going hot with, yes, fear. It was one thing for Sam to stay with Bex during the run of *Follies,* but what she was asking was quite a bit bigger, and even if Fergus thought it was inevitable, Bex's big brown eyes had gone wide as a doe's. Her two main dimples sank deep into her cheeks. "I'm sorry, did you just imperiously lay claim to me?"

And then Bex raked her fingers through Sam's hair and kissed her.

She pulled away, just a few inches, and looked Sam over, her eyes very dark. "I will hand you the keys to this house—even though you already have a set of keys, I'm talking a symbolic set—if you tell me something right now. Tell me about the project you've always wanted to take when you were accepting shows with spaceships and leather corsets and red-haired detectives you weren't allowed to touch while you said the corniest lines in detective television so brilliantly that no one noticed."

Sam liked this question. She finally knew how to answer it. "I want to do a movie that isn't about what I look like. It will be the kind of movie that gives the audience an excuse to cry about all the feelings they're holding back, and it will be so gay that a cinema history book about queer movies has no choice but to mention it for a hundred years."

Bex kissed her, softly, and this time Sam pulled back. "And maybe I want to direct it. Bex?"

"Yes."

Sam took a deep breath before she said the last thing. "You're my Bex." Then she had to take another breath and swallow over the lump in her throat at the emotion she saw reflected in Bex's eyes. "I want us to be everything to each other. We can go to battle together. Spend too much time and too much money solving more mysteries if anyone else asks us to. I want to be the one who makes sure you have enough of your weird herbal teas and mixes up the clay mask for your skincare routine, and I know some people would say it's too soon for any of that to happen, but—"

"We've already waited too long." Bex pressed her face to Sam's neck. "I missed you so much. Never leave me."

Sam smiled, remembering Vic saying the same thing to Frankie. She took a deep breath of the crown of Bex's head, smelling co-wash and styling products and her one, true, forever person. "I love you."

Bex was breathing fast and shallow, smiling like a purring cat. "It's funny you say that, because I have a plan for what to do right after."

"You have a plan that kicks in right after I say 'I love you'?"

Bex tipped her head to the side, her smile widening. "I don't know if it's a plan, exactly, or more of a fantasy? But it starts with my coming home, and you're here—"

"I'm in your house in this fantasy?"

"Waiting for me. In all of my fantasies the past six months, when I came back, you were here, waiting in my house like you always used to be. And I took you by the hand and led you to my room—"

"What was I wearing?"

"In my fantasy?" Bex laughed. "You want me to tell you what you were wearing? You tell *me* what you're wearing. You've been costuming your life for as long as I've known you. What does Samantha Farmer wear when Bexley Simon deflowers her in her absolutely messy bedroom? I put that last part in so you won't be shocked when you see what's happened to any semblance of housekeeping since I had the falling out with Olive."

"Well, I did buy this shirt with you in mind," Sam said. "When I was in Vancouver."

"This see-through shirt?" Bex smoothed her hands down Sam's arms.

"Because I spent a lot of time thinking about how to disarm you so I wouldn't get so freaked out by how smooshy and vulnerable you make me." Sam shifted, moving her body over Bex's as Bex slid off her lap and leaned back into the sofa's cushions.

Bex fisted the front of Sam's shirt and pulled her close, wrapping a leg around one of Sam's. Her kiss started out as a smile against Sam's mouth but quickly got serious, turning into another conversation that was deep and slow, until it needed more of their attention and Bex slipped from underneath Sam's body and turned her over, making her intentions clear—her intention to learn the texture of Sam's skin everywhere, to take her kisses to all the places she touched, to strip away their inhibitions as easily as their clothes, and to savor Sam's body and love on a foundation of friendship and years of intimacy and care.

Sam was so grateful she'd made it here. She would never assume again she had plenty of time left to ask for what she wanted.

"Take me to this messy bedroom of yours," Sam demanded between kisses and tastes of Bex's skin.

Bex kissed her, finishing this one with a smile. "I'm so glad you didn't *ask*."

Acknowledgments

Thank you to the architects of our own comebacks, Tara Gelsomino and Pamela Harty. Long may we reign. Your unfailing support and creative, values-first agenting gets us through the labyrinth of inspiration to reach our readers.

All of our unending love to our children, August and James. Life with you, life in our family, means that we've become constitutionally incapable of writing a lone wolf book. We can't stop, won't ever stop, making sure found and natal families surround our characters—messy and loving, hard and soft. You remind us what all of this is for and how persistence can look so many different ways. You remind us why we answer to love.

We have so much gratitude that the Hollywood Detective series found our editor, Alex Sunshine. You are sharp, tireless, fierce, and love Bex and Sam as much as we do, but you aren't afraid to be their genius director and tell them to "run it again, but this time with *feeling*." This series wouldn't turn heads like it does without you. Is there an Oscar for editors?

Our covers are illustrated by the fantastic Becki Gill, who has the rare ability to get an imaginary character in her mind's eye and bring them to life stylishly, with wit and an ineffable sparkle. We're so grateful you've brought Bex and Sam to life and that you like Easter eggs as much as we do.

Thank you, thank you, truly thank you, to the folks at Kensington. Larissa, you know *everyone* and have brought us to so many great people and experiences. You are truly the queen of mystery. Michelle, you never miss an angle to get a book to the readers who will love it. Jackie, you stepped in to pinch-hit for Alex with such aplomb. Robin, you put up with a million picky changes. We have enjoyed so much uplifting and experienced support from our extraordinary team.

The culture raises every one of us, and the movies and music that had their part in shaping us continue to speak to so many. Our readers will be able to spot our influences. We remain amazed that this is the life of art. It reflects the moment of its making, but it is also full of stories from its past, and it resonates into the future. So much of this book is about how systems make hard work look like overnight success and the long life of an artist look like a series of comebacks. With this story, we hoped to give solace, inspiration, and validation to our readers and fellow authors. We see you. We see the value in your rest, in your voice, in your wild successes, in your setbacks. We've got this, despite it all.